PINCH

THE NEW BRADFORDS
BOOK 1

TIA LOUISE

This book is a work of fiction. Names, characters, places, and incidents are products of the author's imagination or are used fictitiously. Any resemblance to actual events or locales or persons, living or dead, is entirely coincidental.

Pinch
Copyright © TLM Productions LLC, 2025
Printed in the United States of America.

Illustration by Laura Moore, LCM Designs.
Cover design by Kari March Designs.

All rights reserved. No part of this publication can be reproduced, stored in a retrieval system, or transmitted in any form or by any means—electronic, photocopying, mechanical, or otherwise—without prior permission of the publisher and author.

PLAYLIST

"Cheer Down" - George Harrison
"We Are the Champions" - Queen
"Another One Bites the Dust" - Queen
"NOKIA" - Drake
"You Shook Me All Night Long" - AC/DC
"(It Must've Been Ol') Santa Claus" - Harry Connick, Jr.
"I Want It All" - Kat & Alex
"The Heart Wants What It Wants" - Selena Gomez
"Infinitely Falling" - Fly By Midnight
"This Girl" - Hunter Hayes
"Steal the Show" - Lauv
"Tangled up in You" - Staind
"Lullaby" - The Chicks
"Mandy" - Barry Manilow
"She Blinded Me With Science" - Thomas Dolby

Scan to Listen!

THE BRADFORD FAMILY

1

Haddy

"Who says you can't be a beauty queen *and* a scientist?" My best friend, roommate, and first cousin Gigi Bradford slides her brush through the silky coat of a tall dog with a long nose secured in a large, empty tub.

As soon as the envelope appeared in our mailbox, I snatched it out and ran to her small grooming studio in our converted she-shed behind our rented house in Los Feliz.

I didn't want to open it alone, which is silly, I know. It's just a check in an amount that will cover my entire tuition, room, and board for my next semester of graduate school. Still, my fingers tremble as I carefully unfold the green paper and read the dollar amount.

A letter with a golden-embossed "Congratulations, Princess!" printed across the top is also enclosed.

"It's kind of embarrassing." My voice lowers as I recall Dr. Warwick's face when I told him why I wouldn't be returning as his graduate assistant in the fall.

Winning International Princess Woman will allow me to focus on my lab work without the extra strain of grading papers and proctoring exams.

"Why are you embarrassed?" Gigi's nose wrinkles. "It's simple genetics, same as in the dog world."

"Don't say it..."

"You're just like your mother."

"You said it." I fall back against the porcelain-tiled countertop.

My cousin pauses, cutting her green eyes at me. "More like Princess Drama Queen."

"You can't be a princess and a queen. It's redundant."

"Whatever. Your mom is a meteorologist, which is why you love science, and your grandmother was Miss Georgia World. You're a natural for the nerdy International Princess Woman. It's in your blood."

"So you're saying I'm bred for it?"

"Exactly!" Gina shakes her head talking in a baby voice as she rubs both of her hands on the golden dog's muzzle. "Those silly scientists should understand. It's in your DNA. Yes, it is!"

It's annoying, but as a dog breeder, groomer, trainer, and judge in championship dog shows, it's how my cousin views the world.

I have a pedigree. My family excels in science *and* pageants with ridiculous names that pay a lot of money.

I study the large check. "For a program that awards millions in scholarships every year, I don't understand why they have to have the word *princess* in the title. It's demeaning. They should just call it 'International Scholarship Woman.'"

"But they give you a crown?" She tilts her head, glancing up at me.

"Yes."

"And you wear it at events along with an evening gown and a sash."

I exhale a heavy sigh. I can't argue. Such commitments do come with the title.

"Some women like to be princesses." Gina straightens, picking up a pair of sharp scissors.

"My professors are so confused." I fold the check and slip it into my pocket. It's too big for mobile deposit, so I'll have to make a special trip to the bank. "Calling me a princess only makes it weirder."

Gigi pushes a lock of strawberry-blonde hair behind her ear and leans closer to trim the dog's whiskers. "Your dad is the one who should be confused. He has enough money to cover all their bills and yours. You don't have to keep doing these pageants if they embarrass you."

"No." I shake my head determinedly. "I'm paying my own way. If I keep taking money from them, I'll always be a spoiled nepo-baby. No one will ever take me seriously."

Gigi's lips twist. "I'm pretty sure your mom married Uncle Hen because of that same independent streak. She understands you better than you think."

The woman smiling back at me from the cover of the pageant brochure has perfectly coiffed, wavy blonde hair, and she's wearing a white, strapless dress with a red and white striped sash that reads *International Princess Woman*. It's basically how I look at events, only my hair is dark brown and long waves, which makes my blue eyes more noticeable.

"It doesn't matter." I shake it off. "Winning this means I'll be able to finish my research without having to worry about money. I'll happily pivot, hold, smile, and wave all day for that privilege."

"Don't forget you're riding on the *Welcome Back* float in the parade tomorrow." The screen door slams as our other cousin and third roommate Maverick Murphy enters the room. "We're rolling out at 10 a.m. sharp."

Gigi puts the scissors aside and unhooks the dog's leash. "We're just happy to be your ladies in waiting. Aren't we, Haze?"

"That dog's name is *Haze*?" Mav's dark brows furrow. "He's not even purple."

"*Her* name is Some Like it Hot Hazel, but I call her *Haze* for short."

"What the fuck?" He goes to the cabinet and opens the door, digging around. "What dog is going to come to *Some Like it Hot Hazel*? 'Here, Some Like it Hot Hazel!'" He pretends to call the dog, who doesn't even move. "See? Dog breeders are nuts."

"She's got better hair than I do." I walk over to slide my hand through her silky coat.

"She's an Afghan Borzoi. She'll be on the float with us tomorrow." Gigi helps the large dog out of the grooming pen then goes to our cousin. "Why are you digging in my supplies?"

"I need to borrow your good tweezers." Mav takes out the stainless-steel tool. "I've got something stuck in my blade."

"Maverick, no." Gigi reaches over his shoulder in an attempt to grab it. "I can't afford to have you break those. They cost two hundred dollars!"

"I can afford to replace them." He dodges her arms.

Gigi is five-eight like me, but Mav is six-two and wily. I shake my head at them wrestling like they're still kids as I head for the door.

Maverick makes enough money as the star right winger

for the LA Champions to buy twenty sets of tweezers. He doesn't have to live with us. He just likes the company—and driving us crazy.

"I've got to finish grading papers. See y'all in the morning."

"Wave pretty," Maverick calls after me, and I wave my middle finger at him over my head. "That's my Princess. I'm so proud."

"Just like your mom," I yell back.

Mav's mother, our aunt Dylan, actually cried when she discovered that after years of trying to guide him into the "safe sport" of golf, her only son is the best hockey player in the southern region.

There was a lot of interest in him when he became a free agent, and he chose LA because we were here. He was only supposed to stay with us until he found his own place, then he never left.

We have an adorable two-story bungalow with four bedrooms and two bathrooms in the best part of LA, and not far from Caltech, where I attend school.

We weren't looking for a third roommate, but with the cost of everything these days, we were glad to have another person to share expenses.

He was more than happy to stay, especially since we all grew up like siblings. Say what he wants, Mav's a total family guy and an excellent chef, which Gina and I are not. So, perks!

"I'll bring the purple drink!" Gigi shouts after me, and I snort a laugh.

Purple drink is a New Orleans beverage made of purple Kool-Aid and Everclear. It's been in our family since before we were born, so of course, we ran off with the recipe as soon as we turned twenty-one.

"Purple drink before ten in the morning?" I turn, pushing the door open with my butt.

"Our mammas raised us right!" she replies with a wink.

If we're going to start the day with purple drink tomorrow, I definitely have to lock up in my bedroom tonight. It's possible I could be out for two days, and these finals won't grade themselves.

"Why is it so cold?" I stand at the back of the line of cars with Maverick's coat around my shoulders. "October is supposed to be one of the best times to visit LA!"

"Talk to your mom," Gina quips.

"She'll just blame global climate change."

Maverick shoves a red Solo cup into my hand. "More purple drink. It'll warm you up."

"Hold my cup a second." I smooth my dark hair behind my shoulders before placing the crown on my head. "Help me pin this, Geeg."

"Hold Haze's leash." She passes the sparkling strap to me before taking the hairpins.

Under Mav's bright purple and black team jacket I'm wearing a sequined white dress with black accents to match the Champions' jerseys.

My *International Princess Woman* sash is in place, and a helper waits with the oversized bouquet of white and black roses I'll carry in the parade.

"Where do they get black roses?" Gina squints at the bouquet. "Will you be able to hold those *and* the safety bar?"

"Of course." I take the Solo cup from Mav. "This isn't my first rodeo."

Or pageant parade.

"Hurry up—it's almost time." He nods at my cup.

I take a big gulp, pulling my chin back as I swallow. "How much Everclear did you put in this, Gigi? You're not supposed to be able to taste it."

"Mav made it. I had a doggy emergency last night."

My blue eyes widen at Mav. A maniacal grin is on his face, and he nods, sticking out his tongue. "Extra strength, Princess!"

He takes another big gulp, but my stomach drops. "Maverick..."

I'm about to fuss at him, about how as a representative of the International Princess Woman Scholarship Program, I can't be drunk on a float, when a lady on a bullhorn orders all riders to take their place.

I'm already feeling the effects of too much grain alcohol when I take my first step up the short flight of stairs to the platform that will carry us through the crowd of fans lining the streets.

"Why didn't you warn me?" I hiss as I stow Mav's jacket behind the decorated podium I'll hold as I wave. "What's a doggy emergency anyway?"

Gigi arranges my skirt then positions Hazel and her own show dog, a white standard Poodle she calls Spanky (short for Spank My Bottom) at her side.

"One of the breeders had a breakdown. It might've been related to her messy divorce." Gigi makes a worried face. "By the way, we're fostering a dog for the next few weeks."

Before I can argue that *we said no more fostering dogs*, the attendant shoves the massive bouquet of roses into my arms.

"Hold these over your shoulder..." He proceeds to push my hair behind my back again. "Then hold this strap around your wrist."

"I need something sturdier than a strap." I'm still

speaking as the guy walks to the edge and hops off the float. "Wait! I'm in three-inch heels!"

Not to mention I've had two cups of extra-strength purple drink.

The guy doesn't look back as he blends into the crowd of organizers preparing to roll.

Gigi steps closer. "Grab my arm if you get wobbly."

"And throw these flowers everywhere? They're heavy!" For a reason called *purple drink* mixed with the lingering, horrifying memory of dog vomit from our last foster pet, I want to sit down right here and cross my arms. "Who is this foster dog, anyway?"

"Oh, she's the cutest little thing!" Gigi smiles enraptured. "She's a little teacup poodle named Princess Petunia. You'll love her. She's practically made to be your pet!"

"I don't want a pet. Where is she now?"

"At the house." Gigi's eyes narrow. "Are you okay? You're swaying, and we haven't started moving yet."

She's right. I didn't eat breakfast, and it feels like the float is already rolling.

I'm in trouble.

"Hey, ladies!" Maverick waves at us from where he stands at the side of the float. "I want y'all to meet my new teammate. He's going to be staying at the house a few days while he finds his own place."

"Maverick!" Gigi's voice is loud and cross. "We didn't discuss this first!"

"You're one to talk." I'm still cross about our surprise foster-dog. "If this new dog barfs in my bed like the last one—"

"You're going to love her," Gigi interrupts me.

Our cousin waves over a big guy with shaggy brown hair,

then holds out a red Solo cup to him as he hustles up to give Mav a bro-hug.

"That's my man!" Maverick is still yelling, pointing at the guy whose back is turned.

The lady is on the bullhorn again, giving us all the ten-second warning.

Doing my best to shake off this buzz, I roll my shoulders back and adjust my posture. The float does a sharp lurch forward, and I wobble on my heels, jerking hard on the strap.

"Whoa..." It's a low yell, and Gina grabs my hand.

"Are you okay?"

"Yo, Princess, Maid Marian, over here!" Mav is yelling, and now his arm is looped around the new teammate's shoulders. "I present to you Gavin Knight of the dynamite, unstoppable Gav and Mav hockey duo!"

The tall fellow lifts his square chin, and ice-blue eyes blink up to mine. When they clash, cold water surges through my bloodstream followed quickly by fire.

He's standing there, all six-foot-two, broad shoulders, rounded biceps, square jaw with that dimple right in the middle of his cheek. Full lips part over straight white teeth, and my stomach dips.

I'm frozen as my mind tumbles back to my college days in Chapel Hill, North Carolina, my roommate Karen crying her eyes out on the sofa because the man she loved, the man she trusted, her first college boyfriend, was sleeping with every girl in the Tri-Delta sorority house.

I don't know when he started going by Gavin, but *Lane* Knight is the most notorious playboy I've ever met. He has the body of a god and the heart of a villain.

"No!" My voice is sharp, and I release the strap, taking a step in the direction of my cousin. "Not him!"

I guess purple drink makes me think I'm going to do something right here in the middle of a parade in my dress, crown, and three-inch heels.

The float starts to roll, and the words morph into a scream as I throw white and black roses into the air.

Spanky lunges forward, dragging Gina with him, as if he'll rescue me, but it's too late. Nothing is going to stop me as I fly through the air.

Nothing except the rock-hard chest of the world's biggest jerk, who I vowed to my college roommate I'd never speak to again.

With an *oof!* I land, Cinderella-style in his arms.

He has the nerve to catch me.

"Well, hello, Hayden." His chin dips, and he grins at me like the player he is. "Nice of you to drop in. I hear we're going to be roommates."

"Put me down." I struggle to get out of his strong arms.

He doesn't let me go. Instead, his eyes narrow. "I guess that's your funny way of saying thank you for saving your life."

"You didn't save my life. You only broke my fall." I push his chest, and he relents. "Like you break everything."

I said the last part under my breath, but I can tell he heard me by the way his jaw tightens.

I'm all set to walk away and take my place on the float again, when my heel catches in the hem of my gown, and with a loud rip, the bottom of my skirt disappears along with my appearance in the LA Champions official Welcome Back Parade.

2

Gavin

Yesterday...

"You can't do this to me, Chip, the moving truck's already on its way to your house." My brow is tight, and anger burns in my throat.

I'm trying to keep my voice down as I stand in the terminal in Atlanta waiting on the plane train.

"Sorry, Gav, the missus decided she wants to stay. I can't get her to budge."

"What am I supposed to do?" I pinch the bridge of my nose, dropping my chin as the silver doors open and passengers stream out. "You're leaving me homeless."

"Don't you have a teammate you can crash with?"

The coast is clear, and I take my place on the train beside a woman with a dark-haired little girl.

"Probably. If you'd told me a week ago, but I'm arriving in LA today."

"I'm really sorry. Can you afford a hotel room?"

Of course, I can afford a hotel room.

"This is really short notice, Chip. What about all my stuff?"

"Tell you what..." His tone brightens like he didn't just ruin my entire day. "I've got a friend who owns one of those pod rental places. I'll ask him to give you a month for free, since I left you hanging."

Lifting my chin, I stare at the ceiling of the car as I exhale. "Sounds like I don't have a choice. Text me the address, and I'll try to get in touch with the driver."

"I'll have some guys there to unload it and everything." He sounds like he's opening a bag of chips, which makes me even more annoyed. "You won't have to lift a finger."

I'm thinking of lifting a finger. Now I've got to find a place to stay until I can track down a replacement home near the practice stadium in El Segundo.

I end the call as we approach the B terminal, and my eyes land on the little girl. She's holding the hand of a woman who could be her mother or an aunt or I guess a nanny.

Dark curls frame her chubby pink cheeks, and her bright blue eyes are fixed on me.

I give her a smile and a wink, and she buries her face between the woman's legs so fast, the woman has to take a step forward. I exhale a chuckle, looking at the overhead guide.

We're approaching our stop, and when I glance down, she's peeking at me again. Another wink, and she gives me the tiniest smile. A dimple appears at the corner of her mouth, and she's a little cutie.

The train comes to a hard stop, and I hesitate as people start to exit, doing my best to hold the door for them. We step off, and the little girl releases her companion's hand. She presses her hand to her mouth and blows it at me.

The woman stops just in time to see. "Harper, are you flirting?"

Harper's eyes squint, and I chuckle. The woman straightens, looking up, up, up at me, and her lips part with an "Oh!"

I give her a nod. "Gavin Knight. Sorry, I started it all."

The little girl tugs her arm. "Ask him to play with us, Mommy!"

Her mother squints an eye, smiling up at me. "Would you like to play, Gavin Knight?"

I'm not sure whether to pick up the double entendre or let it go. I don't see a ring, but I do see the clock ticking down. My layover is pretty tight.

Instead, I bend to a squat in front of Harper. "I'd love to play with you, but I've got to catch my plane. Where are you headed?"

"My grandma lives in Santorino," she lisps, lifting her chin proudly.

"San Antonio," her mother explains.

"Ah, fun town." I reach in my bag and pull out a small LA Champions logo sticker. I'm not even sure where I got it. "Maybe you'll see me play sometime."

Harper takes it and smiles up at me. "Look, Mommy!"

"Hockey player." Her mother nods slowly. "I wouldn't have guessed with the…"

She gestures to her mouth, and I rise to my full six-foot-two height. "I promised my mom I'd protect my teeth."

"Good luck with that." She laughs.

"Have a safe flight."

With a wave, they step onto the elevator. The little girl waves as hard as she can, which makes me chuckle. I'm only thirty, starting a new life in a new town, but I look forward to having one of those one day.

My phone buzzes, and I pull it out to see my buddy Maverick Murphy's name on the screen.

MAVERICK

What's your ETA, bro? Need help moving in?

Walking to the gate, I use text-to-speech to reply.

GAVIN

Boots on the ground at five, but I have a problem. Chip left me homeless.

It doesn't take long for my best teammate to reply.

MAVERICK

WTF? What happened?

GAVIN

Wifey decided she didn't want to leave.

MAVERICK

Can she do that?

GAVIN

Isn't there some saying about it's a woman's prerogative to change her mind?

MAVERICK

Do you have a backup plan? Need a place to stay?

GAVIN

Got a hotel room for tonight, and I guess the duration.

MAVERICK

Fuck that, you'll stay with me. I've got plenty of room.

My brow pinches, and I think about it. Maverick and I played together in Atlanta for three years before he signed with LA. It's because of him I got the great offer to come here as a last-minute trade when the Champions lost their right defenseman to Toronto.

We're "Gav and Mav," the unstoppable duo, and the fans go crazy when we're on the ice together. He's a star right winger, and although I'm a defenseman, we've played together so long, we can read each other's minds. Together we get the entire stadium on their feet.

I might not be the biggest D-man in the league, but I'm the strongest skater. I'm not afraid to take it to the boards, and I'm good in a pinch.

GAVIN

You sure I won't be imposing?

MAVERICK

No way! Stay as long as you need. We've got a spare room and everything.

GAVIN

Thanks, brother. You're a lifesaver. See you tomorrow at the parade.

MAVERICK

Bring your stuff. You'll come home with me.

I give him the thumbs up as my phone rings. I press the button at once, and my mom's face appears on the screen.

"Did I catch you between flights or are you jumping on a plane?" Mom's smile is big, and her bright blue eyes have faint laugh lines in the corners.

"Yes, and yes. I'm between flights, but I'm about to jump on a plane. Everything okay?"

My mom is tiny, petite and pale, with dark purple hair and ink on her shoulders. She was a tattoo artist when she met my dad, a former national guardsman turned private eye.

They never married, but they've always stayed close.

"Elaine wanted me to call and see if you're getting settled. I'll tell her you haven't gotten there yet."

"She's not still mad at me, is she?"

My stepmom let me know she's not happy about this move.

"She's just pouting. It was a lot easier to get to Atlanta from Wilmington than it will be to get to LA."

I was really lucky to grow up with two sets of hyper-supportive "parents." My dad got the biggest kick out of me telling my elementary school teachers I had two mommies when I was a little guy.

It makes disappointing any of them extra hard.

"It was a great deal, and I'm out here with Mav. Y'all love Mav."

"You know she's really worried you're going to have her grandbabies out there. I'm a little worried about that myself."

Her nose wrinkles, and I know she hates putting pressure on me.

"You know, you do have other children."

"That's part of Elaine's problem." Mom pokes out her lips as she nods. "Teenage boys are so quiet and broody. She should've had one more baby."

"She teaches middle school."

"It's not the same."

"Tell her to hang on. He'll grow out of it and start talking again."

That makes her laugh. "True. I'm not sure Sabrina will, though."

I think about my half-sister, Mom and Slayde's daughter.

She's petite like mom, pale with long straight dark hair. "She'll come around. She's a lot like you."

"You're a good big brother." Her smile is warm. "I want to visit when you're all settled."

"Okay, and tell Elaine not to worry. I'm about as far from settling down as I can get."

The memory of that little beauty queen on the plane train drifts across my mind, and something like regret tightens my stomach.

Mom doesn't miss a thing. "What's that look about? Something you need to tell me?"

"No." I huff a laugh. "It was just... This little girl blew me a kiss on the plane train. It was cute."

I'm pretty sure cartoon hearts pop out of my mother's eyes. "Lane Knight, you are just like your father. Ladies can't help but love you."

"Okay, okay. I gotta go. They're calling my zone."

She purses her lips, and I can tell she knows I'm trying to get off the phone now.

When either of "my two mommies" starts on the baby talk, it can get intense, and ever since what happened in college, I haven't had any interest in wading back into the girlfriend waters, which I realize presents a problem.

I made a clean break after that burn. I even changed my name from Lane to Gavin, something they can't seem to remember.

"Fly safe, Laney. I love you."

"Love you, too, Ma."

We say our goodbyes, and I disconnect. My eyes catch on the thin red ring around my left thumb. Mom inked it there when I was leaving home for the first time. It's an old Japanese legend about a red thread that holds us together across space and time. Her ring is on her pinky finger.

She's sentimental like that, and as I wait, a thought like a whisper drifts through my mind. It's a thought inspired by brunette hair and bright blue eyes, a combination as familiar to me as home.

One person...

Who I have no intention of ever speaking to again.

I've effectively put my bad college experience in a box I never intend to reopen. I learned a hard lesson that year, and when hearts are involved, you can't trust anyone.

It's UNEXPECTEDLY cool the morning of the parade. I'd been led to believe LA would be warm in October, but I was also told it's unpredictable. I've got my jacket on as I make my way through the crowds lining the parade route.

Maverick told me to head to the last float, where the queen of the parade would ride with all of us players walking along beside her. We're supposed to be handing out toy pucks, stickers, and other team paraphernalia to the fans.

Even though I'm the new guy, I still get cheers as I pass people in black, purple, and white attire. Excitement hums in the air, and I'm looking forward to seeing my old buddy.

Mav and I both come from big, close families, and we bonded at once in Atlanta over the perks and drawbacks of it. We also wouldn't change it for the world.

"There he is!" I hear him yelling to me, his dark hair catching the breeze.

He's holding up a red Solo cup, and I shake my head. It's 10 a.m., and I'll bet he's drinking something strong. It's probably that infamous purple drink his aunts like to make.

"Get over here, my man." He pulls me in for a hug, and we slap each other's backs. "Has it been a whole year?"

"Yeah, but it goes fast when we're playing all the time."

"That match in Atlanta last year was the worst."

I nod, taking the cup of dark purple death he's holding. I'm pretty sure I won't be having any of this so early.

"Yeah. It was hard being on opposite sides."

"I kept waiting for you to pass the puck to me." His hazel eyes shine, and I nod.

"That would've gone over really well."

"They'd have kicked my ass." We're about the same size, and he's got his arm around my shoulders. "Come over and meet your other roommates."

"Other roommates?" My brow furrows. "I thought…"

"Eh, I decided I didn't want to live alone, so I crashed with Gina and Haddy." My chest tightens, and I stop.

"I don't—"

"It's okay, there's four bedrooms, so you'll have your own space."

"It's not that. I just…"

"Yo, Princess, Maid Marian, over here!" Mav yells as he drags me to the side of the float. "I present to you Gavin Knight of the dynamite, unstoppable 'Gav and Mav' hockey duo!"

My throat is dry when I look up at her. She stands in the middle of the float, perfect poise, long, silky hair streaming down her back. Her elegant white gown fits her body perfectly, slim but with curves in all the right places.

The crown is on her head, and she's holding a massive bouquet of flowers in our team colors.

Hayden Bradford is the most beautiful woman I've ever seen in my life. The first time I met her, I forgot how to speak.

Now when our eyes meet, it's a shock of cold water followed by an angry blowtorch.

"No." Her tone is sharp. "Not him."

My sentiments exactly, Princess. Hayden Bradford might be insanely beautiful, but the history between us makes sharing a house less than desirable.

She takes a wobbly step in our direction just as the float starts to roll, and her words morph into a scream. Her arms fly up, and the roses fly in an arc above her head.

Everyone, even the two large dogs lunge in her direction, and instinctively I dash toward the float as well.

With an *oof!* she lands, Cinderella-style in my arms, and our eyes meet. Crystal blue like a punch in the chest.

We're both stunned, and I can't help a grin at what just happened—the ice princess just fell off her float.

"Hello, Hayden." My brow arches. "Nice of you to drop in. I hear we're going to be roommates."

"Put me down." Her full lips purse, and she wiggles her body in my arms.

It feels unexpectedly good. She's light but soft, and she smells like fresh flowers.

"I guess that's your funny way of saying thank you for saving your life."

"You didn't save my life. You only broke my fall." She pushes my chest, and I lower her to her feet. "Like you break everything."

She says it under her breath, but I hear it. I also know what it means.

She hasn't gotten over what happened at UNC any more than I have, and I wonder if it's too late to check into that hotel again.

3

———

Haddy

"Yes, Mrs. Higgins, I realize it reflects poorly on the International Princess Woman program, but you see I had a wardrobe malfunction." Chewing my lip, I pace our small backyard doing my best to control the damage. "My heel got caught in the hem of my dress, and it ripped off the bottom half of my skirt."

"I would think someone with your level of experience wouldn't have such *wardrobe* issues." The older woman's tone is infused with impatience. "We disappointed the fans, the little girls who were there to see you, and the entire Champions nation."

"The players were still there." I winced as the words slipped unbidden.

"That is not the point, Miss Bradford, and you know it."

"Yes, ma'am." I do my best to sound penitent. "I could make a statement?"

"I think it's best if we let it be. The less attention, the better. But I have my eye on you."

"I won't let you down again."

"I sincerely hope not. The International Princess Woman Scholarship program is one of the oldest in the nation. We are royalty. We are *not* commoners."

My lips press together, and I nod as she disconnects the call.

Looking at the screen, where I had the TMI site open when she called, I frown at the image of me in my white sequined dress with the crown on my head in the arms of Gavin Knight.

His biceps bulge, and he's holding me like I'm freaking Cinderella under a headline reading, *He's a Hot Hockey Player <u>AND</u> a White Knight!!!!!*

"Exclamation points and all," I mutter under my breath.

Clearly, they don't know him like I do.

Taking a slow inhale, I lift my chin to the sky above and exhale a quiet *Thank you* that I didn't lose my scholarship. I don't have to go back to work for Dr. Warwick, and I'm still on track to finish my degree on time without racking up debt I'll never be able to repay on a professor's salary.

I slide my phone into the pocket of my maroon silk pajama bottoms and tighten the belt on my pink terry cloth robe before entering the kitchen. Maverick is the first person I see.

He's sitting on the edge of the bench seat at our reclaimed wooden table, an expression of guilt on his face. Gavin is across the table from him, his eyes fixed on his phone, and he doesn't look up.

"What did she say?" Maverick's voice is low. "Did she take away your crown?"

"No."

"Thank goodness." His brow relaxes, and he falls back. "Mom would've killed me."

I think about his mom, my aunt Dylan, who was already frustrated with him for becoming a hockey player, which is a million times more dangerous than playing football—the Bradford family sport.

She made him promise to protect his head... and his teeth... and not be a player who sleeps with all the puck bunnies in every town. I don't even ask about that last one, and I won't even allow myself to ponder the question when it comes to Gavin.

He has never been my business.

"Next time, I'd appreciate a warning before you serve me triple-strength purple drink on an empty stomach."

Maverick pushes off his knees, crossing the room to hug me. "I'm sorry, Hads. I didn't mean to get you super drunk and make you fall off your princess float."

My eyes roll, and I shake my head. "If I'd known you were mixing them, I'd have eaten a sausage biscuit. Or only had one."

Maverick prides himself on his extra-strong drinks. He never considers they could be hazardous to your health or your livelihood.

I put my hand on his shoulder. "I can't lose my scholarship, Mav."

His chin drops, and I feel Gavin's blue eyes slide to me.

My skin prickles, and I wait for him to make some remark about irresponsible alcohol use, *as if*. Instead, his attention returns to his phone.

Probably because he knows as well as I do this living arrangement is not going to work, and anything he says will only add fuel to the fire. Not that there's a fire. I feel no heat toward him.

Other than the heat of justice.

"Everything okay?" Gigi enters the room, followed by

two large dogs. "Haze and Spanky were so worried, they almost dragged me off the float trying to save you."

"Yeah." My shoulders droop, and I pet the curly head of her white poodle. "I acted like a total amateur out there. I wouldn't have blamed Mrs. H if she'd put me on probation."

"I've got something to cheer you up!" Her tone changes to a high-pitched doggy-voice, and she pulls out what looks like a little brown muffin. "Haddy, meet your new baby, Princess Petunia."

She holds the fluffy brown ball out to me, one hand around its middle and the other cupping its butt. Huge brown puppy-dog eyes blink up at me, and my heart melts into my stomach.

"Oh my gosh!" I take the teeny-tiny dog from her hands. "Gina! How is she so little?"

"Isn't she precious?" My cousin steps closer to where I'm holding the warm little bundle of fur against my neck.

"She's so cuuute!"

"I told you you'd love her." Gigi strokes the tiny dog's head with her index finger. "Does that make you feel better?"

"It does." I pucker my lips. "Softness signals safety to your nervous system. That's why petting animals lowers your blood pressure."

"And she's a princess." Her eyes brighten. "Peepee is perfect for you!"

Maverick does a spit-take, and even Gavin ducks, lifting a large hand to cover his mouth.

The muscles in his forearm flex attractively, and I don't know why I'm tracking his every movement like a magnet to steel.

I need to remind myself how he treated Karen. It doesn't

matter that he's as hot as molten lava—or one of Aunt Dylan's spicy peppers. He *cannot* be trusted.

"We're not calling her *Peepee*." I shake my head.

"Why not?" Gina snorts a laugh. "I give all the dogs nicknames."

It's true.

I lift Princess Petunia in my hands and give her a good inspection. She's an adorable, cinnamon-colored teacup poodle, and she fits perfectly in my palm.

"How much bigger will she get?"

"Ten inches is the usual height for toys, and they usually weigh six to ten pounds."

"Is she house-trained?"

"She uses a puppy pad." Gigi makes her own version of puppy eyes. "But if you take her out regularly, she'll go outside."

Gina's hands clasp under her nose, and she blinks those green eyes at me.

"Okay, she can stay."

A shriek of joy causes Peepee to shiver, and I tuck her curly brown body against my neck as my cousin throws her arms around my shoulders for a jumping hug.

"Yay! You're not going to want to give her back when Tori gets herself together."

"I *will* give her back." I don't have time for my research, my pageant obligations, *and* a dog. "And we're calling her Patsy."

"I'm calling her Peepee," Mav yells from where he's digging in the refrigerator.

My eyes drift to Gavin, who is looking down and doing his best not to laugh. Damn that stupid dimple in his cheek.

Maverick made a valiant case for him staying with us. It seems yesterday, on the second leg of his flight here, the house he was planning to buy was taken off the market at the last minute. Gavin had nowhere to go, and since he and Maverick are such good friends, my generous cousin said he could live with us until he finds a new place.

Maverick's argument is that between practice and games and grad school, we'll never even see each other. However, I've already seen him too much since my cousin made that pronouncement.

"That just leaves one last thing." Maverick steps out of the fridge holding a neon-green Mountain Dew.

He tilts his head in the direction of the table, and Gina's lips twist. She's a total softie. She would never turn Gavin out in the streets, even if by "streets" that means he'd move to a luxury hotel downtown.

Neither of my cousins knows about our history or my objection to his staying here, and it's not like me to be the bad guy, so I shrug. As loyal as I am to Karen, we were raised on hospitality. Our parents would never forgive us if we turned away someone in need.

For the time being I can put a pin in the past. It doesn't mean I've forgotten or that I'm disloyal.

"We do have an extra room." Gina looks at me for the final vote.

"Mav's right," I concede. "I'll be spending most of my days in the lab, and they're basically at the practice rink or playing nonstop."

"It's settled then." Maverick holds up his hand for an air high-five, which Gavin returns. "You're going to love it here. Monday's movie night, so add your nominations to the fishbowl."

"Maverick..." A warning tone is in my voice.

"What?" He holds out his hands. "If he's going to have to watch movies, he should have a vote, and for once I'll have some backup against you two. I might have a chance of seeing a guy film for once."

Shaking my head, I carry Patsy to the stairs. "Call me when dinner's ready."

GOLDEN STRING-LIGHTS HANG from the metal roof of our bungalow over the wooden back porch where a black wrought-iron table and chairs are arranged. A long serving table is against the house, and Maverick has arranged platters of tortillas, a covered dish of steaming fajita meat, and two bowls of guacamole and salsa, along with all the fixins, plates, and utensils.

"I used Mom's special habañero picanté sauce tonight, so be careful," he warns, passing behind me to get in line with his plate.

"Are you saying we should not try to put the fire out with beer or water?" Gina holds out her hands like she's a flight attendant explaining safety protocols. "We have vanilla ice cream in the freezer if you feel overwhelmed. Or tomato juice for the lactose intolerant."

"No one here is lactose intolerant." Then I glance at Gavin, who appears confused. "Sorry, are you lactose intolerant?"

"My mom is, but I'm not." He shakes his head, turning those heart-stopping blue eyes on me. "What's going on?"

"It's the standard warning they give before Dare Night at our family restaurant back home," I answer as I turn away.

I'm not looking to engage in a long conversation with him.

"Cooters & Shooters." Maverick throws his arm around his friend's neck. "We should go sometime. It's wild."

"Cooters?" Gavin's forehead wrinkles.

"It's the common name for the river turtles that live around south Alabama." Gina explains.

I take two warm tortillas from the folded napkins in the basket. "It's from the African word for turtle, *kuta*."

He nods, following my lead. "I forgot how smart you are." I deny the warmth flooding my chest at his compliment. "Are you still doing your sneezing studies?"

It helps that he just killed it.

"They're not sneezing studies." My tone is final, and I continue to spoon fajita steak from the covered dish.

A spoon of guac and some sour cream to cut the heat, and I walk over to sit at the table while my cousins and our house guest finish their servings.

Mav hands his friend a Dos Equis Amber, but I'm sticking to sweet iced tea tonight.

Gigi hops up after her first bite of dinner. "I need a glass of milk! Anybody else?"

"I'm good." I wave. The fajitas are spicy, but I love spicy food.

"Wimp!" Mav calls after her, but Gav dips his chin after his first bite.

"I'll take one." He slides his beer to the side. "You said that won't put out the fire?"

"What's the matter, Boomer?" Maverick teases. "Can't take the heat?"

"Boomer." Gavin snorts, walking over to the cooler and taking out a piece of ice. "I'm the ice man."

My eyes catch on Gavin sliding the piece of ice up and down his tongue, and I shift in my seat. Refocusing my gaze on my plate, I decide I'll finish early and head upstairs.

"Here you go!" Gina places a glass of milk in front of him, and the three dogs are now with us on the side porch.

It's a pretty sunset. The sky is gradually shifting from golden to blue and purple. I hear a little squeaky bark beside my chair, and I lean down to pick up Patsy.

"Yay!" Gigi does a fast air-clap. "You love her already."

"I don't want her to get stepped on." I pretend to be so stoic, but when she does two little circles in my lap then curls into a little ball, I know I'm in trouble. "As long as she doesn't barf in my bed like the last one."

"Something was wrong with that dog," Maverick calls from the other end of the table. "He was always humping my foot."

Gavin nearly chokes on his milk, and Gigi sits back in her chair, crossing her arms. "He might've had a urinary tract infection. It's hard to know when dogs come from bad situations."

"Alls I know is that couch pillow will never be the same again."

"Ew! Which one?" I drop my fork, ready to throw them all in the garbage.

"The one with the big red flowers."

Gigi clutches her cheeks. "That's my favorite pillow! Did you clean it?"

"Why would I do that?" Mav shakes his head like she's being ridiculous.

"Thanks for the warning," Gavin manages to say through his coughs.

"Are you okay?" Gigi reaches across the table to touch his forearm, and my stomach tightens, which is ridiculous.

"Yeah, thanks. You guys gotta warn me." He gives her a wink, wiping his mouth with a paper napkin.

My eyes narrow, and I'm not hungry anymore. Pushing away from the table, I tuck Patsy under my arm. "I'll load the dishwasher."

"You're not finished?" Gigi frowns up at me.

"You can't load the dishwasher and hold a dog. Give me Peepee."

"We're not calling her that." I walk over and hand the tiny poodle to Mav. "Dinner was delicious, thanks."

I walk to the table to start collecting the serving platters when Gavin's chair scoots away from the table. He stands and starts helping me, which is not what he's supposed to do.

"It's okay!" My voice is too sharp. "I have it. Just enjoy your dinner."

"Don't be prickly, Princess." He dares to give me that cocky grin. "I'm a guest. It's good manners to help out."

"It's nice to see you've picked up manners along the way. What's that like?"

"I guess you'll have to let me know." He takes the cast-iron meat platter from my hands. "Don't worry. I won't break it."

A hint of sarcasm is in his tone, and it's like a brand of fire.

I take the remaining items off the table and start for the kitchen. "Unlike the hearts you've broken in the past."

4

———

Gavin

My jaw tightens as I watch Hayden standing at the sink in those track pants and cropped tee.

Her back is turned and she's doing her best not to acknowledge my existence, like she's been doing all evening. It seems wrong that a woman so damn prickly should have a body that fine.

Still, she didn't veto me staying here, so I decide to extend my own olive branch.

"You never told me about your sneezing study." I place the heavy iron platter on the counter beside the sink.

Her blue eyes flash at me, and it's like a punch in the gut. *Gorgeous.*

Dammit.

"That's because it's not a *sneezing study*." Her eyes cut, and she turns to place the rinsed plates into the dishwasher.

"Set me straight, then." I do my best to sound friendly as I open the cabinet doors, one after the other. "What's so fascinating it's held your attention since college?"

With an impatient breath, she stops what she's doing. "What are you looking for?"

"Something to hold these leftovers."

"I'll take care of it. You finish here."

We trade places, and she walks over to a cabinet behind us. While she takes down a square plastic storage bin, I take the now-empty sauce bowls and give them a rinse before placing them on the top rack.

Glancing over my shoulder, I see her spooning leftover steak into the container. "Would it be more correct to say you're a virologist?"

Her shoulders fall, and she puts the lid on the plastic container, going to the refrigerator and placing it inside before closing it and leaning against it with her arms crossed.

"I wouldn't say anything to you. That's not what we're doing here."

I shut off the water and turn my back to the sink, mirroring her stance. Now's as good a time as any to have this conversation, and I'm older now.

I no longer lose the ability to form sentences when she hits me with those blue eyes framed by that wavy curtain of dark brown hair.

"If it makes a difference, I didn't know we'd be roommates when I took Mav up on his offer. Thank you for saying I could stay."

Her full pink lips tighten. "You're Mav's friend, and you needed a place to crash. It doesn't mean we're suddenly friends."

"Understood." I want to add I haven't forgiven her either for what it's worth, but I don't. "What happened in college was a long time ago. I'm willing to put it behind us if you are."

"I'm still friends with Karen."

It's like a hot punch to the gut. My jaw clenches.

"And you still believe every word she says?"

"She's an International Princess Woman. We have a code."

Shaking my head, I look down. "Right. No one ever breaks it."

"I realize that can be difficult for some people to understand."

I look up at her standing there with her arms crossed, her blue eyes focused on me, and I wonder how it can be so easy for her to be so certain.

"She's not like you, Hayden."

"Are you saying you didn't sleep with every girl in the Tri-Delt house?"

That makes me laugh. "I didn't sleep with every girl in the Tri-Delt house."

"We really don't have to dig all this up again." Her arms uncross, and she takes a step to the door. "If you've got that under control, I've got work to do before class tomorrow."

"Yeah, I'll finish up here."

She doesn't say goodnight. She doesn't say anything as she leaves the room, and I look out the window wondering how long it'll take for me to find a new place.

It's my last weekend of not having to be on the rink all day. I'm coming in late, and we're heading into the regular season.

"Hey, man, that is a very serious look on your face." Mav hands me a beer, and I take it. "What's bothering you?"

"Just thinking about finding a place with all we've got going on."

"Ah, don't worry about that. You're welcome here as long as you need."

"I wouldn't go that far." My eyes go to the place where she was standing.

"You're not worried about Haddy?" He leans against the counter. "She's just stressed about keeping that scholarship. She's really mad at me, not you."

I blink back to my friend standing there grinning, his floppy brown hair hanging in his hazel eyes. Mav's got an easy way about him. It's difficult to imagine anybody being mad at him for any period of time.

"I think it's more than that."

"Nah." He leans beside me, rinsing his bottle before putting it in the recycling bin. "Haddy's really focused on finishing school this year. She's got a lot on her mind."

A lot of *wrong* things on her mind. Whatever.

"Come on. I'll show you your room." I follow him through the living room, grabbing my bag from the couch. "You'll be upstairs with the girls."

That makes me stop. "Where will you be?"

He points to a door down a short hall. "That's my room."

My lip curls as I look up the dark staircase. "I don't know. I could probably get my room back at the hotel."

"You're not spending another night in a hotel room. You need a home with food and TV, and the girls won't mind."

"I'm not so sure about that." The idea of bumping into Haddy in the hall unexpectedly is not appealing.

"Just be sure to lower the toilet lid. Gina gets all honked off if the dogs drink out of it."

I glance at the clock. It's pretty late, and two nights in a hotel room did leave me wanting to be in a house—preferably my own.

"I'd feel better sleeping down here. I could sleep on the couch."

"We have a perfectly good room upstairs. Come on."

With a shrug, I follow him to the second floor.

MY EYES OPEN BEFORE DAWN, and it takes me a minute to figure out where I am and what time it is. *West Coast, LA, Mav's house, guest room.*

I stretch across the bed. It's firm but comfortable, and the wooden blinds on the windows do a good job keeping out the light pollution. Still, I can feel it. My heartbeat picks up, and I know I'm not going back to sleep. My body's still on Eastern time.

Shit, I'm too young for jetlag, but I've got three hours before I have to be anywhere. Rolling onto my side, I take out my phone and start to scroll.

I'm not looking for her, but we made all the gossip sites with what happened on Saturday. Of course, some dude with a phone was right there snapping pictures. Someone else even got video, and they all sent them to TMI.

In the video, I watch as flowers fly through the air. Haddy's hair swirls in a glossy cascade as I reflexively jump forward to catch her. Her hand is on my shoulder, and she looks amazing even in disarray (and a little drunk).

Studying the still photo, I notice things I didn't have time to notice when it happened. Maverick's face is stretched in an expression of pure surprise. Gigi is on the float leaning forward with her arm stretched out. Her eyes are wide with horror, and both dogs are in pointer positions like they'll throw their bodies between her and danger.

The expression on my and Haddy's faces is more curious. I almost appear pleased, and she almost seems relieved.

Damn, she's pretty.

And it's five o'clock in the morning. I've got to stop

looking at these pictures and sleep some more or I'll regret it later.

When my eyes open again, it's full sun outside, and I've overslept. *Fuck.*

Throwing the blankets aside, I head for the hall bathroom so I can pee and get rid of my morning wood, which has nothing to do with the last picture I saw.

It's not about her.

Only, the bathroom is occupied. The sound of a shower running comes through the door. *Double Fuck.*

I'm about to run down the stairs when a shriek echoes from the other side of the door, and it flies open.

"Spanky!" Hayden yells, and the giant white poodle dashes out of the bathroom with a thick white towel clamped in its jaws.

I've never seen a dog smile, but I'm pretty sure this dog is smiling.

"Come back here with my towel!" Haddy continues yelling as she runs out of the bathroom completely naked, and I swallow air.

She freezes directly in front of me, and I can't move.

All at once, I take in what's happening, and if I thought Hayden Bradford was gorgeous in clothes, she's impossibly beautiful out of them. Her breasts are perfect teardrops, high with tight dark nipples. Her stomach is flat with muscle lines on each side. Her skin is so smooth, glistening wet, and her dark hair is slick against her shoulders, her pussy is bare, and on her left hip is... a tattoo?

Her blue eyes widen, and my morning wood is now full-on erection.

"Fuck me," slips from my lips—at the same Haddy lets out a blood-curdling scream.

She slams her arms and hands over her body. "What are you doing up here?"

"I... I'm sleeping in the—"

Gigi's door opens, and she staggers into the hall with her eyes still closed. "What's happening? Who's screaming? Haddy?"

"What is *he* doing up here?" Haddy has dropped to a squat, balling into herself as she tries to cover her body.

"It's the only empty room!" I squint both eyes shut as I rip my T-shirt over my head and try to hand it to her to cover up. "Maverick told me to sleep up here."

"Why didn't he tell us?" Haddy snatches my shirt out of my hands, quickly pulling it over her head.

I keep my eyes on the ceiling overhead, holding both hands over the tent in my shorts. "I told him it was a bad idea."

"Go away, Gavin!" she screams, and I turn in the direction of my bedroom.

But this won't fucking work. "I've really got to pee."

"Oh my god!"

My eyes are closed, but I can hear as she makes her way to her bedroom and slams the door.

"Looks like the coast is clear." Gigi's voice is muffled, and I think she's trying to hide her laughter.

Scrubbing a hand over my forehead, I step into the bathroom before hesitating.

"The dog stole her towel," I try to explain.

"I know." Gigi's voice is drowsy. "Spanky's a towel thief. Be sure you close the door all the way, and if you're staying up here, you'd better lock it."

"I'm really sorry. I didn't mean to..."

"It's okay. She'll survive." Gina closes her door much more gently than her cousin did.

I'm pretty sure her eyes never opened the entire exchange.

I close the bathroom door and do my best to pee, but the image of Hayden Bradford's perfect breasts is imprinted on my mind.

She looks fucking incredible naked, and it's the last thing I need to know.

5

———

Hayden

"Miasma was thoroughly debunked by early scientists." I stand at the podium before a small panel of graduate advisers explaining the premise of my graduate thesis. "While miasma led to things like better sanitation, germ theory was in direct response to the notion that the air could hold sickness.

"And while germ theory does explain transmissions of many illnesses, it was the adamant refusal to acknowledge the possibility of aerosol transmission that led to the rapid spread of the virus in early 2020. Scientists were so focused on germ theory, washing hands, cleaning surfaces, they didn't properly account for the transmission through air."

"You'll bring in the case of the choir..." Dr. Vera Cross, my graduate advisor, prompts.

"Absolutely, the tragic story of the Sagkit Valley Chorale in Seattle was the first indication we were dealing with something more than skin-to-skin transmission. They followed all the CDC protocols. They washed their hands, they social distanced, they cleaned all surfaces. Yet after that one rehearsal, fifty-two individuals were diagnosed with the disease and three tragically died."

"What will be your contribution to the body of knowledge, Miss Bradford?" Dr. Becker, the director of graduate studies, makes notes on his legal pad.

He's very old-school, and most of my fellow students are afraid of him. I welcome his questions. He's a good professor, and he challenges us to tie up every loose thread.

"Kawasaki Disease is a rare syndrome that mostly affects children under the age of five. It's a terrible disease that causes extreme cardiovascular damage and can ultimately lead to death." I swipe through my notes. "To this day, researchers still don't know what causes it. It's not spread by person-to-person contact, however they have identified a pattern that coincides with the wind and dust storms sweeping from China into Japan, where the illness most often occurs. Here on the west coast, Kawasaki outbreaks have been linked to weather patterns and strong winds coming off the Pacific Ocean."

My throat tightens as two of the professors mutter something under their breath to each other that doesn't sound encouraging.

"It's still highly theoretical," I continue. "I'm collaborating with a researcher at the Japanese Society of Kawasaki Disease, and if we were able to establish a link between air currents and the transmission of Kawasaki, it's possible we could protect babies at these critical times and potentially save hundreds of lives."

Dr. Becker straightens in his chair, crossing his leg and fixing his dark brown eyes on me. "That's quite an ambitious goal."

"Yes, sir, it is." I look down at my iPad. "Researchers have been trying to solve this problem for five decades. I hope I can do my part to help advance our knowledge so no more babies will die from this terrible illness."

"I look forward to seeing what you're able to learn." He stands, and my shoulders relax.

Dr. Cross steps forward to take my hand. "Well done, Haddy. I've never felt so inspired."

My lips tighten, and I watch as the three other members of my advisory committee close ranks to chat.

"I hope I didn't over-promise. I don't think I'll find the cause, but I want to advance the ball down the field."

"A football metaphor?" The older woman's nose wrinkles with her smile. "If you take after your dad, you certainly will."

Dr. Becker walks over, extending his hand. "Nice presentation, Miss Bradford. Correct me if I'm wrong, but isn't your mother Raven Bradford, chief meteorologist at KCLA?"

"Yes, she is." I smile, knowing what's coming next.

"And you're an aerobiologist. I guess studying air currents runs in the family?"

"Mom always says understanding the weather can save lives, although she was hoping to be the next female Jim Cantore."

He breaks into a chuckle. "What in the world is she doing in LA?"

"I guess you can blame me for that. She came here to be with my dad."

"Of course." He lifts his chin. "This research has a lot of potential. I'm glad to be on your advisory committee."

"I'm glad to have you."

We exchange a few more pleasantries, and I head to the lab where I'll spend the majority of my time this semester.

It's a big white room with large computer monitors showing wind currents and tracking models.

It's a lot like what my mom uses at the television station, and even if she is miffed at me for continuing the pageant tradition, she's pretty stoked about my studies.

"How'd it go?" Timothy Grant walks up and leans against the counter where I've placed my iPad and phone.

He's studying tickling. It's the kind of research topic we get a lot of negative publicity for, but if the haters would dig a little deeper, they'd find out he's actually working on something extremely useful in diagnosing autism in infants.

"They're all pretty psyched about it." I give him a smile, and he blinks at me a second like his mind blanked.

He quickly clears his throat, giving his head a little shake. "All you have to say is 'saves the lives of babies,' and people start throwing money at you."

"Nobody's throwing money at me yet, unless you count the International Princess Woman Scholarship Program."

He huffs a laugh. "I still can't get over that. I mean, obviously you're beautiful, but princess, whoa. Unexpected."

"Right." My lips press into a frown. "Let's just keep it between us, okay?"

The only reason Timothy even knows about my pageant money is because he saw the letter sitting on my desk in the lab and asked. And I'm a terrible liar. If someone asks me a difficult question, I completely freeze up and blurt the truth.

"My lips are sealed." He does a little zipping movement in front of his mouth. "Want to head out and grab a beer? It's quitting time."

"Can I get a rain check?" His brow furrows, and I explain. "A while back my cousins and I set up this standing date night to be sure we spend time together each week. It sounds silly, but we're all so busy with all our jobs and Mav's games. Monday seemed like the best night, because you know. *Monday.* When he's not playing, of course."

"Rain check accepted. Maybe we can try again Thursday?"

"Oh..." My lips twist. "Thursday is game night."

"As in..."

"It's when Gigi and I go to watch him play when he's in town, because you know. *Thursday.*"

"I'm not sure I do know." He laughs, but it seems less convincing the second time.

"They're the two days nothing much happens. Monday's the first day of the week, and Thursday is the day before the weekend starts amping up."

He nods, "I concede to your scientific approach to the weekdays. How about Friday, then?"

"Yes!" I hold out my hand for a shake.

He takes my hand, and my shoulder lifts at the way he caresses it. Did I just agree to go on a date with Timothy?

"Drinks on Friday," I reiterate just to clarify.

I'm not sure dating him is such a good idea, especially since we share a lab space.

"TGIF."

Scooping up my things, I head for the door before things get weird.

"I HAVE THE FISH BOWL!" Maverick marches into the living room, using his announcer voice as he raises a plastic bowl filled with little slips of paper. "Who's doing the honors tonight?"

"I think you put Pepper X in dinner tonight." Gina

complains, eating another spoonful of Ben & Jerry's Fudgy Flan. "My tongue is still burning."

"I told you it was just jalapeños," he argues.

"Who puts jalapeños in hummus?" Gavin emerges from the kitchen where I assume he finished loading the dish washer.

I did not offer to help with clean-up tonight. After our horrifying encounter in the hall this morning, I haven't even looked at Gavin Knight all day, and I'm still a little pissed at Maverick for putting him on the second floor with me and Gina and not warning us.

It's always been just us girls up there, and he knows Spanky is a towel thief. Gigi blames it on the way we used to laugh when he was a puppy and stole all our things. He still thinks it's a game.

"It's pretty good, isn't it?" Maverick joins his friend behind the couch.

"It's different."

A tingle passes over my shoulders at the sound of Gavin's chuckle, which I immediately dismiss. I'm a grown woman and a scientist. So what if he saw me naked?

Gigi hops onto her feet on the couch, looking up at them. "I think Gavin should do the honors, since it's his first Monday Movie Night!"

"What do I do?" I'm not looking at them, but I can feel every time his eyes drift to where I'm holding Patsy under my chin and pretending to be completely absorbed in checking my social media.

Of course, it's all pictures of me flying through the air like a doofus off the parade float straight into his waiting arms. That, or people reenacting me flying off the float accompanied by strings of laugh-crying emojis.

Sometimes I hate this timeline.

"Now, open the paper to see what you picked," Maverick explains. "If we all hate it, you can put it back and draw again, but we all have to hate it."

"Somebody won't hate it," Gina argues. "They put it in there!"

"Majority rules," our cousin replies.

"It says... *Jurassic Park*." Gavin looks at each of us, and it's like a thermal laser when his eyes glide over me. "Everybody good with that?"

My cousins all agree, but I don't look up from my phone.

"Haddy!" Gina finally shouts. "Would you stop looking at your phone and pay attention?"

"*Jurassic Park* is fine," I answer, still not looking at them.

Gigi exhales a noise, but Maverick has the remote in his hand to pull up the movie.

"Just because Gav saw you naked, doesn't mean you have to give us all the silent treatment." Gigi grouses, and I glare at her. "Well, it doesn't!"

"I'm not giving you the silent treatment. I had a pretty tough day. I'd like to decompress."

"What made it so tough, Hads?" Maverick sits on the floor in front of my chair and leans his back against it.

I reach out to thread my fingers in his thick dark hair, and give it a sharp pull. "For starters, no one warned me a guy was on our floor."

"Ow!" He laughs, pulling his head forward. "I didn't know you were planning to flash him!"

"I wasn't."

Gavin walks around to sit on the other end of the couch from Gina, which puts him closer to where we are. My skin prickles with heat, but I keep my eyes on the opening scene of the raptors being delivered to the park.

"It's so much like *Jaws*." Gigi's knees are bent, and she

has a pillow on top of them to hide her eyes. "The way the girl gets yanked all over the ocean?"

"I'm getting more Indiana Jones vibes," Mav counters. "What about you, Princess?"

My lips twist and we watch as the movie shifts to the archaeologists in the field. I know what's coming with the pile of poop, and I remember my reference to miasma this morning.

"This movie made me want to be a scientist." My voice is quiet, and I feel Gav's eyes drift to me.

"You wanted to shove your hands in massive piles of poop?" Maverick leans his head back to look up at me.

"I have never done that once."

"But you *are* the super poo—"

"Maverick!" I yell, pushing his head. "Shut up."

Gigi falls to the side on the couch laughing. "You are so dead, Mav."

A smile is on Gavin's face as he watches us. "I feel like I'm missing something."

"You're not." My throat tightens, and I feel my face heating.

"Well, I think it's pretty cool that you're a scientist." Gavin's tone is warm.

"Thank you." I still don't make eye contact.

We continue watching the film. Gigi buries her head in the pillow when the T. Rex pushes the kids around in the car, when the raptors chase the kids in the kitchen, when they barely escape the island. Of course, we tease her.

"We've watched this movie a billion times." Maverick stands, stretching as it ends. "I can't believe you're still hiding from dinosaurs."

"It's scary!" Gigi stands, and Spanky trots up to her side.

I stand as well, and Patsy stirs in my hold. "I'm taking her out. Want me to take Spanky, too?"

"Please!" Gigi clasps her hands before catching the bannister and trotting up the stairs.

"Come on, bad boy." I snap my fingers, and the white puff ball jogs up to my side.

To my dismay, Gavin stands as well, following me. "I'll help you."

"I don't really need help." We walk through the kitchen to the back door, and I walk across the wooden deck to put my tiny guest on the grass.

She hops more than walks, and I can't help a smile. "She's so tiny!"

"Hey," Gavin touches my arm, and it's like a little shock. "I'm really sorry I saw you naked this morning. It was a total accident."

"We really don't have to talk about it." I blink up at his blue eyes, which are stupidly gorgeous.

"If it helps, you have a really nice body."

A flash of heat fills my stomach. "It doesn't help," I answer quickly.

My face is red, and I angrily fight against my involuntary physical response to him. It's simple biology, as I well know being a scientist. I can control it.

"Your breasts are perfect." A naughty glint is in his eyes.

"Please stop talking."

"It was like one of those movie scenes when all of a sudden, a perfect rack flashes across the screen. Like *Airplane!* Or what was that high school movie with girls in the showers?"

I know exactly what he's talking about. My mom is a total movie buff, and I was raised on old films.

"They don't do that anymore."

"Doesn't mean little boys don't know how to track them down."

My eyes slide to his. "I take it you tracked them down? That sounds right."

Player.

"You bet I did. There's nothing better than perfect breasts. They're works of art."

Patsy is hopping back to where we stand after doing her business. I walk forward and scoop her off the ground. "I'm going to bed now."

He laughs, a full-throated hearty sound I don't want to like. "I'm just messing with you, Haddy. Can't we be friends?"

"I think you know the answer to that."

He puts his hand on the porch railing, leaning forward. "Maybe I'll grow on you."

"Good night, Gavin." I turn on my heel and head to the door, the noise of his chuckle echoing behind me in the night.

6

———

Gavin

I sail around the rink, keeping my eye on Mav as he guides the puck across the ice before shooting it to the left winger. One of my new teammates glides in my direction, playing opposition, and the puck appears in my path.

Moving fast, I skate straight up to the guy, putting pressure on him to move away. He's not expecting it, and I quickly swipe the biscuit, sending it over to Mav, who slams it into the net.

The guys yell, and the player I pinched gives me a playful shove into the boards. Mav is right behind him pulling me into a neck hug.

"That's what I'm talking about." We glide across the ice to the bench.

"Nice pinch, Knight." Saxon Walsh, the left winger hops off the ice, dropping to sit beside us. "Keep that up, and they won't know what hit 'em."

We're having a good practice, and as Mav predicted, I'm

fitting right in with the Champions. They're good guys, precise, no hotshots. As always, Mav's the team beautician. He playfully slaps hands with everybody, his hair sticking out from under his helmet, sure to be the inspiration for all the little boys.

"That was dirty!" Aiden Akers, the goalie I slipped it past, laughs, reaching out like he'll give me a face wash.

I block him at the last minute, and the whistle blasts, calling half of us back onto the ice. Mav and I hang back, having earned a break. He leans forward yelling at the guys on the rink as they move around, passing swiftly.

"Ready for tomorrow night?" He looks up at me.

"I'm ready now." It's true.

Adrenaline surges in my muscles, and I can't wait to get out there for real. Nothing's better than being on the ice with the guys.

Well, one thing's better, but that's not happening any time soon.

"What's up with you and Haddy?" Mav's teasing frown catches me off-guard, and of course, her naked body flashes through my mind.

Clearing my throat, I school my expression. "What do you mean?"

I'm pretty sure I know what he means.

"You're the best guy I know. Haddy's the best girl I know. Everybody always likes both of y'all. Yet you don't seem to like each other. I'd go so far as to say you have difficulty being in the same room as each other."

He's studying my face, and Mav might be a hockey god, but he's smart. He has no idea how conflicted I feel about his cousin, how confusing it is for her to be so attractive, yet so cut off at the same time.

"We knew each other in college." It's the safest reply.

"Yeah, you both went to UNC, which makes no sense. That's basketball country."

"I grew up in Wilmington." He lifts his chin in understanding. "You're one to talk. You're from a football dynasty in south Alabama."

"It's true." He nods. "But back to Haddy. What happened?"

Pressing on my knees, I lean back not really wanting to get into this with him. "I dated her college roommate, and things went... bad."

Understatement of the year.

Mav twists his lips, then nods. "Haddy is loyal. You hurt her friend, it's like you hurt her."

"I've noticed." Even if she doesn't know what she's talking about. "She also jumps to conclusions and doesn't allow for the possibility she might be wrong."

"Whoa..." Mav holds up both hands. "Sounds like I touched a nerve."

The whistle blasts, and it's time for us to get back on the ice.

"It was a long time ago." I swallow that old anger trying to resurface. "I'm willing to let bygones be bygones, but I don't think she is."

"I'll talk to her. You'd be surprised. My cousin is a really great gal. Very understanding."

I can believe Haddy is great. I've seen her with her friends, but as far as *understanding* goes, that has not been my experience.

"Don't worry about it, Mav. I'll find my own place soon."

He glides over to pull my head into his chest. "But I am worried about it! You're my guy."

"Get off me." I push his arm from around my neck and straighten my helmet. "Let's do this."

"Gav and Mav." He growls playfully. "Or should I say Mav and Gav?"

"You had it right the first time."

I'M dead when we get back to the house, but Maverick is in the kitchen blasting music and dancing as he sautees something on the stove.

"I had no idea he could cook like that." I hold a Dos Equis Amber, watching as Gigi drags a brush through her tall, white poodle's fur.

"Yeah." She nods, the messy bun of her reddish-blonde hair bobbing. "He started learning with his mom, our Aunt Dylan... gosh, I don't even remember when. He inherited her love of hot peppers, even though she couldn't eat or cook anything spicy when she was pregnant with him. The two of them had the best time. She wanted him to be a golfer."

"I've heard." I exhale a laugh, taking a sip of my drink. "I can't imagine Mav on the golf course."

We glance over at him shaking his ass in front of the stove, and we both chuckle.

"He is way too crazy for golf," his cousin agrees. "He's a lot like my dad. So much personality."

A little cinnamon-colored puff ball hops into the kitchen, letting out the tiniest bark, and my body tenses. I feel her before I see her, the air growing electric with anticipation.

Haddy breezes into the room wearing tennis shoes, thick white track pants with black stripes down the sides, and a top that looks like lingerie. It covers her stomach, but it has thin straps and the tops of her perfect tits are smooth and visible beneath triangle cups.

"Do I have time to go for a walk? I've been sitting on my butt all day." Her dark, silky hair hangs down her back, and I swallow the desert in my throat.

"I think so." Gigi continues brushing.

"Hey, Mav," Haddy yells. "How much longer til dinner?"

He doesn't even look up, yelling back, "Seven-thirty."

"Perfect. Will you keep an eye on Patsy for me, Geeg?"

"Of course." Her cousin continues brushing, and the naughty poodle lifts his white head like he's preening as she brushes under his neck.

Haddy starts for the door, and an unexpected surge of protectiveness rises in my chest.

Straightening, I set my beer on the counter. "I'll go with you."

She takes a little stutter-step, and her full lips part. "That's not necessary."

"I..." *am fumbling for a reason. What am I doing?* "I'd like some fresh air myself."

Her slim brows furrow, and she glances from me to Gigi, who continues brushing like she's not part of this.

"I'm not going for a stroll, Gavin. I'm power-walking."

"Sounds good." I straighten to my full height, which puts her head at the center of my chest. "I'll keep up. My legs are longer than yours."

Her lips tighten, and I can see her trying to find an excuse to say no. I don't give her a chance.

With a smile, I rub my hands together. "Ready?"

She exhales a little growl, but I don't care. I don't like her walking around at this time of day alone, dressed like that.

Out on the sidewalk, she lifts her sassy chin and bends her elbows, walking like some kind of sexy soldier. I'm beat from being on the ice all day, but I keep up with her pretty easily.

"You didn't have to come with me." Her dark hair fans behind her in the breeze, and she huffs a little with each word. "I'm not leaving the neighborhood."

"If Mav is cooking dinner, the least I can do is make sure nobody messes with his cousin on her walk."

She rolls those blue eyes up at me. "It's a very safe neighborhood."

My eyes drift to her breasts, which do a little bounce with every step, and there was no way in hell. I don't understand this feeling, but if something were to happen to her and I didn't...

"I was just sitting around. What do they say? Sitting is the new smoking?"

"I'm sure you had a very active day at practice. Whereas I have to fit in that silly pageant dress on a moment's notice."

We continue walking, and she takes a turn at the stop sign. I look both ways, but there's not a car in sight. In fact, the entire neighborhood seems to be settling in for the evening meal in the waning twilight.

Through windows, I see a mix of families moving around making dinner, couples sitting at tables, singles walking around their living rooms. It does seem like a nice neighborhood.

My eyes drift to her with the great posture, the focused expression. "You know, I think all this princess stuff is really cute."

"Back the eff up, Knight."

"I've noticed you don't swear." I arch an eyebrow. "What's that all about?"

"The International Princess Woman scholarship program doesn't approve of us using coarse language." It sounds like she's reciting a textbook, then she gets more casual. "I don't want to get in the habit and slip up."

"Makes sense." I nod, looking at the road ahead. "Either way, I don't mind being your knight."

"Too bad your armor's tarnished. And I've seen under it."

She has no idea. "Sneaking peeks, Princess?"

Her eyes slide up to mine. "No sneaking required. Your behavior was on full display in college."

Shaking my head, *this girl.* I almost have to admire her for her stubborn loyalty.

"I'm not so bad."

"I prefer nice men."

"Who are you? Princess Leia?"

"You're so arrogant. I guess that would make you Han Solo?"

"Sure." I give her a wink. "I'm as confident as that guy any day of the week."

"Or cocky." She takes another right, and I realize we're headed back.

A sheen of sweat glistens on her upper lip, her neck, the top of her shoulders. She's moving fast, and we're nearly at the house. I put my large hand on her smooth shoulder, stopping her progress.

"What?" She huffs, frowning up at me.

"You're saying you'd prefer a lukewarm Luke Skywalker over Han Solo?"

"I prefer someone without the ego."

"I call bullshit."

Her lips part. "What?"

"You don't want that. Nobody as smart as you would ever settle for boring."

"As if you know anything about me."

I take a step closer, and she's breathing fast. She's also blinking fast, and the pink glow on the tops of her cheeks is from more than exercise.

She feels it the same way I do. I'm not sure what it means or what to do with it, but after seeing her naked body, I'd like to find out.

"I know you better than you think I do."

Her lips part, and watching her pretty blue eyes, I can tell she's got a comeback locked and loaded. But she doesn't shoot.

Instead, she turns to storm off, kicks a crack in the sidewalk, and pitches forward. My hockey reflexes kick in, and I lunge forward to catch her.

Her back is to my chest, and we're both breathing fast now. The scent of flowers is in her soft hair, and I want to lean my face forward and take a deep breath.

My arms are tight around her narrow waist, and she grip my forearms. "Let me go." It's soft and a little breathless.

I can't resist. "Feels too good?"

"It feels wrong." She pushes my forearms, and I release her.

Without looking back, she jogs up the steps, leaving me on the sidewalk watching her sexy little ass run away.

7

———

Haddy

Years of poise, grace, calm under pressure, and one week with Gavin Knight has turned me into one of the three stooges. I trip over nothing, and did I mention he saw me naked?

He's right behind me as we enter the living room. The table is set, and Mav has Patsy under his neck, a flustered expression on his face. Gigi's arms are crossed, and she's giving him the stink-eye.

"What's wrong?" My eyes go from one to the other.

"Dude, I thought I sat on Peepee." He holds the shivering dog under his chin, and his hands are so large, they cover her entire body. "I flopped on the couch, and that stupid toy squeaked. I nearly shat my pants."

"I've told you to watch where you flop when we're fostering puppies." Gigi shakes her head, going to where he's standing and giving Patsy a gentle pet. "You yelled so loud Spanky ran and got under the bed."

"I thought I'd killed her. Then what would Haddy say?"

"I would've strangled you." I calmly walk over to take the trembling little dog from my oversized cousin. "Her owner would never have recovered."

"She's a fragile human." Gigi's green eyes are sad as she nods at me.

Gavin enters the room, and I continue quickly into the kitchen, cuddling my puppy to calm my jumpy insides.

He does not make me jumpy. I almost fell, which is why I'm understandably flustered.

"What's for dinner? It smells delicious." I stop at the stove, surveying a glass dish of rice and assorted vegetables.

"Nothing major. Just paella."

"Just paella," I huff a laugh. "Don't some people consider that one of the hardest dishes to make."

"I don't know why." Mav makes amends by scrubbing Spanky's neck with his fingers. "It's just rice, chicken, and vegetables."

"Which pepper did you use?"

"Cayenne." He swings his legs off the couch, walking over to where we're congregating in the kitchen.

Gav leans his back against the sink, placing his hands on the counter beside him. It stretches the white tee he's wearing attractively across his chest, but I don't raise my eyes to his.

My cheeks have started this annoying habit of blushing every time he grins at me. Partly because he smiles at me like he's remembering what I look like without my clothes on, which makes my neck all hot.

The guys are animated at dinner, discussing practice and how well Gavin fits in with the rest of the team. Gina's on the edge of her seat, but I finish quickly, leaving her to help clean up. I'll take my turn tomorrow night when the boys are at the rink.

Also, I'm taking my shower right now, when I know our new upstairs visitor won't be wandering around.

I'm in my room, post-shower, dressed in my cotton PJs when Maverick taps on my door.

"Fresh sweater for you." He hands me a new, massive white hockey jersey with the purple and black Champions logo on front and a big number 74 under the name *Murphy* on the back.

"Tight." I shake it out, excited to wear it to the game this week.

Gigi and I always sit in the center, front row so we can cheer and see what happens without people in front of us. I've only just started following hockey since my cousin moved here, which means Gigi has to tell me what's happening most of the time.

They grew up in the same town, so she got to sneak off to all his games with Kimmie Joy and our other cousins. I'm kind of glad I wasn't there, because I suck at keeping secrets. If I'd spilled the beans to Aunt Dylan, they'd have all been mad at me.

I don't mind playing catch-up now. The games are so exciting, and hockey players are hot.

"Come here, Peepee." Mav takes the tiny dog off my bed before sitting on it and looking up at me. "She's really cute."

I smile, scrubbing my fingers in his long hair. "You're really cute. I should set you up with one of my pageant friends."

"You think I need help picking up women?"

"I don't know." I give his nose a playful tweak. "I haven't seen you with one."

"Speaking of, Gavin's a good guy. He's like me, focused on the game and minding his own business. He's not into bunnies. He's loyal..."

My shoulders tense the more he speaks. "Loyalty is not a quality I've seen in your friend."

"Maybe you don't know him as well as I do."

I think about the past few days. It's not long enough to know anything, but I don't want to argue with my cousin.

"You know, I could say the same thing to you." He stands, and I smile up at him. "I was there, Mav. I saw his behavior with my own eyes."

"I still think there's more to the story. I know my friend, and people don't change that much."

He has a point, and I guess I didn't spend a whole lot of time around Gavin in college. I was always buried in the lab or in classes or doing pageant events to pay for it all.

"They say if you don't put the past behind you, it'll keep checking you into the boards."

My nose wrinkles. "I don't know what that means."

"It means if you live in the past, you'll never get over it. Just give him a chance. For me."

"I've been trying to do that." I look down at the sweater in my hands, and he pokes me in the ribs.

"Try a little harder, Princess."

"I'll try." I chew my bottom lip wondering what that would look like. Then I remember. "Hey, would you do me a favor?"

"If I can."

"One of the PhD students said I could have some of their old equipment. It's a giant monitor and several smaller things. Would you be able to swing by tomorrow and help me move it to our lab?"

"Don't you have student helpers for that?"

"Not really. I share the lab with Timothy, but he's kind of... not very strong."

"He's a wimp?"

"I was trying to put it nicely." I don't include the part about how if Mav helps me move the equipment, I can casually suggest he join us for drinks as well.

That way I'll be doubly sure Timothy doesn't think we're going on a date or anything.

"Come by around five, and I'll buy you a beer to thank you."

"Say less," he laughs, going to the door. "See you tomorrow night."

"Can't wait!"

WHEN GINA and I arrive at the hockey arena, the speakers are blasting "We Are the Champions" by Queen followed immediately by "Another One Bites the Dust," which are the team's hype anthems.

Fans crowd around the glass to watch the guys warm up, and we're dressed like it's the middle of winter in leggings and our Number 74 jerseys (excuse me, *sweaters*) for Mav over white turtlenecks.

Okay, some of the fans only wear jackets, but I was surprised how cold my first game was. I guess I should've expected it to be cold being so close to the ice.

Our seats are right up front, and we watch the team stretching and skating around. Some of those stretches make me wonder how they don't freeze their junk off. I guess they wear cups.

When it's finally time to start, Gigi and I cheer as loud as we can for Mav. She says we have to cheer for Gav now, too, and I go with it. I promised Mav I'd try harder, after all.

Our cousin glides by our seats waving at us and giving a

thumbs up, and of course, we turn around and show off our Murphy sweaters.

When I turn back around, I don't miss the frowny twist of Gavin's lips. I'm not sure what that's about, but I can't worry about him. It's not like I can read his mind.

Fun fact about hockey games: They're a blast! They're fast paced and energetic, and Gigi and I are constantly jumping up to yell and cheer. Mav scores, and we scream our heads off. Of course, a fight breaks out, and we hold each other's arms. I cover my eyes.

Half the time, I don't know what's going on. Gigi tells me to watch the players instead of trying to track the puck, and of course, my stubborn eyes keep going to Gavin.

He's so fast, it's hard to believe at his height. He's really intense, like all the guys, but his blue eyes are fixed on the opposing players, watching every move.

At one point he goes to the boards and does some maneuver where he blocks the opposing guy from moving forward. Then he swipes the puck away and sends it to Mav, who whacks it into the net so fast, I almost don't even see it.

The arena explodes, and Gina grabs my arm, shaking it so hard.

"What happened? What did he do?" My eyes are wide, and I smile looking from her to the ice, where the guys are gliding like whatever just happened was a piece of cake.

"It's called a pinch, and it's a super risky move, but he nailed it!" She's screaming as she jumps up and down, chanting *Gav and Mav* along with the rest of the crowd.

"He made it look so easy," I muse, then I'm chanting *Gav and Mav* along with the rest of our fans.

We win 2-0, and the crowd floods down to the glass to cheer for the guys. We wave enthusiastically at Mav, and I chew my lip watching as Gavin chats with some girls on the other end of the bench.

They're all young and wearing tight clothes, and they're smiling and blinking fast. It makes my throat feel tight, but I push it away. I am not jealous of Gavin Knight. Good lord.

"Ready?" Gina grabs my arm, and I tear my eyes away from him smiling at a bosomy blonde in a tight purple sweater.

"Let's get out of here."

~

"DO YOU WANT THIS FILE CABINET?" Lucas digs behind a stack of air samplers, incubators, and a large microscope to drag out the last of his folders and put them in the banker's box.

I'm obsessed with the ancient microscope he appears to be abandoning. It's large, black metal with an oversized base and brass accents, and it looks like it's from the early 20th century.

"Not really, but I'd love this old microscope." I lean down to look through the eye piece. "Where did you get it?"

"It belonged to one of the microbiology professors. He retired, and I guess he just donated it to the lab. Or he forgot it."

"How could you forget something like this?" I put my hand around the arm to try and lift it, but I give up pretty quick.

It feels like it weighs fifty pounds, and I don't want to drop it. *More for Maverick to carry.*

"Take it." He stops to give me a hug. "I'm heading out. Good luck with everything, Hads. I'm sure we'll cross paths again."

Lucas got a job with NASA, which means the chances of us working together are slim, but I don't see the need to point that out.

"Thanks so much for all of this. I'll put it all to good use."

He gives me a wave, and I stand back, surveying the large flatscreen, the microscope, and the file cabinet. I pull out the drawers, reconsidering my rejection. Everything I do is stored on my computer now, and we don't have any hard copies in the lab.

"Still, it's a neat old relic..." I muse as a light tapping on the door draws my attention. "Gavin!"

"Hey," He stands to his full height, putting his hands in his pockets. "Mav said you needed help moving some stuff?"

"He was supposed to help me."

"He had to do some publicity stills, so he sent me instead. I hope that's okay?" He grins lightly, raking his fingers through the dark scruff on his square jaw. "You might not realize it, but your cousin's pretty famous."

"I realize it. He's on the billboard outside the arena."

The side of his mouth curls upward, and my lips twist. I don't ask him what they did last night. Gigi and I always go home after the games, but the guys like to go out for drinks and whatever else they do.

Mav says he's way too amped up to sleep after they play, but whether Gavin was with purple sweater is none of my business, even if he does look like he didn't get much sleep.

Blinking my wandering thoughts away, I gesture to the items on the lab table beside the microscope. "It's just these things. I think the two of us can make it in one trip."

"Let me see." He walks over to test the weight of the monitor, the microscope. The gray tee he's wearing can barely contain his broad shoulders and rounded biceps.

Which is good, since I need someone strong to help me move this equipment.

"Is this stuff expensive?" he asks, and I nod. "I don't mind making two trips."

"I can at least show you the way." He scoops up the microscope easily, reminding me how easily he caught me falling off the float... and tripping on my walk. *Good grief.* "How did you find me?"

"A guy in your room said you were down here."

"That must've been Timothy." I remember my plan to drag Maverick with us to have drinks, so Timothy wouldn't get the wrong idea.

I guess I can drag Gavin.

We enter the open lab space, and I notice my fellow grad student behind a computer. His eyes lift to us as we enter and promptly narrow.

"Over here." I lead Gav to my work space, where he puts the items on the table beside a monitor showing the direction of wind currents over the ocean.

Straightening, he surveys the stuff on my desk, my iPad, the notes I've made on a map of the Pacific, the calendars with dates and storm seasons highlighted.

"This is really high-tech." His blue eyes land on mine, and I squirm a little under his gaze. Then he nods to the wall behind me. "What's that about?"

I look over my shoulder at the "Women in STEM" poster. "That's Heddy Lamar, Natalie Portman..."

"I recognized Queen Amidala."

"They're famous actresses who were also scientists." We take a step closer, so he can read the captions.

"Invented a simple method to demonstrate the enzymatic production of hydrogen from sugar." His brows lift, and he tilts his head. "Sounds like you've got competition."

My stomach tickles, and I almost laugh. "It's not a competition. It's inspiration. These are all beautiful, successful women who are also scientists."

"I'm just messing with you. One day you'll be on that poster with them."

I can't stop a smile as a mixture of pride and hope tightens my stomach. "I hope so."

"Hey, Haddy." Timothy walks up to where we're talking, an annoyed expression on his face. "Are we still getting drinks?"

"Yes! Although, ahh..." I glance up at my hunky helper. "I was going to invite Gav to join us, since he's helping me and all. As sort-of a thank you."

Timothy's brow lowers, and he blinks from me to Gav and back. "Hockey player?" I nod. "Those guys are used to hard work. He'll be okay."

"Don't be grumpy, Tim." Gav puts a hand on Timothy's narrow shoulder, giving it a playful shake.

Timothy shrugs him off. "It's Timothy."

"My bad."

I'm not sure, but I think Gav is intentionally giving my lab mate a hard time.

Then he puts his hand on my lower back, leaning down to speak in my ear and sending heat swirling through my stomach. "Should we get the rest?"

I glance up at his cocky grin and my breath catches. Which is silly.

"Yes." I turn to Timothy. "Last trip and we can go."

Timothy is not happy, but he didn't say I couldn't bring a friend.

～

"A PRIVATE TUTOR." Gavin says the punch line loudly over the bar music, and I'm clearly feeling my frozen margarita.

I've only had one and that was a total Dad-joke, but I almost do a spit-take.

"Private tutor!" I cry, holding my nose.

"Hilarious." Timothy grumbles, finishing his beer.

His sour grapes response makes me want to laugh more, but I swallow it, clearing my throat instead. I can't help it. He's just so sulky in his baggy pants holding his Trader Joe's tote bag with a baby-blue Labubu attached to the strap.

At five-foot-eleven, he's the exact opposite of Gavin, who's leaning his muscled forearms on the high-top table across from me, watching me with that panty-melting grin. The dimple in his left cheek deepens, and his blue eyes sparkle like he's winning this round.

"I've got plenty more where that came from, Princess." He reaches across the table to hook my pinky finger with his, and Timothy puts his empty bottle down on the wooden surface a little too hard.

"I'm gonna get going." His voice is not breezy. "See you next week, Haddy."

"You're leaving?" I frown at Gav, and he gives me a wink. "But it's so early."

"It's too crowded for my taste."

The small off campus bar is only half-full, but I'm not going to argue with him. "I'll see you in the lab next week."

Reaching out, I give his arm a friendly squeeze, and his eyes travel over my head to Gavin. "Maybe we can try again another night."

"Maybe." I keep my tone bright, not overly encouraging, and he looks at me once more before heading to the door.

Once he's gone, I slowly turn to face my roommate-helper who's wearing a smug grin.

My eyes narrow, and I poke his rock-hard bicep. "You did that on purpose."

"You are *not* interested in that guy. He is way too Luke Skywalker."

"I didn't say I was interested in him, but you could've been nicer."

"I was very nice!" Gav straightens, holding his hands out. "I told the worst jokes I knew, and he still got pissed and left."

Another snort slips through my nose, and I lift my hand. "Private tutor was pretty funny."

He flashes that killer grin, catching my hand again. "He didn't even try to fight for you."

"Fight?" My eyes widen. "This isn't a hockey game."

"Yeah, but he was a dork. Did he have a doll on his tote bag? Also, why did he have a tote bag?"

"I think he's a teaching assistant this semester, which means he probably has papers to grade."

"Haddy. No." Gav shakes his head, so disapprovingly. "You cannot tell me you're interested in that guy."

Doing a little shrug, I stab my straw in my frozen margarita. "We share a lab. We should be able to have drinks together as friends."

"Trust me, Timmy does not want to be friends."

My nose wrinkles, and I take a sip of my drink. "I know. Thanks for coming with me. I was worried it might get awkward."

"Glad to help." He studies me as I hold my frozen drink and take another sip.

The music in the bar is some ancient Beatles song or maybe it's only George Harrison... my mom would know. Either way, I bob around to the familiar song until I realize

Gav is still watching me, only now his smile has morphed into something like satisfaction.

"What?" I stop bobbing and step closer. "Do I have a bat in the cave?"

I reach up to wipe my nose, and he catches my wrist. "No. You're beautiful as always, Princess."

Straightening, I clear my throat, feeling silly. "Thank you."

"Tell me something." His dark brow lowers. "Why don't you date?"

"I date. You saw me date in college."

"Right." His expression turns to disapproval. Again. "You dated Rob the knob Westcoat."

Again, I almost do a spit take. "The *knob*?"

"It's a British expression. It means dick." He hits the word hard.

"You're not British."

"No, but I like the insult. I bet they'd even let a princess say *knob*."

I shake my head. "Not likely. You have no idea how strict these pageant people are."

"Back to my point, you dated Rob the knob…"

"He was a total knob, too. He was way more excited about dating a beauty queen than a scientist." My chest heats at the memory. "He acted like my thesis was a hobby, and he always made little comments like wouldn't I enjoy majoring in fashion design more?"

"Knob." Gav is still watching me with that smile.

He's thinking about me naked. Which makes me wonder about him naked. Which makes my skin prickly and my body hot, so I slurp up the last of my frozen beverage.

"Don't you get horny?" he asks.

This time I do send frozen margarita through my nose. "Ow!" I squeal.

He laughs, handing me a napkin. I press to my upper lip squeezing my eyes shut against the burn.

"That was the least princess-ey thing I've ever seen you do." Then he pauses as if remembering. "Except for when you fell off the float... and tripped over air."

"It's all your fault." I blow my nose into the napkin, and he hands me another. "I've never had such a time until you showed up. I'm a total mess."

"You're welcome." That dimple's back, and I narrow my eyes playfully.

It *is* nice to relax for a little bit.

Then he shifts gears, leaning forward and giving me a serious look. "Tell me about your work. I've asked you a few times now, and you always dodge the question. I really want to know. What has you so consumed in the lab every day of the week."

"It's not every day."

"Quit stalling, Bradford. Tell me."

Clearing my throat, I slide my dark hair behind my shoulder. "Okay, I'll tell you."

8

——————

Gavin

I already knew Hayden Bradford was the most beautiful woman I'd ever seen, but tonight, watching her light up from within telling me about her research project... It adds a dimension I never expected.

She's amazing.

"Imagine if a virus could fly around the world on air currents alone." Her blue eyes sparkle, and her hands are spread wide in excitement. "If a disease could spread without person-to-person contact. No sneezing in your face or on a surface, which you then touch."

"That's terrifying."

"It is, but if we could show a correlation between the wind storms blowing into Japan from China every fall and the resultant outbreak of Kawasaki disease, we could protect more babies and potentially even stop the disease in its tracks."

"Damn." I say the word on an exhale. She's had me on

the edge of my seat since she started talking about it. "That's really cool."

"It's not as cool as figuring out the actual cause of the disease." She leans back with a sigh. "But think of how many children we could save."

"Why would anyone call what you're doing a hobby? You're saving lives."

She holds up both hands with her fingers crossed. "Not yet, but one day. I hope." Then she seems a little embarrassed. "Sorry, I'll go on and on once I get started."

Reaching across the table, I cover her hand with mine. I can't seem to stop touching her.

"It's incredible. Is that why you went to UNC?"

"Not really. I always wanted to live in North Carolina. It has a fun, cultural vibe, and they have a great STEM program. What about you?"

"I grew up in Wilmington."

"Still, it's a basketball town." She gives me a playful nudge I kind of love. "You were being a rebel."

"UNC was *not* me being a rebel. *Hockey* was everything my parents didn't want me to do, but I loved it." I exhale a chuckle. "My dad couldn't understand why I didn't join the military like him. He would always say, 'if you want adventure, join the guard.' My mom Elaine made me promise I wouldn't fuck up my teeth. Only my mom Kenny seemed to understand."

"Wait..." Her brow furrows, and she blinks at me a few times before grabbing my arm and pulling me closer. "Your parents are in a throuple?"

"What?" It takes me a second, then I break into a real laugh. "No, hell no. My parents were never married. Dad married Elaine, but my mom Kenny was always a part of my life."

"Aw!" Her pretty head tilts to the side. "That's so sweet! And how very evolved of them."

"Dad and Kenny were always really good friends. It was one of those drunk accident kind of things. Lucky for me, they decided to keep me."

"Oh no!" She cups her hands over her face, giving me wide eyes. "Was giving you up a possibility?"

"I don't think so. Mom was a widow, but she always wanted to have a baby. Dad had plenty of money, and he'd never tell her no."

"Your mom Kenny was a widow? That's so sad. She must've been young."

"She was, but then she met Slayde. Now they're married with a daughter."

"Yay! A happy ending!" Her face lights, and she does a little air-applause.

She's so pretty, I wonder if she'd ever consider turning our truce into something more like friendship.

Then she jumps and pulls out her phone. "Somebody's texting me... Oh. Oh no." Her shoulders droop. "It's Mrs. Higgins. I'm delinquent on my community outreach."

"That's a strong word. What crime did you commit?"

"I have to do some kind of community outreach every quarter, and since I fell off the parade float, I'm missing my project for this one."

"Come with me to the hockey clinic tomorrow."

"I'm not sure how that will help me."

"We do a charity hockey clinic for little kids every year, and I bet they'd love to see a real princess, especially one who's also a scientist. It's our official community outreach, so I don't know why it can't also be yours."

"Really?" Her pretty blue eyes blink wider. "I think it would count if a parade counted. What time?"

"10 a.m."

"We'd better get going then." She scoops up her phone and her iPad. "I'll have to get up early to put on my face, and I can't look hungover."

"You've only had one drink!"

"Let's go, Knight." She grabs my arm, and I chuckle, leaving enough cash to cover the bill and a healthy tip.

That's right, I'm her knight, and she took my arm that time.

WE STEP out of the ride share in front of our house, and Haddy wobbles back against my chest.

"Whoa." I catch her like I always do. Like I've really grown to like doing.

"Sorry, I lost my balance when I stepped out." She snorts a laugh, but her grip tightens on my forearm.

I escort her up the front porch steps to the door. "You really are kind of a lightweight. No wonder you fell off the float."

"I fell off the float because I hadn't had breakfast."

Tapping in the code to unlock the door, I scan her slender frame in front of me. "You need dinner."

"I think Mav's gone to bed."

"Nah, too early. He's out." Shaking my head, I open the door and hold out my arm for her again.

"I've got it!" She waves me away. "I just stepped out of the car funny."

"Okay." I hold up both hands. "I'll make us some dinner."

Fifteen minutes later, I'm sliding a perfectly toasted

grilled cheese sandwich from the cast-iron skillet onto her plate. "See what you think of that."

She actually licks her lips. "It smells delicious."

"It's my specialty." I scoop the remaining sandwich onto my own plate and follow her out the side door to the porch, where we sit at the table under the twinkle lights.

"I made my special lemonade." She places two glasses beside our plates.

"Really?" I take a big gulp from mine. "That's really good. Did you use real lemons?"

Her head ducks, and she snorts a laugh. "It's Country Time."

"Aw," I grin. "Got me."

Soft music drifts from the speakers on the corners of the house. The dogs are out here with us, Spanky resting on his stomach with his head perfectly poised. The little one is curled at his side like a baby.

We both immediately start stuffing our faces.

"Oh, my gah!" She groans, leaning back and covering her mouth with her hand. "That's so good!"

I grin, taking another bite of my own sandwich and thinking about how sexy that little groan sounded, thinking about how sexy it would sound with her on my lap, those perfect breasts bouncing in my face.

I've got to stop before I pop a boner. "Thanks."

"You know, Gina's a scientist too." Her brow arches. "She's a cynologist."

"What's that?"

"It's the study of domestic dogs." She takes another big bite, and I like watching her devour the food I made for her. "She had to learn all the different breeds, their behavior, human-dog interactions, their history..."

"That's really cool. Maybe she could bring Spanky and that other one to a clinic."

"Little kids love dogs." She nods, polishing off her last bite.

"It's true, they might be too distracted to play hockey."

"Thanks for dinner. You're a really good cook."

"I think anybody can make grilled cheese."

She stands, picking up her empty plate and mine and starting for the kitchen.

I'm on my feet at once, picking up our glasses. "I think it's cool to live in a house full of smart women."

She holds the door with her back, looking up at me. "Smart enough to pick some good eye candy for roommates."

I pass in front of her, warmth in my stomach. "We even cook."

"And move heavy stuff!"

We're both at the sink, and I take the plates from her hands. "And catch you when you fall."

My voice lowers, and she seems a little embarrassed. We're standing so close here at the sink. The water runs, but I can't break this moment. She lifts her chin, blinking up at me, and I'm ready to drop the plates, pull her into my arms, and devour those soft lips.

Leaning my face a little closer, she doesn't pull away. Her scent of fresh jasmine surrounds me. Heat flares stronger with every heartbeat. Her tongue slips out to wet her bottom lip, and I can taste the cool lemonade we drank on my tongue.

I'm so close, but as if waking from a dream, she lifts her hand quickly, resting it on my chest like she's holding me back.

"I'd better go to bed." Her voice is raspy. "I have to get my beauty sleep."

"You couldn't be any more beautiful, Princess."

A pretty shade of pink colors her cheeks. She picks up her little dog and with a soft goodnight, she leaves me wanting more.

9

———

Haddy

"Are you really a princess?" A little girl in the white hockey helmet squints up at me.

Her curly brown hair is styled in two pigtails on either side of her head, and she's dressed in skates, black leggings, and a kid-sized white Champions sweater with Mav's name and number on the back.

She looks like she's probably in first or second grade, and like all the kids, she's holding a hockey stick. She's in the box with me and the other camp participants her age waiting for their turn with the team on the ice.

"I sure am." I smile down at her.

Gavin is in the rink with Maverick and about ten of his other teammates. They're leading a mixed group of boys and girls through basic hockey plays, culminating in a chance to slam the puck into the net.

I'm pretty sure the Champions' goalie is only pretending to try and block, since they all score. Still, he puts on a good act, and they all get so excited to get it past him. It's really sweet.

I'm wearing a fluffy white jacket and black leggings along with my small tiara and a sash that says International Princess Woman.

I didn't go all out, since it's not a parade, but the coach asked if I would make an inspirational speech. I only found out about it this morning, and I've been working on it ever since.

"Is your dad a king?" Another little girl jumps up and down, causing me to scoot my feet back to protect my toes.

"My dad's a football player."

"My dad says football is way less awesome than hockey." The first little girl's nose wrinkles.

I'm about to reply when an oversized little boy sitting on the bench and swinging his feet yells, "My dad's mean as a snake!"

Chewing my lip, I squint my eyes, unsure how to respond to that one.

"Do you think girls can play hockey?" The little jumping bean has stopped jumping, and she's now holding my hand.

She's a cutie, and I lean down to whisper in her ear. "Girls can do whatever they set their minds to."

Her dark eyes widen with excitement, and she nods. "That's what my momma said!"

"It sounds like you've got a smart mom."

A whistle tweets, and Gav swirls up to where we're waiting. "Next group, on the ice!"

The other kids have gone to sit on the bench across from us, and the little ones who were surrounding me flood into the rink with cheers and yells.

Gav hangs back, leaning on his arm against the plexiglass partition. "How are you feeling?"

"Good." I smile up at him. "They're really cute."

"Yeah. We'll do a round with this group, then you'll say a few words, and that's it."

"I'll be ready!"

His smile is adorably crooked, and he skates backwards a bit before turning to join the other guys. I'm not cold at all as I watch him guiding the little hockey girl through a play, culminating in her slamming it into the net. Up next, he shows the little boy with the snake-dad how a pinch works, which I only know because Gigi explained it to me.

Maverick waves at me, and I lift my chin with a smile. I'd already gone to bed when he came in last night, but if he stayed out late, you'd never know it. He's as smiling and energetic as the rest of the guys.

Another twenty minutes pass quickly, and the little ones are sweaty and thirsty. They return to the bench area, and I step back to let them grab water bottles and flop on the seat.

Two of the team players quickly unroll a red carpet leading to center ice for me, and the coach skates over to where I'm waiting.

"Thanks for coming out, Miss Bradford. We're ready when you are."

No matter how many times I do this, I always have a mini-panic attack before addressing a large group of strangers. I've learned to lift my chin, straighten my shoulders, and put on a confident smile as I step out in my stilettos. Still, when I get to the center of the rink, my stomach dips when I turn to see twenty giants in full hockey gear standing in a line facing me.

I blink a few times, doing my best to project confidence, until Mav lets out a taxi whistle and starts clapping. "All right, Haddy!"

He's quickly joined by Gav, who claps and also shouts a "Yeah!"

The other guys start clapping, and the kids all beat their sticks on the wooden boards. It breaks the tension at once, and I exhale a laugh.

"Thank you for that." I look around at the little kids on the benches. "Is it okay if they come out and join us, too?"

"Sure." The coach motions to the little attendees. "Come on out!"

They all hop up and quickly take their places in front of the big guys facing me. I notice the little girl with pigtails skates right up to Gav, taking his hand. She looks up at him, and he gives her a warm smile as he holds her little hand in his big one.

It helps me relax, and I take a beat, doing my best to make eye contact with each of them. "Now I don't have to yell."

Polite laughter fills the gap.

"You're probably wondering who I am." All the little heads nod rapidly. "I'm Hayden Bradford, this year's International Princess Woman, and Maverick Murphy's first cousin."

At that the children gasp, turning big eyes from me to Mav and back again.

"I'm also a scientist. Do any of you know what that means?" I get a mixture of nods and shrugs.

One girl raises her hand. "It means you work in a lab and do experiments!"

"Yep, that's part of what I do. I also do a lot of math, and I build models on computers."

"My dad said girls aren't good at math." It's the little boy with the snake-dad.

"It's a common misconception," I reply. "Have any of you heard of the STEM program?"

Several hands shoot up, and the little girl holding Gav's hand waves hers wildly.

I point at her, and she yells, "It's science camp! I go every summer!"

"That's great! Do any of you have STEM programs at your school?" About half the group nods, so I press on. "Then you know that just like hockey, being a scientist involves a lot of hard work and sometimes even failure."

I continue talking to them about what to do when an experiment fails or we lose a game (dust yourself off, see what you learned, and try again), and we talk about the value of hard work and team work and not being afraid to take chances or ask hard questions.

After a few more minutes, I wrap it up. They're tired, and I don't want to make them stand too long at their age. Also, their pick-ups are arriving to take them home.

"With that in mind, remember always to do your best, stay curious, and look for ways to help others shine."

Everyone claps, and I quickly thank the coaches and the players for having me.

Little Pigtails releases Gav's hand and skates up to me. "I think I'll be a princess now, too!"

"You can do it!" I give her little shoulder a squeeze, and she holds her arms up for a hug.

I lean down, and she hugs me so hard, it makes me laugh. Then she skates to her waiting mom, who gives me an apologetic wave. I wave back, smiling. It's totally fine.

Gav glides up to me expertly on those skates. I still can't get over how fast he can move on those things.

That cocky grin splits his cheeks. "You're a natural."

"I could say the same for you. I think that little girl

would've come home with us if she knew we all lived together."

"This is my favorite outreach we do." He's serious, watching them all meet up with their adults. "They're so earnest."

"You're really unexpected, you know that?" My head tilts to the side.

"I could say as much for you." He gives me a wink.

"Other than Mav, I haven't met a lot of guys who have the patience for little kids."

"It's not about patience. They just want somebody to listen to them and care."

My eyes follow his to a beefy man in a Champions sweater picking up the boy with the "snake-dad." I hold my breath a second as he excitedly shouts to his dad everything he learned today, including "a lady who's a princess *and* a scientist!"

The man laughs, holding up his hand for a high-five, and he puts his arm around the little guy as they walk to the exit.

We both exhale a laugh, and I take Gav's arm as I walk up the red carpet to the bench where I left my stuff. "I don't know what I was expecting from that guy."

"Something more sinister?" Gav's tone is serious. "I was waiting to see what he'd do."

"He must hide his snakeyness under a bushel." I pick up my stuff. "Or maybe it was a joke, and his son didn't get it?"

"Hard to know." Gav shrugs. "Do you need a ride home? Give me a second, and I'll get changed."

It's not long before he's helping me into a black SUV that will take us home. Mav likes to drive his own car, but the team all have drivers available if they need them.

I notice my cousin standing with one of the little attendees and talking to reporters. They take pictures, and another reporter has a mic and a television camera.

"You don't have to do that?" I nod in their direction.

"Not yet." He's in jeans that stretch attractively over his thighs and a black hoodie. "I'm the new guy, but I expect that'll change before long."

His confidence is pretty much on par with all the hockey players I've ever met, but I can't argue after watching him. "You and Mav play really well together."

"We always have. It was tough when he left Atlanta, but he's the reason I'm here."

"I can understand wanting to play with your friends. Your schedule is about to go crazy."

Every fall it's the same. Mav's games start up with a vengeance at the same time I go back to school and Gigi heads into dog show season.

She's as busy with all the training and qualifying. It's like dog-pageant-world.

It's also the reason we came up with a schedule for spending time together. Otherwise, we'd be ships passing in the night, "same planet, different worlds."

"I don't know how you guys do it." I look over at Gav. "You play so much all the time. You must be exhausted."

"Nah, we love it." He gives me that grin that makes my stomach tingle.

Clearing my throat, I look out the window. "I was surprised how many little girls were at the clinic today."

"Girls can do whatever they put their minds to."

"Right." I glance back at him. "I noticed one little girl was a big fan of yours."

"She was a good little player—and she wants to be a princess now, too."

I think about that. "They're not that different, you know.

Pageants and hockey, I mean. Not when you get down to it. They're both hyper competitive, and some participants take it way too seriously."

"Are you saying pageant girls draw blood?"

"They can, figuratively speaking. I hate to take my mom's side, but I'm not sure I'd want my daughter to do either one."

"You're making both our moms right," he chuckles.

"I'm not sure how I'd handle it if my daughter wanted to play."

"I think I'll have to support my kids whatever they decide to do."

More unexpectedness. I study his wistful expression. "You've thought about having children?"

"Sure, I always wanted to have kids, although Karen kind of killed that for me."

"How did she do that?"

His eyes drift to mine before moving around my face. "She told a lot of lies. She damaged my trust... and the trust of others."

We're at the house, and I don't know how to respond. It almost feels like he's talking about *my* trust, but I don't know what his having children would have to do with me.

Either way, if he's trying to act like he can't get a girlfriend, I'm not buying that for one second.

Gripping the door handle, I open it before the driver can make his way to me. "I'm sure you'll find somebody to help you with that."

The man takes my hand, and I step out, heading to the house without looking back.

"Haddy, wait." Gav slams his door, but I'm already up the front steps.

I hear him jogging up behind me, and I have to stop to enter the code to unlock the door.

"Why are you mad?"

"I'm not mad." My fingers tremble, and I enter the code wrong. "Stupid door. Why can't we just use keys?"

"Stop." He puts his hand on mine, turning me to face him. "Talk to me."

"About what, Gavin? I don't know what you want me to say."

"I want you to say for once you'll give me a chance to tell you my side. I know she's your friend, but is it possible there's more to the story?"

Crossing my arms, I step away from him. He's too close and too overpowering.

"Okay." Exhaling a sigh, I look up at him. "I'm listening. Tell me your side."

He exhales deeply, looking down and putting his hands on his hips. Then he turns, taking a step away, to the side of our small front porch and shoving both hands in his hair before turning back.

When he faces me again, he's disheveled and earnest and his eyes are too blue.

His broad shoulders heave, and he speaks as if he's making his confession. "I realized things weren't going to work out with Karen the day I met you."

My eyes blink wide. "But you stayed with her."

"Because it wouldn't have made a difference. You were friends, and even if we'd broken up, you wouldn't have dated me. Would you?"

"Of course not. She was my roommate and my friend."

His lips tighten. "She wasn't anybody's friend. She definitely wasn't mine, or she decided our relationship was non-exclusive and forgot to tell me."

"Are you saying *she* cheated on you?"

"I walked in on her on her knees in front of my team-mate. A few weeks later, my cousin Dex confessed she'd tried to get with him, and he didn't want to tell me..."

"So it was all Karen, and all those other girls simply made up stories about sleeping with you."

Reaching up, he scrubs the back of his neck. "No."

"That's what I thought." I turn to start entering the code again, but again, he stops me.

"I slept with a few Tri-Delts."

"A few?"

"More than a few." He won't meet my eyes now, and his brow is furrowed. "I didn't care about them, and it wasn't right. But I was on a rager after Dex told me. Then next thing I knew, she found out and she turned it all around. She said it was all me... and you stood by her, just like they all did."

"I never had a reason not to believe my friend. I've known Karen since we were teenagers."

"I'm giving you a reason." Intense blue eyes lock on mine. "I'm telling you it was a lie."

10

____

Gavin

I don't know if she believed me. I told her my side, and she pressed her full lips together and nodded. She didn't say anything. She only entered the code on the door and went into the house, scooped up her little dog, and went to her bedroom.

Mav eventually came home as did Gigi. We had dinner together, and Haddy acted like she always does, friendly but not really making eye contact.

It twists in my chest, and I want to pull her aside and make her tell me where she landed.

That would be a mistake, so instead we chatted about the charity clinic. Mav bragged about his cousin, and how she inspired a whole generation of princess hockey stars, male and female.

Haddy's cheeks flushed a pretty pink when I joined him in praising her popularity among those future hockey stars.

She even laughed when I mentioned the little boy with the dad who is allegedly mean as a snake.

"That doesn't sound very good," Gigi frowned, patting Spanky's fuzzy head. "Are you guys mandated reporters?"

"I don't think so," Mav polished off his last habanero-spiced black bean burrito. "Coach might be, but not us."

"You don't seem too worried about it," she pressed.

"I was concerned at first." Haddy leans over to put her little dog on the porch. "Then his dad showed up, and they interacted like any father and son, no fear, all shouting and happy excitement."

"The guy seemed okay," Mav agreed. "I think the little kid might've overheard his friends joking around or something."

Gigi seemed satisfied. "Well, I'll tell you who was *not* shouting with happy excitement."

"Oh, no." Haddy leans forward to squeeze her arm. "Was it elimination day?"

"First round contestants for the West Coast Regional dog fair." She shakes her head. "I don't know why I do this every year. I've done my best to scrub our address from the Internet, but keep your eyes open."

"Not this again," Mav groans.

"What the fuck?" I look from Gigi to Mav. "Is something going to happen?"

"Somebody's going to toilet paper the house or stink-bomb the mailbox," Mav explains.

"Which is a federal offense, by the way." Haddy stands, walking over to where Peepee is trying to climb back up the steps from the yard to the porch.

"We should figure out a way to booby trap it!" Mav is on his feet collecting plates, which prompts me to do the same.

"And have it go off on sweet Mr. Nelson?" Gigi cries. "Never! We'll deal with the stink if it comes."

"Maybe we could teach Spanky to be a guard dog,"

Haddy observes, collecting the serving dishes and following her cousins into the house.

"I don't know if Spanky is discerning enough for that," Gina says. "He might attack the wrong person."

"I'm not sure anyone would be afraid of a poodle," I tease.

It's a small space, and Mav and Gina are busily rinsing and loading the dishwasher. I put the stack of plates I collected on the counter, and I notice Haddy waiting with the serving dish in one hand and Peepee in the other.

"Here, I'll take care of those." I try giving her a smile.

She blinks up at me briefly, giving me a hint of a smile in return. "Thanks. I guess I'll head on up, then."

I pause, watching her go to the stairs without looking back.

We're headed into a time when I'll be at the arena most nights, not to mention traveling. It would be easy to bury myself in the sport like I've done for so long, since college, and forget these past few weeks ever happened.

Only, I don't want to forget.

We finish up in the kitchen, and Mav and Gigi curl up on the couch to watch some reality TV show, but I head upstairs to my room.

I hear her finishing in the bathroom. I hear her open the door, and I picture her going to her bedroom. It's a longshot, but I snatch the jersey I bought last week off the back of my chair and open my door before she closes hers.

She stops, looking straight at me in a way that tenses every muscle in my body.

With a blink, I take her in. She's wearing soft cotton pajama pants with tiny mermaids all over them and a thin, long-sleeved cotton shirt. Her soft hair is gathered in a messy bun on her head, and her face is freshly washed.

Today at the arena, she was in full pageant mode, with thick black lashes, glossy nude lips, and all the glitter and sequins. It was all very glamorous, but I like this way better.

Tonight, she looks so young. I walk down the hall to where she's standing, and the closer I get, I see the faint freckles on the bridge of her nose.

"I got this for you after the last game." I hold out the sweater with the Champions logo on the front and a giant Number 5 on the back under the name *Knight*.

"It's your jersey." She takes it in her hands, turning it over and holding it up to her body.

It's pretty big, but so was the one she wore for her cousin.

"I noticed you were wearing Mav's jersey last game." I don't say it made me angry in a way I didn't expect. "I thought you might wear this to the next home game. It only seems fair. Mav already has one beautiful lady cheering for him."

Her lips poke out then twist. "I don't think he'll like you poaching his fans."

"He's got plenty of fans. I'm just getting started in a new town."

"You're not doing too bad. I noticed you talking to a group of girls after the game." She slants those pretty blue eyes up at me.

Could that be a hint of jealousy in her tone? I decide to put a pin in it.

"What do you say?" I rest my hand on the door jamb above her, hanging on the edge of my seat for her answer.

Her eyes scan my chest quickly, moving up my arm, before quickly returning to the jersey, a touch of pink in her cheeks. "I think I can do that."

A laugh huffs through my lips, and I take a step back,

feeling like a weight has been lifted off my chest. "Okay, then."

She might not have said she accepted my side of the story, but I take this as a promising sign.

OF COURSE, our next four games are on the road.

Time is moving fast. The season is in full swing, and we're playing at least three games a week, sometimes more.

I'm starting to understand the cousins' call for dedicated nights to spend together, and with October winding down, I'm looking forward to finally having a game at home.

As we warm up on the ice, my eyes go to the spot where the girls always sit. A crowd is gathered at the glass to watch us stretch and hopefully catch a puck.

We won all our games on the road, most involving killer plays, a trip that resulted in a slap shot, a high-risk pinch that had me on my stomach sliding it through the goalie's legs. Mav and I are on all the highlight reels, and it's turning into Atlanta all over again.

Fans have started doing a hand signal that's a combination of the *G* and the *M* in American Sign Language. Basically, it's a fist with the thumb under three fingers for the *M* that they shake into a point for the *G* while chanting *Gav and Mav*.

After a while it's impossible to know if they're doing the *G* first or the *M*, and of course my number-one supporter Maverick Murphy likes to insist they *always* start with the *M*.

Either way, we both toss pucks for it.

I'm in a lunge, stretching my hamstrings, when I look up to see Gigi and Haddy setting up at their designated seats behind the glass. Adrenaline spikes in my veins, and I hop to my feet so I can skate closer.

It's the first time I've seen her in almost a week because of our schedules, but I lap the rink before going straight to them. I don't want to seem too eager. Still my eyes are fixed on her body.

She and Gigi are both in tight black pants and long-sleeved white turtlenecks under their sweaters, and from the front they look identical with the Champions logo on the front.

Chewing my lip hard, I cross center ice, moving in their direction, when Haddy turns around to put her jacket on the seat behind her, and I see a big Number 5 peeking out from beneath her hair.

"Yeah," I laugh, picking up speed and skidding to a hockey stop in front of them.

It only creates a small spray, but I've got a puck in my hand. She straightens, and before she turns around, she sweeps her long, wavy hair into a high ponytail revealing the massive *Knight* across her shoulder blades. *Fuck* yeah.

She turns around, and her eyes land on mine through the glass. They sparkle blue, and her lips press into a tight smile that makes me laugh again. I hold up the small, black biscuit, and she steps forward to catch it from me.

I toss it gently, and she catches it, waving it at me and giving me a wink.

We're going to win this one.

Colorado's team is killer, and for the first half of the game, nobody scores. They got close on us several times, but Saxon and I are strong defenders. If I'm not there, covering Akers, I know he is, and vice versa.

In the second half, we come out strong. Mav almost has it, when a defender swipes his skates, sending him to his stomach. Still, he flips the puck and nearly makes it past the goalie's mitt. A fight breaks out as a result, and Mav is landed in the sin bin for two minutes, which is bullshit, since their D-man clearly tripped him.

The clock is beating down, and we're moving fast. I look up to see a Colorado winger coming down the boards, and it's go time.

Heading straight for him, I know Sax will cover my spot. I'm tight on the guy, sending my stick through his skates and scooping the puck right out of his possession. Mav's ready, and I slap it to him, but it hits another player's skate and flips into the air.

Without hesitation, Mav bats it with his stick, and it flies straight past the goalie's head into the net. The stadium erupts, and we're finally on the board.

It's 1-0, and we just have to hold them a little longer.

But Colorado didn't come here to lose. These guys are beasts, and I'm slammed into the boards more than once. Another fight breaks out, this time landing one of the Cliffs players in the penalty box, which I guess is meant to make up for the previous, lousy call.

I glance over at the girls to see they're on their feet, clutching their hands. Haddy is hiding her eyes, which makes me chuckle, and I get checked into the boards, which wakes me up.

No more distractions.

We're in the third period, and the Cliffs are going for a tie. I'm guarding their left wing when the center shoots through the middle. Saxon stays with him, but at the last minute, the guy does a hockey stop, a skip, turn, and shoots the puck right past Akers.

Shit. We're all frowning as we glide into formation. The clock runs out, and it's sudden-death overtime.

Mav's jaw is set, and he skates up to me. "You know what to do?"

I nod, and it's time to pull out the move we perfected in Georgia. The Cliffs have the puck, and their left winger is bringing it down the boards.

"Come to Papa," I say under my breath, skating towards him fast, until I've scooped the puck away from him and shoot it over to Mav.

Mav shifts into lightning speed, scooping it out and running it down center ice to the goal. I'm headed back as well, and he shoots it across to me, catching their defender off guard. I bring it around behind the net, and send it back to Mav, who immediately slaps it past the goalie for the win.

"Boom!" Mav yells, spinning around to grab my shoulders and giving me a shake that makes me laugh.

"Tic-Tac-Goal!" Donovan shouts, grabbing Mav around the ribs and playfully slamming him against the boards as Saxon sails past us on his stomach.

The stadium is on their feet cheering. I'm a sweaty mess, but I glide over to where the girls are doing the *G-M* sign with their hands over their heads. I put two fingers to my lips as if to blow a kiss, which I turn into a point at Haddy. She points back at me, and I'm too fucking happy to care how it looks.

11

Haddy

Halloween is on a Friday this year, which happens to land perfectly for our annual celebration. Usually, we have to adjust our date to accommodate Mav's schedule, but they have a rare Friday night off.

They'll be back on the road Saturday, but it's for a game in Anaheim, so not too far.

We all love Halloween. When I was a little girl, my fall break always fell around this time, and Mom and Dad would pack us up to head south to Newhope to spend the holiday with all the Bradfords.

Besides Christmas, it's the holiday I most associate with my cousins, and every year we go all out.

"What do you think?" Mav stomps into the kitchen, where Gina and I are stringing the Styrofoam balls we've covered in cheesecloth.

They're cute little ghosts, and we'll hang them everywhere, inside and outside the house.

Our cousin is dressed in what looks like a hairy ape-like

costume with a pink ribbon in its hair and a pink belt tied in a bow around his waist.

"What are you?" Gina frowns. "Mrs. Chewbacca?"

"There's no Mrs. Chewbacca," he groans. "I'm Big Foot!"

Tilting my head to the side, I squint up at him. "Did Big Foot wear a pink ribbon in his hair?"

"He does on the clock app. Haven't you seen the video of him walking with the purse?"

"Yeah, I didn't know what that was supposed to be about."

"You should just go as regular Chewbacca." Gina stands, carrying four ghosts on her fingertips to hang on the front porch.

Mav pretends to snore, and I bump him with my hip as I pass, carrying more ghosts to hang outside. "I'm going as Princess Leia. We can be a pair, like they were in Cloud City in *The Empire Strikes Back*."

"Haddy!" Gigi whines from where she's climbing the ladder at the front door. "You changed your costume?"

"I didn't change it!" I walk over to where she's stringing ghosts along the orange twinkle lights.

"But she wears that puffer vest in Empire! I thought you were wearing the white dress from the awards ceremony at the end of *A New Hope*."

"You're going as Princess Leia?" Gav walks up from where he just finished hanging bat silhouettes in the trees.

His cap is on backwards, and the short-sleeved black tee he's wearing makes me wonder if any of his clothes can accommodate his muscular physique. It's stretched so nicely over his pecs.

"It seemed like the obvious choice." I shrug, and my stomach tingles when our eyes meet.

"Obviously, Princess." He winks at me, and I blink down,

fighting a goofy grin and wishing my cheeks didn't flame red every time he did that.

We haven't had a chance to talk for real since the day of the charity clinic, but I've thought a lot about what he said. I've thought about what Mav said about how people don't change that much. Every time, it leaves me feeling uneasy.

I can't believe Karen would lie to me, but I don't know why Gavin would lie to me either. It was all so long ago, I'm not sure why he still cares about what I think today.

Except... I think I do know why, and the reason makes my insides all hot and zippy.

He was genuinely disgusted with Rob "the knob." He gave me his sweater to wear to the games. *I was ready to break up with her the day we met...*

"What are you going as, Gav?" Gina climbs down the ladder and folds it.

"I hadn't decided yet, but now I have an idea."

"If Mav goes as Chewy, and Hads is Leia... What can I be?" she pouts.

"You could be Cruella Deville!" I suggest excitedly.

"Haddy! She was breeding dalmatian puppies to use for a dog-fur coat! That's pure evil."

"It's Halloween," I counter. "You're supposed to be pure evil."

"Princess Leia's not pure evil. She's good."

It's true. "You could be Rey from *The Force Awakens*."

"Why doesn't Star Wars have any strawberry-blonde characters?" My cousin frowns up at Mav, who is strutting around with his hand up like a prissy Big Foot.

"That is a good question, girl!" He sticks out his index finger and boops her nose.

"What the hell are you?" Gav frowns at his friend. "Lady Chewbacca?"

"There is no Lady Chewbacca!" Mav groans.

"If there were no lady Chewbaccas, how would they get the little Chewbaccas?" Gina bats her eyes at him as she lifts the wooden ladder and starts to carry it into the house.

Gavin steps forward quickly to take it from her. "Let me help you."

"You can be Glinda the good witch," Mav suggests.

"Do you know how many times I've been Glinda?"

"What about Pretty Woman? Or Danger-Prone Daphne?" I try.

She waves her hand, following Gav into the house. "I'll figure it out."

Stepping back, I survey our decorations, from the orange twinkle lights framing the front door to the large bowls of candy we'll hand out to trick or treaters. The party will start after dark, after the kids are finished making the rounds, which looking up, I realize is about to begin.

"I've got to get dressed! Mav, are you ready if kids show up?"

"Ready with the full-sized Hershey bars." His eyebrows waggle, and he rips the plastic off the packages. "Best house on the block."

"Never grow up," I tease, dashing up the stairs to get changed.

"Another Maverick Murphy!" I exclaim, handing the little boy a full-sized chocolate bar. "That makes ten."

"Ten Mavs and only six Gavs." My cousin tilts his Yeti head, pretending to be sympathetic. "Looks like I'm winning, bro."

"Don't get cocky." The sound of boots clomping up behind us makes us turn, and I swallow air.

Gav walks up in tight brown pants and black boots, a long-sleeved white T-shirt, and a black thin-puffer vest. A belt with a silver buckle is slung low on his narrow waist, and on his leg is a band with a black water gun attached.

"I'll be danged, it's my ole buddy Han." Mav reaches up to pull the pink bow out of his "hair," and with the flick of his fingers, the pink belt is gone.

Then he emits a near-perfect Chewbacca roar.

"That's more like it." Gav steps up beside his friend, and they both look down at me standing there with my mouth open. "What do you think, Princess?"

I think I just ovulated.

Clearing my throat, I manage to get out, "You look really good." Before we're interrupted by loud voices yelling *Trick or Treat!*

The side of his lips curls up with a sly grin, and heat flashes from my stomach to my toes. Turning quickly, I grab more candy bars for the kids. It's almost time for trick-or-treating to end, and cars are starting to arrive for the adult party.

"I've got the eyeball Jell-O shots all ready to go!" Mav heads to the kitchen to fetch a tray of red plastic cups with eyeballs suspended in them. "Don't worry—there's plenty more where these came from."

"Did you make them?" My eyebrow arches.

"You know it!" He grins, handing me a cup. "And there's purple drink in the Ninja."

"You've been warned." Gina whispers in my ear, and I turn to see she's wearing a long greenish-black wrap-dress, and her hair is in thick spiral curls all around her head with little google eyes attached to the ends.

"Are you…?" I frown, unsure.

"Medusa, of course!" She holds up a platter with a tiny jack-o-lantern on it.

The mouth is open, and a massive amount of guacamole is pouring out like vomit. She has a big bowl of blue-corn tortilla chips in her other hand.

"If I didn't know that was delicious, I'd barf," I laugh.

"Let's do this!" She puts the appetizers on the table laden with food and scoops up two Jell-o shots.

We do them together, and I realize the eyeball is made of chewing gum. "It burns!"

"Purple drink for the princess and one for the Gorgon." Mav puts two insulated cups in our hands, and continues to greet the gang pouring through the front door.

Halloween music blasts through the speakers, and I laugh, scanning the room for Han Solo. He's near the entrance to the kitchen, and of course his blue eyes are locked on me.

My stomach tingles, and I make my way through the crowd of hockey players, neighbors, and friends to where he's standing with his arm propped on the door jamb.

"Hey." He leans down to me.

"How are you liking your first Halloween party in LA?"

"Not bad." He grins, arching an eyebrow and giving the room a quick sweep before returning his attention to me. "How about you?"

"It's my favorite party of the year." I hold up my cup of purple drink. "Have some."

"I think I will." He takes the metal cup from my hand.

Snapping my gum, I'm feeling sassy from the shots and the purple drink and the music. I'm feeling like it's Halloween, the holiday where anything goes. Where you're supposed to be naughty.

"You take that one, and I'll get another."

I slide past him into the kitchen, and he places his back against the wall, watching me as I pass.

"One for you." Maverick hands me a solo cup this time filled with purple drink. "I expect to see you making out with somebody before the night's over."

He elbows me in the side, grinning as he not so subtly tilts his head in the direction of his friend behind me.

Without missing a beat, I take a sip of my drink. "I'd just as soon kiss a Wookie."

"Or Han Solo." My cousin points a finger at me. "I can arrange that."

12

Gavin

Purple drink is no joke. Hell, I don't know what Maverick puts in it, but halfway through the night, it looks like the whole gang is hammered. Except Haddy. She's holding what looks like a glass of her "special lemonade," and I grin, watching her work the crowd.

She's so poised and pretty. She really is a natural at this princess thing.

I've held myself to the one cup she gave me, and a few Jell-O shots. We've got to play tomorrow, and I've got my sights set on my Princess Leia across the room.

She turns, and our eyes meet. I lift my chin, and she nods for me to come on over... just as Donovan slams into me, dumping frozen alcohol all down the front of my shirt.

"Holy—" It's ice-cold and running onto my pants.

"Fuck! I'm sorry, Gav." He grabs a napkin off the table and tries to blot it.

"Ah, don't worry about it." I glance up at Haddy, who's now giving me a frustrated grimace.

Huffing a laugh, I turn and quickly jog up the stairs to change my shirt.

The party is in full swing below, and the thump of bass is audible through the floor. I strip off my vest and the long-sleeved tee, and drop them onto the floor beside the dirty clothes hamper.

I don't have another white shirt, which means my costume is pretty much ruined. With a heavy exhale, I take off my fake gun and all the belts. The front of my pants is wet, too, so I strip them off as well.

I'm full commando, crossing to my dresser, when the door opens, and a figure in all white slips inside. It's Haddy, and she closes the door with a giggle. Then she turns around, and her blue eyes land on my naked body.

"Oh, shit!" She falls back against the door. "Oh my gosh!"

She's so startled, she almost hits the floor, but I lunge forward to grab her, pulling her flush against my chest.

"Hey, Princess. What are you doing here?"

She's breathing fast, her hands on my biceps, and her eyes blink everywhere but to mine.

"I'm sorry," she whispers. "I came up to see if you needed help with... anything."

"I can think of several things you can help me with right now." My voice is low, and the heat racing through my pelvis centers in my growing erection.

"Gavin." She gives me a little push, and I release her.

She takes a wobbly step backward, but she doesn't rush out the door. Instead, her blue eyes move quickly down my chest to my cock, where they linger. She actually gulps, which is a major turn-on, and I take a careful step closer.

"Like what you see?" My voice is low, non-threatening.

"You look... good." Her soft breasts rise and fall with her pants, and she blinks up to my stomach. "Very good."

"Thank you." I put my hand over hers, lifting it to my lips. "Likewise."

Her eyes move to her hand at my lips then up to my eyes, and for the first time I see something I've only dreamed about.

Hayden Bradford's blue eyes are dark, full of lust and desire, and directed at me.

Releasing her hand, I lower it. "Touch me, Princess. Don't be afraid."

"I'm not afraid..." she whispers, not finishing her sentence.

I don't want her to finish if there's a *But* at the end.

"I'm your knight." I give her a wink. "I'll never let you fall."

She's panting, and I can see the wheels turning, so many thoughts going through that beautifully brilliant mind. Her full bottom lip disappears briefly into her mouth, then she steps forward quickly, putting her hand on my upper chest.

"Your body is amazing. It doesn't look real." Her fingers lightly trace the lines in my chest before moving to my shoulder.

When her blue eyes meet mine again, I can't resist. I lean down to cover her mouth with mine. She exhales a soft whimper, and I cup her cheeks, tilting her face as I part her lips.

Our tongues curl together, and another soft noise slips from her throat. My cock is a steel rod, and I groan deeply when her soft hand wraps around it, tugging slowly.

"Fuck, Princess." My mouth moves to her cheek, kissing a line to her ear. "That feels so good."

"You're so big," she whispers, looking down at my dick in her hand.

She touches me curiously, and I'm going to come if she keeps doing it.

"Turn around." My voice is low, and her eyes lift to mine.

Without hesitation, she does as I say, and I unzip the dress she's wearing. It falls to the floor, and I quickly unfasten her bra. Wrapping my hands around her, I lift her perfect breasts in my hands, holding her back to my chest as I kiss the side of her neck.

"You are so fucking beautiful." Looking over her shoulder, I gaze at her full tits in my hands, lifting and squeezing them like I've only done in my fantasies. "I've wanted to touch you ever since I saw you naked."

Her head falls back against my shoulder, and she reaches behind her waist again to play with my cock.

"I don't think it will fit." A naughty tone is in her voice, and I'm ready to find out.

"It'll fit. I just need to get you good and wet."

I lift her off her feet, carrying her to my bed and placing her onto the mattress. Lowering to my knees in front of her, I reach for her waist, sliding the string of her thong underwear down her legs and shoving them under my bed. I'll just be keeping those.

Her fingers thread in my hair, and she leans forward to kiss my temple. "I can't believe we're doing this."

I slide my thumbs over her hardened nipples before leaning forward to suck one into my mouth. "We're doing it."

Kissing my way down her stomach, she leans back on the bed as I cover her pussy with my mouth and start to lick. She moans loudly and her hips match my movements.

I plan to make up for all our lost time tonight. With one

hand, I squeeze her breast, pinching her nipple as I continue to focus on that tight little bud between her thighs, as she whispers *yes, yes.* . With my other hand, I gently slide a finger into her core.

"Fuck." I break off with a groan. She's dripping.

"Feels so good," she sighs, and I return my mouth to her pussy.

Sliding my tongue over and over her clit, I slip another finger inside her and slowly start to stretch her, getting her ready.

Another pass of my tongue, and her stomach trembles. Her body jerks, and she cries, "Oh, that's it!"

She's coming on my fingers, and I know it's time. Kissing her stomach, I move higher, pulling a tight nipple with my lips before meeting her eyes.

"I'll use a condom if you want, but I've been tested. I'm good."

"That's good." She nods quickly, threading her fingers in the side of my hair and rising to kiss me. "I'm good."

I kiss her parted lips, swiping my tongue inside to meet hers with a groan. My stomach is so tight, and the thought of being with her has me right on the edge.

Holding my cock, I guide the tip to her entrance, slowly pushing into her, watching her pretty eyes darken, her lips part. She's a fucking wet dream come true.

"It's so big..." she gasps, and I lean down to kiss her lips, pulling them with mine and swirling our tongues together.

"You're doing so good, Princess." She's so fucking tight, at the same time I feel her stretching to accommodate me. "Relax and take it."

Her thighs tremble, and she exhales another *Oh...* My forehead is tight, and it's so hard to go slow. She feels too good, and my animal instinct fights to take over.

"Almost there, beautiful." Another slow push, and I'm all the way in, holding for an excruciating moment. "You okay?"

She nods quickly, her hands moving from my shoulders to my hair again. "I'm so full."

Fuck me. I groan, kissing her jaw, her lips. I move my hips, thrusting slowly, and she gasps, hiccupping a moan as she squirms beneath me. Her pussy clenches, and I almost come on the spot.

"You take me so good." I kiss her neck, and she nods, moving her hips again.

"Just getting used to... oh!" My thumb covers her clit, and I circle it over and over that sensitive spot.

She moans another *Oh,* and her hips start to jerk as her orgasm reignites.

"More," she whispers, and I rock a little faster.

Her body trembles, and my mouth covers hers. Our tongues slide and curl, and she starts to move. She meets my thrusts, sending shocks of pleasure through my pelvis.

I kiss her neck, her ear, sliding my nose into her jasmine hair as I thrust faster.

She gasps and shudders. Her moans are ragged and her cries broken.

We're fucking now, and I can't hold back anymore. I want to wait for her, but my control has slipped. My cock starts to pulse, and at last, she breaks, her core spasming as her fingers curl and grasp against my shoulders.

With a low groan, I come, spilling into her. It's so good, I can't stop. Her body is everything. Her soft breasts are flush against my chest, and her soft pussy squeezes and holds my cock.

She was made for me, and all I can think about is doing this again.

13

Haddy

My eyes open slowly as the room lights with the first glow of sunrise. Blinking slowly, the night comes blasting into my memory.

Gavin's mouth on my body, kissing every part of me, between my legs, my waist, my lower back, my breasts. I lost count of how many times we made love, but when I move, I can feel it was a lot.

I've never been with anyone like him, so hungry and eager. We did it in every position, some I've only seen in videos. I sat on his lap, rising and falling with my knees bent as he squeezed my ass with both hands.

His cock is so big, I was certain it would hurt, but somehow it didn't.

Now I'm lying on my side with my back to his broad chest. His palm is spread over my stomach, and I feel the beast against my right butt cheek.

Heat twists in my stomach, pulsing higher with every heartbeat, and so many feelings swirl in my chest.

It was wonderful. It was impulsive. I can't believe I did it. I'm never like that, but when I saw him naked, I didn't have a choice. I mean, seriously. The man is utterly, perfectly gorgeous. He's unreal.

A low rumble comes from his throat, and panic hits my stomach. He rolls onto his back, and I slide out of the bed, falling softly to the floor in a crouch.

My white dress and bra are in a pile on the floor, and I snatch them to my chest.

His arm lifts, and I hear him inhale deeply, scrubbing his face with both hands. Without a look back, I creep to his door and slip through it, closing it softly behind me then dashing on tiptoe down the hall to my bedroom.

Patsy squeaks from her crate as I stand with my back to my closed door, trying to catch my breath. Her little front legs march side to side as she looks up at me with big, brown eyes.

"Sorry, Pats." I speak in a soft, high voice as I cross the space to my closet. "Didn't mean to ditch you last night. I'd blame the purple drink, but I only had one."

I quickly put my costume dress on a hanger, then I go to my dresser and pull out a fresh pair of cotton underwear, black capri leggings, and a jog bra. I could use a shower, but I'll have to wait until the guys leave for Anaheim. I don't want to take a chance of bumping into him, or him joining me, although that might be interesting... *Would he do that?*

Pulling a hoodie over my head, I open the door of the crate and scoop out the tiny dog. "Let's go for a walk."

She's under my arm when I step into the hall. Then I turn around, and my heart flies to my throat.

"Oh my gosh," I gasp, slapping my hand over my mouth. "You scared the crap outta me."

Gigi is standing in a similar outfit as I am, and she has Spanky on a leash. "Going for a walk?"

"Yeah, you?"

"Spanky needs to, and I figured I'd get some exercise."

Gav's door at the opposite end of the hall starts to open, and I grab her arm, pulling her to the stairs.

"Let's go then!"

Out on the sidewalk, Gigi frowns, rubbing her eyes. "I was going to make coffee to go first."

"We can stop at Rise and Grind. I've been wanting to check that place out since they opened."

It's a lie. I was there last week, but I had to get out of the house before Gavin said something. He and I have got to talk alone, in private, and decide what in the world we're going to do before anyone knows what happened.

If anyone will ever even know what happened. I don't even know what happened. Okay, I know what happened, but I don't know what it means.

"What happened to you last night?" My cousin's nose wrinkles, and I startle thinking she read my mind.

"What do you mean?"

"You ditched the party, and when I walked up to check on Peepee, you weren't in your room."

"You are not still calling her that, are you?" I'm carrying the little dog under my arm as we walk, since she's too little to keep up with us.

"It's funny, and you're dodging the question."

Spanky pulls us to a stop at a small patch of grass, and I put Patsy down so she can use the bathroom as well.

"I uhh... fell asleep in Gav's room." My ears are hot, and I wish I'd grabbed my dark sunglasses on the way out the door. I am the world's worst liar.

"Whaaat?" Gina's brows rise, and suspicion is in her

green eyes. "What were you doing in Gav's room, Princess Leia?"

"Too much purple drink." I answer quickly. "I think I passed out."

I did pass out, only it wasn't from too much purple drink. It was from too much dick.

"Well, that's a let-down." Her lips twist into a frown. "He was so hot as Han Solo. I thought you guys might wind up doing a little smooching before the night was over. You looked amazing."

"Did you do any smooching? That Donovan is a hottie." The guys' hockey captain is a massive six-foot-four brute with red hair and flirty brown eyes. "He's got kind of a Prince Harry thing going on."

She shakes her head. "You know I don't like gingers."

"But you're a..."

"Don't say it!" She points a finger at me as she picks up Spanky's poo with a plastic bag.

I laugh as I scoop up Princess Petunia. "So you can say *I'm* just like my mom, but I can't accurately note *you're* a ginger?"

"Being just like Raven Bradford is not an insult."

"Neither is being a gorgeous strawberry blonde." She rolls her eyes at me, and I quickly add, "It's the way you say it."

A car horn makes us jump, and we both turn to see our cousin Maverick slowing down on the side of the road in his bullet-gray Range Rover. His window is down, and he waves at us.

"Can I get some fries with that shake?" He's teasing, and I notice Gavin in the passenger's seat looking straight at me.

His lips tighten, and his blue eyes narrow slightly. Heat

rises in my chest, and I turn to search for Patsy's poo in the patch of grass. I guess she didn't go.

"We'll be in Anaheim all day," Mav tells Gigi. "But we should be back in plenty of time for dinner if y'all want to wait."

"You don't want to check out the bunnies in Anaheim?" Gigi teases, and her question seriously pisses me off.

I'm being ridiculous.

"Nah, I'm tired, and I expect I'll be even more exhausted after we play." Mav's voice rises. "What happened to you, Princess? Too much purple drink?"

I squat down like I'm shielding the little dog from running into the street. She just sits on her little cinnamon butt and looks up at me.

"Something like that," I call over my shoulder.

"You are such a lightweight," he laughs. "I made yours especially mild."

And I gave it to Gavin. I have no excuse. I only wave at him over my head.

"Okay, we gotta get out of here. See you tonight."

I wait until the sound of his Rover fades, then I scoop up Patsy and smile at my cousin. "Let's get some coffee!"

RISE AND GRIND IS PACKED, and I put in my order for a skinny cappuccino. Gina gets a soy matcha latte. We pay, and then we walk over to a table in a crowded corner to wait.

"I hope all these people means it's really good." She looks around the room.

"Don't worry, it is." The words are out of my mouth before I can stop them.

"I thought you said…" Her green eyes narrow, and I panic.

"I forgot I came here a few weeks ago. It just sort of slipped my mind. Probably because I've been so focused on school and all. That's all. School."

I'm talking too fast, and if anybody knows me, it's Gigi.

"You're acting weird. What are you not telling me?"

The guy calls our names, and I hand her Pats. "I'll get them."

Walking to the counter, I do some quick mental calculations. I could tell Gigi what happened, but then she'd be invested, wanting to know what comes next, if we're serious, if we're going to start dating, if we don't start dating are things going to get weird at the house, if we do start dating does that mean I'll move in with him and break up our happy cousin home? What about Karen?

These are all my panicked thoughts, which I'm sure I'm projecting onto my cousin. Especially since I'm the only one who knows Karen and Gav's history.

"Glad to see you back!" The scruffy barista hands me our paper cups, giving me a flirty smile.

"Oh, thanks. We live in the neighborhood."

He looks like he might say more, but I lift the cup in a friendly, platonic gesture. He gives me a wistful smile in response, and I head back to where Gigi is sitting, studying me suspiciously.

"It really is amazing how guys lose the ability to function when you smile at them." Gigi takes a big gulp of her tea. "You should date more."

"I don't know." I sip my coffee, wavering on telling her the truth.

"I was reading online how Jennifer Aniston is dating a

hypnotist. Did you see that?" She turns her phone to me, and I lean forward to read the headline.

"A hypnotist?"

"I know." Her nose wrinkles. "Are you thinking what I'm thinking?"

"Did he hypnotize her? I mean, he's not bad looking, but this is Jennifer Aniston we're talking about."

We both snort, and this feels better.

Laughing with Gigi and gossiping about celebrities helps me regain my bearings after a night of mind-altering sex with a hockey god who has the body of a Michelangelo sculpture.

Trust me, that can really throw you off-kilter, especially when you've spent almost a decade thinking he was not a nice guy.

He might still be bad, but when it comes to orgasms, he is all good. A bubble of laughter tightens my throat, and I have to stop thinking about it before my face turns all red.

Thankfully, Gina's eyes are on her screen. "I've actually been looking into this whole area of pet hypnosis and how it can be used to help dogs with emotional issues... Which leads to the whole area of pet psychics."

"Wait..." I take a too-big sip of coffee and squeal from the burn. "What the hell?"

She's not fazed at all by my near spit-take.

"I agree with you, the psychic part is ridiculous. I mean, how can anyone even prove that? Are they speaking dog language? It's silly." She shakes her head. "But the hypnosis part is very interesting. They say it can soothe behavioral problems related to stress, that it can help calm anxiety and promote relaxation."

I can't drink any more coffee now that I've scalded my

entire mouth and throat. "I guess it makes sense. Therapy can be calming"

We stand and start for the door. "I wonder if it would work for humans."

I'm mostly teasing. I actually wouldn't mind having a psychic tell me what's going to happen when the guys return this evening, or even what's going to happen, period. Do I dare to trust Gavin Knight? Is that even what he wants? Is he really a player who'll break my heart as easily as he'll snatch a puck?

"I think Gavin is working out well." Again, it's like she's reading my mind. "I mean, it was a big surprise to have a fourth roommate all of a sudden, but he's a big help. He seems like a really nice guy."

"He seems that way." I look ahead at the sidewalk, trying to reconcile the past and the present.

"Mav said he went to UNC. Did y'all know each other?"

I shrug. "Not really. He dated my roommate Karen, but it didn't last."

"I can see that." Gigi polishes off her latté and drops it in a bin. "She always struck me as sort-of a loose cannon. Can you say that about a girl?"

I frown at her. "I don't know. Why would you say that?"

"That time she came home with you for spring break? She was hitting on all the guys at the beach."

My throat tightens. "Are you sure? She's really a friendly person."

"She wasn't very friendly to me. I got the impression she wished I would take the dogs for a long walk and not come back."

The tightness in my throat moves down to my chest. "You think she wanted something bad to happen to you?"

"I think she wanted me to get lost so she could have all the boys to herself."

I snuggle Patsy under my neck unsure how to take this. "You didn't know her very well."

"No, but I've met the type before. Why are you defending her?"

"I've known her a long time. She's an International Princess Woman, so every summer, we spent a few weeks together. It was like camp."

"Maybe you didn't know her as well as you think you did." Gina arches her eyebrow, pushing the front door open with her back.

"I thought I did." Only now I'm feeling less confident. "And we shared things."

My cousin frowns. "Like what? Clothes?"

A knot is in my throat. I've never told anyone this. "Remember Rob Westcoat?"

"The guy you dated in college?"

I nod. "I found out he was cheating on me junior year."

Her jaw drops, and she reaches over to grab my wrist. "No!" I nod, and she steps closer to hug me. "That bastard. I knew I hated him."

"The same thing happened to Karen, and I guess it sort of made us closer."

"You bonded through trauma." Gigi nods, giving me another squeeze before stepping back to meet my eyes. "I guess if she was a good friend to you when you needed her…"

"Don't tell anybody that." I look down at my hands. "It's so embarrassing. It kind of messes with your head, like why didn't I see it? Or why wasn't I enough?"

She grabs my hands in both of hers. "Hayden Lucille Bradford. You are gorgeous and kind and smart and the best person I know. That guy was never good enough for you, and he always had some dumb opinion on everything."

"He was a knob." I exhale a bitter laugh, thinking of what Gavin said about his pompous ass.

"Rob the knob. Is he the reason you stopped dating?"

I shrug. "Numbers, data, wind currents, these are all things I can understand, things I can control. Men are... unknown variables."

She gives me a tight hug. "You don't have to convince me men are rats, but not all of them, right? Mav's doing pretty well, and Gav..."

"Maybe."

"At least he's no love bomber." She exhales a sigh, walking ahead of me into the house.

I don't argue with her. I think about college and everything that happened. I think about what Maverick said and how Gavin has acted since he's been here.

I built my hypothesis on the evidence I had at hand. But new evidence keeps emerging, and I'm not so sure things were the way I thought they were in college.

14

Gavin

I hate opening my eyes to an empty bed. Especially after a blazing hot night with a woman I've been low-key trying not to obsess over for almost a decade.

Turning onto my side, I buried my head in her pillow, inhaling the lingering scent of fresh jasmine as the memories flooded my mind.

I worshipped her body like I'd wanted to do since she flashed me in the hall my first morning here. She's perfect in every way, from her beautiful mind to her beautiful breasts to her sweet pussy to her red-painted toenails.

My mouth covered every inch of her body, and I was looking forward to doing it again. Instead, she was gone, leaving only her scent and my conflicted emotions.

I tried hating her.

She took one look at me in college and decided my cheating ex was more trustworthy than I was. When did I forget how she stood by Karen?

The minute her trembling fingers touched my bare

chest, and she looked at me with those blue eyes so full of wonder and lust. I had to have her, grudges be damned.

To be fair, we didn't really know each other in college. She was Karen's roommate. Of course, she believed her friend over me.

What's worse is I gave Karen the tools she needed to kill my reputation. If I hadn't gone on an anger-fueled rampage and slept with those Tri-Delts, I might've been able to fight back.

But we hadn't announced our breakup. No one knew except me she was sucking off any guy who wasn't my friend. Shit, some of them were my friends—or they were supposed to be. That cut the deepest.

Then I discovered she went after Dex. He's like a brother to me. He's my dad's partner's son, and we basically grew up together. My mom Elaine and his mom Melissa were best friends before they even met our dads.

Of course, he felt like shit telling me, but I wish he'd said something sooner.

Which brings me here, to the most incredible night of my life with Haddy, and she sneaked out of the bed before I even woke up. Then she turned her back on us in the car, and wouldn't even look at me.

She still believes the story.

She still doesn't trust me.

She's still holding onto misplaced loyalty.

It's been a minute since I've slept with anyone, and what we shared was beyond anything I've ever experienced. I want to talk to her. I need to talk to her and find out where we stand.

A whistle blows, and an arc of ice shavings fans in front of me, snapping me out of my rumination.

"Hey." It's Mav, and he's in my face. "What's up with you? I'm reading your mind, and it's not in the game."

"You're right. I'm sorry." Shaking my head, I glance around to see the team watching me with worried eyes.

"TTG?" Mav bumps my helmet with his before heading to formation.

"Yes." *Tic-Tac-Goal.*

It's our winning play, and we've done it a hundred times. Hancock brings it down the center, and I'm on the left winger headed straight at him.

The puck goes to Mav, and he "unexpectedly" sends it over to me.

I dig in, taking it around the back of the net before chipping it to Mav as soon as I clear the goal, but it catches the post and flies high into the air.

I raise my stick to bring it down and instead hit the opposing defensemen on the shoulder.

One of his teammates body-checks me into the boards, and a fight breaks out. The guy I clipped punches me straight in the face, and blood fills my mouth. Donovan grabs him, throwing him off me, and we all go to town, throwing punches.

Fighting feels good right now, even if it doesn't solve anything. I don't catch another fist, but when the refs finally break it up, I'm headed to the bin on a high sticking penalty.

It was an accident, but I'm out of the game for five minutes. We ended up losing by a point, and to make matters worse, it was my fault. Because I was thinking about a girl.

Hanging my head in the shower, I felt like a total amateur as the hot water washed the blood off my cheek. Needless to say, the drive home with Mav was no picnic.

He was pissed, but he didn't lay into me. We've all had bad days on the ice, but I was completely off my game today.

"Anything you want to talk about?" Mav's brow was furrowed.

Shifting in my seat, I looked out the window at the growing dark. Flashes of Haddy's sweaty body flooded my mind, her long, dark waves sticking to her skin, covering her soft breasts with my mouth, the taste of salt on my tongue, the sound of her soft moans in my ears.

"I think I had too much last night." *Too much sweet pussy.*

"Nah." He shook his head, taking the exit. "I've seen you play with a worse hangover than that. I think your problem is you need to get laid."

Shifting in my seat, I cleared my throat. "I don't know."

He has no idea.

Finally, I just said, "I'm sorry, Mav. I played like shit, and I let you and the team down. There's no excuse for it."

We drove a while with only the radio playing until our driveway was in sight.

Reaching over, he grabbed my shoulder and gave it a firm shake. "Don't worry about it, bro. We're still Mav and Gav. We'll get 'em next time."

"I think you mean Gav and Mav."

"Don't make me kick your ass."

Exhaling a chuckle, I climbed out of the Rover ready to face whatever was waiting for me inside.

"I LOVE THIS MOVIE SO MUCH." Gigi coos from where she's curled up on the couch beside Maverick.

"I'm just waiting for Fred Willard to ask if he can take a

Shih Tzu on his luggage." Mav chuckles. "Then I'm going to bed."

"Nooo," his cousin wails. "You have to watch the whole thing with me. Or at least until Hubert. He's my favorite."

"Why didn't you name Spanky 'Butch'?"

"Because Butch is a bitch." Gigi shakes her head like it's so obvious.

Sitting across from Haddy at dinner had been a torture test. She's so gorgeous. The few times she glanced at me, I was struck by her sapphire eyes made even more intense by her dark hair and slim dark brows framing them.

Storms raged in those pretty eyes, and I could feel all the words we needed to say to each other radiating at me with each passing glance. I wanted to slide my hand over hers, but I couldn't in front of Mav and Gigi.

Mav had whipped up a quick black bean dish with tomatoes, bell peppers, onions, and jalapeños. He served it over pasta and called it "Tex-Mex chili." It was freaking fantastic, and I have to hand it to him. I never knew my old teammate was such a good cook.

Once everything's cleaned up, Gina puts on her favorite movie, the Christopher Guest mockumentary *Best in Show*, about a fictional dog show (no surprises there).

We all make our way into the living room, where she and Mav take their spots on the couch and get it rolling. Haddy hesitates behind them, holding her little dog, until she makes a quiet excuse about having a headache before leaning down to kiss the tops of their heads.

I let a few minutes pass, watching the zany dog owners with their pedigreed pets get ready for a national show, then I head upstairs as well.

I don't feel the need to kiss any heads or make excuses.

Mav knows how I performed in today's game, so he can come up with his own reason for my early retirement.

When I make it to the second floor, she's stepping out of the bathroom, her face freshly washed, and her hair up in a messy bun.

She stops with a little stumble, like she's startled by my presence. "Gavin..."

It's a soft exhale that makes my dick twitch. It hasn't even been twelve hours since I had her moaning my name in ecstasy, and my body remembers so well.

"Hey." I keep my tone gentle. "I thought we should talk. About last night."

Her back is to the wall, and I can see her pillow breasts rising and falling with her breaths. Her lips are parted, and mine warm remembering her kisses.

We're so fucking compatible, it hurts, but we have to talk. We have too much history to ignore.

"Okay." She leads me to her bedroom, where I see Peepee is in her crate.

Once I'm inside, she closes the door, putting her back to it and facing me. Her eyes blink quickly to mine then away again, and she seems so small in her bare feet in front of me.

"I'm surprised you could walk today," I say, trying to lighten the mood. "I'll have to do a better job next time."

"You did a fine job last night." She takes a step forward, passing me as she clasps her hands together. "I have a hickey on my inner thigh."

I lift the hem of my T-shirt, where a large purple hickey is visible on the side of my ribs. "Twins."

She glances up at me, and I give her a wink, which seems to melt the tension.

She exhales a laugh. "Sorry, not sorry."

I take a careful step closer. "Talk to me, Hads. What are you feeling right now? Regret?"

"No." She shakes her head, and relief washes through my chest. "At first I was embarrassed, considering..." She does a little wavey, hand gesture towards my ribs. "Everything we did."

I can't help a grin. "Nothing to be embarrassed about. We just did what came naturally."

"Yeah, but I realized today, I don't really know you." Her brow furrows, and her blue eyes meet mine full force this time.

It's a little breath-taking. "We're hardly strangers."

"I know, but we never hung out in college. Then everything happened, and, well..." She seems to be choosing her words. "I'd like to know you better before we... I don't know. Whatever."

She presses her lips together like she showed her cards, like she might want to do a little more of what comes naturally.

That little slip is all the encouragement I need. "What do you want to know? I'm an open book."

"I don't mean right this minute. I mean, we need to take a step back, take some time to actually talk to each other without all the other stuff clouding the issue."

I don't know what brought about this change of heart, why she's giving me a chance now, but I'm not letting it slip away.

"My schedule is hell right now, and we're headed to Vegas then Tempe. We'll be gone more than a week." My jaw clenches, and I try to think. "Give me your number, and we can text or FaceTime..."

Hell, I'd even email if that made her happy.

We quickly exchange numbers, and I look at my phone a

second, seeing her face in the contact photo. Her nose is wrinkled and she's winking, sticking out her tongue. She's adorable.

Suddenly a text appears on my screen.

HADDY

I'll talk to you soon.

Lifting my chin, I meet her eyes, which shine with interest. I want to step forward and pull her to me. I want to kiss her again. I want to chase her lips with mine, curl our tongues together. I want to trace my lips down her neck, pulling the skin between my teeth, marking her as mine. I want to hear that sexy little moan again.

Instead, I tap quickly on my phone.

GAVIN

Looking forward to it, Princess.

15

───────

Haddy

Daniel Ito is my counterpart in Japan. We've never met in person, and we don't really know each other. We were assigned to work together by our graduate advisors.

Mine is Dr. Vera Cross. She works closely with a researcher at the Japanese Society of Kawasaki Disease, and the two of them are the leaders of this study.

Daniel and I are simply two of the many graduate students contributing to their work.

He doesn't speak English very well, and I know zero Japanese, which means we communicate mostly in smiles and nods and Google Translate.

We both look forward to helping save many lives. As it is, we're mostly tracking wind currents and noting timelines and directions on spreadsheets until something major happens or a pattern appears.

Despite all my excitement talking about the potential of my studies, for the most part, it's pretty boring work.

It reminds me of the astronomers who sit out and listen to space noise. We're the true believers. I think of Jodi Foster in that movie about aliens, *Contact*. I have always related deeply to the scene of her putting on headphones and leaning back on the hood of that car.

Maybe one day all of this watching on our part will lead to us cracking the code. Until then, we're documenting the trade winds.

Glancing down, I see a text on my screen.

GAVIN

You have a tattoo on your hip. What is it?

My brow wrinkles, and I quickly send a reply.

HADDY

Aren't you supposed to be practicing?

GAVIN

We have a break, and quit stalling. What're you trying to hide?

HADDY

IPWs are not supposed to have tattoos.

GAVIN

I always knew you were a rebel. What is it?

HADDY

An axolotl.

GAVIN

WTF is that?

HADDY

Only the cutest little sea creature ever to live! Google it. I'll wait.

I do wait.

Gray dots float across the screen.

I wait a little longer, then his answer appears.

GAVIN

It's smiling… Is that for real? That's the cutest little thing I've ever seen. Is it a lizard? What is it?

Warmth floods my insides, and I'm grinning as I reply.

HADDY

It's a paedomorphic salamander.

GAVIN

Okay, smarty pants, WTF does that mean?

HADDY

Paedomorphic means it retains juvenile features. Basically, it's a cute little salamander that never grows up.

GAVIN

Is that bad? It seems really cute.

HADDY

I don't think it minds being a Peter Pan lizard

GAVIN

Are those little things around its head whiskers?

HADDY

They're gills. It never grows out of them.

GAVIN

And you got this because…

HADDY

It was my favorite stuffed animal as a baby, my aunt Mimi made them for me, and I've always loved them. They're very good at regenerating limbs, they symbolize immortality…

GAVIN

I don't think I'd want to live forever. After a while, you're all alone. All your friends have died.

HADDY

So no vampirism for you—got it. What's the word you have on your ribs? Kombucha? Big fan of the fermented tea?

GAVIN

Komorebi. It's a Japanese word… kind of hard to describe. It's the way sunbeams filter through the leaves on the trees. Serenity, beauty…

HADDY

Unexpected.

GAVIN

My mom Kenny's a tattoo artist. She said it's the way you feel when you find the person you'll spend the rest of your life with.

My brow furrows, and I tilt my head at the words on the screen as emotion warms my chest

HADDY

You're very romantic.

GAVIN

Only with you, Princess. Gotta run—they're calling us onto the ice.

GAVIN

What's your nickname?

I'M CURLED up in my bed, Patsy is secure in her crate, and I'm just drifting to sleep when my phone screen lights up with his question. Twisting my lips, I reply.

HADDY

Did Maverick tell you to ask me that?

GAVIN

No…

HADDY

My nickname is Haddy.

GAVIN

Why do I feel like it's also something else?

HADDY

Do you have a nickname?

GAVIN

When we played in ATL, fans started calling me Boomer, but it was because Maverick would yell Boom every time we made a big play.

HADDY

He called you Boomer when you first got here. When did you pick up Gavin? You were Lane in college.

GAVIN

After all that stuff with Karen, I wanted a break from the past.

HADDY

But why Gavin?

GAVIN

I was in this play in elementary school where
I was Sir Gavin the Gray, a fictional Knight of
the Round Table. He seemed like a good
guy, so when I arrived in ATL, I went with it.

HADDY

I like it, Sir Gavin.

GAVIN

Your turn… you're clearly hiding something.
Out with it.

HADDY

It's not a nickname. It's more an inside,
family joke about my dad.

GAVIN

Quit stalling, Princess.

HADDY

Super pooper.

Gray dots float...

More gray dots...

I feel my throat tightening with embarrassment. *Why did
I tell him that?* I guess he could've gotten it out of Maverick.
Mav *loves* telling that story.

GAVIN

HADDY

Stop.

More minutes pass, and my cheeks heat with embarrassment. I'm ready to put my phone away when his reply
appears.

GAVIN

Do you break toilets or something?

HADDY

When I was a baby my dad couldn't change poopy diapers without gagging, and I think they exaggerated my baby poops because he was such a drama king.

GAVIN

It's okay, Princess, I've been known to break a toilet in my day.

HADDY

I don't break toilets! My bowel movements are as normal as anybody's!

GAVIN

I don't know how I feel about you checking out other people's BMs. Have you ever been kicked off a flight because of excessive bodily functions?

HADDY

Goodnight, Gavin.

GAVIN

Favorite TV show as a kid… I'll go first, The Suite Life of Zack and Cody. I thought living in a suite looked so cool.

HADDY

Did you ever live in one?

GAVIN

Yep—when I was in ATL, I had my own penthouse suite.

HADDY

Fancy. Was it everything you dreamed it would be?

GAVIN

Pretty much. But I like living in a house with my best friend, two beautiful smart women, and a couple of dogs. Hell, that sounds like a show right there.

HADDY

Sometimes it is

GAVIN

What was yours?

HADDY

Hannah Montana

GAVIN

That show was funny as shit. Dolly Parton was on it once.

HADDY

A lot of people were on it. I liked how she could be a pop star and a regular kid at the same time.

GAVIN

Kind of like you—a princess and a scientist. What got you interested in pageants? You said your mom isn't a fan.

HADDY

My mom hates pageants. She was forced to be in them as a girl, and she couldn't believe I wanted to do it. It was like I'd betrayed her.

GAVIN

But someone took you to those competitions, bought your dresses, paid your admission fees...

HADDY

She doesn't need your help. She already has Dad

GAVIN

So what was it? Besides the fact that you're naturally beautiful… and you have really good posture.

HADDY

We train for that. Ever heard of books on the head?

Taking a second, I inhale, looking around the science lab to where my poster of Heddy Lamar and Natalie Portman is hanging.

Nowhere is it written that you can't be a beauty queen and a scientist.

HADDY

My grandmother was Miss Georgia World. When I was little, I found a box filled with all her old pageant pictures, and she seemed so confident and controlled. I wanted to be like that.

GAVIN

She must be really proud of you.

HADDY

She died before I was born. I never knew her, but my mom said she would've been thrilled. The way she said it… I got the impression they didn't get along.

GAVIN

I'm sorry.

HADDY

It's family stuff. You know. Kind of how your parents didn't want you to play hockey.

GAVIN

They're just over-protective, but they support me. I think it's really cool that you're a beauty queen. Especially when you turn around and start explaining paedomorphic salamanders. Hot.

HADDY

Thanks, Gav

Hesitating a moment, I study my phone screen. I think about a video I watched earlier of the team getting off the bus that transported them from their hotel to the arena.

My interest grew as each of the massive players filed off dressed in designer suits, smiling at the camera, occasionally winking or pointing.

Maverick looked really good, but when Gavin stepped out, my mouth went dry.

His expression was so focused. His dark brows were lowered over his ice blue eyes, and he looked like a runway model in a gray suit with his dark hair slicked away from his face. I couldn't take my eyes off him.

My core grows hot and slippery at the memory, and I decide just to tell him.

HADDY

I miss you guys. When will you be back?

GAVIN

Friday. Then we'll be back for a while. You'll probably be wishing we were gone again.

HADDY

I don't think so.

GAVIN

See you soon, Princess.

GAVIN

Another win! I think Mav's finally forgiven me for my post-Halloween meltdown.

HADDY

You melted down? Why?

GRAY DOTS FLOAT, and I snuggle deeper into my blankets. The weather is getting cooler, and Thanksgiving is fast approaching.

GAVIN

My head wasn't in the game. We'd just had our night, and then when we saw you on the street, you wouldn't look at me. I couldn't stop thinking about it… wondering why.

HADDY

I'm sorry. I guess I was kind of freaked out.

GAVIN

Don't apologize. It was pretty earth-shaking.

HADDY

Things were definitely shaking.

My legs for starters. The memory sends heat from my chest to my stomach to my core, and I might need a visit with my battery-operated boyfriend, a.k.a., Bob tonight.

GAVIN

Would you say I shook you all night long?

HADDY

Or did I shake you 😏

GAVIN

Sassy. I like it. I think we're a good match,
like puzzle pieces fitting together.

HADDY

Are you implying I have a Gavin-shaped
hole?

GAVIN

You do now, Princess. Perhaps I can fill it
for you.

HADDY

Night, Gav.

Yep. I put my phone on the charger feeling all hot and
flustered. Reaching into my bedside drawer, I take out the
smooth purple device. It's not as big as the gray knight's
dick, but it gets the job done.

A few well-placed vibrations, and my back arches, my
legs shake, and I'll get through another night without him.

~

GAVIN

Boarding the plane, wondering if you have a
favorite food?

HADDY

Tater tots.

I CLOSE the door to the oven, standing back and crossing my
arms. They'll be back tonight, and I can't keep the zippy
feeling out of my stomach. My throat is tight, and I can't stop
smiling.

GAVIN

You're kidding...

HADDY

Crispy tater tots with salt and ketchup are the best thing on the planet. Like God's little gifts of deliciousness.

GAVIN

Hayden Bradford, you never stop surprising me.

HADDY

Is that a bad thing?

GAVIN

It's one of my favorite things about you, Princess.

16

Gavin

The flight from Arizona to California feels like forever. I'm leaning forward, looking out the window of the small, chartered plane the team uses when the pilot tells us to prepare for landing.

Texting with Haddy has brought us closer, and it's also put this unexpected ache in my chest. I can't wait to see her. It's been so long.

It's dark when we touch down at the airport, but the nice thing about having our own plane is when we land, we can leave. We don't have to deal with waiting for our luggage to show up in baggage claim, and Mav's gray Rover is parked in the private lot right outside the small terminal.

He hangs back, of course, chatting with Saxon about our next game in a few days, but I'm in the passenger's seat with my phone in my hand, wondering if I should text her.

Finally, my friend gets in the car, but I can tell he's not in a hurry to get anywhere. I'm about to crawl out of my seat. I wish I'd offered to drive.

"Want to stop off and grab something to eat?" If Mav were driving any slower, we could walk.

"I'm good. Let's get on back."

"What are you so eager to get home for?" He glances over at me, my hands clenched on my thighs. "The girls don't cook when I'm gone. They'll probably just have pizza and tater tots on the stove."

The mention of tater tots makes me smile, and I picture Haddy with that messy bun on her head, sitting at the bar munching on a little golden potato nugget with salt and ketchup.

"I could go for some tater tots right now." Mixed in with the sweet taste of Haddy's lips.

"Napoleon, give me some of your tots," Mav imitates the bully from the movie *Napoleon Dynamite*. "Now you've got that in my head!"

"You said it. Think you could light a fire under your ass? I'm tired of being in this car."

"Dang, keep your shirt on," he complains, but he does hit the accelerator a little harder.

The Halloween decorations are all gone when we arrive at the house, and now the porch has turkeys and scarecrows on it.

"I can't believe we're closing in on Thanksgiving already." Mav slams his door, and I do my best not to jog up the steps. "Damn, the time starts flying when our season begins. Next thing, we'll look up and it'll be Christmas."

"It's true." I'm tapping the code on the lock, the breath tightening in my lungs in anticipation of seeing her.

A little hiss, and I open the door. Stepping inside, the downstairs is empty. A light is on in the kitchen, but the girls are nowhere to be seen.

Maverick bustles past me, carrying his suitcase to the laundry room just off the kitchen.

"What did I tell you?" His blazer is already gone when he returns. "Pizza and tater tots."

I follow him to the small area where he takes a plate from the microwave oven. Several slices of pepperoni pizza are on it, and he puts a bowl of tater tots on the counter.

My shoulders fall, and I can't believe she didn't wait up. Not even after our text conversation. Glancing towards the stairs, I wonder if I might tap on her door.

"I think I'll head on up." I turn, suitcase in hand.

"Hey, hang on. You can't go to bed on an empty stomach." Mav stops me before I can make it out of the room. "What if I order up some burgers and wings for us? Pop open a beer, and I'll see if I can get express delivery."

I look toward the dark landing above. How could she go to bed so early? She knew we were coming home tonight. Is it possible I'm the only one who started to get invested in our daily conversations?

"Big Kahuna burger?" Mav is on his phone tapping in an order.

"Is that really a thing?" I frown at him, and he nods.

"One for you and one for me with a side of fries? Actually, they have tater tots if you want more."

I'm about to tell him to skip it when the back door leading to the patio opens, and Gigi bursts through it laughing and holding Spanky's leash. She's talking to someone behind her, but when she sees us, her eyes light.

"You're home!" She cries, running forward to give her cousin a hug.

My breath disappears when Haddy steps inside after her, smiling and looking like the best thing I've seen all day. Hell, she's the best thing I've seen all year.

"Lookin good Mr. Knight. I love a sharp-dressed man." Gigi turns, crossing her arms and nodding at me. Then she elbows her cousin. "Where's your suit, Mav?"

"Laundry room." He starts for the living room, calling to me. "Throw yours on the pile, and the cleaners'll pick em up tomorrow."

I don't answer him. I'm still facing Haddy, who's standing quietly inside the back door with her little dog in her hand. Her blue eyes blink up to mine, and her full lips press.

My stomach is tight, and I want to pull her into my arms. Instead, I put my suitcase down and take a step closer. I'm about to speak when Mav returns, passing me and going to his cousin.

"I prefer knowing where she is before I sit anywhere." He takes the little brown dog from her hands. "Did you miss us, Peepee? Food should be here in ten minutes, Gav."

He carries the dog into the living room where Gina and Spanky are waiting, and Haddy's arms fall to her sides.

"We made tater tots." Haddy's voice is quiet, and she motions to the stove.

Her voice sounds so good after texting for so long.

"Yeah, Mav showed me." My voice is equally quiet, and I take a step closer.

"You do look nice in a suit."

"You look beautiful."

"In this?" She huffs a little laugh, shaking her head.

She's wearing black leggings and a white, long-sleeved tee. Her face is freshly washed, her dark hair is piled on her head, and her lips are glossy.

She looks like sunshine after weeks of rain. She smiles and warmth fills my entire body.

"It's really good to see you again, Hads."

Her eyes blink quickly, and she goes to where the leftovers are still sitting on the counter, lifting the bowl. "Want one?"

Exhaling a breath, I take the bowl from her hand. "I've been thinking about these since you mentioned them."

"I was just putting them in the oven when you texted."

She looks up at me, and her full lips part. We're all alone in the kitchen. The sound of Gigi and Mav's animated conversation echoes from the living room.

I swallow quickly, placing the bowl on the counter, my eyes fixed on her mouth. "I'd really like to kiss you right now."

Her eyes darken. She glances down then steps closer to me. Reaching up, she puts her slim hand on the front of my blazer, and rises onto her toes.

Fresh jasmine surrounds me, and she closes her eyes before pressing her lips to my cheek. She's on her way back down when I catch her, cupping her face in my hands and leaning forward to seal my lips over hers.

A soft whimper slips from her throat, registering straight to my cock, and I open her mouth with mine. Our tongues slide together, and heat twists my stomach. Her fingers curl on the lapel of my jacket, pulling me closer. *Fuck, it feels so good.*

Wrapping my arms around her, I hug her body up, closer to my chest, and her arms slide around my neck. I'm lost in our tongues chasing, our lips pulling, the softness of her body pressed against mine, the soft sounds of reunion.

All at once, her hands grip my shoulders, and our lips part with a little smack. She's out of my embrace, turning quickly to the counter so her back is to me.

"Food's almost here!" Mav bursts into the kitchen, going to the refrigerator and taking out a beer.

I'm breathing fast, feeling shaken. It's like I was just

swept up into a tornado and then unceremoniously dropped to the ground again.

My buddy is oblivious to what's going on. He shoves a beer in my hand and starts for the living room. Haddy has the bowl of tots in her hand when she turns to face me again.

She slides a finger under her bottom lip, and shakes her head. "I'm sure you're hungry. Mav never stops eating during the season."

I'm hungry all right, but not for food.

Haddy seems to read my mind, and she catches my forearm, giving me a little pull. "Come on. We can't stay in here all night. They'll start to wonder."

I couldn't care less, but I let her lead me into the living room. When our food arrives, Mav spreads everything out on the coffee table. My stomach growls at the scent, and I guess I'm hungrier than I thought.

Or seeing Haddy has eased one hunger, making room for the other.

It doesn't take long to polish off the burgers, fries, and tots. Mav fills the girls in on our winnings on the road. We're only one game down at this point, thanks to my disorientation after Halloween night with Haddy.

I don't regret it one bit.

I'm sorry I let the team and the fans down, but damn, it was worth it.

"I'm fading." Mav stands, collecting all the papers and crumpling them up, stuffing them in the brown bag. "We've got games all week, but I'll get something together for dinner."

"I've been dreaming about your sweet potato soufflé," Gina says, standing and following him to the stairs.

"You'll have to wait for that one. Mav continues to his bedroom, calling a goodnight before shutting the door.

Gigi pauses before trotting up the stairs. "Be sure to start the dishwasher before you come up, Hads. Night, Gav!"

Haddy nods, giving her cousin a wave. We both stand as if frozen until we hear Gina's door close upstairs. In one fluid movement, I catch Haddy's hand in mine. She's right behind me as I lead her through the kitchen to the small room where a large washer and dryer are situated.

She's just through the door when I shut it, turning her and pushing her back against it as I cup her face in my hands again, sealing my lips to hers.

"Gav," she whispers between kisses, threading her fingers inside my blazer and pushing it off my shoulders. "We shouldn't be doing this. It's too risky."

"They'll never know." I shrug the garment to the floor then my hands are on her waist again, moving beneath her shirt, higher to flick the clasp on her bra.

Her breasts spill out into my hands, and I lift them, squeezing and sliding my thumbs back and forth over her tight nipples.

She moans into my mouth. Our tongues slide, and her hands are on my cheeks. I'm ravenous for her. My cock presses against my pants, straining for release. I'm about to undo my fly when she pulls away, looking down.

I groan as she unbuttons my pants, lowering the zipper, and sliding her palm up and down my erection. "Fuck, that feels so good."

She licks her lips, lowering to her knees, and I think I might pass out when she pulls my dick into her warm mouth, sliding her soft tongue along the length of my shaft before curling it and flickering under the tip.

One hand braces the top of the door, and my other

threads in her soft brown hair. She holds her tongue against the tip of my cock, sucking it like a popsicle as she pumps my shaft with her hand.

Orgasm races through my pelvis, and I groan as she takes me to the edge so fast.

"Get up here before I come down your throat." I reach down, lifting her off her knees. "I'm not going to ask how you got so fucking good at that."

"Gay porn," she gasps, her lips swollen. "I figure they have the best technique, since they have the equipment."

"I love your scientific mind." I'm quickly shoving my pants down as she removes her leggings. "Let me taste that pussy."

I lift her in one easy move, sitting her on the washer and wrapping my arms around her thighs. With a gentle lift, I adjust her so I can bury my face in her sweet center. She's already so wet as I trace my tongue all over her clit.

"Oh shit... Gavin," she gasps, her fingers threading and pulling my hair. "I'm right there. I'm going to..."

She doesn't finish the sentence when her thighs break into shudders at my ears. She moans, and I kiss her right on the clit. Then I kiss the inside of her thigh, her belly, before straightening to line up at her entrance.

"Ready for me, Princess?"

"Fuck, yes." she gasps, reaching for my neck.

I almost come hearing that word from her guarded lips, and I'm literally on the edge when I start to enter her slippery core. I plan to take it slow, give her a chance to adjust, but once my tip is inside, she grabs my hips, pulling me closer.

"Fuck me, Gav." It's a desperate groan, and I'll be damned if I make her ask twice.

Holding her around the waist, I brace one hand on the

appliance and thrust in hard and fast. Her moans are loud, and I reach up to cover her mouth.

Only, it doesn't help for my own noises. She's hot and wet and eager, and my groans are guttural and feral.

"Fuck, Haddy, you feel so good... I'm gonna come."

"Come," she hisses, leaning forward to pull my ear between her teeth.

That sharp little bite of pain sends me over the edge, and I hear the washing machine squeaking on the floor as I thrust faster.

Two more, and I hold, moaning deeply as my cock pulses again and again. I'm flying through space, swept away in a surge of orgasm. Her insides spasm and pull, and I moan words of satisfaction. I don't know how, but being with her in this cramped room is even better than the night we spent in my big bed.

We're both breathing fast, holding each other as we drift down again. Turning my head, I find her mouth, pulling her lips with mine, licking my tongue inside to hers. Her palms smooth my hair back, and she kisses my cheek, my eye.

I'm right with her, kissing her temple, the line of her hair, holding my nose to her scalp to inhale the sweet scent of her shampoo. I want to commit every part of her to memory. I never want to forget this.

When we've caught our breath, she slips off the appliance. "Oh..."

Her nose wrinkles, and I quickly scoop up a T-shirt from the pile of dirty laundry. A small sink is in the corner, and I dampen it.

"Here." I use it to clean her legs, wiping her thigh then kissing her hip.

"Gavin." Her fingers thread in my hair, and she bends down to kiss the side of my cheek again.

Looking up at her, I can't deny the pressure in my chest. The strong emotions pulsing on every heartbeat. She's here. This is real. I don't know what to do with it.

"We should probably get upstairs." She looks at the door then back to me. "I'll go first. Give me a minute or two before you come up."

Standing, I smooth her hair back from her face, gazing deeply into her pretty, pretty eyes. "I'm really glad to be home, Princess."

17

Haddy

Lying in my bed, I can't seem to keep my eyes closed as I think about what just happened with Gavin. My insides are warm and throbbing from his rough invasion, and my breasts tingle from his kisses and sucks.

I'm relaxed from that incredible release, but I can't seem to sleep. *I wish...*

My eyes drift to the door, and I wonder if anyone would notice if I sneaked down the hall. Gina usually sleeps late, and I could set an alarm. My heart jumps when the door opens on its own.

A large figure slips into my room, and without a word, he lifts the blankets. His warm body slides into bed with me, and he puts his large, strong hand on my waist.

One inhale floods my senses with his scent of soap and leather.

"Gavin," I whisper, reaching up to cup his cheek, finding

it impossible to keep the smile off my face. "You read my mind, only... we're really close to Gigi's room here."

His warm lips press gently against mine. "It's okay. Just sleep. I want to hold you."

He turns me so my back is against his chest, and his arm is tight around my body. I'm not sure I'll fall asleep with his warm breath at my neck, but soon my eyes are growing heavy.

The next thing I know, I'm blinking my eyes open to the sun streaming through my windows. Gavin is gone, and I sit up, looking around to see Patsy stamping her little feet to be let out of her crate. A message is on my phone.

GAVIN

Hope you slept well. You're beautiful in the sunrise.

My stomach tingles, and my lips part. I don't know if this is going too fast. I don't know if I can stop it if it is.

I do know I have a lot to do at the lab today and I need a shower and Pats needs to go out. Throwing the blankets back, I jump out of bed and open her crate.

"HEY, Super P, it's about time you remembered where your parents lived." Dad pulls me into a hug. "Where are your cousins this evening?"

"Mav has a game and Gigi is judging a dog show."

He takes my hand in his large one, and I follow him into my childhood home, a gorgeous Frank Lloyd Wright style concrete mansion in the hills.

I loved growing up here with him and Mom and all our

little rituals, the movie nights, the game days, trips south to visit our family.

As we pass through the living room, I spy a football on the couch—no doubt being used for a pillow at some point.

One thing my dad always had in his arms besides me or Mom was a football. When he finally retired, it was a total given he'd take a job as one of those sports guys on ESPN. He's a natural on television, and with his outgoing nature, everybody loves him.

"Haddeee!" Mom calls from the kitchen. "Get in here and give your mother a kiss."

"Hi, Mom." I go to where my gorgeous mother stands barefoot in front of the stove whipping up her famous shrimp and veggie stir-fry with fish sauce.

Her dark hair is styled in a ponytail and her curves are accentuated by the red, flowered wrap dress she's wearing.

"What's new in the atmosphere? Saved any lives lately?" It's something she's actually done in her line of work.

"I wish." I open the refrigerator and take out a can of sparkling water, hoping it'll settle my stomach.

Mom's shrimp and veggie stir-fry is one of my favorite dishes she makes. It's restaurant-quality, but for some reason, my throat tightens at the scent.

"It's been pretty slow this semester," I continue. "Daniel and I've resorted to working on our language skills. Check me out, *Kazamuki wa?*"

Her slim brows rise, and she makes an impressed face. "What does that mean?"

"Which direction is the wind?"

"That's pretty cool, P!" Dad reaches into the refrigerator for a bottle of white wine. "Now you're bilingual. Heck, it won't be long before you know everything."

That makes me snort. "Not everything, Dad."

Dad is six-foot-two, and I inherited his bright blue eyes. My dark hair came from my mom—along with my perfect sense of style and love of old movies.

"Who's Daniel?" Mom arches an eyebrow, but I shake my head, sipping my water.

"Just a student at the Japanese institute that's co-sponsoring our research. Trust me, it is not a love connection."

"If you never date anyone, Hayden Lucille, how will I ever get a grandbaby?"

"Give me time. I'm almost finished with my master's, then I have to decide if I'll get my doctorate."

I'm still on the fence about getting a PhD, but it helps if I want to be a professor. I really just want to finish this study.

"Babies won't keep you from achieving your dream. I hadn't done anything when I had you."

"But you had Dad."

"Not at first." Mom lifts the spoon from the sauce. "Taste this and let me know what you think."

The gesture fills me with warmth. Our family has always bonded over food and music... and in my house movies. Stepping forward, I meet her eyes remembering being a little girl watching her skip around the kitchen in her bare feet and singing "Good Morning, Baltimore," which was her talent when she was in pageants. It made me so happy.

The spoon comes closer, and I hesitate. The scent meets my nose, and again, my throat tightens strangely. My stomach trembles as if in warning.

"Here, let me do it." I take the spoon from her hand and carefully pull just a tiny bit into my mouth.

As soon as it hits my taste buds, my stomach drops, and too much saliva pools in the back of my throat.

"What's the matter?" Mom's forehead crinkles. "Is it bad?"

She takes the spoon from me, finishing the bite, when a gag pulls me forward.

"Oh..." I clap a hand over my mouth.

"Get to the bathroom, quick! Your dad's a sympathetic barfer!"

"What's happening?" Dad turns worried eyes from me to her and back again. "Why is Haddy barfing?"

Flying to the half bathroom beside the kitchen, I slam through the door and flip the lid up just in time to lose all my sparkling water in the toilet bowl.

"Oh my gosh," I groan, pulling the lever to flush it as I brace a hand on my forehead.

My arms tremble, and I wait several seconds for my stomach to unclench. When I'm pretty sure I'm done, I stand slowly, turning to the sink and scooping water into my mouth. I do it several times, doing my best to get the taste of that sauce off my tongue.

"It tastes good to me..." Dad's voice is quiet when I return to the kitchen. "You okay, honey?"

"I don't know." My face feels cool and hot at the same time.

"Want some ginger ale?" Dad carries a can to where I pull out a chair at the small table in the kitchen.

"I think I'm going to wait."

"Is there a bug going around school?" Mom walks over to put her hand on my forehead. "You don't have a fever."

"To be honest, I've felt kind-of off all day. I had a chicken salad sandwich from the cafeteria at lunch... maybe it had turned?"

Dad goes back to where he left the wine. "I never get anything with mayo on it anywhere but here."

"That's probably a good rule of thumb." Mom returns to

the stove, where she turns the fire off under the wok. "Would you rather some broth? Chicken noodle soup?"

"No, thanks." I stand slowly, picking up my purse. "I might just head back to the house. If I do have a bug, I don't want to give it to you two."

"Oh, no!" Mom makes a pouty face. "We didn't get enough of a visit with you, and I'd cued up *Mermaids* for us to watch tonight."

"I love that movie!" I make a pouty face as well. "It's perfect for this time of year."

"I know." She hugs me close. "It's okay, baby. Cher, Winona, and Christina will be here when you're feeling better."

"What are your plans for Newhope? I've got two weeks left in the semester, so I'll be pretty slammed, but I'll try to get back over here before y'all leave town if I can."

"Don't stress about that." Mom tucks a piece of hair behind my ear, looking into my eyes with concern. "We're headed down next week, but we'll be glad to see you kids at Christmas."

Gigi, Mav, and I always fly to Newhope together as soon as Mav plays his last game. He gets a whole three days off for Christmas, and we do our best to cram in as much family time as possible.

Chewing on my lip, I think about Gavin and Christmas.

For the entire month, we've been sneaking around at the house. It's been risky and uncontrolled and sexy. Perhaps the most dangerous was when he slipped into the shower with me.

The music on my phone had suddenly grown louder, and the exhaust fan switched on. My mind went straight to *Poltergeist,* until he stepped inside the shower curtain fully naked, with that perfectly chiseled body on full display.

His physique really is perfect. I know from Maverick they train with weights and stretch and do cardio in addition to playing strenuous games almost every night of the week. Seeing him like that, with his muscles so defined and his cock erect and ready, I was instantly wet.

He gave me one order. "Put your hands on the wall and don't scream." Then he took a knee.

It was probably the hottest experience of my life, and I can't believe no one heard us.

So for the past four weeks, we've been sneaking around, and now the holidays are here. We haven't talked about it, but I'm sure he'll visit his family in Wilmington, which is miles away from our family in Newhope.

We're not official. We're fooling around, right? We haven't said what we're doing, but every night when he slips into my bedroom and holds me in his arms, I grow a little more attached.

The guys have a game tonight, but when I walk in, I see Gigi. She's eating a bowl of pasta on the couch and watching *Isle of Dogs* with Spanky lying on the floor at her side and Patsy curled in her lap.

"What are you doing home so soon?" She puts her bowl on the coffee table and sits up straighter. "Y'all didn't have an argument... Did your mom offer to pay for college again?"

I shake my head, still unsettled. "My stomach's messed up. I barfed, and I decided I'd better come home and go to bed."

"Oh, no! Can I get you anything? Chicken soup?"

"No, it's okay." I put my hand on the stair railing. "I probably just ate something weird."

"I've got Peepee, so don't worry about her." She lifts the

little dog off the couch, and I take a beat to give her little brown head a pet before heading upstairs.

Sitting at my desk in my bedroom, post-shower, I rub my fingers against my forehead still thinking. My chest is tight, and I don't like the nervous path my logical brain is following.

Mom said I've always been so analytical, working out problems, finding solutions. She said I get it from her, the need to have an answer. Knowledge is power, but it's also security.

Only this knowledge is terrifying me.

After our reckless Halloween hook-up in which I did something I never do, I went straight to the gynecologist and got a fresh box of birth control patches. I'd been a little careless about changing and reapplying them, but after that night, I'd been a "perfect" user.

Still, the painful knot in my throat reminds me I hadn't always been.

I pull up the calendar on my phone, counting the weeks since Halloween. Friday will be five weeks, and I haven't had a period since...

My face flashes cold then hot, and I slide off my chair onto the floor of my bedroom. The first of October was my last period. Bending my knees, I press my eyes against the backs of my hands. *Don't borrow trouble, Haddy... Don't borrow trouble.*

After allowing myself a ten-second freak-out, I straighten my shoulders and crawl across the floor to my bed. Lifting the blankets I climb under them and hug my knees to my chest.

It's dark when I feel him join me. His large hand slides to the hem of my sleep shirt, going under it to cover my bare skin. Most nights I relax into how good his touch feels. Most nights it leads to us having quiet-as-possible sex.

Tonight, I'm too panicked to relax into his embrace. I can tell he notices my stiffness when his hand moves from caressing my bare stomach to holding my shoulder.

"Something wrong?" His voice is warm, concerned.

Pulling the blanket to my mouth, I swallow a sob.

Clearing my throat, I manage to whisper, "I was sick this evening. I think I have a stomach bug."

"Shit, I'm sorry." He rises up on his elbow, but I don't dare look at him.

I know if I meet his gaze, he'll see the fear in my eyes, and I don't want to have this conversation with him until I'm certain. It could still be bad chicken salad.

Oh, God, please let it be bad chicken salad.

"I don't want to get in your face in case it's a virus."

"Dang." He rolls onto his back with a deep exhale that I feel all the way to my toes. "We had a great game tonight. Another win..."

"That's so good." I reach behind me to give his rock-hard forearm a squeeze.

Nothing would be better than to give myself to him, pretend my mind isn't paralyzed by dread. It's not going to happen tonight.

He rolls toward me again, pressing his lips to the back of my shoulder. "Want me to go?"

"Not really, but I think you'd better. To be safe."

His lips press against my arm, and my eyes squeeze shut as he hesitates. "Okay, but if you need anything, send me a text. I'll sleep with my phone in my hand."

"I expect I'll sleep all night. Don't worry."

"That's kind of not possible, Princess." His voice is so gentle, it aches.

One more kiss to the top of my shoulder and he quietly slips out, leaving me to toss and turn all night.

18

───────

Gavin

Haddy is not okay.

We've been playing nonstop, and we're finally getting a break. Only it's not much of a break, as Mav has us all preparing for Friendsgiving in December—pushed back a week, because our schedule didn't have any time in November.

I've been slipping into her bed every night we're in town since that first time, and it's been heaven. A lot of times I just hold her, but other times, in the silvery dawn, before I sneak out to head back to my own room, I'll take her.

I can't help it. I always want her.

For the last week, though, I've been sleeping alone in my own bed, and it sucks. She says she hasn't been feeling well, but I have a sinking feeling it's something more. Particularly because she doesn't seem to want to meet my gaze, and the few times she does, she doesn't hold it for very long.

It's starting to make me a little crazy. I've started to feel attached, and I had wanted to ask her out on a real date, see how she's feeling about our sneaking around. I wanted to ask if she might consider going public.

"A little more to the right…" Gigi is on the ground directing me to hang a giant turkey in the palm tree in front of the house.

It's all made of paper, but it's almost as big as me. I'm up on a ladder, and she's waving her hands as I pull the rope.

"There!" She gives me two thumbs up, and I tie it off. "Now we can put up this garland, and we'll be done."

Gigi is really into decorating for the holidays. I thought we went all out at Halloween, but she's got more decorations than I've ever seen. I didn't even know they made Friends-giving decorations.

I've been up and down ladders all day while Mav's been in the kitchen whipping up turkey burgers. I told him I thought that sounded disgusting, but he told me just to wait.

I've learned over the past few months not to question him. He hasn't made a bad dish yet.

"Hold this side." Gigi is on a ladder across from me holding the other side of the streaming curtain.

"Thankful for you… bitches?" I slant my eyes at her.

"Two of my dog-breeder friends are coming. They'll get a kick out of it."

"What about everybody else?"

"Let's see… it's your friends Donovan and Saxon, and Haddy said her lab partner Timothy is coming. I don't think any of those males will care."

"I think it's funny." I shrug.

If I recall correctly, Timothy's a little bitch. He might care, but I don't say it out loud.

Gigi's pretty feisty, but I'd never call her a bitch. I'd probably punch anybody who did… unless it was a girl, then I'd have to be growly and make the offending female apologize.

"Bitches, Gina?" Haddy's voice lights my entire body. "Seriously?"

She's standing at the foot of the stairs frowning at the sign, and she looks so pretty. Her dark hair is styled in large curls around her shoulders, and she's wearing an oversized brown sweater that hangs to her thighs. It's almost like she's trying to cover her sexy body, but I know how hot she is under all that yarn.

"We're hosting dog people, *Hayden*." Gigi's nose lifts as she climbs down the ladder. "I don't tell you what pageant people will think is funny."

I take a step in Haddy's direction, but the doorbell rings, cutting me off. She shakes her head, going to answer it, and a bustle of noise precedes my giant teammates entering the house.

Donovan leans down to give Haddy a hug, and I swallow the jealous knot in my throat. I'm not jealous of Donovan, jeez.

She turns and gives her cousin a pointed look. "The guys are here, Gigi."

Gigi's eyes narrow, and she waves her away. "I'll let Maverick know."

Again, she tries to pick up that heavy ladder, and I have to take it from her. "You stay. I'll let Mav know."

Her hands are on her hips, and with her back to our guests, she cuts those green eyes at me. "Are you two in cahoots?"

Holding up my free hand, I shake my head. "I don't know what you're talking about."

Whatever Haddy is up to, I'll support, as long as it keeps her attention on me and not either of those knuckleheads.

Gina gives a big smile, turning to the guys. "There's beer in the kitchen. Follow Gavin. He'll show you."

They take off, following me as the doorbell rings again. I take a quick glance to see it's Lisa, one of Gigi's dog-breeder friends. She points at the sign and bursts out laughing. Gina gives Haddy the "I told you so" treatment, and I grin, leading the guys to the beers.

It's another party like Halloween, only without the costumes. Mav plates the turkey burger patties and heads out the back door to cook them on his big green egg. I step back to the living room, wishing I could get Haddy alone.

Instead, I see her greeting Timothy at the door. He gives her one of those weird little monster dolls dressed in a turkey outfit.

"Isn't that cute?" She takes it from him, turning it in her hands. "I'll have to find a place to put it."

I have an idea for a place.

"Time to eat!" Mav calls from behind me, and Haddy looks up, her pretty eyes meeting mine.

She blinks quickly, almost seeming startled, and my brows lower. *What's going on, Hayden?* I wait as she and Timothy head in my direction to the table. He stays by her side, but when she gets closer, I trace my finger over the back of her wrist.

Her hand turns, and without looking, she gives it a gentle squeeze. It's not much, but at least it's positive.

"I don't know how you guys can keep up that schedule." Timothy is on his third glass of red wine. "When do you ever have time for a personal life? Or is that something you even want?"

I don't know if he's aiming that comment at me, but I'm ready to answer when Donovan jumps in ahead of me.

"It's not so different from any other demanding job. The hours are just different." He straightens in his chair, putting his hand on the back of Gigi's beside him. "We prioritize relationships just like doctors or firemen or people in the military. They're all pretty tough schedules, yet they manage to have personal lives."

"Don't forget scientists!" Mav jumps in with a laugh. "Haddy works just as long hours as we do sometimes."

I've noticed my girl hasn't touched her wine. She's barely eaten anything, and I don't like that. Is it possible her stomach is still messed up? It's been a week. We really need to talk.

"Not so much this semester," she counters. "That was when I was assisting Dr. Warwick and had to grade all those papers. That was rough."

"That reminds me..." Timothy is running his mouth again, only this time, he clutches her arm, and my eyes narrow. "I'm assisting Dr. Becker next semester."

"That's amazing, Timothy!" Haddy moves her arm out of his grasp and pats him on the shoulder. "No papers to grade in that job."

"Nope, just processing grad school applications."

"You're selecting the next generation."

The two of them share a laugh, and I stand, collecting the empty plates. "I gotta hand it to you, Mav, I didn't know you could do that with ground turkey."

"That was turkey?" Saxon's eyes are wide, and Donovan stands to help me clear the table.

"It's Thanksgiving!" Mav explains how he infused the turkey with onion powder and grated mushroom, and as I expected, Haddy stands to collect their empty plates as well.

Timothy tries to stand, but she puts her hand on his

shoulder. "No, no—you're a guest. Stay right here and have dessert."

He tries to argue Donovan is helping, but she argues she'll take over for him. Our team captain appears in the doorway, and Haddy puts her hand on his arm.

"Guests don't clean. Go sit and have dessert." He starts to argue, but I back her up, taking the glasses from his hand and nodding to the other room.

I'm glad she and I are on the same page about being alone in the kitchen.

As soon as the plates we're holding are rinsed and put in the dishwasher, I catch her around the waist. "I'm thankful we finally have a little alone-time."

Her hands are on my chest, and her lips tighten. "We need to talk, Gav. Wait here."

I don't like the sound of that, but I do as she asks, listening to her telling Gigi she'll take the dogs for a walk and finish cleanup when we get back. Gigi and her friend offer to help, which elicits another complaint from Timothy.

Haddy handles them, and as soon as she returns, she shoves Spanky's leash into my hand and grabs my wrist, pulling me to the door.

"Come with me. Hurry."

She's got Peepee under her chin, but the serious expression hasn't left her face. We have to talk. She wants us to be alone, and I can't tell if it's a good or bad thing.

We're a block from the house, and she's still quietly holding the tiny poodle. I've got Spanky's leash, and that spoiled mutt has sniffed every bush we've passed and hasn't stopped to go yet.

"I like all your family rituals," I say, hoping to break the ice.

She nods. "Family is really important to all of us. We were raised on it."

"Me, too." I glance over at her worried expression. "I think that's why Mav and I are such good friends."

"It's true." She says it in a way almost like she's remembering something. "He thinks a lot of you."

"He's a great guy." And this is a weird conversation.

Spanky finally stops at an open patch of grass and starts acting like he might go. Haddy puts Peepee on the ground, and while the two dogs do their thing, she crosses her arms, looking up at me. Her blue eyes are so round, my stomach dips.

"What's going on, Haddy?" I take a step forward, putting my hand on her arm. "Whatever it is, you might as well say it and let us both off the hook."

Uncrossing her arms, she shakes her hands like she's loosening up. "I've never been this nervous before."

A frown pulls at my lips, and I couldn't be more lost. "It's okay, you can tell me anything."

Her lips part, and she exhales a deep *Oh, man...* Then she inhales again, walking away and back again, stopping beside a bush covered in purple flowers.

Squaring her shoulders, she clears her throat and looks up at me. "I don't know if there's a good way to say this. There's definitely not a good way to find out about it..."

"Jesus, Haddy, what the hell?" I do my best to keep my voice gentle, but dang, she's killing me.

The dogs are coming back to us, Spanky at a bounding run and Peepee doing her little hop. Haddy doesn't pay attention to them.

Her sapphire blue eyes hold mine, and she gulps air before stopping my heart. "I'm pregnant."

19

———————

Haddy

The words have just left my mouth when a streak of white jumps in front of me, and I fall back with a yelp, landing slap in the large California lilac bush behind me.

Gavin dives forward, grabbing my upper arms and catching me before my butt hits the ground.

I'm surrounded by purple flowers, and Spanky stands in front of me wagging his stumpy tail. I swear he's smiling.

"Are you okay?" Gavin lifts me out of the bush like I weigh no more than a doll.

"That's not how I pictured it going." I pluck broken twigs off my sweater, out of my hair.

Gavin holds me around the waist, touching my chin so I'll look up at him. "You're... *pregnant*?"

The sun is setting, casting both of us and everything around us in a shimmering hue. It's what movie makers like to call the "golden hour," but my heart is beating out of my chest.

This moment is not golden. It's more like panic stations.

"It wasn't a virus." *Or bad chicken salad, thanks, God.*

I blink briefly at his eyes, but it's too intense.

I took three pregnancy tests in the small, unisex bathroom at the science lab, and every single one came back positive in less than thirty seconds. Since then, I've been sort-of wandering around in a state of shock.

"Shit." He exhales the word, then he looks past me at the bush where I fell.

Clearing my throat, I hold his forearms and step out of his embrace, doing my best to get my bearings. This is no time for panic. We have to be logical, scientific.

"I was using the birth control patch, but I guess I was kind of sloppy before Halloween. I wasn't having sex, and I didn't keep track of how long I'd wear one." Swallowing my nerves, I straighten my shoulders. "It's my fault."

My neck is hot, and I don't know why my silly eyes heat. I am *not* going to cry. I'll accept whatever shock or outburst he might have with strength and dignity...

"No way!" He steps forward quickly, covering my clasped hands with his large one. "It's as much my fault as yours. I didn't use a condom."

"But I told you it was okay."

He looks down at the pavement before lifting his blue eyes to mine. "What do you want to do?" His brows pull together, and he almost seems in pain.

I swallow air, and my chest trembles. Chewing my lip, I inhale slowly before I say it. "I..." *exhale a terrified breath.* "I want to keep it. I figure..."

"Oh, man, okay. That's good." His words come out in a rush, and he scoops me into his arms before I can finish my sentence. "I was so scared to ask that question."

Now my eyes really are burning, and my stomach twists.

Gripping his arms, I step out of his hug once more.

"Yes... well..." My throat is thick. *No crying, Haddy.* "I figure I won't start showing until late next semester, I hope. I'm almost finished with my degree. If I can just graduate before anyone notices—"

"What do you mean?" He's frowning again. "Why does that matter?"

"My scholarship." Besides telling Gavin, losing my scholarship is my next biggest fear. "I can't be pregnant and be an International Princess Woman. I'll be stripped of my title if they find out."

"What the fuck, why?"

"We have a code, Gavin. I can't be pregnant."

"Why not? You're a *woman*. It's in the title."

"An *unmarried* woman. We're supposed to set an example to little girls, other pageant participants. IPW has standards—"

"You have the highest standards of anyone I know. Hell, you don't even swear."

"I can't change the way the program works. My only choice is to hope they don't find out before next semester ends."

His jaw tightens, and he blusters with protective rage. I kind of fall in love with him a little bit for it. Not that I could actually *be* in love with him. We've only really known each other a few months.

"Would it change anything if I proposed?" His brow is lowered. "They couldn't kick you out if you were getting married, could they?"

Shaking my head, I exhale a laugh. "We can't get married to save my title. I mean, I appreciate the offer, but I'll just lie low and hope for the best."

His eyes hold mine, and I see all the thoughts going on

there. We have a lot to discuss, logistics, how this would even work, how much he wants to be involved.

I know it's a risky decision to stay pregnant when I don't even have a job and I'm not even finished with college. I know it's because I have the privilege of rich parents who love me, a big family that loves babies, security...

Even with all of that, I want to do this myself. My independent streak is fierce, and I've never liked people taking care of me. It makes me itchy and restless to think I owe someone or I'm dependent on someone to live.

At the same time, I want this little baby so much. I don't even know why, but it already feels like this little person is meant to be.

Gavin steps closer, taking my hand again. "What if we got married because we wanted to?"

"What?" My eyes snap to his.

"We could try it. If it doesn't work out, no harm, no foul. Your title is safe, the baby is covered..."

"We can't get married because I'm pregnant. We hardly know each other."

"That's not true. I know a lot about you. You're incredibly smart, you're doing this study to save babies."

"That's not exactly what it's about..."

"You love *Hannah Montana* and axolotls and tater tots. You make cute little snorty noises in your sleep..."

"I do?" My cheeks heat with embarrassment.

"You're a super pooper—"

"You are never allowed to say that." I cut him off quickly.

"Haddy." He slides his thumb over the back of my palm. "Couldn't we try?"

"No." I shake my head, scooping up Patsy and walking in the direction of the house. "This isn't a science experiment.

We're not being reckless. We've been reckless enough as it is."

"Slow down." He's behind me holding Spanky's leash. "Why are you mad?"

"I'm not mad. I'm taking this seriously."

"I am, too."

We stop at the front steps, and I turn to face him in the growing dark. "We need to think about what this means, what we want. We both have a lot going on right now. You're in the middle of your season. I'm on the verge of graduating, defending my thesis..." He reaches for me again, but I hold up my free hand. "I'm going to have doctor's appointments. I've got to get through Christmas... We need a plan."

"I plan to go with you to those doctor's appointments."

Inhaling slowly, I nod. "Okay. But we can't tell anyone—not Maverick, not Gina. Until I graduate, this is top secret."

His lips tighten, and again he frowns. I know he's angry about that part, but he doesn't understand. I can't lose this scholarship.

"Please, Gavin." My voice is quiet, and when he looks at me again, the anger melts from his expression.

He steps forward, pulling me into a hug. "I'd never do anything to hurt you, Princess. I catch you when you fall. Right?"

"I'm not falling anymore. Starting now." Now too much is at stake.

"Hey, Hayden." Timothy's voice on the porch makes both of us jump. "Did you fall? You do have some twigs stuck to your sweater here."

"Timothy—how long have you been standing there?" My voice trembles, and I take the dried twigs from his fingers. "Spanky jumped at me, and I fell into a lilac bush. It's no big deal."

My lab partner nods, his smile tight. Then he glances up at my escort briefly. "I'm just taking off. Final grades are due next week, and I've got a stack of papers."

"Of course. Thanks so much for coming." I hold out my hand to shake, blocking his attempt at a hug. "Sorry we didn't get to spend more time together."

"Yeah." His annoyance is plain. "I'll see you in the lab."

We hesitate, watching as he walks up the sidewalk to the car. I do a little wave as he gets in and drives away.

"That guy." Gavin grumbles watching him leave.

I scrub my fingers over Pat's little head before going into the house. "He's the least of my concerns."

"Happy Ho-ho-ho to you!" Harry Connick, Jr., blasts through Cooters & Shooters, my family's restaurant on the coast, and everyone dances and sings along.

Gigi's dad, my uncle Garrett, and our honorary uncle Craig are dressed in red-velvet shorts, red velvet Santa jackets and hats, and they're on the bar with a few of the wait staff—also dressed in skimpy Santa costumes— shaking their butts to the jazzy Christmas song.

Christmas Eve is on a Thursday this year, and everyone's at the restaurant having spiced egg nog, habañero-ginger hard apple cider, cayenne pepper-dusted brownies, and cheese balls covered in jalapeño pepper jelly. It's a Christmas-themed Dare Night, and even the candy canes are spicy.

Our whole family is in town. Mav is dancing with his mom, and Gigi is across the room sitting with Miss Gina, the sweet old blind lady she's named after, who is basically our honorary grandmother.

"Hey, Super P." My cousin Kim walks up and hands me a glass of hard cider. "Why do you look like you're trying to disarm a nuclear weapon?"

"Thanks." I take the tumbler from her hands, unsure what to do with it. "I've just got a lot on my mind."

"Like what?"

Like Gavin Knight. He's been on my mind since he pulled me out of that lilac bush, threatened the entire International Princess Woman program, then proposed to me. Twice.

The next day, the guys left for an out-of-town game, and the whole time they were gone he checked in via text to ask if I still had nausea, if I had any spotting... *How would he even know that could happen?*

I sent him the date of my first ultrasound in January, and he put it on his calendar. Then our last night in town, he sneaked into my bedroom. It was the first time he'd done it in almost a month, and my chest ached at his closeness. My body longed for his...

It's impossible to know how much of my reaction is pregnancy hormones and how much is real. Our past hasn't changed. We've just been hit with a really tricky plot twist.

Lying on his side facing me, he traced a lock of hair off my cheek so gently, as if I were made of glass. "I'm not trying to muddy the waters." His blue eyes were so warm, so full of affection. "I know you need space..."

Did I need space? I was trying to remember why.

Oh. Because he supposedly cheated on my roommate with a bunch of sorority girls, and the last thing I wanted was to risk my heart again with a guy like that.

Only, is he really a guy like that? He doesn't act like it. Can I trust myself to be right this time?

"My moms are complaining I haven't been home since

June," he continued. "Otherwise, I'd make an excuse to spend Christmas in Newhope."

"It's a family holiday." My voice was quiet.

His brow furrowed, and his eyes flickered to my lips. "I know. That's why I thought…"

He didn't finish his sentence, but I knew what he was thinking. *His family. Did he mean me now?*

Then he'd kissed my cheek and told me to have a safe trip before he slipped out again.

"So why do you look like the saddest Christmas elf on the shelf?" Kim leans against my shoulder.

"I'm not sad." But my eyes are on my untouched drink.

We're standing at the small bar in the back of the room near the pool tables while the rest of our family dances and celebrates. I look up and see my own parents moving their hips in time to the Bo Diddley Christmas beat.

"Mm-hm." Kim arches an eyebrow. "Let me guess, it's a guy."

Kimmie Joy is our oldest cousin. She moved to Newhope as a baby with my uncle Jack before any of our parents even met. For a while it was just her and Aunt Dylan and her dad. Then slowly, the entire family started making their way home and having babies.

All except my parents, who stayed in LA for work.

Now Mav and Gigi are with us in LA, but we come back to our original family home on the coast as much as possible. We all grew up together, and nobody knows me as well as they do.

"It's not! I've just got a lot going on." But my voice goes weirdly high, giving me away.

"What's his name?" Kim straightens beside me, crossing her arms, and I know she's not letting me out of this one.

I glance around to make sure no one's headed this way. "Gavin Knight."

Her amber eyes widen. "Mav's teammate? Does he know?"

"No." I grab her arm fast. "Nobody knows, so don't say a word."

Her brow arches. "So what's the problem?"

I shrug, playing it off. "I'd like to get to know him better, before the entire world finds out and goes crazy."

"You don't trust him. Why not?"

Dang Kimmie Joy Bradford. She's six years older than me, and I've never been able to get anything past her. Who am I kidding? I've never been able to get anything past anyone. It's some sort of miracle Mav and Gina don't know about Gavin and me—or a testament to how busy we all are.

"We went to college together, and he dated my roommate Karen. When they broke up, she said it was because he cheated on her. He says it was the other way around."

Kim's nose wrinkles. "You don't know who to believe?"

My shoulders drop. "I want to believe him... Mav says he's not a player."

Kim lifts her chin. "If Mav vouches for him, he's a good guy. Your cousin would never lead you wrong."

"But what if Mav doesn't know him like I do?" I've been burned before. "Why is trust so hard?"

Her lips twist, and she puts an arm around my shoulders. "Is he hot?"

Nodding, I pick up a spicy candy cane. "Very."

"Eh, I say take a chance. What's the worst that could happen?"

Boy, if only she knew. I'm so close to telling her when our aunt Allie dances up to us.

"Here are my girls!" She pulls me into a hug.

She's actually Kim's step-mom, but we would never, ever call her that. It sounds too Disney-villain, and Aunt Allie is the best human on the planet beside my mom... and all our other aunts.

"You two better get on that dance floor, or I'm going to go get Austin and Edward to make you."

"Austin's here?" My voice goes up, and I'm so excited.

We rarely get to see Allie's son from a previous marriage anymore. He moved to Texas to play football, and he's a big star—just like Uncle Jack was before he retired.

Austin was always one of the big boys when we were little, but he was so sweet to us anyway. He'd give us rides and tease us. I think we all had baby crushes on him.

Kim's back stiffens, and she seems suddenly nervous. "I just remembered I have to take care of something at the house."

Aunt Allie makes a complaining noise, but I catch Kim's arm before she disappears. Our eyes meet, and she steps to me, giving me a hug and pinching my upper arm playfully.

"Don't worry, Hads. You're the smartest girl I know. You'll make the right decision." Then she whispers in my ear. "Keep me posted."

I watch as she makes her way out the back screen door at the same time as Austin and Edward enter through the front. They're grown-up men now, and handsome as ever... although, I guess I'm a grown-up woman, too.

With a big fat secret in the middle of my big ole family, and only one person who knows the truth.

20

———————

Gavin

"**A**nd for Lane, a brand-new mouthguard!" My mom Elaine is playing Santa this year, and as soon as she pulls the purple and white guard from the red sack, my mom Kenny throws a sock at her.

"You did not get him a mouthguard for Christmas!"

"You got him socks!" Elaine argues. "This has the Champions logo right there in the middle. Isn't that fun?"

"Mom, I told you I'd protect my teeth." I pull her into a hug, then I make a fist and noogie the top of her blonde head.

"Patrick Lane Knight!" She squeals, and my dad chuckles from where he sits in his recliner, a stack of gifts on his lap.

It's Christmas morning, and we're opening gifts at Dad's house in Wilmington. My half-brother Finn is sitting on the floor with his back to the couch in front of my half-sister Sabrina, who sits beside her dad Slayde, my mom Kenny's second husband.

My family can get a little confusing with all the halves, especially with my two moms insisting we keep everybody close. I'm not complaining—I love my big, twisted family.

"That gift is rank, and you should stop dead-naming Gavin," Sabrina grumbles under her breath.

"Easy, Tiger." Slayde scolds his daughter in a low voice, giving her a nudge. "It's Christmas."

A former boxing champ, Slayde's past is pretty dark, but he loves us as much as we love him. He also works at my dad's private investigation firm as one of their lead trackers.

"I'm just saying, he asked us to call him Gavin." My teenage sister pushes her long dark hair behind her shoulder. "We should respect his wishes."

"Good grief, Bree, we respect your brother." Kenny fusses from where she sits, looking more like Sabrina's twin sister than her mom.

They're both petite with pale skin, dark brown hair, and big blue eyes. The blue eyes are the only thing I got from my mom Kenny. Otherwise, I look exactly like my dad.

"What is dead naming?" Elaine frowns from where she's digging in the bag again.

"Calling him Lane instead of Gavin," Sabrina explains.

"My sister, the social justice warrior." I lean forward to tug her foot. "I don't expect them to remember after all this time."

Elaine drops her hands looking up at me with sad eyes. "Does it really hurt your feelings, Laney? I'll try to do better."

"It's all good." I wave her away. "Aren't you going to open your gifts, Dad?"

"I'm too busy enjoying the floor show." He picks up a small box, turning it in his hands. "I hope this isn't jewelry."

"Open it!" Kenny cries, and I guess it's from her.

He tears the paper back then shakes his head. It's a pewter badge that opens like a locket to reveal a picture of all of us in it.

"That's different." He turns it so we can see.

"Found it on eBay," she explains.

"I think it's cute," Elaine jumps in, taking it from him to study.

We continue unwrapping our gifts, sitting on the floor beside the Christmas tree, and it's good to be here with my family. My mind jumps ahead to next year and a little baby ripping through all the paper, looking for gifts. It tugs a smile at the corner of my lips.

I guess next Christmas might be too soon for a baby to be walking, then I realize I don't even know Haddy's due date.

My stomach tightens, and I remember her face, her worried eyes, the way she told me then fell straight into the bushes.

"What are you grinning about?" Dad nudges me with his foot.

We're all lying around now inspecting each other's' gifts, being together.

I glance up at him, thinking about our past and how our mixed-up family came to be. "Can I talk to you about something?"

His brow lowers, and he uncrosses his foot to stand. "Anybody want some coffee? Gav and I are treating."

Five yeses ring out.

We take everybody's orders, and he gives me a nudge as we start for the door. "See if Starbucks is even open. We might have to improvise."

We do manage to find a coffee shop that's open, and

while we wait for all the different specialty items to be prepared, I decide to come clean.

I've always been able to talk to my dad, and he's good at keeping things between us until I give him the okay to share. Probably because he's a PI.

"What's on your mind, Gav?" He takes a sip of black coffee.

I'm having the same, but with cream. "It's this girl I know, Haddy Bradford. She's actually one of my roommates. I really like her a lot, but I kind-of blew it."

Dad's brow lowers, and he takes another sip of coffee. "How'd you manage that?"

"Remember how I was dating that girl Karen in college?" He nods. "Haddy was her roommate, and she got this wrong idea about me back then."

He's watching me intently, and I shift in my seat, embarrassed to say the next part.

"I found out Karen was cheating on me, and I kind of lost it." The back of my neck grows hot, and I reach up to rub it. "I slept with some sorority girls, but it was before we'd officially told people we were broken up. Karen twisted it around and said that was why it ended, and Haddy believed her."

Dad exhales a low *hmm*, leaning back in his chair and pressing his lips together. "She believed her friend over you."

"She didn't really know me. She's really, *really* smart, so she studied a lot, worked in the science lab." I look at the paper cup in my hand, remembering how excited she got telling me about her work. "I was so busy with hockey, I just put my head down and powered through it."

"And now you want something different?" Dad's eyebrow arches, and I nod, glancing up at him.

"I don't know how to change her mind. I *did* sleep with those girls, but I never cheated on Karen. I never would have."

"I know you wouldn't." Dad reaches out, giving my shoulder a squeeze, then he shakes his head with a chuckle. "It's pretty crazy how much you're like me... without even knowing it."

"What do you mean?"

"Ahh..." He exhales heavily. "Before you were born... before I even knew your moms, I proposed to this girl, Stacy. We were going to be married, and one day, I got home early to surprise her with flowers and all the things..."

He looks down, and I sit straighter, my eyes widening. "No."

His lips tighten, and he nods. "Yep. I walked in on her with some other guy."

"Dang." I shake my head. "I'm sorry."

"Then I went on my own rampage. I was determined to do everything differently, and I tell ya, I got into a lot of trouble. I almost lost your mom Elaine over it."

"You were acting that way with Elaine?"

"No, nothing like that." He holds up his hands. "It was more like, my past came home to roost, and she was rightfully upset about how I'd acted. She left me over it."

"But..." I point in the direction of the house and back to him. "You were able to fix it. How?"

"I wallowed in guilt for a little while. I beat myself up for being an idiot." He looks me straight in the face. "Then I got off my ass and went and got her. I showed her how much I loved her. I showed her the man I really was, that I'd never let her down again. Anything she needed, any time, I was there for her."

My jaw tightens, and I look at my hands, thinking about what he's saying. "You were there for her."

He gives me a nudge. "You've got an advantage I didn't have. You live in the same house."

Nodding, my mind is miles away, on the coast in south Alabama.

My chest aches, and I know what I have to do. "Would you apologize to the moms for me? I've got to go."

A smile splits his cheeks, and he pats me on the back. "Sure thing. Good luck, son. I believe in you."

It's after dinner when I pull into Newhope, and Cooters & Shooters is all lit up and full of people. I've never been here, but Mav has talked about it so much, I feel like I know the place.

The ride share driver helps me with my luggage, and I give him an extra tip before walking to the door. The "closed" sign is out, but they're all inside playing music and laughing.

It looks like the entire Bradford clan is here, and my eyes go to her at once. She's standing beside a man about my size who must be her father. She has his eyes, even though her hair is darker. His arm is around her back, and she leans her head on his shoulder.

My chest twists, and a smile curls my lips. She's so relaxed and happy here. I can tell this is her safe place, her home, and I want to be a part of it.

It's more than that. I want to be the place she goes for safety.

Walking to the glass doors, my palms are a little sweaty, but I wipe them down the front of my jeans before reaching out to try the handle. It's locked, but Mav sees me and lets out a yell.

"What the hay?" He runs over to unlock the door, flinging it wide and pulling me in for a bear hug. "Bruh, what are you doing here?"

Shit, I'd been thinking so much about seeing Haddy again, I didn't give much thought to a good excuse for appearing on their doorstep.

"You talked about this place so much, I wanted to see it." I give him a shove, as Gigi jogs up to where I'm standing.

"Gavin!" She throws her arms around my neck, and I give her a hug. "Merry Christmas!"

She's a little wobbly, and I chuckle. "Merry Christmas to you. I'll have what you're having."

"It's this ginger-spiced hard cider." She puts her hand on my chest, leaning closer. "I'm addicted! I'll get you one."

She dances off to hook me up, and like a little earthquake, my eyes meet Haddy's. She's still standing with her dad, but a smile is on her lips, and she blinks at me a few times before walking over to where we're standing.

"Gavin..." She stretches up to give me a hug, speaking low in my ear. "What are you doing here?"

"Couldn't stay away, Princess." I give her a wink, and her cheeks flush a pretty color. "Figured you could use some support abstaining."

"Abstaining?" Her eyebrow arches, and our roommate appears.

"See what you think." Gigi shoves a copper mug of hard cider into my hand. "Aunt Allie came up with it, and it's delicious. It warms your whole body."

I lift the mug at Haddy, and her eyes narrow.

"Sure you don't want some, Hads?" Gigi turns to her cousin.

"No..." She moves a hand over her midsection. "My stomach is still kind of weird."

She sticks her tongue out, and I give her a knowing look before taking a sip of the beverage Gigi gave me. It's actually pretty damn good, and she's right, it does warm me all the way to my toes.

"Who's this kid?" A big man walks over to where I'm standing, slapping me on the shoulder.

I straighten to my full six-foot-two height, but I'll be damned. This guy's got two inches on me.

"Grizz!" A petite woman runs up behind him and jumps on his back. "Are you trying to intimidate my son's best friend?"

He catches her under the legs, yelling, "Get off me, Banshee!"

A dark, curly head peeps around his shoulder. "Are you *the* Gavin Knight I've heard so much about from my little boy?"

Her amber eyes twinkle, and I'm immediately at ease. Mav's mom reminds me a lot of Elaine. She sticks out a hand from over her giant brother's shoulder.

"Yes, Ma'am." I reach up to shake it. "It's really great to meet you all. Mav's told me so much about all of you. I had no idea he was such a good cook, and Gigi said we have you to thank."

"That's my little ginger snap!" Dylan calls to our other roommate, who looks up from where she's swiping on her phone to give us a happy wave.

"That's my daughter Gina." The big guy glares down at me. "Don't be getting any ideas, hockey boy."

"No, sir." I shake my head, taking a step back and holding up both hands. "Gigi is safe with Mav and me."

From the corner of my eye, I see Haddy's hand cover her

laugh quickly, but I hold my expression steady. He has no idea how safe his daughter is with me.

His brother's daughter, on the other hand...

"Stop being a party pooper, Grizz." Mav's mom tilts her head to the side, then hops off her brother's back. "You kids have fun. You're only young once."

"That's terrible advice," Grizz the Giant complains.

"You're one to talk!" his petite sister argues.

"Come on." Haddy catches my arm, pulling me away from the group through a screen door in the center of the dining room.

She doesn't even try to hide our exit, which I take as a good sign, and I follow her out to a playground facing the bay. It's enclosed by a fence, but she leads me through it, down to the water, where we take off our shoes and dip our toes in the surf.

"You left your parents on Christmas day to come here?" She squints up at me. "What did you tell them?"

The moon is bright in the sky, and I look up at it then out at the waves tipped in silver. I have no idea what my dad told them.

"My dad said I should be here with you, so I came."

She stops in her tracks, turning to face me. "You told your dad about us?"

"Yes, and no." I tilt my head side to side, but I can see she's worried. "I told him we knew each other from college, and I had strong feelings for you. He said in that case I should be here, with you, and I decided he was right."

Her chin drops. "You have strong feelings for me?"

"You know I do. I haven't tried to hide it."

She starts walking again. I follow her, and we take several steps in silence, the only sound the shushing of the tiny ripples on the water.

"I'm glad you're here." Her voice is quiet. "I've been thinking about all of this so much, trying to understand how it happened. Based on where I was in my cycle, I should not have gotten pregnant when we were together... although, there have been studies that show females will ovulate if they're aroused by a suitable male."

Her scientific approach is too much. "Are you saying I make you ovulate, Princess?"

She looks up at me, wrinkling her nose. "I think it's possible. I would never have disregarded common sense like that if I hadn't been significantly aroused."

"I was pretty horny for you, too. I never have sex without a condom."

"We've been having nothing but condomless sex since Halloween."

"It's true." I give her a wink. "You make me reckless."

She exhales a teasing scoff. "You don't need my help to be reckless."

The return of Sassy Haddy makes me smile. She's adorable, and fuck, I'm glad I came here. I wouldn't want to be anywhere else right now.

"I'm glad I came, too. It helps me understand you better, why you aren't afraid to do this."

Her chin lifts, and she looks out at the water. "It's hard to be afraid of anything in Newhope."

"I get that. You've got this incredible mob of family in your corner, but I can give you something they can't."

"What's that?" A sly grin is on her lips.

Reaching out, I catch her arm, pulling her close. Her hands are on my chest, and I lean down to kiss her. Our mouths seal and part, and I sweep my tongue inside to curl with hers.

A soft whimper slips from her throat, and her body

relaxes in my arms. It feels so good. Cupping her chin, I tilt her head so I can kiss her deeper.

Her back arches, and her soft, perfect breasts press against my chest. I groan, tracing my lips to her cheek, closer to her ear. "I can definitely give you that."

"Hmm..." She takes a step back, her blue eyes stormy. "I'm not sure we can do *that* here. Not without getting caught."

"I bet I can sneak it in."

"I don't know, it's pretty big."

That makes me laugh out loud, and she reaches up to cover my mouth with her small hand, shushing me.

"They'll hear you." Shaking her head, she exhales a soft growl. "How did I end up with so many secrets? I've never been good at lying. I've always said I'm glad I wasn't here when Mav was sneaking around playing hockey. If anyone would've slipped up and told Aunt Dylan, it would've been me."

I lean against a large oak tree, crossing my arms and smiling at her cute frustration. "You won't have to hide for much longer. Mav and I are leaving tomorrow."

"Then I'll be alone again, watching everything I say."

"You're never alone, Hads. I told you, whatever you need, I've got you covered."

"I don't know how you can say that with your schedule the way it is."

"Trust me. If you call, I'll be there." I take a step closer, tracing my thumb along her jaw. "We can make this work."

She looks up at me, and a little smile curls her lips. "I believe you."

"It might be easier if we at least start dating—with Mav and Gina, I mean."

"Won't that put us all over the gossip sites?"

"Hockey's a pretty insular community. We might be hot for a week, but I expect it'll cool off pretty fast. I'm not as big a star as your cousin..."

Poking my chest with her finger, she says the last word at the same time as me. "Yet."

My stomach tingles, and I huff a laugh. Damn, this girl. I haven't smiled or laughed this much in a long time. I've got to do what Dad said. I've got to show her I'm not the man she thinks I was.

I'm committed, and I'm going to win her.

21

Haddy

For our fall semester wrap-up, Daniel and I worked together to show how even though we didn't find any strong correlations, it's just as important to have data on what's not happening as what is.

So much science is built on what didn't happen, what didn't work. Our study hasn't failed. It simply hasn't demonstrated what we want it to... *yet*, to quote the father of my child.

A flush of heat moves through my chest at the thought. After he and Mav left, Gigi and I stayed in Newhope through the new year.

The guys were playing nonstop, and we were able to watch several games with the whole Bradford clan at Cooters & Shooters. The place was also packed with customers, most of whom were cheering for Maverick as well.

Aunt Dylan did her best to stay busy and away from the big-screen televisions behind the two bars.

The few times we held her in place to make her watch, she stayed beside one of the large posts, ducking behind it and hiding her eyes whenever a fight broke out or Mav got body-checked into the boards.

"Oh, my... Oh!" She'd squeal. "This is worse than football!"

One night, amidst all the uproar, Kim pulled me aside to whisper in my ear. "Gavin is gorgeous!" Her amber eyes twinkled with excitement. "He said he came to see the restaurant and Mav, but it was clear he came for you."

I chewed my lip and tried to act aloof, but I couldn't do it. We both fell together in giggles, and it was so good to have her there, knowing about us, at least, as much as she could know safely.

Soon they'll all know about the baby, but I'm months away from that happening.

Today, I'm hanging out in the waiting room at the New Beginnings Birthing Center in Pasadena. I couldn't ask a friend or colleague for a doctor's recommendation without provoking questions, so I turned to Google and spent hours reading reviews. New Beginnings is supposed to be one of the best, and Dr. Barry has all five stars.

I'm chewing my fingernail, standing just inside the glass door waiting for Gavin when I see him hustling up the walk. He's got the hood of his jacket over his head, and he's wearing dark sunglasses.

Even in that disguise, he's very noticeable at six-foot-two with his athletic build, messy long hair, and his square jaw dusted in scruff. People will either think he's an actor or a sports star.

Now I can't believe I didn't come up with a sneakier plan, and I grew up with a celebrity dad! See? I'm terrible at hiding things. We're playing with fire.

He ducks into the waiting room and walks straight to where I've scurried to hide behind a Ficus tree.

"Did you check in?" His voice is low.

"Not yet. I was waiting for you." Again, a total amateur move.

I look around the room. It's not crowded, and the few women who are here are either preoccupied with their own tiny babies or they're pregnant. Thankfully, they all seem to be distracted, which means it's possible we're safe.

"Wait here," I whisper, going to the window to sign the clipboard.

I have to fill out a questionnaire, and Gav turns to the wall, keeping his hood up and studying his phone. Thankfully, it's not too long before they call my name.

The nurse is very pleasant, taking my vitals and getting my weight. She leads us to a small room with a bed and assorted ultrasound equipment and monitors, then she says the technician will be right with us.

When she leaves, I look up at Gavin. "I don't know why I'm so nervous."

He pushes the hood off his head and puts his sunglasses on the counter before pulling me into a tight hug. I'm surrounded by strong muscles, the scent of soap and leather, and comfort.

"It's going to be fine. You've been sleeping well, no spotting. These are all good things." I've always been strong, but he's really good at this. "It helps knowing exactly when conception happened. You should be in the tenth week, which means the baby is the size of a strawberry..."

Pushing out of his arms, I squint up at him. "How do you know all this stuff?"

His brow lowers. "I've been reading *The Expectant Father* on my phone. My dad said it's the book he read when they were expecting me. I also downloaded *From Dude to Dad*, but I like the other one better."

I only blink at him with my jaw dropped. We've been home a week, and with school starting and hockey games, I haven't been paying a lot of attention to his reading habits.

Hell, I've never paid attention to his reading habits. I didn't even know he read. Now, the thought of him studying baby books has me melting inside.

"I didn't know you were doing that." My voice is soft.

"You're not?" The side of his lips rises in a half-grin. "I figured you'd be way ahead of me on all of this."

Pressing my lips together I climb slowly onto the ultrasound chair. "I haven't read anything... other than Google."

"I don't believe that. You're the scientist. You study everything in detail. I've heard you talk about wind currents and viral transmission."

"I know!" I cringe. I'm sitting with my legs hanging off the side of the chair, and I cover my face with my hands. "I guess I've been in denial? I finished up the semester and visited with my family and set up the lab for spring... I've done everything but think about this tiny being inside me."

He lifts one of the chairs from beside the wall and places it right in front of me. Then he reaches up and takes both my hands in his.

"Maybe it's too theoretical... or you could still be in shock. The books say it can take as long as the first diaper to feel a connection with your baby." He holds me so securely, my eyes heat. "They say not to shame yourself about it. You'll get there when you do."

"Gavin..." My voice is a whisper, and I don't know what I'm about to say.

The door bursts open, and a friendly woman enters.

"Hello, Bradfords! I'm Dr. Mandy Barry. Yep, just like the Barry Manilow song, easy to remember."

Her hazel eyes dance, and her blonde hair is streaked with white. Google reviews for the win!

"I'm actually the Bradford," I nod towards Gav. "He's a Knight."

"A white knight. I love it!" She reaches out to shake Gav's hand.

"Gray night, actually," he corrects, but I can tell by his response and the tone of his voice he likes her as much as I do. "Nice to meet you, Dr. Manilow."

"Ha!" Dr. Barry points at him. "Good one. I hope that gray knight thing doesn't stand for 'morally gray.'"

Gav is quick to answer. "Not at all. It's more a mix of Gawain and Galahad."

"Galahad was the greatest knight ever. I love it."

She pulls up her sleeves, turning to me. "Ready to get a look at what's going on in there?"

"Yes." I smile, feeling more relaxed than I have in a month.

The doctor takes the wand out and squirts warm gel on my midsection. Then she puts the half-moon-shaped wand on my flat stomach, and the large monitor lights up with a grainy, black and white field.

A black hole is in the center, and my breath catches in my throat when the profile of a blurry little baby-looking figure appears. We're surrounded by the sounds of rhythmic swishing, and my hand tightens in Gav's.

"This right here is your baby." The doctor circles the bright white image with her pen. "And that sound is the heartbeat, good and strong."

She taps on the keyboard, taking pictures, and my eyes fill.

Gavin leans closer to me, speaking softly. "You okay, Princess?"

I nod, blinking tears onto my cheeks and meeting his gaze. "I made it. I'm there."

He slides a large hand around the back of my neck, pulling us closer as he presses his lips to mine. My heart expands, filling with so much love.

DR. BARRY UPLOADED our ultrasound pictures and video to our patient portal, and I've probably spent too much time gazing at our little boy or girl on the screen. Gavin was right. We're at ten weeks, the baby is perfectly healthy, and we're not due back for another month.

When I presented the latest portion of my graduate studies to my committee, both Dr. Cross and Dr. Becker commented on how healthy and glowing I am as we walked back to the lab.

Timothy scowled from where he sat, making notes on one of his tickling videos, which struck me as funny.

Daniel logged on and we discussed our division of labor this semester. It takes a lot of coordination to work with someone on the other side of the globe, but if it's done well, we can keep a 24-hour surveillance going.

We both agree this semester we're going to identify the exact tropospheric wind patterns carrying the disease. We're manifesting. There's always an increase in cases during the winter into spring months, and the windy season is just around the corner.

I've been getting home after dark most days. It's my last semester, and my last chance to make any sort of contribution to the field, unless I continue and get my doctorate.

I was already on the fence about doing that, and now that I'm going to be a mom, I'm feeling less inclined to do it. Also, I won't have the income from my scholarship, and I can't imagine being a teacher's assistant and a mom and working on a dissertation.

The house is dim when I finally arrive. Gigi left me a note on the counter saying she walked the dogs and put Princess Petunia in her crate. She also noted leftovers are in the microwave.

I step over to find a paper box of Mediterranean chicken with saffron rice and hummus waiting. It smells delicious and my stomach growls loudly. I'm about to dig in when I hear the bumping sounds of someone coming through the front door.

The guys had a game tonight, and I poke my head around the corner to see Gavin dropping his bag on the floor beside the stairs. He looks up, and when our eyes meet, the greatest smile curls his lips.

"Hey, Princess." He crosses the living room to where I step into his arms.

He lifts me off my feet in a sweep, and my legs go around his waist. Carrying me into the kitchen, he sits me on the counter, leaning down to kiss the side of my neck, my jaw.

"I want to fill your Gavin-shaped hole, but I've got to eat something before I die."

A laugh snorts through my nose, and I lift the box of leftover Mediterranean. "How do you feel about chicken shawarma, saffron rice, feta, and hummus?"

He groans in a way that lights my core. "I feel like put it in my belly now."

"My thoughts exactly." I lean over to grab the fork I set out on the counter.

He grabs a fork from the drawer beside my leg, and we

fight over who can eat the fastest. At one point, we cross forks, which makes me laugh. The leftovers are gone so fast, I'm not sure we had enough.

Tilting my head, I wrinkle my nose at him. "Tater tots?"

"Please."

I give his shoulder a little shove, and lean over to hit the preheat button on the oven. We'll have to wait a few minutes for them to bake, but the edge is off our hunger.

He reaches into the fridge for a beer, nodding at the ginger ale in my hand. "Morning sickness?"

I shrug. "I like ginger ale."

"That's cool." He smiles. "You're almost to the second trimester."

"Baby is the size of a plum."

"You've been reading." He grins, and warmth floods my chest.

It's hard to remember the fear that gripped me at Christmas. Now all I can think about is the tiny plum inside me, wondering if it's a boy or a girl, if it'll have dark hair, blue eyes, be tall or petite, athletic or scientific...

"Do you want a boy or a girl?" Gavin takes out the cookie sheet, arranging the tots on it before sliding them into the oven.

Chewing my lip, I hesitate. I know the correct answer, but I clasp my hands, holding them in front of my nose as I say it. "I want a healthy baby."

"Cut the crap, Princess." He straightens, putting both hands on either side of me on the counter, caging me in where I'm still sitting.

I put my hands on his shoulders, leaning closer to his handsome face. "What do you want?"

He kisses my cheek, the side of my hair at my ear. "I'd like a little girl who looks just like you. I'll get her a crown..."

"There are no crowns in Star Wars," I counter.

"There are crowns. They're just smaller." He reaches over to tap on the face of his phone, and music starts to play.

It's a slow and sultry song about wanting it all, and he holds out his large hand. "Dance with me."

A smile curls my lips, and I hop off the counter, going to him and resting my head on his chest. His strong arms surround me, and we sway to the words about falling for someone.

He kisses the top of my head, sending a rush of warmth through my veins, and it's so perfect.

Those protective walls I've kept around my heart are gone. I know what I want.

22

———

Gavin

This is how it's supposed to be. Haddy fits just right in my arms, and her cheek is against my chest. My lips are in her dark hair, and I inhale the sweet scent of jasmine as song lyrics about wanting it all float around us.

I want it all.

"You've been so good to me in all of this." Her voice is soft as she blinks those pretty blue eyes up at me. "Thank you."

I smile, tracing my finger along her jaw. "You're welcome, but you don't have to thank me for taking care of what's mine."

Her cheeks flush, and she blinks quickly, nodding. "I've decided I don't care about the past or what might or might not have happened in college. I want to give us a chance."

As much as I've wanted her to say that for so long, the way she frames it makes my insides twist.

I take a step back, my expression tight. "Really, Princess? You're still there?"

"What do you mean?" Her brow furrows. "Are you angry? I just said I don't care about the past."

"You should care." I shake my head, releasing her. "If you still believe what Karen said, you shouldn't want to be with me."

"I'm confused. I thought this was what you wanted."

"It is." My chest is hot and twisted. "But I don't want you to make peace with someone you think is capable of cheating. I want you to believe me."

Her lips press together, and I see her take a little gulp. Her cheeks are pink, and she looks down, which makes my stomach sink.

Her voice is just above a whisper. "I want to, but it's really hard for me. If I hadn't seen it happen…"

My jaw tightens. Her words are a knife to the heart.

"I'm going to bed."

"Gavin, no." She starts to follow me. "We made tater tots."

It's a sad little plea, almost like she's trying to smooth this over, but I'm not hungry anymore.

"You can have them."

The weight of that fucking past is on my shoulders, the lies, the way I was betrayed.

I don't know what more I can do to show Haddy I'm not that guy. I've tried to demonstrate my commitment. Shit, I haven't slept with another woman since we've been together… and we're not even officially together.

Like that matters. The thought of being with anyone else leaves me cold. She's in my veins, and I'm not getting her out. I'm frustrated, and yeah, I'm fucking angry.

I hear her cleaning up downstairs when I finish

brushing my teeth. I showered at the arena, and this isn't how I envisioned the night ending when I got home.

Instead, I'm in my room, climbing into my bed alone.

Dad didn't say how long it took for Elaine to change her mind. I should call him tomorrow for a pep talk, because I really feel defeated right now.

My arms are crossed, and I can't seem to relax when I hear the sound of my phone buzz on the nightstand. A few seconds pass, and it buzzes again.

I don't want to pick it up, but the pressure of wondering if it's her finally gets the better of me. I pick up the device and yep.

HADDY

I'm sorry.

HADDY

I don't want you to be mad at me.

Rolling onto my back, I exhale deeply, staring at the ceiling in the dark. I consider not replying, but that's not my style. I won't leave the mother of my child on read, especially when she's trying to make amends.

GAVIN

I'm not mad at you, Princess.

HADDY

I think you are...

GAVIN

I don't want you to settle, even if I know it's not true. I want you to be proud to be with me.

I don't say it, but if we ever do cross paths with Karen, I

don't want Haddy to hide or feel like she's betrayed her friend by choosing me.

HADDY

I'm very proud of you.

GAVIN

I want you to believe me.

She doesn't reply, which I decide to mean she's thinking about what I've said. Putting my phone aside, I close my eyes and somehow manage to sleep.

23

Haddy

The computer screen is a series of lines and dots that adjust by fractions every thirty seconds. They show the direction of the wind currents, and I'm comparing the number of cases reported by the Japanese institute to the strength and direction of the storms.

It's tedious and repetitive and not yielding the results I want, and it's exactly what I need. Facts. Observable. Measurable.

Gavin's been distant all week, and I don't know why it makes me feel guilty. I was trying to extend an olive branch, to tell him I didn't care about what happened. I really don't, which is a pretty big step for me.

He's shown me how devoted and caring he can be, whether it's for the baby or for me, I can see it's real.

Whatever happened between him and Karen is their business. I wanted to be honest with him. I didn't expect him to take it as an insult.

I tried to apologize, but he's still mad.

Leaning my head on my hand, I squeeze my eyes. Crying is the most ridiculous response to what is going on. Still, knowing he's angry is a lead weight in my chest.

I was looking forward to sharing his bed that night. Instead, I slept alone and we're in this place of distance, not really speaking, barely texting, but not technically fighting.

I debate just saying I believe him, it's all over. But I'm the worst liar. He'd see right through me, and then it would be worse.

Why isn't it enough that I don't care anymore?

In the morning, when my alarm goes off, I don't even want to get up. I want to curl deeper under the covers and cuddle Patsy.

A buzz on my phone makes me jump, and I snatch it up fast, hoping it's him. It's not, but it's something almost as good.

KIMMIE

I just found out our moms and our dads have their own group chats 😺 Why don't we have one of those???

KNOX

Because you're my big sister, and that's weird.

GINA

I love this idea… let's do it! I do think it should be girls only, tho. Knoxey's right. We can't talk about everything with the guys in the group.

SAGE

I only text with vets. Otherwise, call if you need me.

GINA

At first I thought you meant the military 😏

SAGE

Veterinarians 🐴

MAV

You might be a cowboy if you prefer talking to horses instead of people.

SAGE

Horses are good, people are crazy.

KNOX

I thought it was God is good.

MAV

Why aren't Austin and Edward in here?

KIMMIE

It's a cousins-only chat.

GINA

Austin's a cousin! And Edward's an honorary cousin...

KIMMIE

Where's Haddy? Back me up on this please.

Exhaling a smile, this is just what I need to distract my mind from obsessing over Gavin.

HADDY

Austin's more of an uncle... Edward, too, I guess even tho y'all are closer in age.

KIMMIE

How old do you think I am?

KNOX

This needs to be boys v girls. Mav, Sage, we're getting off this crazy train.

GINA

Our train isn't crazy! We have puppies 🐶

KIMMIE

Fine, Sage, Knox, Mav, form your own group… we'll talk about you behind your backs.

SAGE

I don't mind seeing what the girls have to say.

GINA

You are so Uncle Zane 😍

KNOX

Just wait til they start talking about their periods.

MAV

It's good. We can have a separate chat for the men.

KIMMIE

We'll have a separate chat for the girls.

GINA

The women?

KNOX

If the word discharge appears on my phone, I'm out.

KIMMIE

What if you discharge a pass?

KNOX

I throw passes.

HADDY

Mav could discharge a puck…

MAV

I don't even want to imagine how that might happen.

KIMMIE

Y'all hit those pucks pretty hard... don't bend over.

SAGE

Is that what you call bull hockey?

HADDY

MAV

That doesn't happen.

SAGE

Similar to horse hockey...

GINA

Sage!!!! 😅

KIMMIE

Bell rang—time for class. I expect all important information to be reported here.

KNOX

I'm being heavily recruited to play for the Saints.

KIMMIE

Knoxey!!! Mom is gonna cry 😭

KNOX

Don't say anything... I don't want to get her hopes up until I'm sure.

KIMMIE

See, this is the kind of thing we share. Girls, we'll have our own chat for periods. The boys can have their own to discharge their duties...

SAGE

KJ said doody 💩

Everyone signs off with *love yous* and hearts, and I put my phone down, feeling better than I did five minutes ago.

It's time to check in with Daniel before I leave for the day, but I look up to see Timothy watching me pointedly.

"Everything okay, T-man?" I do my best to be very neutral-friendly, no romance.

He's practically sneering. "You're really into that hockey guy, aren't you."

"I guess we're getting to know each other better."

"You know those hockey guys are all players, right? They call their female fans *bunnies*."

My cheeks sting, but I won't let him shame me. "I don't know if that's always true."

"You deserve somebody who'll treat you with respect, Haddy. Who won't run around on you."

Sitting straighter, I think about the way Gavin reacted to what I said about his past with Karen.

"I think Gav would agree with you." Timothy's eyes narrow, but thankfully my computer rings, alerting me of my virtual meeting.

"This is Daniel." I wave my phone at him, not really interested in continuing this conversation.

It's none of Timothy's damn business what I do. Putting on my headphones, I'm ready to talk data.

"I REALLY LIKE the idea of a cousins group chat." Gina has Spanky's leash, and we're power walking around the neighborhood before the game tonight. "I don't know why we didn't think of that before."

"Same. It'll help us keep up with each other, especially with Sage and Knox." I'm carrying Patsy in a doggie backpack I saw online. It has a little "window" she can stick her head through, and I can swing my arms as we walk. "They're like 'same planet, different worlds.'"

"Of course, Knox is a quarterback. He's Uncle Jack's son. But who knew Sage would turn out to be a cowboy?"

"Uncle Zane loves working with horses."

"And he's so funny, I love it!" She cuts her eyes at me, giving me a sly smile. "Speaking of love, are you going to wear Gav's jersey tonight?"

My stomach tingles at the thought of seeing him play. He's so sexy on the ice, flying around the rink. Even when he fights, I hate it, but it's also a little thrilling.

We only go to the games once a month, so I haven't had a chance to show my support since our *disagreement*. The way he's keeping me at arm's length is killing me inside. *Is it killing him?*

"I don't know about love, but he needs our support, too. He's the new guy."

And it might help smooth things over between us.

"I don't know about that. He's getting a lot of support from the fans, the female fans in particular."

A knot twists in my throat. "He is?"

"Well, I mean, they're into him, but he doesn't seem interested in reciprocating, which is strange. He's so handsome, and Mav is always so full of adrenaline after their games. I wonder why Gav never hooks up with anyone."

I don't like anything about this conversation. It's making me itchy and my teeth grind.

"I wonder..." It comes out as a little growl.

"Oh, shut the front door, Haddy!" Gigi yells at me so unexpectedly, Spanky jumps and barks.

I put a hand on my chest. "What?"

"You know it's because of you! Stop playing it off and confess. You two have been flirting since Halloween. He gave you his jersey to wear to the games, and then he flew all the way to Newhope for what? To see our *family restaurant*?" She practically groans the words. "Give me a break. What do I look like? A dumb blonde?"

"I... We..." My mouth drops wider and wider the more she speaks. "Well, technically you're a ginger."

Gina shoves a hand on her hip. "Don't even try to deny it. In fact, I'm pretty sure I heard bumping and muffled sounds coming from the shower a few weeks ago."

Heat flames in my cheeks, but I can't deny it. We were fucking in the shower. A word I don't say out loud, but it's kind of the best description of how it goes. Gav is excellent in bed... In laundry room... In bathroom...

Her lips twist into a knowing smirk. "Just clean up after yourselves."

Spanky finally finds a suitable grassy place to do his business, and we stop. I take off my backpack and squat down to let Patsy out. She hops like a little brown bunny after her giant white doggy friend.

"We were going to tell y'all after Christmas, but..." My shoulders droop under the weight of my misery.

Gigi squats beside me, brow furrowed. "What's wrong?"

"I think I kind of blew it."

"How in the world could you have done that? I'm telling you, Hads, that boy looks at you like you're a rib eye steak and he's on a diet."

"He does not!" I push her shoulder, and she falls onto her butt with a little squeal.

"He does, too!" She hops up at once, shoving me onto my butt with a cackle.

Then she dives on top of me, and we roll to the side, which of course makes Spanky bound over and jump on us as well. Patsy hops around squeak-barking.

"Ow! Spanky," I groan, doing my best to guard my midsection. "Seriously, Geeg, he is out of control."

"No, he's not!" She sits up, hugging her big white dog, bits of grass clinging to her strawberry blonde hair. "He's a sweetie."

Patsy hops around us excitedly, letting out her little squeaky barks. "*This* is a sweetie. He's a menace."

I pick up the little dog, poking out my lips like I'll kiss her. She happily licks them in response.

"And you didn't want to foster a dog." Gigi shakes her head at me. Then she imitates my voice in a high-pitched range that sounds nothing like me. "Oh, Gigi! She's going to barf on my bed!"

I'm not hearing it. "You know that dog barfed on my bed any time the door was open."

"He had a nervous condition." My cousin climbs to her feet, catching my hand and helping me up. "I hate to tell you, but we might have to return the princess soon."

"No!" I wail, hugging the little pooch to my chest. "She's so happy here."

"I know, but that's the meaning of the word *foster*. It's temporary. Peepee's mommy misses her."

My heart hurts at the thought of Gav being mad at me *and* losing my little companion. I don't think I can take any more suffering on top of trying to keep a massive secret from my best-friend cousins.

"When?" My tone is pouty.

"I'm not sure." Gigi catches my hand. "But start preparing yourself."

We hold hands as we walk slowly back the way we came. I cuddle Patsy under my neck rather than putting her in the backpack.

"We'd better hurry or we're going to miss warmup." Gigi runs up the porch steps when we get home. "And I know you want to see Gav stretching."

Heat pushes out the misery, and I chew my lip. I do want to see him so much.

24

―――――――

Gavin

We keep winning, and for the first time in my hockey career, I wish we weren't.

I love the game with all my heart, but the more we win, the longer our season lasts, and Haddy needs me.

Her due date will be in July, which is kind of perfect. Even if we go to the championships, I should be finished by then, but I don't want to be on the road if she goes into labor or has any issues or complications.

Still, I can't let the guys down. Nobody wants to go home in April. So I fly around the rink, playing my best, putting pressure on the forwards, working with Mav on our signature plays.

He slaps another shot into the goal, and I'll be damned. My best friend just scored a hat trick.

The arena is on their feet roaring, and I look up to where the girls are sitting. They're jumping up and down hugging each other, big smiles on their faces.

Haddy is wearing my jersey, and she and Gigi wave in time to the beats of "Nokia" by Drake, which has somehow become one of our celebration songs. I think it started because of the part where he says *Ice like Gretzky.*

Even if I'm frustrated with her, I can't stop a chuckle when I see the two of them shaking their cute butts and pumping their arms in celebration. I mean, hell, our roommate slash their cousin slash my best friend just pulled off a major score. Another win for the Champions.

Haddy's been sending me little texts every day. Mostly they're about how she's feeling, the fact she's officially in the second trimester, and the books are right. She's feeling great, looking beautiful, and so far, still not showing.

Standing under the shower after the game, as the hot water runs down my face, I smile thinking about her. I won't lie, I can't wait for the day when her belly pops, and she's walking around with that bump showing.

When I talked to Dad again, he told me to be patient. Security is important in relationships. Trust is the foundation. I need to fucking find Karen and make her confess the truth.

I've been turning that idea over in my head since that night in the kitchen. I lost track of her after college, but I imagine she wouldn't be too hard to find on social media. She was one of those International Princess Women, after all.

I'm still thinking about it when I arrive for Haddy's doctor's appointment the next day.

My hood is over my head, and I'm wearing dark sunglasses. Even though I'm pretty sure no one is following me all the way out to Pasadena, I still make the driver let me out a block away. I'm being extra careful for my girl.

When I see her in the waiting room, she looks up at me

with so much hope in her pretty blue eyes. She's doing her best, and I want to pull her into my arms and kiss her. It was so hard to go straight to bed last night after the game. I wanted to go straight to her.

Still, I have to be strong. I don't want a relationship where she thinks I'm capable of betraying her. I want her to believe in me.

Dr. Barry starts with the ultrasound, and like always, she's peppy, telling us the baby is the size of an avocado now.

"A chip off the ole guac, you might say," she teases.

"That's terrible!" Haddy groans through a laugh as the doctor slides the wand over her belly.

"Just giving the big guy here some ideas for dad jokes."

I lift my chin to the petite physician. "Appreciate it."

"Well, everything looks great. All that's left is the blood-work." She takes some tissues out of a box, handing some to Haddy and using the others to wipe off the tool. "Don't be worried, it's all standard procedure, and I'll have the results back pretty quickly. You won't have to obsess too long."

We thank her, and I walk with Haddy to the phlebotomy station. The woman places six glass vials on the tray, and Haddy sticks out her tongue.

"That's a lot of blood," she mutters, not sounding happy.

My protective instincts kick in, and I take the seat beside her, pulling her hand into mine. "Squeeze my fingers if it hurts."

"It shouldn't hurt, but it will take a minute." The dark-skinned nurse smiles, tying the rubber tourniquet around Haddy's upper arm. "I'm pretty good at this."

"I know, it's all routine." Haddy returns her smile, but I've gotten to where I can tell the difference between her confident smiles and her "putting on a brave face" smiles.

I hate thinking she's nervous and doing her best to be strong. Fuck, I never want her to worry.

"It's all going to be good." My voice is quiet. "You're young and healthy. We both are."

"Scientifically speaking, the odds are very much in our favor."

"Is *The Hunger Games* scientific?"

"Not really." She blinks a few times, clearing her throat. "The game was so much fun last night. I think you and Mav will be sharing that billboard next season."

She's nervous-talking, but I won't argue with her. "I think you might be right."

"Oh, my goodness," the nurse exclaims, looking up from where she's switching out the vials. "You're Gavin Knight! I had no idea you were expecting. Congratulations... both of you!"

"Ahh..." I clear my throat, catching the panicked look on Haddy's face. She's pale, and it's not from loss of blood. "You know, we're kind of trying to keep this quiet. The paparazzi and all are pretty relentless."

"I get it." She nods, removing the needle from Haddy's arm and applying a Band-Aid. "And I expect this would be big news."

"We really want it to be a special time just for us." Haddy's voice is quiet, and she smiles up at the young woman.

"Your secret is safe with me."

I'VE GOT to get back to the arena for a game tonight, so I'm not able to stay with Haddy while she's freaking out about me being recognized.

I know she's freaking out, because I've also come to recognize the way she presses her lips together as she twists her fingers. Annoyed or not, I feel like a shit leaving her at the clinic, but I think she'll be okay for a few hours.

We win again, and Mav is on me to go out with the team and celebrate.

"Bruh, you've only gone out with us twice this whole season." Mav tries to snap me with his towel, but I catch it, pulling it out of his hand.

"Don't even."

"How are we supposed to bond if you go home?"

My shoulders are tense, and I can't believe this guy hasn't figured us out yet. I look down, trying to find a reason I haven't been with anyone since October—as far as he knows.

When I glance up, mischief is in his eyes. "What are you not telling me?"

I pull the tweed blazer over my shoulders, thinking about how at Christmas, we'd decided to let our roommates know we're dating. Then we'd gotten cross-ways with each other.

My hair is still damp, and I turn to face my friend who's pulling on jeans and a hoodie to go out. "I'm going to tell you something, and I want you to be cool about it."

He straightens, shoving both hands through his shaggy hair, pushing it out of his face. "What?"

"I'm really into your cousin. We've known each other since college, and I think she's a great girl. She's smart and obviously beautiful..."

Mav's expression tightens, and I can't tell if he's going to pull that protective cousin shit on me or try to hit me or what. Instead, he completely surprises me.

"Dang, I'm sorry." Shaking his head, he looks down. "I

don't know how to tell you this, but she's not really into you. She's got this wrong idea in her head, and I tried to tell her you're a good guy, but I don't know if she listened."

My shoulders relax, and I huff a laugh. "Yeah, we talked about that. Her roommate..."

"Yeah, that Karen chick. She's a real—" He stops himself, adjusting his reply. "She said some shit about you I know isn't true."

Nodding, I consider how to say this. "If I could change her mind, would you care if I dated Haddy?"

"Hell no!" He grabs my shoulder, giving it a shake. "Ask her to the gala. She's really good at shit like that, and you can show her what a great guy you really are."

"I like that." I smile like I hadn't already thought of asking her.

"So now I get why you're headed home all the time." He grins, giving me a shove. "You and Haddy. It's good. It makes sense. Now get out of here."

We clasp hands, and I slap him on the back. I'm headed to my waiting SUV, when I see the paparazzi waiting for us.

"Go, I'll take care of them." Mav steps in front of me as I steal around the back of the large black vehicle.

Looking out the window, I see him hamming it up with the female reporter as my driver slips us out the back way.

He waves his hand, and I'm sure he's making some joke. She laughs, her eyes flashing with excitement, and I shake my head smiling.

My buddy has never met a camera that didn't love him, and after meeting his uncle Garrett, I get the feeling it's genetic.

I'm quiet on the drive from the stadium to our little cottage in Los Feliz. I gotta say, when my original housing fell through, and I saw where Mav was living, I thought I'd made a mistake. Now I really like the quaint, neighborly location.

The house is dark when I arrive, which I don't expect. Granted, it's a Friday, but Gina usually is sitting on the couch watching a dog movie. Haddy stays late at the lab during the week, but on Fridays, she's usually home hanging with her cousin.

Or at least, that's how it used to be. We haven't been talking as much lately. Damn, I'm going to feel like a loser sitting here alone on a Friday night if they've gone out.

My phone is in my hand to text her as I jog up the stairs to drop my bag in my bedroom, and I skitter to a stop on the landing. The light is on under her door, and I hear noises coming from inside.

I step forward, hesitating before I knock, and my stomach drops. The door isn't closed all the way, and I realize she's crying. Without really thinking about it, I walk right in to find her sitting in the middle of the floor.

She's dressed for bed in a thin, white tee and those mermaid pajama pants. Only, her legs are crossed, and her chin is tucked. Both her hands are in her lap, and her shoulders hunch forward, shuddering with every sob.

Fuck me, it's like a punch in the chest.

Dropping my bag, I rush forward, hitting my knees and pulling her hands into mine. "What happened, Haddy? Is it the baby? Why are you crying?"

My whole body is tight, and I feel like I'm right on the edge. Her eyes squeeze shut and big tears fall onto her cheeks as she shakes her head. "No... it's not that."

A box of tissues is on the floor in front of her, and she grabs several, holding them to her nose as she sniffles another sob.

My stomach twists, and I carefully place my hand on her chin, forcing her to look at me. "Tell me what's wrong."

"It's Patsy." She nods in the direction where the small crate used to be, and I realize it's gone.

Shifting onto my butt, I look all around the room. All of her doggy things are gone.

"What happened to her?"

"Her owner wanted her back. Gigi was here, and she took her..." Another little cry cuts off her words. "I couldn't do it, and when I came back and saw the empty place, I just... I can't stop crying." Another shuddering inhale. "I guess it's hormones?"

Her brows furrow and her face wrinkles as she cries more. She's actually pretty when she cries, which I don't have time to think about right now.

Reaching out, I pull her into my arms. I lift her into my lap, and she faces me with her legs in a straddle. My arm is around her waist, and I hug her to my chest, sliding my hand up and down her back.

"It's not hormones, baby. You loved that little dog."

She nods against my neck, and her voice is muffled as she speaks. "She was so sweet. She made those little squeaky barks, and I would cuddle her under my chin..." She snuffles again.

"Look at me." I lean back, smoothing her hair away from her face and sliding my thumbs over her damp cheeks. "I'll get you a dog. Whatever kind you want. I know we don't talk about it very much, but I actually have quite a lot of money. We can get you one just like Peepee or if you prefer something different, a bigger dog or a different breed. Gigi could probably help us get one tomorrow."

Her brows pull together again, and her lips pull down.

She's adorably pitiful looking up at me. "Gavin?"

"Yes, Princess?"

"Please don't be mad at me anymore."

And with that, she breaks me. My chest splits open leaving my heart for her to steal.

Too late—she's already stolen it.

Cupping her face in my hands, I wipe more tears off her cheeks with my thumbs. "I told you, I'm not mad at you."

"But you are, and I need you, Gav. I miss you so much." Her nose wrinkles and more warm tears float down her face. "I have a Gavin-shaped hole."

I try to hold back a little longer... and fail. A smile splits my cheeks, and I drop my head back with a groan. "You're killing me, Princess."

She leans closer, and her warm lips press against my throat. "You said you'd be there if I needed you, and I need you now."

Her lashes are damp, but she's not crying anymore. She's reaching higher, pulling my neck down to her. It's no use, I'm gone for this girl.

Our mouths seal, and our lips part. Our tongues slide together, and she rises onto her knees. Her hands move into my hair, and our kisses turn hungry.

It's been too long, and I want her too much.

I briefly squeeze her ass before sliding my hands higher to the hem of her shirt, under it to the clasp of her bra. Unfastening it, I slide my hands around to lift and knead her breasts as her kisses move along my forehead, down to my ear.

Her soft sighs register straight to my cock, which is hard and aching for her.

"Princess," I groan as her soft lips trace a line along my temple.

"Love me, Gav."

With a groan, I move her off my lap briefly so I can stand. Then I lift her into my arms like Cinderella, carrying her down the hall to my bedroom. I toss her onto the bed as I close my door and turn the lock.

She sits up, her blue eyes dark as she pulls the thin T-shirt over her head and drops her unfastened bra to the floor. She's a fucking goddess on her knees topless in the middle of my bed with her dark curls falling around her shoulders.

Her perfect breasts are fuller, nipples tight, and my mouth waters at the sight of them. I can't wait to get my hands on her body, but first...

Crossing the room, I hold her face, tilting her head so I can kiss her like I've been wanting to do for a week. She holds my wrists, exhaling a whimper as she does her best to keep up with my hungry bites, my desperate pulls, my tongue invading, claiming.

I take a moment to remove my blazer, tossing it onto the chair. Then I reach behind my head to pull the black T-shirt off my body. Her teeth bite down on her bottom lip at the sight of my bare chest, and it's the sexiest thing she's done all night.

My inner cave-man comes alive. *Mine.*

She's as tempting as the first night she saw me naked, the night I put our baby inside her, and I walk over, lowering to my knees. I've been wanting to do this for weeks.

My hands are large enough to span her midsection, and I pull her stomach to my face. It's still flat and tight from years of toning, preparing for pageants and staying in shape, but I know what's hidden inside.

I press my forehead against the top of her ribcage, gazing down to where our little avocado is growing.

"I love you," I whisper, kissing her belly, right beside her navel.

"Gavin..." It's a soft whisper, and she threads her fingers in my hair.

Turning my head, I place my cheek against her skin, my palm over her stomach, and I close my eyes, thinking of what's coming, not wanting to miss a thing.

She bends forward to kiss my ear, and I straighten, meeting her beautiful eyes. Fuck, I can't say I love you to her yet, but I do. I love our little baby growing in her beautiful body, and everything, from the moment she fell into my arms until now, every piece of the puzzle, every brick in the wall, it's all right here... My entire world.

It scares the fuck out of me, and I don't want to think about it too hard. She has a Gavin-shaped hole, and I'm ready to fill it.

Straightening, I meet her gaze. Her blue eyes are so warm, and her cheeks are flushed. She smiles, placing her palm against my cheek before kissing my lips again.

I cup her breasts in my hands. Everything about her is blooming with life, and she sighs as I lean down to pull a taut nipple into my mouth, giving it a firm suck. I trace my thumb over the other before kissing across to pull it into my mouth.

"Gavin," she whispers as I move my lips down to her ribs, nipping the skin there between my teeth, leaving a mark.

I want to mark her entire body, like I did the first time. Her belly, her inner thighs.

She squirms, moaning beneath my kisses. I kiss her belly again. With my thumbs, I catch the sides of her pants, taking her underwear with them as I drag them down her legs.

Her thighs fall open, and I cover her bare pussy with my mouth, making her moan loudly as I circle her clit with my tongue. Her back arches and her fingers stab into my hair as I pull and suck her clit between my lips. I'm relentless and eager, hungry for her moans, for her wetness on my fingers, my cock.

Every gasp, every soft moan makes me harder. I kiss the crease in her legs, biting the top of her thigh, and she jumps and squeals. I look up once more to meet her eyes, shining with desire, her full lips parted in a smile.

"Ready to come for me, Princess?" My voice is rough, and she nods, licking her lips.

I can't resist moving up quickly to kiss her mouth before returning to the place I know will make her scream. She's almost there, and I want to feel her pulsing and throbbing when I fill her.

25

Haddy

My back arches off the bed, and I see stars.

Gavin's head is between my thighs, and holy shit, fuck me, he's so good at this. My fingers thread in his shaggy hair, and I pull... pull... pull...

"Oh, God!" My thighs jerk and shake, and the top of my head is on fire.

Orgasm races through my body, and he doesn't stop. His lips pull my clit into his mouth, and his warm tongue circles right on it until my back bows, jerking me forward.

"Yes..." My voice is ragged, and I'm somewhere between laughing and screaming.

Until I'm squirming, unable to take anymore. I'm too sensitive, but he's not finished.

Rising onto his knees, my stomach twists in anticipation. My eyes fall to his thick cock, long and hard in his hands. A whimper slips from my throat as he draws closer, and I lift my legs, holding my knees for him. I want this so much, and he doesn't make me wait.

He drags it up and down my pussy before lining it up with my core. "You're dripping. Just like you need to be."

A gentle nudge is followed by a forceful drive. A gasp catches in my throat, and the sting is as erotic as the sensation of fullness.

"Oh, shit," I gasp, moving my hips to adjust to his size. "It's so big."

At the Halloween party, when I saw him fully naked for the first time, my stomach dipped. His cock is so big and hard and thick, I didn't know if it was going to fit, and it was a little terrifying... but also exciting.

Here we are today. I'm pregnant, and all I want is him to get inside me and make me see stars.

"You're doing so good, Princess." He leans forward to kiss my cheek, tracing kisses to my ear and sending chills through my body. "Relax and take it."

"Yes," I gasp, wrapping my arms around his shoulders, covering his neck with my mouth as I wrap my legs around his waist to pull him deeper into me.

He turns, sealing our mouths together in such a possessive way. I love the way he kisses me, like I'm the air he needs to breathe.

Gavin Knight loves me like I've never been loved. Rough, possessive, yet careful like I'm so precious. I never knew it was possible to be taken and cherished at the same time.

He breaks our kiss, grunting as he thrusts faster, and every deep hit flashes light behind my closed eyes. Fire races through my stomach. He finds a place inside me I didn't know existed, and it's electric. It's mind-altering. I exhale a primal moan as intense orgasm takes hold.

Digging my fingers into his hard shoulders, I pull him closer to press my teeth against his skin. His face hovers just above mine as he groans in ecstasy. A drop of sweat lines his cheek, and I lick it away, savoring his saltiness on my tongue.

He smells fresh like soap and sultry like leather. He's amazing. He's everything.

The way he pressed his face against my stomach, kissing my abdomen and whispering words of love to our baby melted me completely. My eyes heated, and the words *I love you* appeared in my brain as I watched him. It was there, fully formed, but I can't say it out loud yet.

He groans, thrusting harder. "Feels so good. Fuck, you're so good."

When he comes, his muscles tense. His hips hold, and a shuddered groan ripples through his stomach and chest. It's so sexy. I feel him pulsing, filling me.

My mouth is on his neck, and I suck and pull the skin. It makes him groan and pulse deeper inside me. When I break away with a little smack, a mark is left behind, and satisfaction warms my stomach. I've never done that before him. Now I've done it twice.

I've marked him. He belongs to me.

He cups the back of my head in his palm, tilting my face so he can cover my mouth with his. Our lips chase each other's, and our tongues curl together. He's still buried deep inside me, and we're panting, coming down together.

"Fuck, Princess, you're like a drug." His arms go around my back, dragging me higher onto his bed without pulling out. "I can't get enough."

I exhale a satisfied sigh, resting my cheek against his chest. I couldn't agree more, and his large hands cover my back, sliding up to my shoulders before surrounding me in the most amazing hug. I'm practically hidden, so secure in his embrace.

For a moment, we only breathe together, every part of our bodies melting, skin against skin. I've never been so calm, so peaceful.

My breathing returns to normal, and he leans down to kiss the top of my shoulder. I lift my chin to meet his eyes.

He blinks, sliding a piece of hair off my cheek with his thumb. "It kills me to see you cry."

His voice is low, tingling in my belly.

"I've forgotten why I was crying." Mine is soft and high in comparison.

A smile lifts his cheeks as he huffs a laugh. "Peepee had to go home?"

"Oh, right." I nod, wrinkling my nose.

"I'll get you another dog. Say the word, and it's done."

"I think we should have a baby instead."

Another deep chuckle thrills my insides, and he blinks slowly. "If you say so."

Rolling me onto my back, he kisses the top of my shoulder before standing, placing a hand on my hip and telling me not to move. My knees fall together, and I melt a little more at the sight of his perfectly toned ass flexing as he walks across the room to the door.

He peeks out, making sure the coast is clear before going to the bathroom quickly. When he returns, he's holding a damp washcloth, which he uses to clean us up. Then he pulls back the blankets and we scoot beneath them facing each other.

We don't speak immediately. We only gaze at each other like lovesick puppies. I put my hand on the top of his chest, and he reaches out to trace his thumb over the top of my brow.

"I told Maverick I wanted to ask you out."

"What did he say?"

"He suggested I invite you to our charity gala next weekend. It's to help pay for repairs at the planetarium."

"That sounds fun. Will there be a space theme?"

"I'm not sure, but you know I love your Princess Leia outfit."

I lean closer, whispering. "Your Han Solo costume makes me ovulate."

"I guess I know what I'm wearing." His eyebrow arches, and my stomach tingles.

I stretch closer, kissing his lips through a contented sigh. I'm so happy to be back in his arms, to have him smile at me, his blue eyes so full of love.

"I bet I can find something you'll like."

"I like what you're wearing right now." It's a low rumble, and the tingles turn to heat filtering through my inner thighs, all the way to my toes.

Arching my back, I put my hands on his cheeks, pressing my lips to his. He rolls me onto my back, kissing my jaw, making his way down my neck, and I exhale deeply, surrendering to his possession.

"ECHOES OF GALILEO" is the theme of the gala, and I'm wearing a flowing white dress with a scooped neck and a large silver necklace, similar to what Princess Leia wore at the end of "A New Hope." It's a fancier version of my Halloween costume, which makes my insides all zippy at the thought. Good thing you can't get pregnant twice.

It's not a very forgiving dress, and I spread my hands over my stomach, checking every angle in the full-length mirror to be sure I don't look pregnant.

At this point, I haven't popped. None of my clothes fit, and I'm thick in the middle, but I've been hiding it in leggings and oversized sweaters. I can't hide my chubby cheeks and bigger boobs, so I've been making a big show of eating my breakfast in front of Gigi and Mav.

The baby books suggest raiding your husband's closet at this stage of pregnancy, and while I'd love to wear Gavin's clothes, I think the husband envisioned in that advice wasn't a six-foot-two hockey player.

Walking down the stairs, I try not to blush when Gigi squeals and Mav grins, nodding.

"Our little girl is all grown up," he quips.

He's dressed in a traditional black suit with a light purple shirt and dark purple tie for the Champions colors. He looks very handsome, but my eyes search for my man.

Gavin stands with his shoulder propped against the doorjamb leading into the kitchen. He's wearing black slacks and a black tee with a brown suede bomber jacket on top and a cocky smirk curling his lips.

It's not quite Han Solo, but it's pretty damn close. His dark hair is shaggy around his head, and when our eyes meet, I feel something distinctly like a baby kicking inside my stomach.

The books all say we're right in the zone of the baby's first movements. I want to tell him so badly. I want to grab his hand and press it to my stomach, but I have to settle for smiling as my eyes heat with happy tears.

Don't cry, pregnant Haddy! I internally scold myself. How would I possibly explain that?

"Y'all look so good," Gigi gushes. "I wish I was going now."

"Dude." Mav's shoulders drop, and his dark brows pull

together. "I could have totally hooked you up if you'd said something. Donovan asked—"

"It's okay!" She cries, waving to the three of us. "Stand by the fireplace so I can take a picture to send the family. Or would it be better outside under the trees? Or on the patio under the twinkle lights!"

Her green eyes widen, but Mav puts his foot down. "The car is waiting outside, Gina. Just take it by the fireplace."

"You are going to have to get over that attitude when you have kids of your own," she fusses.

"I'll worry about that when it happens, now get it done."

Pictures taken, Gavin pulls my hand into the crook of his arm, leaning closer. "You're gorgeous, Princess."

"So are you, my knight." I rise on my tiptoes to kiss his cheek, and his expression changes slightly.

It's almost like me saying those words hits him differently tonight. My chest squeezes and the other three words I've been thinking over and over since our reunion night press hard against my lips.

The gala is at the Griffith Observatory, and the entire place is decorated like a 1960s space event with shiny silver accents, planetary table toppers, silver balloons, and rockets.

Maverick's date meets us at the door. She's a blonde in a gorgeous red dress. Gav tells me she's one of the reporters who covers the team, but he doesn't think it's serious.

I'm not so sure his date got that message when I see the way she looks at him. Sometimes I don't think Maverick understands the power he has over women.

Flashes go off nonstop as we walk up the red-carpeted stairs. The guys pause, nodding and giving friendly smiles to all the photographers shouting their names.

They yell "Princess Leia" at me, and while I haven't

encountered photographers at this level in my pageant career, I've definitely been trained in how to stand. Shoulders square, hand on hip, smile slowly, side to side.

The guys are the celebrities at this event, and I'm happy to fade to the background so they can have all the attention. A man in a black tux with a black shirt beneath shakes Maverick's hand then pulls Gav in for a photo with his arms over both their shoulders.

"The dream team," he shouts to the photographers, and the flashes go crazy.

Gav finally breaks away from the line, catching my hand in his and hustling up the steps. "You're going to love this."

I follow him deeper into the observatory, holding his arm so I don't fall as I look up and all around the iconic structure.

"Check it out." He pulls my back to his chest, wrapping his arms over mine. "The Tesla coil."

My lips press into a smile, and I nod. "I love this place. It's in all my favorite movies."

"Which ones?" He steps back, sliding his hand down my wrist to hold my hand again.

He's so playful and happy, and as we walk through the ivory-marble hallways, it's like I'm in one of them.

"I don't know," I shrug. "*Rebel Without a Cause, LaLa Land, The Terminator…*"

"The Terminator?" he laughs, frowning.

"I'll be back!" I lean into his chest.

We step up to the large, circular portal to watch the pendulum clock swinging below. Above us is the mural of the four winds, and I can almost hear the music playing from *LaLa Land*. It's like a magical dream.

"Mav told me your mom is kind-of an old movie buff?"

"Kind of?" My voice rises, and I laugh. "It's her passion."

He walks around the viewing station to pull me closer to his chest. "I'd like to kiss you right now, Princess."

"I'll allow it." I smile, tilting my chin higher.

He presses his warm lips to mine, and I exhale a hum, leaning into him. We don't go full-on make out mode, since we're surrounded by gala attendees.

"I feel like we could waltz into the stars right now," I blink up at him, so happy.

"Is that from a movie?" He looks down at me, his blue eyes so full of emotion.

I nod, and I feel it again, only this time it's stronger. My eyes widen, and I grab his wrist in my hand. "Come with me!"

His brow furrows, but he follows me as I dash from door to door, finally finding one that will open to the balcony surrounding the upper floor. We have the space to ourselves, and I spin to face him.

"Give me your hand." I grab his wrist, pressing his palm flat against the thin fabric of my dress over my stomach.

We're both breathing fast, and we wait, only the sound of our pants filling the space.

His eyes are wide when they meet mine. "Is it happening?"

When I hear the excitement in his tone, I nod. Of course, he knows it's time. "It happened at the house, when I saw you in this outfit."

"Han Solo works every time."

He exhales a low chuckle, and the vibration lights every nerve ending in my body. It also activates our baby, who gives my stomach a direct kick.

"Oh my gosh!" I gasp at the exact same time he hisses, "Oh, shit!"

Large hands cup my cheeks, and he pulls my face to his,

kissing me so hard, it makes me cry. Tears I can't stop fall onto my cheeks, and he presses his forehead to mine.

"You are so fucking amazing, Princess."

My hands are on his wrists, and he has no idea.

"It's all because of you."

26

———————

Gavin

"What are you looking at?" Haddy leans her head on my shoulder.

I kiss her forehead then turn the screen for her to see. We're sitting in the waiting room of New Beginnings Birthing Center, and I'm scrolling through pictures on my phone of the two of us at the gala.

The photographers picked up on our personal theme right away, and they had a lot of fun with us being Han and Leia. Some enterprising reporter even put together that Haddy was the same girl I caught falling off the welcome back float last October. Those headlines were a lot of fun.

WHITE KNIGHT IS THE REAL HAN SOLO!!!!

"I love those pictures," she smiles.

Her pretty sapphire eyes meet mine, and my stomach twists. Leaning down, I plant a kiss right on her mouth.

Haddy was actually glad they figured out she's an International Princess Woman, because she said she can use the gala as her community outreach this quarter, which she said she completely forgot. I don't blame her. We've got a lot on our minds.

These past few weeks have been really great around the house. Being out to Gigi and Mav, has taken a lot of pressure off us. It's really cool to be able to pull her in for a kiss without having to make sure nobody's about to walk in the room or pop out from behind a corner.

Still, we try to keep the PDAs to a minimum out of respect, and I've quietly been looking for our own place. I don't know how Haddy will feel about leaving her cousins, but I think once the baby comes, we'll need it. Still, I'm checking for something in the neighborhood.

I've returned to sleeping in her bed, spooning her body with mine and placing my palm over her stomach, not wanting to miss a single kick from our baby. It's fucking amazing this little being is already making his or her presence known.

It makes me think of some of the more outgoing members of both our families. Is it possible those personalities start so early?

What's even better is she's starting to show. In the mornings, she'll climb out of bed to use the bathroom, and when she comes back sometimes her sleep shirt is hitched up over her bump. When that happens, I always have to sit up and pull her to me, kiss our little sweet potato good morning.

Only one thing could make me happier. I've been thinking about it a lot—every time I catch her smiling at me, every time I see her in the stands dancing and cheering in my jersey. I have images saved on my phone, and I've even planned out how I'll do it...

"Bradford-Knight?" The familiar nurse holds out her hand, and we both stand, following her through the doors to the check-in area.

Haddy is weighed, measured, we go to a treatment room, and Dr. Barry pops in with her usual smiling, jokey manner.

"How's it growing?" She gives Haddy a wink.

"So far, so good." Haddy's eyebrows rise as she looks down at her midsection. "I think the baby's finally sticking out some."

"It's usually that way in first pregnancies." Dr. B squirts the blue goo on Haddy's stomach. "You get thicker and thicker, then all of a sudden, Pop! There it is." She taps on the screen of the iPad she's holding. "Your measurements are good; all the tests came back negative. Ready to see what's cooking?"

We both answer yes at the same time, and I lean forward to take Haddy's hand. Today's the day. We're having the ultrasound where we find out if it's a boy or a girl. I'll be glad with either, but I still hope it's a little princess just like her mama.

She's reclining in the chair, and I can feel the tension in her muscles as well. We're both excited for the big reveal.

"Keep in mind, if we don't see anything, that doesn't mean it's a girl. Sometimes those little guys like to hide their junk. Still, with the 3D ultrasound, we've gotten a lot more accurate."

Haddy and I exchange a glance, and she asks quietly. "Can we check again if you're not sure?"

"Definitely!" Dr. Barry reaches out to give her forearm a squeeze. "Wouldn't want you to buy a bunch of baby dolls for a little guy." She hesitates, arching an eyebrow. "Although it might not hurt him to have one, am I right?"

My chin drops, and I exhale a laugh. "You might be onto something, Doc."

"I think it's good for little boys to know how to care for

babies." Haddy's voice is small. "But Gav is doing really well, and I don't think you had any practice."

She wrinkles her nose at me, and I lean forward to kiss her cheek. "I'm a fast learner."

"Well, let's see what we can see," the doctor says.

We watch as Dr Barry moves the wand around Haddy's stomach. It is impressive how clear we can see the baby's features in 3D.

All of our eyes are fixed on the screen as she focuses on the leg area. "That's its little butt..." She uses the wand to push gently. "Come on, baby, spread 'em."

We both laugh softly, but at that moment, baby seems to understand the assignment. Its little body moves, and the tiny legs part.

"I think we have our answer." Dr. Barry's eyebrow arches, and she looks at us.

I look at Haddy, and her eyes are filled with tears. She reaches for my neck, and I lean forward to kiss her firmly on the mouth.

I've never wanted to tell everybody something so bad in my life.

MUSIC PLAYS IN THE KITCHEN, and Maverick is singing some country song while he works on dinner. I've been watching the ultrasound of our baby on my phone since our visit with Dr. Barry.

I can't keep a smile off my face, and I'm already planning all the fun stuff we're going to do. I wonder if I'm glowing. Do expectant dads glow?

The books only talk about gaining "sympathy weight," but with all the skating and weight training and nonstop games, I can't imagine how much I'd have to eat for that to happen.

Gigi bustles through the door with Spanky on his leash. Her brows furrow when she sees me sitting on the couch.

"Is Haddy working late again?" Spanky jumps all around and she leans down to unhook him. "She usually comes home early when y'all don't have games."

"Yeah." Standing, I put my phone on the coffee table. "She texted that she has a video chat with Daniel and their faculty advisers. They're examining the composition of the air... Or the density of the particulates or somethin-gorother..."

I stop before it sounds like I know what I'm talking about. Haddy told me exactly what they're doing tonight, but it's a lot of sciency jargon.

"I should probably let you read her text."

Gigi waves at me, putting her jacket on the stand. "Don't bother. I can probably infer what they're doing from what you just said."

"All I know is saving babies." I grin, thinking of my girl being awesome. "She's on her way now, though. I just checked our tracking app."

"You are so cute!" Gigi skips over to give me a hug. "It's a little stalkery that you track her location, but it's also really swoony."

"She shared her location with me." I look at my phone feeling guilty. "I shared mine with her..."

"You two." Gigi pokes my shoulder. "Where is she now? I'm starving."

That makes me laugh. "So it's okay for me to stalk your cousin if you're hungry?"

"Definitely. I'd even go so far as to say it's mandatory!"

Opening the app, I see she's pulling into the driveway.

I'm about to tell Gina when my best friend appears in the kitchen doorway glaring at me.

"Hey, Mav! What's the ETA on... dinner..." My tone goes from upbeat to confused when I see his expression.

His jaws are clenched and his shoulders are bowed up. His brow is lowered, and he looks like a raging bull. I can almost see the smoke blasting from his nostrils.

I drop my phone as he storms across the room, headed right at me. Squaring my feet, I brace to stop him when he grabs the front of my shirt and slams me against the wall, forcing an *oof* from my lungs.

"What the fuck?" I grab him by the shoulders, trying to shove him back, but he's pushing into me with equal force.

"I told Haddy you were a good guy!" His fists are clenched, but I'm ready to block if he tries to punch me.

"Maverick!" Gigi's voice is loud. "Stop this! What's wrong with you?"

"This is wrong with me." He lifts his phone, shoving it at my face.

Pulling my chin back, I release his arms so I can take it from his hand. There on the face in all caps, bold black text with a string of exclamation points reads, **CHAMPIONS' KNIGHT SCORES OFF THE ICE TOO!!!!**

"What the fuck is this?" I frown, trying to understand what I did.

"It's a picture of you leaving a birthing clinic in Pasadena," he shouts. "The article says you've been going there every month, meeting some chick."

"Birthing center?" Gigi gasps, and my stomach pits.

"You tell me you've been secretly dating my cousin since Halloween, and now I find out you got some chick pregnant?" Mav comes at me with a forearm to my neck, slamming me against the wall again. "Who is she?"

"Jesus, Mav," I grunt, trying to get him off my windpipe. "You don't understand..."

He's holding me hard, and sparks appear in my vision. "You made a big mistake messing with a Bradford."

"Maverick!" Haddy shouts, her voice echoing in the living room. "Stop it! What are you doing?"

"I'm throwing this fucker out of our house. I'll teach him to break your heart, get some girl pregnant..."

"It's me, Maverick!" Haddy is right beside us now, pulling Mav's arm away from my neck.

Thank God, because I was starting to black out.

"What?" The pressure disappears from my throat entirely, and I lean forward, holding my neck.

I do my best to catch my breath. Spanky bounds over and licks me right in the face. I guess he thinks this is all a game.

"I'm the pregnant chick," Haddy explains.

"What?" Gigi's voice goes high with a mix of wonder and excitement, and Spanky jumps, letting out a happy yip.

Haddy pulls up her oversized sweater to reveal her cute little baby bump poking through her pregnancy pants. Hell, I think the baby's gotten a little bigger since the ultrasound. We are at the mango stage, I guess.

"Haddy, oh my God!" Tears flood Gina's eyes, and she throws her arms around her cousin. "Why didn't you tell me? Look at that cute little bump! How far along are you? What is it?"

"Dang, bro." Mav rubs the back of his neck, looking confused and sheepish. "I'm really sorry I tried to kill you just now. I had no idea."

"No worries..." My voice is rough, and my throat hurts from being crushed by his muscled forearm. "I would've wanted to kill me, too, if I thought what you did."

He shakes his head, rubbing his face. "I didn't want to believe it, but I saw those pictures and, well, there was all that past shit."

It burns to know Karen's lie still casts doubt on my name, but I accept his apology. "You love Haddy. I get it."

"Although..." His tone changes. "You knocked up my cousin. Are you planning to marry her?"

My eyes meet his, and I hesitate. I think he sees the thoughts I've been turning over in my mind, and a flash of understanding is there.

It's like when we're out on the ice, and we know what we're about to do, but Haddy walks over to shove his shoulder.

"You are so old fashioned, Maverick Murphy! First you try to kill your best friend, and now you're trying to marry me off like I don't have a say in the matter."

He bites back a grin, but I shake my head to let it go. It's not time.

Changing his tone, he shrugs. "I just wanted to know where we stood."

"Where we stand is absolute, top secrecy." Her blue eyes are sharp, and she points a cute finger up at her cousin. "No one can find out about this, understand?"

"No..." Mav frowns down at her.

"Haddeeee..." Gigi hugs her waist, resting her strawberry head on her cousin's shoulder. "I want to start shopping and buying little outfits and doing all the things. We need to have a shower and a gender reveal party and we have to tell the family..."

"We can't do any of that, Gigi." Haddy takes her arm, turning to face her cousin. "If the IPW finds out, they'll strip me of my title. I'll have to pay back all the scholarship money, and I've already spent it on tuition."

The old anger in me is reignited hearing her say all of these things. "I told her it doesn't matter. I can help her with tuition…"

"Strip you of your title?" Outrage infuses Gigi's voice, and I couldn't agree more. "That is absolutely the most patriarchal, discriminatory, misogynistic…"

Haddy only holds up her hand, shaking her head. "Maybe it is, but my term is almost over. It's just a few more months until the next girl is crowned, and then I'm off the hook."

"I don't like it." Mav's voice is quiet. "I'm with Gina and Gav. These pageant people need to get over themselves. It's not like you're a teenager or something, not that it would matter then either, I guess."

"It's their rules," Haddy argues. "If I'm going to represent their organization, I have to abide by them."

Gigi's lips tighten, and I wonder if she's thinking the same thing as me. Haddy has the highest standards of anyone I know. She's beautiful and smart, and I'd let her represent my organization any day of the week.

She's also a dirty, dirty girl in private, but I can't start thinking about that right now.

"I know you want to protect me." Haddy goes to her cousins, pulling them into a group hug. "And don't think I haven't considered telling them myself, but it's almost finished, and I don't know. I worked really hard for a long time to win that crown. Maybe it's dumb, but it's the top prize, and I earned it."

Her nose wrinkles, and the way she says it, like it's a guilty confession or something, hits me right in the chest. I know what it's like to work hard and feel a sense of accomplishment over something you achieved, something hard.

"You did earn it, and you should be able to keep it." I

step up behind her, joining them in the hug, wanting her to have everything her heart desires.

"If you put it that way... I guess I understand," Gigi sighs. "Okay. Top secret."

"I won't rat you out, Hads." Mav lifts his phone to her. "But I don't know how you're stopping this. The cat's out of the bag, and these gossip sites are going to be stalking Gav like crazy."

"What does the article say?" She takes his phone, scrolling through the story, her lips pressed into a straight line as she reads it quickly. "It looks like they only know about Gavin. They only have these photos of him through the glass doors."

"Isn't there some kind of privacy thing for patients?" Gina's tone is fussy. "What does HIPAA say about this?"

"That sounds right," I agree, thinking about it. "Mav and I are considered celebrities, but I don't know about Haddy. Are pageant winners celebrities?"

"I think if it were Miss America or Miss USA, it would be." She looks up at me. "I should be protected."

"I don't know," Mav cautions. "Those guys use that excuse to get away with all kinds of bad behavior."

"In that case, we'll have to outsmart them." I grab my friend by the shoulder. "It'll be like on the ice. We'll have them looking one way, and we'll send you around to the other side for a fast pass, slap-shot score!"

Haddy's nose wrinkles, but when she starts to laugh, it relaxes the tension in my chest. We're a great team, and I have a good feeling about this.

27

Haddy

"Look how cute you are here!" Gigi lifts a picture out of the box she carried down from my room.

It's my stash of old pageant memorabilia, including publicity photos, ribbons, and certificates. All my old trophies are at Mom and Dad's house.

"Let me see." Gavin takes the photo from my cousin, and I lean over to check out which one it is.

It's a picture of me at twelve, when I won the International Princess Girl competition. It was my first big win, and I'm sitting on a kid-sized pink velvet sofa. My hair is enormous, my dress is all fluffy white tulle, and I've got a wide sash across my chest with my title on it in pink.

"I can't tell which is bigger, that smile or that crown." I huff a laugh, taking a bite of taco.

"You've been doing this so long." Mav straightens from where he was looking over my shoulder as well.

Tonight he made us suadero tacos with jalapeños, avocados, and pickled onions. My mouth is on fire in the best possible way, and I'm glad my baby doesn't hate spicy food like Mav did in utero.

"I think you're adorable." Gav grins at me in a way that makes my stomach tingle.

I know what he's thinking.

"I loved that scepter." I tell him, pointing out the long, metallic wand I'm gripping so hard my little knuckles are white. "I thought it was the coolest thing... Kind of like a light saber."

"There's my nerdy cuz." Mav noogies my head. "I don't know how you fit in with all those beauty queens."

"They weren't mean girls." I think about the weeks we'd spend at training camps every year getting ready for the big pageants. "It really was like *Miss Congeniality*—you know, that old Sandra Bullock film? Girls would come from all over the country, and we'd hang out and talk about how we felt and our hopes and the silly things we'd done. It was more like a camp than a competition."

"You're saying none of those girls were competitive?" Gina narrows her eyes at me.

"Oh, yeah, we were all pretty competitive, but the IPW program was more about things like talent and public speaking than just beauty. It had a positive vibe."

"You never told me your talent." Gav slides a finger along my neck, moving my hair behind my back.

"She's a singer," Mav answers him. "You should hear her sing. It's pretty amazing."

"Yes! You should hear her," Gigi coos. "Selena Gomez, 'The Heart Wants What it Wants.'"

"I like that song." Gav smiles, and our eyes meet briefly. It's electric.

"Maybe you will one day." I don't mean to say it all low and sultry. It just comes out that way.

"Whoo wee!" Gigi fans her hand in front of her face. "Is it getting hot out here or is it just me?"

I laugh, tossing a paper napkin at her. "It's all those jalapeños Mav put in our dinner tonight."

"I think it might be something more... biological." Mav's eyebrow arches, and he does a little hip thrust.

"And on that note..." I stand, collecting our empty plates. "I've got to get some sleep. I've been exhausted for months now."

"You'd better get your sleep." Gigi hops up to help her collect the plates. "From what I've heard, once that baby gets here, you're never sleeping again."

We head into the house, and between the four of us, the kitchen is clean pretty fast. My cousins curl up on the couch to watch a movie, but Gavin takes my hand, leading me to the stairs.

"Keep it down up there," Mav calls after us. "I don't want to hear how the sausage is being hid."

"Leave them alone." Gigi throws a pillow at him. "If you haven't heard them by now, you're not going to."

"I'm still very conflicted about all this." Mav catches the pillow in one hand. "I can't decide if I should support this or kick his ass, and you know how much I love ya, Gav."

"Leave the ass-kicking to Uncle Hendrix." Gina waves her hands at us. "As you were, love birds. Remember to clean up after yourselves."

Shaking my head, I look up at Gavin, who's smiling down at me. Hunger is in his eyes, and it lights me up from the center of my chest all the way down to my toes.

I don't waste any more time bantering with my cousins. I jog up the stairs straight into his arms. They surround me at once.

"Careful running on the stairs." His lips are at my ear,

and his kisses send chills down my arms. "It's harder for me to catch you that way."

"I told you I'm not falling anymore." I pass him with a little turn, pulling him after me in the direction of his bedroom, thinking how that statement might not be entirely true.

We burst through his bedroom door with our mouths already sealed together. My lips part readily, and I curl my tongue to his as he exhales a low groan. His large hands cup my face, and he lifts my chin, kissing me deeper.

He's so possessive, drawing me closer, surrounding me in his arms. I inhale his scent of clean soap and rich leather. He's so warm, I want to lick my tongue along his neck to taste his sweat. I turn in his arms, putting my back to his chest and holding his wrists.

Dropping my head back against his shoulder, I lift my chin to nibble the line of his jaw. "I've wanted you since you touched me at dinner." It's a breathy moan. "Take me from behind."

"Anything for you, Princess." His lips cover mine briefly before he drags them down my neck, sending feverish chills through my body.

I'm already hot and needy, and I lean forward to quickly shove my leggings to my ankles, kicking them off my feet. When I straighten, I put his large hand between my thighs as I reach behind me to rub his hard cock through his jeans.

"I've been thinking about you singing that song." He slides his thick fingers over my clit in firm circles.

"Make me come, and I'll sing it for you." Stepping forward, I climb onto the bed on all fours and look over my shoulder at him.

"Damn, you are so fine." He takes a step forward, kissing my butt as he unfastens his jeans and pushes them down.

I moan as he drags his tongue all over my most sensitive parts. His tongue slides over my clit, and my body jumps. I'm so close.

"Fuck me, Gav," I whisper.

"Dirty girl," he groans, testing me with two fingers then hissing. "You're ready."

My thighs tremble as he aligns the tip to my entrance then fills me completely with one forceful thrust.

I groan, bending to my elbows and dropping my forehead to the mattress. "God, you're so big."

"You love it." He grips my hips in both hands and thrusts rhythmically, faster.

"I do..." I moan.

"Your body was made for mine."

"Yes..." I reach up to circle my fingers over my clit, moaning as he hits that place inside me. "Feels so good..."

His large fingers cover mine, helping me. I'm so close, I push back against him, arching my back so my ass is higher. "Slap it," I whisper.

He slaps my ass at once, and I turn my face to scream into the mattress. My thighs start to shake and my pussy breaks into flutters.

"Do it again..." I gasp, bouncing on his dick against his stomach. "Harder.

He leans down to kiss my mouth then he straightens, slapping it harder again, then again. I'm moaning and bucking against him as I break. He lets out a loud groan as well, and I feel him pulse inside me, his body trembling against my thighs.

Pushing off the bed, I lean my back against his chest, reaching for his neck, his mouth. Our bodies are still moving. I'm riding out this incredible orgasm, trembling in his arms.

"Fuck, Princess..." He groans, cupping my breasts in both hands and squeezing them, lifting and kneading them. "You're so gorgeous."

He covers my lips with his again, and I shudder. He cups my pussy, sliding his fingers all over my clit, slapping it sharply until my legs shake, until I turn my forehead against his neck with a moan.

"That's my girl." His voice is low, tracing kisses along my shoulders, holding my breasts. "My kinky girl."

They slide lower, moving over my rounded stomach, spanning wide as he kisses the top of my shoulder. I put my hands over his, and we hold for a moment of intimacy, connection.

He pulls out, putting a hand on my shoulder as he grabs a nearby towel to clean us up. I wait, watching with affection as he gently strokes the wetness off my thighs before lifting me in his arms as he moves the blankets away.

We crawl in together, facing each other, and I reach out to touch his cheek as I quietly sing the lyrics to my old pageant song. They're not quite right anymore. I don't believe there are so many reasons we shouldn't be together, but it's still a beautiful song. And my heart does want what it wants, Gavin Knight.

As I sing, his blue eyes warm, and he slides a finger along my jaw. I finish, letting the final note fade away, and he exhales low.

"You sing..." He shakes his head rolling onto his back and shoving both hands into his hair. "I didn't think it could get any better, and then you sing."

Rising onto my elbow, a big smile splits my cheeks. "You like it?"

His hands lower, and he reaches for my face, rising up to kiss my lips. "I love it."

Our eyes hold several seconds, and I think it's possible we're thinking the same thing. The words we don't say out loud. *I love you...*

My stomach twists, and I have to break the spell. Lying down again, I rest the back of my head on his shoulder. "Why does it feel this way? So natural?"

He inhales deeply, tracing his fingers along my arm. "I used to wonder that after Mav and I got so close so fast. I think it's because we both come from big, close families, small towns... we have that common bond, that thread."

His voice goes quiet, and I take his large hand in mine, holding it up to the light, looking for something I noticed before. A thin red line is traced around the base of his thumb, and I turn it over, examining the faint ring.

"What is this?" I touch it gently with the tip of my finger.

"My mom Kenny did that." He turns his hand side to side. "She has a matching one on her pinky finger."

"It's a tattoo?" My brow furrows, and I rise onto my elbow to look at it closer.

"It's an old Japanese fable..."

"Another one?" Our eyes meet, and my nose wrinkles.

"My mom went through a real Buddhist phase after she lost her first husband. She said it helped her make peace with the grief... until she had me."

"I get that." My lips tilt down with a sad little frown. "What does it mean?"

"There's a legend that when people are destined to be together, they're connected by an invisible red string. It's mostly for husbands and wives, but Mom said it could be for family as well. No matter how far apart we are or how much time passes or things change, the thread can tangle, but it will never break."

"You're always connected." My eyes warm, and I trace my

finger over the bright red line that almost looks faded into his skin, almost like it could be invisible, but we've somehow managed to summon it.

"Forever." His voice is quiet.

I blink up again to meet his beautiful eyes. He looks at me with so much depth of emotion. I reach out to place my palm against his cheek, then I stretch higher to seal my lips to his.

WALKING TO THE LAB, I'm still thinking about the red string, imagining a thread stretching all the way from here, walking across campus to the arena, all the way downtown. I picture it thin as spider silk, twisting and straining, yet strong as steel.

My chest warms. A cool, early spring breeze pushes my hair behind my shoulders, and I look up at the sunlight filtering through the leaves on the trees. The soft wind rustles them, mixing up the way the light reflects on the pavement, on my face and hands. *Komorebi...*

It's so interesting how his mother was obsessed with Japanese culture, and I'm doing all this work with the Kawasaki Institute. It feels like fate somehow, and I drift into the large lab, with a hand on my midsection as I ponder the possibilities.

I'm still wearing oversized sweaters, only now I couple them with stretch-front pregnancy leggings. I still think I'm getting away with hiding it pretty well.

I've just arrived at my station when I hear Timothy exhale a disgusted noise. "Looks like lover-boy got himself in trouble."

He has an almost gloating grin on his face, and my brow lowers. "What are you talking about?"

He waves his iPad, and I go to where he's leaning against the counter, studying the screen.

"I told you not to trust this guy. What's the line? Players gonna play?" I don't like the sneering tone in his voice as he turns the device to face me. "It's probably one of those hockey groupies... *bunnies.*"

Heat is in my throat, and I see he's reading the TMI story Mav showed us. I don't like him taunting me with gossip reports, and I'm really pissed he'd immediately assume Gavin cheated on me.

"It doesn't have to be bad." My tone is sharp. "What if he were there to see a friend or a relative?"

"With the schedule those guys keep, he doesn't have time to go all the way to a sketchy birthing center in Pasadena for a *friend*. It's his."

"It is not a sketchy birthing center." My voice turns defensive. "And maybe it's somebody he really cares about."

Timothy blinks at me, and I swallow a soft gulp. Cool air is on my neck, like all the blood is draining to my toes. I can't keep secrets. I'm a terrible liar, and I realize what I just did.

It's too late to take it back, and if I say another word, it'll all be over.

My lab mate's eyes narrow, and I know he's reading it all over my face. Blinking down at the iPad in my hands, I try to change my expression, neutral face, no secrets spilled here.

It doesn't work.

"It's you." Timothy's tone is flat. "You're the chick who's having his baby."

28

———

Gavin

"This is a really nice place." I walk through the massive concrete Frank Lloyd Wright-style home built into the hills. "How long have you had it?"

"Bought it right before Haddy was born, I guess."

Hendrix Bradford is a handsome man, and I can see where my girl gets her bright blue eyes. I follow him onto the balcony, and the view of the city is literally breathtaking.

"You guess?" My brow furrows, and I look over at him.

"Haddy's mom, Raven, is pretty independent. She was sick during the pregnancy, so she stayed with her family in Atlanta until it passed. I was all the way out here, so I didn't know until she told my sister Dylan."

"Wow." My brow lifts. "That must've been a surprise."

"Yeah, but you should've seen her." His eyes take on a faraway look, like he's remembering something that makes him happy. "She was the cutest little thing. You know her first word was *Dada*."

He straightens, as proud as if he'd just been named

athlete of the year... which if I remember correctly, he was a few times. Now he's on the NFL sports shows.

I didn't put it all together when we met briefly at Christmas. I don't really keep track of football, and I had sort-of a one-track mind, which was entirely focused on Haddy and our surprise.

"That must've been pretty sweet." I look at a framed photo of Haddy as a baby asleep on his chest, and I think of our baby doing the same.

"Raven was not thrilled." Hendrix exhales a laugh. "She kept trying to say Haddy didn't know what it meant, but she knew. She was her daddy's girl."

He arches an eyebrow, and I like this guy. It makes my palms a little sweaty, because I want him to like me. I'm not sure how he's going to respond to what I'm about to say.

"She's pretty amazing." I nod, wiping my hands on the front of my jeans. "We met in college, and I always thought she was really cool and smart."

I almost say *and beautiful*, but I don't know if that might be a bridge too far too soon for her dad, coming from me.

"It's hard to believe she's so grown up. That time goes so fast." He squints over at me, putting a hand on my shoulder. "What's on your mind, Knight? I know you didn't come all the way out here for my view, and I know you didn't fly all the way to Newhope just to see Cooters & Shooters either."

My throat tightens. I've never been a nervous guy... until now. Hendrix Bradford and I are about the same size, and even though I'm younger and more conditioned, I wouldn't put it past him to take me down if he wanted.

Clearing my throat, I straighten my shoulders and just say it. "I'm in love with your daughter, sir. I think she's in love with me, and I'd like to ask her to marry me." His brow furrows the more I speak, so I quickly add, "If that's okay with you."

He's quiet for a moment, crossing his muscled arms over his chest. He turns and looks out at the view again, and I stand where I am feeling completely exposed.

Taking a few steps, he stops at the edge of the balcony, placing a hand on the railing before turning back to face me. "What does Haddy think about this?"

My hands are behind my back, and even though his voice isn't raised, I feel like I'm being cross-examined by a drill sergeant. "I haven't asked her yet."

"Haddy's a smart girl."

"Yes, sir." I nod.

"She's got plans and she's very independent." His blue eyes narrow. "How do you feel about that?"

"I think it's great." My shoulders drop, and I meet his gaze head-on. "I admit, her beauty was the first thing I saw, but then I got to know her. She told me about her graduate studies and her work, the things she wants to accomplish." Shaking my head, I look down and speak from the heart. "She's really incredible."

"You think you deserve her?"

"No, sir." I shake my head, exhaling a laugh.

It seems to break the tension, because he laughs, pointing at me. "That's right. We don't deserve them. We're just lucky to be sharing our lives, and don't you forget it."

"I'm not sure I could." I only have to look at her growing our baby to be reminded.

"You seem like a good guy, Knight. Mav speaks highly of you, which carries a lot of weight." He nods. "I'll allow it, but if I ever hear you've made her cry... if you ever hurt her or break her heart, I've got a 45 and a shovel. They won't find you."

We both laugh at that, but I'm pretty sure he means it.

Red alert. Mom said everybody's coming to family game night this year. It coincides with spring break, so she, Kimmie, Aunt Liv, Uncle Jack, and Aunt Allie are all off for the week.

MY PHONE LIGHTS UP as I drive back to the house from Dr. Barry's private office in West Hollywood. She agreed to see us there once we explained the situation with the paps camping out around her Pasadena clinic.

I'd had to miss the last two appointments because I couldn't find a way around them, and I didn't want to miss anymore, especially since we're closing in on the third trimester.

Baby is now the size of a grapefruit, doing great, and Haddy is adorable walking around the house with her stomach pooching out.

She's also completely panicked about Timothy knowing she's pregnant. I told her I'd threaten his life if he told anyone, but she'd rather play it cool. He doesn't have any connections to the pageant program, and she can't see a reason for him to tell.

I can see a reason. I see it every time he looks at me like he wishes I'd take a puck straight to the face. The dude's in love with her, not that I blame him, but he'd better keep his trap shut and his opinions to himself.

GIGI

OMG!!!! I'm so excited to see everybody!
Why didn't my mom tell me this? I just
talked to her!

MAV

Mom said they were waiting on Aunt Raven
to give the green light. The parents will stay
with them, but Kim, Knox, and Sage want to
crash with us.

HADDY

They'll see my baby bump!!!

MAV

Hence the red alert.

Haddy and I drive separately, taking different routes to our doctors' appointments just in case I'm being followed. She's ahead of me, but I pull in right behind her in the driveway.

Her blue eyes are round when she turns to look at me, holding up her phone. "Did you see this?"

"We should just tell them, babe." I walk over to pull her into a hug. "They know how important all the pageant stuff is to you. They'll keep it a secret."

"I know they'll try, but the more people who know about it, the more chances someone will slip up." She wrings her hands as she climbs the porch steps. "And with Timothy knowing, I'm on pins and needles all the time."

"Hey, come here." I pull her into my arms, pressing my lips to her forehead. "If that guy says a word, I'll kick his ass so hard, he'll taste leather."

Her dark head shakes slowly. "You know I don't condone violence. Unless you're in the rink."

"Look at me." I put my finger under her chin.

She lifts her blue eyes to mine, and it's like the first day I ever met her. She's so damn pretty, I forget what I was going to say.

An amused grin curls her lips. "I'm looking at you."

"Have I told you how beautiful you are today?"

Her lips tighten, and her eyes narrow. "Are you trying to distract me with compliments?"

"Nah, it's just the truth." I lean down to kiss her lips briefly. "What I was going to say is everything's going to work out. I don't want you to worry about anything except taking care of yourself and the baby."

"I do want to tell everyone, but they're all so loud and excited. They're about as bad as I am at keeping secrets."

"I think if we're just honest and tell them why, they'll do everything to help you."

A little frown twists her full lips. "I know they'll try."

Studying her pretty face, her soft hair hanging around her cheeks and shoulders, I can't stop thinking about my conversation with her dad. He sent me a picture of the ring he gave her mom, even though they were already married, and I've found a similar design at Tiffany's. I even sneaked a ring out of her room to use for sizing.

Now I'm just trying to gauge her openness to the idea. "Have you thought any more about what you want to do after graduation?"

Her shoulders fall, and she exhales a breath, going to the door. "I'd thought I might go to Japan to visit the team there, see the institute in person. Now I think that's off the table."

My throat tightens at the thought of her going to Japan, but I also don't like the idea of her giving up something that's so important to her.

"I've always wanted to visit Japan. Maybe we could go together."

Her nose wrinkles. "Why do I get the feeling you just made that up on the spot?"

She looks up at me as she hangs her long cardigan on the coat rack. With that garment gone, her baby bump stretches the front of her long-sleeved black shirt and leggings.

It does funny things to my insides, and I can't help reaching out to slide a protective hand over them both.

"*Always* might be a stretch, but now that I think about it, Japan sounds like a cool trip." My eyes meet hers. "I don't want you to give up your dreams because you need help. It's important for our baby's mom to follow her passion."

Her expression changes to something I can't quite read, but it looks positive. "But how could you go with me with your schedule?"

My brow furrows, and I think about what's coming this summer. "If we could fit it in before October, I could make it work."

Haddy's still looking up at me like she's seeing something new when Gigi skips into the room holding Spanky's leash.

"Hey, Little Mama! Hey, Big D!" She gives her cousin a squeeze. "What do you think about the whole clan descending on us in a few weeks?"

Haddy glances up at me once more, and she smiles. I don't think it's my imagination, but she seems less stressed and maybe a little more inclined to lean on me like I've wanted her to do since we found out about our little grapefruit.

She turns to her cousin. "I think we'll just have to make them swear on their lives."

"Haddeee, Yay!" Gigi bounces on her toes. "Kimmie is going to be so excited, and Aunt Deedee, and... oh." Her expression turns suddenly serious. "You'd better tell your mom before they get here or she'll be pisssed."

Haddy bites her lip. "I know. I've been putting it off."

Shit. I don't know why she's afraid to tell her mom, but I've got to tell her dad without her finding out... and without him grabbing that 45 and shovel. Talk about keeping secrets.

"I'll go with you." I put my hand on her shoulder. "We don't have a game Wednesday."

She inhales slowly, looking from me to Gina. "Looks like we're telling them on Wednesday."

29

———

Haddy

My hand is clasped in Gavin's as we drive to my parents' house in the hills. Mav let us use his Rover, because Gavin looks cartoonish all packed into my tiny Honda Fit.

Mom is thrilled we're coming for dinner, and I think it's interesting she didn't even question Gavin's joining us. It was almost like she expected it, and I wonder if it's because of his surprise Christmas visit.

I hope he doesn't think he fooled anybody by showing up like that and claiming it was to see the infamous Cooters & Shooters. Our family restaurant is great, but it's not "leave your family home on Christmas Day" great.

GIGI

Stop being nervous. Bradfords love babies

"Gigi," I murmur, lifting my phone. I show the screen to Gav before quickly tapping a reply.

HADDY

I know, but I'm trying to be responsible.

GIGI

You do know the story of your conception, right? Drunken hotel hookup after Aunt Deedee's wedding? Irresponsible is not a word they would dare to utter.

A laugh snorts through my nose, and I quickly reply.

HADDY

I should've brought you along as backup.

GIGI

You don't need backup. It's going to be fine.

HADDY

I know. It's just so awkward. I feel like a teenager again.

"Why are you laughing?" Gavin's voice draws my eyes away from the device.

Blinking up at him, I think about how he's been since the start of this entire... Adventure? Surprise? Happy accident?

He's been by my side the whole time, comforting me when I'm afraid, threatening to pulverize anyone who would threaten me, placing his large hands over the baby as we sleep.

He even came with me tonight to stand by my side, protecting me.

All of it has pretty much sold my heart to him, but when he offered to go to Japan with me just so I wouldn't have to give up my dream trip. *I want our baby's mom to follow her passion...* It was pretty much a done deal at that point.

"Gigi just reminded me how my parents got pregnant with me."

His full lips curl attractively. "I haven't heard that one."

For a moment, I gaze at his face, his square jaw dusted with scruff, that dimple, those straight white teeth, the shaggy brown hair, and sexy blue eyes holding mine.

I kind of forget what I was saying, which has never happened to me before.

His brow quirks. "You okay?"

I huff a laugh, shaking my head. "I lost my train of thought."

A knowing expression crosses his face. "It happens."

Clearing my lusty thoughts, I look up at the massive concrete mansion where I grew up. So many happy memories occurred here. I love this place.

"They hooked up after my aunt Dylan's wedding," I explain. "It was just supposed to be a one-time thing, but instead, they got me. A big, life-changing surprise."

"Sounds like we've got something in common." He covers my hand with his large one as we walk up the drive. "Don't worry, Princess. I've got you."

"I wouldn't be so confident if I were you. My dad can be a bit... overprotective."

"You don't have to tell me." He laughs under his breath, and I frown, wondering what that means.

I can't remember Gav spending one-on-one time with my dad at Christmas. I guess Mav told him, probably teasing him, getting him ready for tonight. My dad's favorite line is from the movie *Clueless*, "I've got a 45 and a shovel..."

"Mom can smooth things over." I give him a reassuring pat. "She's always had that way with him."

"I like your dad. He seems like a fun guy."

Nodding, I smile up at him. "I can see the two of you getting along. Under the right circumstances."

I don't even have a chance to knock before the door opens and my mother pulls me into her arms.

"I don't know why we have to go so long between visits," she groans, squeezing me so tightly, I'm scared she's going to feel the baby. "We live in the same city."

"You sound just like Dad," I laugh, doing my best to loosen her embrace. "I have dinner with you at least once a month."

I'm wearing an oversized, tan blazer with black leggings and a long-sleeved black turtleneck. I'm doing my best to hide my baby bump until we're able to tell them what's happening.

"Once a month is a lifetime after every day." She looks up at my escort. "Gavin Knight, it's so good to see you again."

"Nice to see you, Mrs. Bradford." He leans down to give her a hug, so polite.

"Well, come on in, I've got meatloaf in the oven and sweet potato soufflé on the stove." She gives me a wink, and I air-clap quickly.

"My favorite!"

"Mine, too." She slides her hand into the crook of my arm, pulling me closer to her side.

We've only taken a few steps into the foyer when she stops, narrowing her eyes and studying my face. "Something's different about you, Hayden Lucille. What is it?"

Her eyes scan my midsection quickly, and my throat tightens. Thankfully, Dad busts up in the group at that moment.

"Hey, Super P!" He pulls me into a hug as I groan at the nickname. "How's my little princess? Gavin, good to see you again, bud."

"Hi, Mr. Bradford." Gavin's voice is more deferential than I've ever heard it as he shakes my dad's hand.

"Call me Hendrix."

"Okay," Gav laughs, and my eyes cut to him.

That's mighty friendly. Mom is still studying me with her hands on her hips, and I feel the back of my neck getting itchy like it always does when I'm trying to hide something.

"Let me take your coat." I can tell by the way she says it, she's sleuthing, and I have to grab the reins on the situation before it goes off the rails... not to mix up all my metaphors or anything.

"First, let's show Gavin the view!" I grab his arm, pulling him closer.

"You want to go out on the balcony?" His voice cracks weirdly, and I look up at him confused. "That's a pretty big drop."

My dad stands beside him, hands in his pockets, and I almost snort a laugh. Does Gavin think my dad will throw him off the balcony?

"I need to take out the meatloaf." Mom waves a hand. "You three check out the view, and I'll meet you in the kitchen. Anybody want a glass of wine?"

"I'll go with you." I follow Mom, but Gavin watches me confused. "You and Dad check out the view, and I'll catch Mom up on all the news."

"*All* the news?" He frowns at me.

"Yes!" I nod, waving my fingers. "Go with Dad."

"Come on, Gav." Dad slaps his shoulder. "The view can wait. I got a bottle of Blanton's waiting to be sampled."

"Yes, sir." Gavin follows after him, glancing back at me.

Once they're gone, Mom pulls me close. "I never expected you to bring home a hockey star."

"That makes two of us."

"He's handsome." She looks back to see him watching us from where my dad is pouring them both tumblers of expensive bourbon. "And serious."

We go into the kitchen, and I try to think about how I want to say this.

"He's really great. Not at all like I thought he was when Maverick said he was moving in."

"That's a good sign." She goes to the range where she lifts the lid off a Dutch oven. "Living with people is a real eye-opener."

I watch as she spoons thick, dark gravy over the meat. I think about my parents and their love, my mom and her dreams. I always wanted to be like her—confident, sure, in control all the time, saving lives…

"I know I disappointed you with all the pageant stuff."

"My goodness, Haddy." She closes the lid and walks over to take my hand. "I've been proud of you every day of your life."

"But I know you don't like all that." I look down at my hand in hers, so similar. "I just wanted to show you I could stand on my own, too. The way you did."

"I stood on my own with a major assist from your dad." She huffs a laugh. "Once he knew about you, he did a lot to help me." She pulls me into a hug, kissing my head. "I didn't want you to be hurt is all. I have a lot of bad memories associated with that world, and I wanted to spare you from them. But I support you, Hayden."

Her voice lowers, and I know she's thinking of her own mom, who didn't provide the same encouragement when she was a girl. I've heard it was a lot worse for my mom.

"I love you, Mom." I hug her back. "And I don't want any distance between us, especially now."

She smiles, wrinkling her nose and smoothing my hair

back. "Why now? Did you bring Gavin Knight here to tell us something big?"

"Yes..." My heart beats faster, and I lick my bottom lip.

I inhale slowly, like they trained us to do when stage fright hits, then I take a step back, unbuttoning my coat.

"I'm going to have a baby."

Her eyes widen, and her lips part. Clasping her hands, she lifts them as her eyes fill with tears. I'm holding my breath, trying to discern if they're happy tears, when she jumps forward with a shriek and pulls me into a hug.

"Haddy!" Her laughter echoes in the kitchen, and tears heat my eyes. "A baby? Is it Gavin's?"

"I mean, yeah, that's why he's here."

"Are you getting married?"

My brow furrows, and I think about the question. "He suggested it in the beginning, but it wasn't a good idea. The timing was wrong. We didn't know each other at all, and... I didn't love him yet."

Mom's brown eyes warm as she cups my face in her hands before moving them to my shoulders. "And now?"

Butterflies swirl through my chest, and I can't keep the smile from splitting my cheeks. "Now, if he asked... I'd say yes."

"Hendrix, get in here!" Mom cries.

She helps me remove my coat, and I'm laughing now, too, touching the tears out of my own eyes.

"I don't know why I was so afraid to tell you."

"I don't either!" She puts both hands on the sides of my stomach. "This is the best news!"

I hear the guys enter the room behind us. Dad's slapping Gav on the shoulder like they're old pals. For his part, Gavin looks way less stressed than he did when we parted ways in the living room. He actually has a smug grin on his face.

"They're pregnant, Hen!" Mom reaches for my dad's arm, pulling him to us. "Isn't it wonderful?"

"Look at you!" Dad wraps his muscular arm around me, kissing the top of my head. "You look healthy and happy. That's all I want for my girls."

A massive weight lifts off my chest, and I lean into him. "Gavin's been so much help to me, Dad. He goes with me to all my appointments, he gets me ice cream when I'm craving it, even first thing in the morning..."

"Are you having weird cravings?" Mom's expression turns to problem-solving. "They say it can signal a vitamin deficiency."

"Not really. I've been craving a lot of spicy food, but Mav has us covered there." I do not mention how horny I've been, or how Gav is very good at taking care of that particular need as well.

My cheeks heat, and I glance up at him. He's still got that smile on his face like this is all going how he expected.

"Which is hilarious, considering how Dylan was when she was pregnant with him," Mom continues. "She couldn't eat a thing, and her cooking was awful. Her taste buds were all messed up."

"I've heard."

"What about morning sickness?" Mom's brow furrows, and empathy lines her face. "I was so sick the whole time I was pregnant with you."

"There was that one time at your house. Once I ate a pear, and it came right back up." I look up at Gavin, and we say the next part together. "So no more pears."

We laugh, and Dad slaps him on the shoulder. "Good work, son."

"Her due date is right at the start of our off-season, too," Gavin continues. "Her doctor has recommended some birthing classes, but that's been tricky with games and everything."

"I can go with you if you need help." Mom rubs my back gently. "Or Gigi. I'm sure she's excited, too."

I nod, thinking how my cousin was exactly right. My family is baby-obsessed.

"I'd really like to be there, so I know what to do." Gavin's warm eyes hold mine, and my stomach flutters... or maybe that's the baby moving?

"So what are you having?" Dad's blue eyes search mine, but Mom pulls his arm gently.

"They might not want to know, Hen." Her voice is quiet.

Gavin is quick to reassure her. "No, ma'am, we wanted to know. We just haven't told anyone yet."

Mom's eyes light. "Is it a secret?"

"Not really." I scrunch my nose, looking up at Gav, who shrugs. "It's all been kind of surprising and fast, and we only just told Gigi and Mav we were pregnant a few weeks ago."

"Spill it, P," Dad teases. "Don't leave us hanging!"

Reaching out, I take Gavin's hand. My chest fills with excitement, and it's like I'm cutting into a confetti-filled cake or popping a smoke-filled balloon.

Gavin smiles, and that dimple pierces the side of his cheek. I've never seen his blue eyes so happy... Well, I have once before, and it was on the day we found out.

He nods, and I turn to my eager parents, holding out my hands and with a breath announcing, "Mom, Dad, we're having a girl!"

Mom lets out another shriek, jumping forward to hug me. "We love little girls."

"I couldn't agree more, Mrs. B." Gavin holds my back.

"You have to call me Raven, now." She grabs his shoulder, pulling him down for a hug. "Have you picked out a name?"

I look up at him again, and he's still giving me encouragement to keep going. "We haven't decided on her full name yet, but we definitely know we want to name her Lucille after Grandma Bradford."

"And you," Gavin adds, nudging my side. "I always thought Lucy was a cute name."

"I love Lucy," Dad says, and it's all noises of agreement.

This night truly is golden, unlike that day in the park when I was so afraid, when Spanky knocked me into a bush. Thanksgiving feels so long ago, and now we're here together, surrounded by love and family.

I can't even remember what I was so worried about...

WE REGRET TO INFORM YOU, you are no longer qualified to represent the International Princess Woman organization. The title of International Princess Woman will pass to the first runner up...

Cold air touches my cheeks as I walk across campus in the late evening twilight. Numbness pushes on my shoulders, and I pull the cardigan tighter around my body. I slide a hand over my growing stomach, thinking about the little cauliflower-sized baby hidden inside me.

To think only a week ago we were all at my parents' house laughing, hugging, talking about baby names and picking out little outfits online.

"It doesn't matter, Lucy," I whisper, comforting the little girl in me. "You're so much more important than a crown."

You will be allowed thirty days to repay the scholarship awarded. If you need longer than thirty days...

It went on to say something about how a payment plan can be provided if I need help repaying the money.

Please return the crown, sash, and all related paraphernalia...

The black type printed on crisp ivory linen paper stands out in my mind like a brand. I stood alone in the sterile, science room reading the thing I feared most.

Looking up, the sky is growing dark now. It will probably rain tonight, since this is the rainiest month of the year. It's kind of perfect timing for rain.

Dark winds lift and bend the branches of the trees, and there is no sunshine. I want to ask Gavin for the word that means the opposite of *komorebi*. This is it.

The house is quiet and empty when I arrive. The guys have a game, and Gigi has a date. Spanky is in his crate, so I walk across the hall to let him out. Gigi will have already walked him, but I'll let him out back to go before the rain starts.

Part of me aches for Patsy, but every time that longing appears, I force myself to think of her loving owner, so happy to have her puppy back. Then I remind myself I'll have a baby soon.

It sort-of helps.

Returning to my bedroom, I pull the old box out from under my bed. The pictures and sashes are all there like before. I lift the new one out and place it on my bed.

With a deep breath, I steady my insides. My throat knots, but I'm trying not to cry. I knew this could happen. I made this choice.

Taking the box off the bed again, a picture falls to the floor. It's the official photo of me being crowned last year. In it, my eyes are damp, and I'm looking up with a huge smile on my face as the previous year's winner passes the title to me.

I remember how much that moment meant to me, and I hiccup a breath. I'm still reeling from the shock of discovering it's over.

Everything I've worked for, years and years of camps and productions and laughter and joy and sisterhood, all stripped away and given to another person like I never even existed.

All gone, because of a biological reality. I'm a woman.

Men don't get stripped of their titles for impregnating women. They get lauded and fist-bumped and treated like they accomplished some great feat.

They came.

The rest is up to us.

Scrubbing my fingers across my forehead, I push against these bitter thoughts. In my case, it's not what happened.

Gavin has been so supportive, so devoted. He's going to be furious when he finds out about this.

The ache in my chest is winning when my phone starts to vibrate with an incoming call. Swallowing back the pain, I lift the device, and I almost can't believe the name on the screen.

"Karen?" My voice is wobbly.

"Haddy?" My old roommate sounds breathless, like she's walking fast. "Oh, Haddy, I had to call as soon as I heard the news. I'm so sorry! I know how much this meant to you, and I just want you to know it's wrong and it's sexist and you deserve that crown, and they shouldn't be able to take it away from you just because you're an unwed mother."

My forehead crinkles, and I look at the phone. "Technically, I'm pregnant... How did you know?"

"Everybody knows." Her voice lowers. "I had to call you right away, because if anyone understands the shame it's me. It's cruel and—"

"I'm not ashamed. I'm more... angry?" I haven't decided.

Too much is happening too fast, and I'm still trying to make sense of it all.

"You should be angry. As soon as I heard, I said you have my support. But what good is it if I don't tell you? Nobody was there when it happened to me, and it was the loneliest feeling in the world."

She's said it twice now, and it feels like she wants me to ask about it.

"I'm sorry, I didn't know this happened to you." I try to remember what she'd even won. "It must've been before we lived together."

"You didn't know?" Her voice goes high. "How is that possible?"

"Was it a state competition?"

"Of course it was, but it went out in the *Princess Woman Gazette*. It's so cruel to tell everyone that way."

"I guess I was so busy with college and my studies." I also never read the articles in the glossy magazine they sent us every quarter. I only looked at the pictures. "What happened?"

"They found out about Thad and me." Her voice goes lower. "They said not only was it against the rules, it also cast doubt on the legitimacy of my winning. Can you believe it? As if I didn't earn my title."

"Who was Thad? I don't know..."

"One of the national judges. You must remember Thaddeus Lyon-Bowes?"

Scrubbing my fingers against my forehead, I try to remember all the judges we encountered through the years. "I guess I should remember him, but I don't."

"He was my first, my only..." She exhales a heavy sigh. "I

tried to say I was with Lane Knight to throw them off the trail. Remember him? The hockey guy?"

"He goes by Gavin now." My tone is crisp. "You told me he cheated on you. You brought receipts."

"Oh." Her voice lowers again. "It was all to throw those pageant bloodhounds off the trail. If I had a hot hockey boyfriend, what in the world would I want with Thaddeus Lyon-Bowes?"

She exhales a light laugh, but the truth hits me like a medicine ball straight in the stomach.

It's what Gavin said, over and over, and I drop to my bed as the ache in my chest twists harder. He only ever wanted me to believe him.

Squeezing my eyes tighter, I'm not sure which question to ask first. "Are you saying Gavin *didn't* cheat on you? Or are you saying you didn't care if he did?"

"What difference does it make, darling?"

"It makes a big difference to me, Karen. I stood by you through all of that. I believed you when you said he'd broken your heart."

"I know you did." She has the nerve to adopt an affectionate tone. "That's why I'm calling you now, because you were my friend when those pageant jerks turned on me."

"But... you lied to me. You were never in love with Gav, and he didn't cheat on you. You cheated on him."

"Lane and I were never serious." Her voice turns huffy as she tries to rewrite history. "I was always in love with Thad. It was the same emotion, just a different person."

"It's not the same at all! I told you about Rob, and you pretended to understand. Did Thad cheat on you?"

"Lord, no!" Karen cries through another laugh. "I might've played the field a little, but Thad would never cheat on me."

"Neither would Gavin."

"I don't know why you're taking it so personally."

"I take lying very personally." My voice is flat. "You're a bad friend, and sleeping with judges is against the rules. But what's worse is I believed you, and you took advantage of my trust. You used our friendship to hurt Gavin, and you used my pain to make me mistrust him."

"I don't know what you mean!" She tries to act so astonished.

"Don't call me anymore. We're not friends, and I never want to speak to you again."

She continues sputtering, but I disconnect the call without another word.

My head hurts. My chest hurts and my stomach hurts. It's like the rug has been pulled out from under me, and everything is falling through the air.

Nothing I believed is true.

No, that's not right. One thing *is* true. It's been true since the beginning, since the day I fell off the float... and tripped over the sidewalk... and fell into the bush...

Gavin is true, and I've got to find him.

I need to tell him right now.

30

———

Gavin

It's a tough game against San Jose. The Killer Whales have come for blood, and it's clear they've been studying all of Mav's and my well-oiled sneak-attacks. We're getting nothing past them tonight.

I try to go in for the pinch, and their right winger slips by me, stealing the puck away and scoring right through the hole I've left vacant. He moves so fast, Saxon doesn't have any time to cover for me.

We're in the third period, and it's 1-0, Whales ahead. Mav gives me the signal to try the Tic-Tac-Goal, and I slip away to try and snatch the puck from their forward. It's our twist on the usual odd man rush. I'm the fastest skater and an aggressive defender.

I race forward to steal it from their winger, but he's a big guy and knows I'm coming. Before I can reach in for the puck, he slams me against the boards and changes direction.

"Fuck," I yell, doing my best to get back in there when

another Whale, Number 67, comes by and slams me into the boards again.

It was an unnecessary hit, and I'm after that asshole, flying down the ice in his direction. He has the balls to spin around and push his stick at me, slamming me against the boards again, but I grab a hold of his jersey and punch him in the side of the helmet.

Whistles go off all around us, and Mav is at my side, body-checking 67 into the boards. Saxon is with us now, yelling, and a straight up brawl breaks out with the linesmen rushing in to pull us apart.

Mav and 67 go down on the ice, but the linesmen are on them. Donovan grabs me by the pads, pulling me away from the fray, but I'm hot around the collar. I'm mad we're losing, and I'm pissed at that guy for taking a shot at me.

"Let it go. It's over." Our captain's voice is low in my ear, and I'm doing my best to breathe it out.

Mav is still in there, and I know he's as fired up as I am that we haven't been able to score tonight. He takes it personally, which I get. He's the face guy of the team at the moment.

The linesmen are sorting it out, deciding who's going to the penalty box, when I look over and see Haddy standing just outside the glass beside our bench.

She's wearing my sweater, and she's jumping up and down, patting her hand on the plastic guard. It looks like she's crying, and my stomach drops to the ice. I push out of Donovan's grip, skating full-speed to where she's standing.

I barely register what's going on behind me or us getting possession of the puck again. Coach sends another player in for me, and I jump over the boards, ripping off my helmet and throwing my gloves and stick behind the bench.

I'm a sweaty mess, but I have to know why she's here. I

have to know what's wrong, if she's okay, if the baby's okay. I don't give a fuck about anything else.

Stepping through the door to the stands, I pull her into my arms. "Are you okay?" My tone is desperate, and I'm touching her stomach, moving her hair back. "Did something happen?"

The baby must be okay, or she'd be at the hospital. I'm so confused.

I don't care that all eyes are on us right now, along with all the phones, the cameras, the jumbotron...

"She lied to me, Gavin." She hesitates, taking a deep breath. "I came straight here. I just got off the phone with her, and she told me everything."

"Karen?" I don't know who else it could be. Haddy nods quickly, and I cup her face, wiping her tears away with my thumbs. "I told you that, Princess."

"But I didn't believe you." A hiccup interrupts her words, and fresh tears coat her cheeks. "I should've believed you."

"You were being a good friend." My voice is raised so she can hear me. "It's okay."

"It's not okay!" She shakes her head. "Rob burned me and I was too afraid to trust you, but I should've trusted you. I should've trusted you the night you asked me to... because... because I love you."

It hits me like a fist of happiness right in the chest.

"What did you say?" I shout over the noise of the arena.

I heard her, but I want to hear it one more time just to be sure—and because it feels really damn good.

She raises her voice, shouting as well. "I said I love you, Gavin Knight!"

Holding the back of her head, I pull her face to mine for a kiss. Our lips part, and she clutches my shoulder pads. Our tongues curl, but I can't keep the smile off my face.

Leaning back to look at her, her watery eyes are smiling.

I'm smiling as I hold her and shout out, "I love you, too, Hayden Bradford."

She takes a shaky inhale. "I could've loved you longer."

"Now you can love me forever like I'll love you."

"You love me forever?"

"Hell, yeah, Princess. I love you bad."

"Me, too!" she laughs. "So bad!"

I pull her to me again for another kiss, and that's when I notice the entire arena is on their feet watching and cheering. At first I think it's for us, and I guess some of it is. The rest are going crazy because Haddy's hotshot cousin has tied up the game, and we're headed into sudden death overtime.

It's possible we could win this thing, but all I care about is the beautiful girl in my arms who just said she loves me. *Forever.*

"THAT'S RIGHT, come for me, Princess." My hands are on Haddy's waist, and she's straddling my lap.

Her hands are on my shoulders, and I'm surrounded by the heady scent of jasmine and sex and sweat. I showered after the game, but I'm fucking happy to get dirty again with my lady.

"So good," she whispers, and her brow furrows.

Damn, she's so fucking pretty riding my cock. Her sexy, fuller breasts bounce at my lips, and I pull a hardened nipple into my mouth, making her moan loudly.

She's so wet and tight around me, sliding up and down my shaft, chasing her orgasm. I grip her ass, helping her move, doing my best not to focus on how good it feels to be inside her.

I'm right on the edge, sweat trickling down my cheek as I try to wait, as my hips lift instinctively.

She moans my name, and I almost come at the sound. It's aching and sexy, and fuck, have I mentioned how gone I am for this woman?

I want her all over me. I want her in my jersey as I take her from behind, I want to worship her beautiful body. I want her to be my queen.

"Gavin!" She stretches, her slim back arching in my hands.

Her sounds get higher, slightly staccato, and all at once, she breaks, bending forward as she shudders. Her insides pull me, and my mind blanks. I relax my hold and let the orgasm race through my pelvis. It's fucking heaven and pure bliss.

I groan, wrapping my arms around her as I lift my hips to thrust deeper into her clenching core. This night couldn't get any better.

Her slim arms wrap around my shoulders and her silky hair flows around us in a soft curtain. Her breathing returns to normal, and a satisfied smile curls her lips.

"You're really good at that." Her blue eyes blink open, and I lift my hands.

Smoothing her hair back from her cheeks, I look at her. "Have I ever told you your eyes are so beautiful?"

Her nose wrinkles and a pretty pink touches her cheeks. "I don't think so."

I stretch higher, and she leans down to kiss my lips. "They are."

"Thank you," she whispers.

"It means a lot that you believe me." My tone is serious. "I was frustrated about it before, because I care about you.

But also because it hurt that you thought I would do that to anyone."

"I didn't know you." Her eyes blink up to mine. "I should've believed you."

"No, it took time." I hold the sides of her hair, sliding my thumbs along her cheeks. "I think we were already there, but I'm glad the past is clear. I'm your knight, Princess. I love you."

She smiles, climbing off my lap and snuggling down into the mattress at my side. "I love you, Gavin."

It's the words I've wanted to hear for so long, and every time she says it, it's like one of those confetti guns going off in my chest. Only, instead of confetti, it's like sparkles of 100 percent pure joy. *Damn.*

"You said something at the arena about the knob?" My brow furrows, and I turn onto my side to face her.

Our heads are on the pillows, and our faces are a breath apart. I could lift my chin and kiss her, but I'm curious.

"What did you mean? Why would he make you not trust me?"

Her chin tucks, and she blinks those eyes away from me. She almost seems embarrassed, which I don't like. She never needs to be embarrassed in front of me. I love her.

"He cheated on me." She says it so quietly, I almost lean forward. "It's why I believed Karen, because I was hurt and humiliated. I thought she and I shared that. I thought you were like him."

Rolling onto my back, I press my fingers to my forehead. All this time, I was fighting to make up for someone else's sins. Someone else had hurt her, and she couldn't let it go.

"Gavin?" She scoots closer to me, her pretty eyes so full of sadness. "Now I know who you really are. I think I knew months ago you could never be like him."

Reaching for her shoulders, I pull her into my arms, careful to avoid crushing little Lucy.

"It all makes sense now." Sliding my hand up and down her slim back, I kiss the top of her head. "And I want you to know, if I ever see that guy again, I'm going to..."

She groans, falling onto the bed beside me. "I hope we never see him again! And you know I don't condone violence... off the ice."

"I feel like you have a big but in there."

Her body bends forward with her laugh. "But you are so hot when you fight on the ice."

"You like that?" Pride swells in my chest as she nods quickly before stretching higher to kiss the side of my jaw. "Okay, babe, in that case, I'll just pants him."

Another burst of laughter comes from her throat. "That would be so hilarious!"

"He embarrassed you. I think it's only right that he should be embarrassed as well."

She relaxes from her belly laugh with a contented sigh. "I'd rather just not see him again. He really damaged my trust, and I just want him to go away and never come back."

"Okay, but just know." I lift her chin to kiss her lips again. "Nobody messes with the mother of my child."

Her nose wrinkles, and she kisses my lips. "Your baby mamma."

"That's right."

"Use the pillow to lift your pelvis into the correct, birthing position." The instructor's voice is warm and encouraging, and Haddy's back rests against my chest.

We're at the New Beginnings Birthing Center taking a

class on water birth, which Dr. Barry tells us sounds old-school and hippie, but is actually the most relaxing way to give birth.

They have actual rooms here at the birthing center with beds and large, shallow pools in the center. When Haddy goes into labor, we will come here and do it all on-site.

We toured them, and they're really nice. Haddy said it looks like a spa, and it's fucking expensive as hell—and I don't give a shit. Anything for my girls.

She's curious, but first, we have to take classes about it, which brings us to this evening.

"Breathing technique and massage therapy are essential for comfort during a water birth." A woman in a chocolate brown yoga outfit is in the front of the room walking slowly through the pairs of expectant couples. "Water immersion promotes relaxation, but it also provides a sense of weight-lessness..."

She's got a soothing voice, and I check out the other couples. They're all listening closely like Haddy, who I'm sure is applying that scientific brain to everything this lady is saying.

"It makes sense that buoyancy would ease the pressure," she whispers in my ear. "But I'm not sure how this helps with delivery."

See? She's already doing the math. It's like I can see the equations floating in the air above her head.

"The most inefficient way to give birth is lying flat on your back," she continues. "Gravity should be used to help bring the baby. In primitive cultures, the women are advised to squat, which makes total sense."

"Whatever you want, Princess. I'm here to help."

Her slim brows are furrowed as she listens to the instructor. I'm enjoying holding her this way, placing my hands over Lucy's foot as it pushes against Haddy's stomach like a little torpedo.

"That doesn't hurt?" I whisper, trying not to laugh.

"Not really." She looks down to where I'm smoothing my palm over the tiny point.

Her hand joins mine, and we're mesmerized by the strange shapes her stomach takes while our daughter swims around in there.

"She's so active tonight." Haddy blinks up at me, and I nod.

"She must be into the water birth idea."

"I think she knows I like being in your arms this way." Haddy kisses my cheek. "She's swimming in endorphins."

My chest rises at the thought I've got both of them in my arms right now. My whole fucking world.

"You're Gavin Knight!" The lady next to me excitedly whispers a little too loudly. "Look, honey, it's Gavin Knight, the hockey player!"

Her partner on her back in front of her looks up at us. "Oh my gosh, and you're the princess?"

Haddy blinks away from them. "I'm just a regular girl."

"You're a lot more than that." I lean down to kiss the top of her head.

"Aw, that's so sweet." The first woman coos. "I saw the video of you two kissing at the game with the teams fighting all around you. That's just good hockey!"

I hold back a laugh as the instructor walks directly in front of us, giving the four of us a pointed look.

"Floating in the water allows you to find the most comfortable position for giving birth..." Her voice grows slightly louder, and I think that's her way of telling us to pay attention. "It also encourages natural movements, which can help the baby reach the optimal position for birthing."

Haddy whispers. "I guess that makes sense."

I look up at the lady, who's giving us a hard stare, and smile.

"I'm curious about that massage therapy you mentioned?" She didn't say it was time for questions, but what the hell? We're already disrupting class. "Is that something I could learn?"

"Yes," she returns my smile, nodding, so maybe we're not flunking the class. "We'll go through the specialized birth massage next week. Thank you, Mr. Knight."

Whoa, she knows who I am, too.

Leaning down, I whisper, "Zip it, Princess."

Haddy snorts, and the lady keeps going, guiding us through movements like squatting, kneeling, and even resting her head on her arms on the side of the birthing pool.

Haddy grows serious as the instructor talks about reduced perineal trauma and different things I don't completely understand. Looks like I've got more homework to do.

When she lets us go, I take Haddy's hand, helping her up from the floor. The leader thanks us for coming, but Haddy doesn't make eye contact. She only nods and mutters a quiet thank you.

I'm not sure what changed in the last half-hour, but I don't pressure her as we walk out to Mav's Rover.

"I guess I need to get off my butt and get one of these before July." I help Haddy into the passenger's side, but she doesn't comment. "We'll have to have a car seat properly installed and all that stuff or they won't let us bring Lucy home."

"Yeah."

Walking around to the driver's side, I feel like I missed

something. We continue for a little bit in silence, but the birth center is a twenty-minute drive from the house. At this time of evening on a weeknight, it's even shorter.

"You okay?" I cover her hand with mine, and she blinks up at me.

"I guess I hadn't thought much about the actual *birthing* part of the process before tonight." Her face is in a sort-of cringe. "I've got to get this baby out through my vag."

To be honest, I haven't spent a lot of time thinking about that part either. Up to now, the only time I think about Haddy's vag is when I've got my mouth on it or when I'm filling it with my cock.

"Are you saying your Gavin-shaped hole might get a little bigger?" I'm going for humor, but apparently that is the *wrong* approach.

Her lips twist, and she shoves my shoulder almost like she's mad at me. "It's like pushing a watermelon through a toilet paper roll. It's going to rip it to shreds."

Damn.

"I guess I hadn't thought about it that way." Clearing my throat, I ditch the humor. "Think you should talk to your mom? She had you... maybe she can give you some tips? At least she'll help you to feel better. She did it."

"Of course, I'll talk to Mom, but don't think that lets you off the hook." She crosses her arms like she's still kind of pissed.

"I... don't." I'm not really sure how I'm *on* the hook, but I know better than to argue with a pregnant lady. "I would never think that."

Sounds like I'll be talking to her dad, although he wasn't there when Haddy was born. Still, he's known them both a lot longer than I have.

We're at the house, but before we get out, I lift her hand

to kiss the back of her fingers. "You can do this, Princess. You're the smartest, most capable person I know. If anybody can figure out the best way to have a baby, it's you."

Her lips press together, and her forehead crinkles. Oh, shit, I know that look.

"I'm sorry, Gav." Tears pop out onto her cheeks. "I guess I'm feeling a little panicky all of a sudden."

"Hey... Hang on." I hop out of the driver's side and jog around to open the passenger's door. Rotating her growing body to face me, I pull her into a hug. "This is a big deal. Of course you're feeling panicky. But I've got you. We've all got you. You're not alone in this."

Her head is on my shoulder, and I feel her nodding as she sniffs. "When that girl said that tonight, I realized... I never told you."

I place my hand on her back, rubbing up and down. "Told me what, honey? What do you need to tell me? You already know I love you."

She sniffs, sitting up and wiping her nose with the back of her wrist. I open the glove box and grab a napkin from some fast-food place Mav visited. It's not the best, but it's better than her hands.

"I lost my scholarship." She dabs her face as my throat constricts. "They took it all away. I have to box up my sash and my crown and everything and send it all back within thirty days."

"Haddy, no..." My stomach churns. "What can I do?"

"We can't do anything, it's over. It's all been decided and announced. That's why Karen called me." She sniffs again, dabbing her face, and the pain in my chest twists hard. "She said it was to comfort me, but after a while, I realized it was just to unload on me."

"In true narcissist fashion." It's a low growl. "Haddy, I'm so sorry."

"It's okay." She shakes her head, doing her best to smile. "I knew it was coming. We're all over social media. How could they not find out?"

"Bastards. They're losing a lot doing this to you."

This time she reaches out to cup my cheek in her slender hand. "It was more important for you to be at those appointments with me. Lucy is more important."

"But it meant a lot to you. Your feelings matter, too."

"Not as much as my family."

This girl. This "regular girl." She has no idea.

Holding her hands, I help her out of the Rover. She leans on my arm as we walk to the door, and I kiss the top of her head as I open it. I wish I could think of something to say. I wish I could make it all right and give her back her crown.

We've just stepped inside the house when familiar, squeaky barks greet us, coming closer as we stand in the doorway.

"What...?" Haddy cries softly as a cinnamon-colored tiny bundle of fur bounces towards us, squeak-barking with each bounce. "Patsy?"

She's on her knees, and I look up as Gigi hops off the couch, running to us, smiling ear to ear. "She's home!"

Dropping to her knees beside Haddy, the two of them pet the little dog, who's frantically licking both their faces.

"The owner said Peepee was so depressed, she wouldn't even get out of her little doggy bed," Gigi explains. "She said she couldn't take it anymore, and if we wanted her back, she'd be glad to send her back to where she was so happy."

"Oh, Patsy!" Haddy hugs her, and the little dog licks all the tears off her cheeks. "I've missed you so much."

Mav walks over, a purple bruise under his eye, and crosses his arms. "I gotta say, I missed little Peepee, too."

"Dude. You got a shiner there." I point at his face.

"Yeah, but we didn't lose the game, did we?"

Shaking my head, I can't argue with that. "Nope."

It looks like we're all where we need to be, and in another week, we'll have the entire family here. I know what I'm going to do.

31

Haddy

"You are so adorable!" Kimmie holds my arms out, smiling as she inspects my baby bump. "How far along are you?"

"Just starting the third trimester." I look down, smoothing my hands over my growing midsection. "Once she popped, she never stopped."

"You've got your new slogan!" Gigi teases, hugging me from behind and resting her chin on my shoulder.

"We might." I laugh, thinking about how much this baby moves in my stomach. "She's a busy little thing."

"What are you planning to do for delivery?" Aunt Dylan sits at the bar munching on a crispy chocolate Easter egg. "Liv had us all doing hypnobirthing. What's the hot new thing now?"

"I'm looking into water birth."

"Oh, my goodness, that was in an episode of *Girls*, remember?" Aunt Allie calls from the couch, where she's sitting by Gigi's mom. "Jessa put her head in the tub and looked between Gaby Hoffman's legs, and they ended up running down the street with her to the hospital?"

Aunt Allie falls forward laughing, and my mom's eyes go two sizes wide. My shoulders tense as I wait for her to freak out, but Aunt Rachel swoops in for the save.

"It's actually not a new method at all," she says calmly. "And it's so much easier on your body. The warm water is relaxing, and you can move around to find the most comfortable position."

"That's what the instructor said." I hang my hand on Gigi's forearm around my neck. "We're just checking it out at the moment. The birthing center at New Beginnings has private rooms with special tubs. It's all really nice. Very upscale."

"I'm sure if your doctor recommended it, it'll be fine." Mom's voice is tentative, and I can tell she's trying, which I appreciate.

"Anyway, Haddy's a scientist," Aunt Dylan adds. "Don't freak out, Raven."

I fight against a laugh when my mom makes a defensive face and exclaims, "I wasn't freaking out."

"I've seen that look before," Aunt Dylan waves a finger, walking over to give her a hug. "You were freaking out a little."

"Nobody will be running down the street with me," I reassure her. "Dr. Barry will be on site the whole time."

"Of course they won't." Gigi's mom narrows her eyes at Aunt Allie, which only makes her snort more.

"It was a funny part of the show," she says defensively.

"Well, I think water birth sounds very cool," Aunt Dylan hops off her stool and walks over to give me a hug. "And I can't wait to have another baby girl. They're so fun with all their little dresses and bows..."

"Speaking of dresses, we've got to get ready for the game." Gigi releases me, jogging to the kitchen table where a large bag is sitting.

Spanky bounds after her, but Patsy is curled up on the couch with the aunts. I walk over to help my cousin distribute the jerseys.

"We got three with Mav's number and two with Gav's," Gigi explains, dragging out the oversized purple, white, and black shirts. "For the record, they're called sweaters in hockey, but you can just call them jerseys."

All our uncles, along with Sage and Knox, are at my parents' place, and our plan is to meet up at the arena. Gav and Mav are already there getting ready for the game.

Gavin's parents are in town as well. He told them about the baby, and they're so excited. We're all planning to meet at the arena, and we're also having lunch together tomorrow.

I'm excited and nervous, and I especially want to meet his mom Kenny and talk about all things Japan and Buddhism and tattoos.

I've been thinking a lot about a red ring around my pinky finger, but it feels premature. Gavin and I have said those three little words, but we haven't talked about marriage or anything official yet.

When we arrive, Dad and all his brothers are standing in a row wearing their Gav and Mav jerseys while talking and watching the rink. They're an impressive, handsome lineup with their arms crossed or in Uncle Garrett's case, trying to put Dad in a headlock.

Knox walks down as soon as he sees us to give Gina and me a hug. "Look at you!" He puts a hand on my stomach, giving it a rub. "Do I get three wishes?"

"Don't be a pest, Knoxey." Kim pushes his head.

"I was just kidding," he laughs, putting his arm around my neck. "Haddy loves me, don't you Hads?"

"When did you get so tall?" I put an arm around his waist, hugging him back.

"Can you believe it?" Aunt Allie grabs his other arm. "He's taller than his dad!"

"Bradford family trait," he calls over his shoulder, continuing down the steps to the wide hallway beneath the stands.

"Where are you going?" I call after him.

He only waves. "Important business. I'll be back."

"Not sure why I didn't get that Bradford family trait," Aunt Dylan grumbles.

It's true, looking up at my four uncles, who all range in height from six-two to Gigi's dad, Uncle Garrett at six-four. When they see me looking, they all yell and wave for me to come up and see them.

Wrinkling my nose, I do a little wave before climbing the rows to where they all want to hug me and ask how I'm feeling, ask about the baby.

"You look good," Uncle Zane bends down to give me a hug. "You're about what? Halfway there?"

"I'm starting the third trimester, so..."

"Wow, more than half."

I nod, and Uncle Jack steps over to give me a hug. "Gavin seems like a good guy. We talked some at Christmas. I got the impression he was there to see you."

"You mean we didn't fool you?" I squint one eye up at him.

"I'm an old hand at sneaking around," he teases. "I know all the signs."

"He played with Maverick in Atlanta," Mav's dad, Uncle Logan says. "He's a good kid."

"He's more than a kid." My dad walks over to pull me into a hug. "How are you feeling, Super P? Don't stand in one position too long. It'll make your back hurt."

"I'm doing good." I hug him back. "Thanks, Dad."

"We are the Champions" by Queen starts up, and the guys all glide out onto the ice as the fans go crazy. Crowds line up around the glass walls to watch them warm up and hopefully catch a puck.

The song quickly morphs into "Another One Bites the Dust," and I spot Gavin at once. He turns, skating backwards and waving at all of us. I don't know why skating backwards is hot, but maybe it's my hormones. Everything he does is hot to me.

"Haddy, look—is that Gavin's dad?" Mom points to a group of four people a few rows down from where we're sitting. "Should we introduce ourselves?"

Our eyes meet, and I duck, smiling nervously. "I guess we'd better!"

Holding her hand, we walk down the rows to where a tall man my dad's age with light brown hair dressed in a tweed sports coat and dark jeans stands beside a woman Mom's age with long blonde hair and wearing a Knight sweater.

A slender, petite woman with long, straight dark hair and a Knight sweater is on her other side, and she's with a muscular man in a short-sleeved, black sweater that does little to hide his tattoo sleeves.

I recognize them at once from Gavin's descriptions.

"Excuse me?" I carefully extend a hand. "Are you Patrick Knight?"

I'm relieved when his hazel eyes brighten at once. "Haddy? Hey—it's so nice to meet you!"

"Yes, sir, it's me, and this is my mom, Raven Bradford." I nervously motion to my mom.

"How do you do," Mom's saying the words as my dad's loud voice comes up from behind us.

"Don't leave me out of this!" He reaches out to shake Patrick's hand. "Hendrix Bradford, Haddy's dad."

They shake hands, and before I know it, Uncle Logan is with us along with the rest of the brothers. Aunt Dylan skips up, and they're all introducing themselves and talking about hockey and us and babies and how long are you in town? And inviting each other to Wilmington and Newhope.

"That was easy!" Gigi's upbeat voice is at my side. "It's like we're not even here."

"Gavin said that's why he and Mav were always so close." I smile watching them chat like old friends. "We all come from big, loving families."

An air-horn sounds, and we notice the teams have moved off the ice, leaving two players at center of the rink.

"It's the face-off." I reach for my mother's arm. "The game is starting!"

"I really like Gavin's parents. They're so nice!" Mom stands beside me, eyes on the rink below. "Wow, look how good they can skate."

I'm about to agree when I feel a hand touching my back. Turning, I see it's Gavin's mom Kenny, and I turn quickly.

"Haddy?" Her voice is soft, and she has bright blue eyes just like her son's. "I didn't get to meet you earlier. I'm Kenny."

"Yes!" I take her hand. "I've been wanting to meet you. Gavin's told me so much about you."

Looking down at her ivory hand in mine, I notice the red ring around her pinky finger.

"He's told me about you, but I think he told his dad

more." Her small nose wrinkles and she leans forward. "He thinks Elaine and I pressure him too much to settle down."

"I don't know about that. He only says good things all the time."

"We love him a lot. I hope you do, too," she laughs, and I like her already. "How are you feeling? How's the baby?"

"So far, so good," I take her hand, placing it on my stomach. "This little girl is active. You might get to feel a kick. Gav and I are always laughing at the crazy shapes my stomach takes."

"He was pretty active when I was pregnant, too." She rubs my stomach gently. "He said you're naming her Lucy?"

"We were also thinking of naming her Kendra if that's okay?"

"I would love that."

Noise on the rink draws our attention to the guys flying around, passing the puck to each other. They're facing off against the Colorado Cliffs again, and I'm bracing myself, remembering what a rough game it was last time.

Mav has the puck and is flying down the ice to try and score when one of their defenders skates right at him, stealing the puck and taking off in the opposite direction.

My hands don't move too far from my face the entire play. I'm ready to cover my eyes when I feel a light touch on my shoulder.

"Haddy?" The blonde woman is at my side, and I quickly reach out to shake her hand.

"Elaine?" I guess, and she smiles, giving me a hug.

"I'm so excited to meet you! I see you enjoy these games about as much as I do." Her nose wrinkles, and we look down at the ice just in time to see a big guy slam Gav into the boards. "Oh! I hate this part!"

Gav skates forward fast, grabbing the guy by the neck of his sweater, and slamming him into the boards in response.

"I think it's kind of hot." I slant my eyes at her, holding my hands over my mouth.

"I can't say anything," Kenny leans over. "I married a boxer."

"Tell me when it's over!" Elaine cries, covering her eyes.

"The linesmen are breaking it up now," I tell her. "It looks like they're more holding each other's sweaters and talking."

The game resumes. The Champions make a goal, and we cheer as "Nokia" starts, doing the dance along with the crowd. Still, it's a tough game.

Gav and Mav go in for one of their signature plays, but a massive Colorado winger slams Gav hard again. We all groan.

Elaine sits down, covering her face with her hands. "I don't know why I said I could do this," she moans. "I haven't been able to watch a game since he was in middle school."

"But you got him that lucky mouthguard," Kenny sits beside her, rubbing her shoulder. "He's wearing it. I saw it when he smiled at us."

The rest of the game is more of the same. Gav goes in for a pinch, but a forward cuts him off, pushing him out of the way, allowing the winger to get it to a center, who sends it past Akers for the goal.

Groans rise up from the crowd, and I can see Mav getting fired up. He hates losing, but it always makes him play harder.

We're in the third period, and it's 2-2. I've been chewing my nails the entire time, and as cold as it is in here, I'm sweating under my turtleneck.

The baby must feel my stress, because she's been swimming around, pushing her little butt out, and bouncing on my bladder. I'm trying to hold it until the end of the game, when Knox and Gigi come to where I'm sitting.

"You have to come with us." Knox reaches down to help me up, but I only frown at him.

"Where are we going?" I look from him to Gigi, who's smiling conspiratorially.

"Come on, Hads, it's a surprise." She steps up beside our cousin, taking my other arm. "Gavin asked us to do this for him."

From the corner of my eye, I see Kenny's hands clasp quickly in front of her face. I glance down at Elaine, who's still sitting, but she's looking away to the side, as if she's trying to hide her excited expression.

Twisting my lips, I let them help me up. I look at the uncles, and they're all smiling, watching us. Uncle Garrett gives me the thumbs up, and it feels like the entire family is in on what's happening.

"Oh, boy..." I take Gigi's hand, leaning into her ear. "I really have to pee."

"Hold it," she hisses back.

"You have clearly never been pregnant."

Knox goes around to my other side, holding my elbow as I descend the steps.

"Why are you treating me like I'm made of glass?" I frown up at him.

My NFL-bound cousin shrugs, pushing his shaggy brown hair out of his eyes. "Gav made me promise I wouldn't let you fall."

My breath catches, and my heart melts a little. "He said that?"

Knox nods, and I put my hand on Kim's little brother's arm. He's such a mixture of Aunt Allie and Uncle Jack, it's hard not to feel completely safe with him... even if he is a cocky little flirt.

"Where are you two taking me?" I look from him to Gigi, who's leading us down to the bench.

"Gav wants you to be close at the end of the game." She puts her hand on my shoulder.

"But not too close to be unsafe." Knox nods at me. "That's my job."

"You're doing a good job, K-man." I give him a little wink.

He exhales a laugh. "You're the only one who ever called me that."

"You asked us to, and I promised."

We're standing inside the glass barrier, and I watch as my guy flies around the ice, so focused on helping make that last, tie-breaking point.

The Cliffs are huge players, and they play rough. It's a true adrenaline rush to be this close to the action after sitting up high in the stands.

Everything is directly in front of us, which I don't realize is a terrible thing until it happens.

I'm standing between my two cousins, holding their hands as we watch Gav, hot on a forward's trail, gliding to the goal.

They're right at the net, the forward slings his stick hard, going for the slap shot. Gavin puts his stick right in front to block it, and almost too fast to see, the black disc ricochets off the stick, flying into the air, and slamming into Gav's face so hard, he drops like a tree.

"NO!" I scream so loudly, almost before I even register what's happening.

"Oh, my God!" Gigi clutches my arm as my knees give out.

Knox helps me land in a nearby seat, but I think I might throw up or faint or both.

Blood spills onto the ice, and Gavin is not getting up. He's crumpled on the ice as trainers swarm around him, checking his vitals, trying to get him on the stretcher.

He's not moving. I can't see his beautiful face. I can't breathe.

Gigi and Knox do their best to hold me, but I'm frantic to get to him. Tears stream down my cheeks, and all I can think is he might not get up. I've heard of players being killed on the ice, and I have to get to him. I have to tell him not to leave me..

"What's happening?" Patrick Knight is at the bench, talking to a trainer.

Knox kneels beside me, trying to calm me down, when another pair of arms circles my body. It's my dad. His strong arms surround me, and he speaks in my ear.

"Come with me, baby girl." His deep voice doesn't soothe me like it usually does.

"He's... Not..." I can't finish my sentence. I'm shaking too hard.

My insides are a tight ball of fear and panic, but my dad holds me tight. "Come on, Haddy. I know where to go."

32

———

Gavin

"That's some ring." Knox meets me in the locker room before I head out to play.

I'm holding a light blue velvet box from Tiffany's with a crown-shaped engagement ring inside it.

Being with me and having our little girl cost Haddy one crown. I bought this ring to give her a new one, to make her my queen.

"You know what to do?" I study his face, and he nods, fully serious.

"I'll get Gigi to help me." He slaps my shoulder. "Don't worry, bro. We'll have her ready and waiting for you."

"Where are they now?"

"She's up in the stands with all the fam. They're where Mav told us to sit."

Nodding, I know exactly where they are, and I picture her in my jersey with all my family. I always play better when she's watching, cheering us on. I like looking up and seeing her there, waving and dancing with Gigi, smiling and blowing kisses.

Okay, the kisses thing is new.

We made a big splash in the tabloids last time with our kissing and the declarations of love during a big fight and ultimate tie-breaker. This time I'm going for the whole enchilada, the proposal, and hopefully her saying yes.

It's a great feeling to know how close we are to making it official. Heading out onto the ice, I turn around to look up at them. It's a big group, but she sees me waving. They all do, and the cheering begins.

Our theme songs blast through the arena, and we do our part, warming up, tossing pucks, giving the fans what they want.

Colorado is a killer team, big and tough. We barely beat them the last time we played them, and it's clear they've been studying all our plays. I doubt we'll have an easy time scoring this go-round.

Sure enough, right off the bat, I'm body-checked into the wall by a massive forward. He didn't have to hit me that hard, and it ticks me off. I go after him, grabbing him by the front of his jersey.

"You sure you want to do this, little man?" he growls back, and it makes me even madder.

"I'm not so little." I have him by the neck, and we're gliding across the ice.

A lineman comes and breaks us up, but I've got my eye on that guy. He's a bully, and I'm not letting him hit me again without a fight. My mom Elaine is here, and I know she hates it when we fight. *Sorry, Mom.*

The whole game is a struggle. We fly up and down the ice, turning the puck over again and again. None of our plays work out. I try for a pinch, and a different player slams me out of the way. They're taking every opportunity to hit us hard.

As I expected, our tic-tac-goal play is blocked, but we still manage to hold it at 2-2 on the scoreboard. Donovan does his best to keep us upbeat and motivated, but Mav is pissed.

He's going for an undefeated streak, and we haven't lost a game since Christmas.

The clock is ticking down, and I notice Knox and Gigi moving Haddy closer to the rink entrance. My stomach tingles with what's to come, and for a moment, I forget to be pissed at how this game is going. It's probably why I get careless.

The forward is lined up ready to go for the slapshot, but I see an opening and reach for it with my stick. I don't have time to think about the miscalculation.

The puck hits the pine, then flies into the air with the force of his blow.

The last thing I remember is pain exploding through my forehead and everything going dark.

33

Haddy

My dad is right.

The first place they take him is to the trauma center at the stadium. He's evaluated, and the trainers decide to send him on to Cedars.

As soon as they say the name of the hospital, I try to fall again. This time, my dad has me.

"It's a good thing, baby. They'll take care of him there. Don't panic."

I'm trying. I nod, but my hands are shaking. I've never seen so much blood, and Gavin still hasn't regained consciousness. They bound his head, but the wound had already started to swell into an ugly mound on his forehead.

It's a horrible, scary injury, and I can't get the sight of it or the possibility of what it means out of my head.

We fly across town to the hospital. He's taken ahead of us in the ambulance, and when we're finally all together, we have to wait in the hall as they set him up in the private room.

Mom is with me, rubbing my back, and Gigi finally appears with Mav close behind her.

"I had to go home and take care of the dogs." She runs to me, hugging me. "How are you doing, honey?"

Fresh tears heat my eyes at her voice. "All I can think about is how much I need him to be okay. He's such a good man. He's done so much for the baby and me. He was always so prepared, and I guess I leaned on him more than I realized." I'm nervous-talking, I know, but I can't seem to stop. "What am I going to do if he doesn't—"

"Stop that, now." Mav puts an arm around my shoulders, pulling me and Gigi close. "He's going to bounce back from this. Gav's a hockey player. We know how to take hits."

"That was a very bad hit, Mav." My voice is thick, and I'm doing my best not to fall apart.

Gavin's dad is talking to the doctors, and his moms are close by as well, listening with wide eyes. Kenny is stoic, unflinching in the face of whatever the doctors say, but Elaine has tears streaming down her cheeks.

My stomach drops, and I can't let my mind go down the rabbit hole of what they might be saying.

"Hold on, baby." Dad seems to know, and he walks over to take my hand. "Everyone reacts to news differently. I'll see if I can find out what they're saying."

"Come on." Mom holds my arm, and Gigi takes the other.

The three of us walk to where a line of chairs is placed against the wall. Mav goes with my dad to talk to Patrick.

"I have to know what's happening," I whisper. "I can't take this not knowing. It hurts."

My whole body aches with every inhale, and I only want to hold his hand, crawl up beside him, kiss his cheek, kiss his warm lips.

More minutes pass, and my dad finally returns to where we're waiting.

"It's not bad news." He starts, and my stomach bottoms out.

A breath hiccups in my throat and fresh tears emerge.

"Hey, hang on," He takes my hands. "Not bad news means good news. He's stable, but he's still unconscious, which is a little cause for concern. They can't fully evaluate the extent of the damage until he wakes up. He has a significant contusion, his front left tooth is broken, and as of now, they're treating him for a concussion."

Concussion. The word sends chills through my body, and all the potential side effects flood my mind. Traumatic brain injury. CTE.

I don't want to think about these things. I don't want to be tormented by knowledge.

"Oh, God." I lean forward, putting my head in my hands.

"Haddy?" I recognize that soft voice.

Looking up I see Kenny standing in front of me, holding out her hand. "I think it would be good if you come in to sit with him. I think he'll feel your presence there."

"Yes! Thank you." I push out of the chair, following her into the small room.

When we enter, my chest aches. Gavin is always so full of life, so animated. I hadn't realized until now that when we're together, he fills all the space around me. I want that.

Instead, he lies silently in the bed. His eyes are closed, and a bandage is around his head.

I take the seat at his side, placing my hand under his large one.

"Here." Kenny hands me a tissue, and I realize I'm crying.

"Thank you." I blot my cheeks.

"I'll leave you here with him so you can talk. I think hearing your voice might help him find his way back to us."

My eyes go to his thumb where the faint red line is inked, and I imagine the string stretching, tangling, but never breaking. I try to remember the exact words of the legend.

The door closes softly behind me, and I clear my throat. "Hey, Gavin... It's me, Haddy." I speak quietly, carefully. "I love your family. They're the best, and they get along so well with the Bradfords. You should see them all together."

Soft beeps and blinking monitors are my only response. My chest sinks. Looking around the room, I think of what to say next.

"I was so excited to meet your mom Kenny, but we didn't get to talk much. Maybe when you wake up, we can talk more."

More beeping. More thinking of upbeat topics.

Studying his unresponsive, handsome face hurts. I run my eyes over his swollen lips, the bandage around his head. His dark hair peeking out, the scruff on his square jaw. The baby kicks as if demanding her time.

"Lucy's been moving so much. I think she misses your voice." I touch the tissue to my cheeks. "I nearly peed my pants at the arena. Dad took care of me, and I was able to find a place to go in the locker room."

I lean both my elbows on the side of the bed, resting my head on my hands.

"I've been thinking she'll probably be an athlete like you. Mom doesn't remember if I moved a lot in utero. She was sick the whole time." I wait a beat, thinking. "Do you remember if you were an active baby?"

Again, the only reply is the quietly beeping monitors.

"Oh, Gavin," I whisper, tracing my fingers along his forearm. "I need you to talk to me. I need you to smile at me and call me princess. I love you so much. I'm just a regular girl without you."

Inhaling a deep breath, I put my head on the mattress.

It's all true. He changed everything just by being himself, being so determined, being so good. If he doesn't come back to me...

ANOTHER DAY PASSES.

The nurses bring in a cot for me to sleep on, and Kenny takes the recliner. Elaine comes and goes, and Patrick is always either in the hallway or in the room with us.

"How long do they expect this to last?" Elaine paces the room, chewing on the side of her finger. "I can't remember him ever being so quiet and still like this. It's making me crazy."

"The doctor said it could be a few days while his brain heals." Patrick puts his hands on her shoulders, rubbing gently. "We have to be patient."

Gavin is so much like his dad, it aches in my chest.

I agree with Elaine. This is all so wrong.

"Hi, everybody." My mom's soft voice joins us in the room. She's carrying a bag with the word *Holbox* printed on the outside, and the scent of tacos makes my stomach growl. "I thought y'all might be hungry, and I wanted to check on my baby."

"Oh my gosh, Mom," I groan, holding out my hands. "I'm starving."

"That smells delicious," Kenny agrees, stepping forward. "Raven, you're a hero."

We all share an exhausted laugh. The food is distributed, and Mom walks over to rub my back.

I unwrap the soft taco and take a bite. "Mmm... so delicious. Thank you."

"How's everybody holding up?" Dad's warm voice joins the room.

Patrick steps over to shake his hand. "Hendrix, good to see you, man."

My eyes go to Gavin's, and I wonder if he can hear this, if it's getting through.

Please wake up...

"I'm worried about you, honey." Mom smooths my hair behind my ear. "Don't you have to get back to class?"

"It's my spring break, too." I finish the last bite of taco.

Which reminds me, I've got to figure out that whole situation.

I must be frowning, because Mom studies me with worried eyes. "What's wrong?"

"Nothing..." It's such a lie. I don't have the money to pay them back, and I don't know where I'll get it.

"Gavin told us about the scholarship." Her tone is gentle, but I can sense her protective anger. "He didn't want to upset us. He wanted to pay IPW back himself, so I showed him how. It was probably better that way, or I'd have given them a piece of my mind."

"He did..." I sit down on the sofa as my throat tightens, as fresh tears coat my cheeks. "Why would he do that?"

Mom sits beside me, sliding my hair off my shoulder. "Because he loves you, Hayden. Your dad stepped up when I was at risk of losing everything. It's what they do."

"But I never asked him to do that."

Dad walks over, concern lining his face. "What's wrong?"

"She didn't know about the tuition. I guess Gavin was waiting to surprise her."

Dad sits on my other side, putting an arm around me. "It's as much his responsibility as yours."

"Not really." I shake my head. "It's my degree. I can't let him do that."

"Yes, you can." Dad turns, making me look at him. "It's his way of showing you his love. He's your family, Hayden. He wants to take care of you."

"That's just it..." My voice breaks, and I press the paper napkin to my face. "He always takes care of me. He takes care of everything. I should take care of my things."

Dad nods toward the bed. "What if he needs you to take care of him now?"

Pain tightens my throat, and I can't think of that possibility.

"I will." I answer firmly. "I'll always take care of him."

My dad's smile warms his eyes. "Don't you see, baby? That's what a family is. You take care of each other."

Looking down at my hands in my lap, I think about his words. I look up at Gavin's three parents. I look at my dear knight still not moving on the bed. *Family.*

"You can start by taking care of the baby." Mom collects the papers, throwing it all away, and stooping to hold out a hand to me. "You need to go home and rest, take a shower..."

Shaking my head, I cut her off. "I can't leave. What if he woke up, and I wasn't here? He wouldn't know... I need him to know I'll never leave his side."

~

"YOU HAVEN'T TOLD me if you have a lucky charm or a game-day ritual." I trace my fingers along the back of Gavin's hand.

It's Day 3 of his coma, and his room is filling with flowers. Fans send little gifts. The coaches and trainers have come to check on him. It all feels very ominous and scary, like they're hedging their bets just in case.

Mav was with us for a while, doing his best to keep my spirits up, telling me how tough they all are. Telling me about the time he played through a broken foot.

I can't shut off my scientific mind. A fractured foot is a long way from a head injury.

Now it's just the two of us again—or the three, including Lucy. The sun is setting, and my eyes are heavy. Still, I hold out hope he's going to blink those pretty blue eyes open and smile that killer smile at me any minute now...

"You probably know Mav drinks a Welch's strawberry soda the morning of every game, then he eats five red M&Ms." I trace my fingers against his skin. "Gigi said it started in high school when he scored his first hat trick. He'd tried a Welch's strawberry soda for the first time, but he'd also eaten all the red M&Ms out of Kim's bag. I think he's not sure which was the lucky thing, so he does them both."

Studying Gavin's handsome face, I inhale a shaky breath. I'm not giving up on him. I'm not giving up on us. No matter what comes next, I'm in it for the long haul.

"Maybe your lucky charm could be an axolotl? They're really cute, and they're all about transformation and healing." My eyes are so tired, and I lean my head on the bed beside his hand. "Or maybe something from *Star Wars*? Something hockey?"

The constant beeping never ends. It's become white noise lulling me to sleep.

Lucy kicks, but I can't keep my eyes open another minute.

34

____

Gavin

Somebody's snoring.

I'm in a room with dim lights, and my head is wrapped tightly. Soft beeping noises are all around me, and I blink hard, squeezing my eyes as I force my brain to remember what happened.

Slap shot to the head. Right.

How that little black fucker manages to find its way past the visor on my helmet is beyond me. I don't remember being knocked out, but as I look around the room, I know what must've happened. *Concussion.*

My stomach twists as my mind races through all the symptoms. I don't feel nauseated. I don't have a headache, but I'm willing to bet they have me pumped pretty full of pain meds.

Lifting my hand, I want to push myself higher in the bed when I realize a soft head is lying on my bedside.

My eyes go to her at once, and nothing matters when I see my beautiful Haddy, tears in her eyes, blinking up at me.

"Gavin?" Her voice breaks, and she's on her feet. "Do you know me? Do you know where you are?"

"Fuck yeah, Princess." My voice is scratchy like I've eaten a handful of sand.

She quickly hits a button on my bedside and grabs a plastic cup with a straw. "Water?"

I pull the plastic straw between my lips, but my eyes are drinking her in.

She's exhausted. Her pretty eyes have dark circles beneath them, and I can tell she's been crying. A lot.

It hits me in the stomach, and I just want to hold her, make sure she's okay. "How long have I been here?"

That sip of water made a world of difference in the sound of my voice.

"Four days." Her nose wrinkles, and she takes my hand again. "We were so worried."

"Holy shit." I push against the mattress, trying to sit up straighter.

That's when the pain hits me hard, radiating through my skull like a spear. I can't speak, it hurts so bad, but Haddy is on it.

"I'll get the nurse. I pressed the call button, but they must be busy..." She starts for the door, right as it opens. "He's awake!" Haddy announces.

My room is suddenly a rush of commotion. Doctors surround me, nurses take my vitals. Lights are shined in my eyes, my heart rate is checked, but all I want is something to kill this pain in my head.

I'm asked a million questions. They assess my cognition, my injury, my recall. What's the last thing I remember? *Trying to block that slapshot.* Who was the first president? *George Washington.*

Finally, I'm given a massive Tylenol, which seems like a

letdown, but I'm not asking for a drug problem on top of whatever this head injury is going to mean for the rest of the season.

For the next however long it takes, I'm inundated with family. Both my moms are at my side holding my hands, but my eyes keep going to Haddy. All I want is to hold her, talk to her, make sure the baby's okay, make sure she's okay.

"I only asked for one thing, Lane Knight," my mom Elaine playfully teases.

I can see in her blue eyes how scared she's been. She's not as practiced at hiding her emotions as my mom Kenny is.

"My mouthguard must've got loose when I fell." I touch the back of my broken tooth carefully with my tongue.

Mom Kenny is right beside her. "I hear they've made wonderful advances in the field of dentistry, Elaine."

I manage a smile, but Elaine shakes her head when she sees my snaggletooth.

"I'm just so glad you're okay." She presses a kiss to my forehead. "I love you, Laney."

I squeeze her arm. "I know, Mom. I love you, too."

MK watches with amusement in her bright blue eyes. I can tell she's relieved as well.

"Maybe we should give you and Haddy some alone time?" She steps forward to kiss my cheek carefully. "Can I bring you anything?"

"Yeah…" I look around, thinking about unfinished business. "I need my phone."

Her lips tilt in a frown. She disapproves that my first request is a screen, but she doesn't know what I had planned to do before it all went to hell.

"I think Haddy has it," is all she says.

"I have to be sure..." I look around the room, lowering my voice, "...something's secure."

She shakes her head, putting the phone in my hand. "I'll be back. Love you, babe."

They all leave the room, and I quickly send a text to Knox.

Haddy returns to my side, her blue eyes so heavy, but a smile is on her face.

Reaching out, I cup her cheek with my hand. "How long have you been here?"

"As long as you have." Her voice is quiet, but it sounds so good.

"Fuck, you must be exhausted." I wish we were back home, and I could spoon her against my chest, holding my hand over Lucy.

She huffs a laugh. "I wasn't leaving until you opened your eyes."

Sliding my hand over her soft hair, I can't stop drinking in her pretty face. "Why didn't you go home and rest?"

Exhaling a *pfft*, she reaches for my hand on her head, pulling it down. "I couldn't leave you. What if you woke up?"

She stayed by my side. I can't put into words how that makes me feel. She never left me. As uncomfortable as she must've been with the baby. As tired as she was.

"Why would you do that, Princess?"

I need to hear her say it.

Pretty blue eyes blink up to mine, and her expression softens. "I'd do anything for you, Gavin."

That's all I needed to hear. Knox hasn't returned my text, and even if he did, it wouldn't matter.

"You can do something for me." I pull her hand into mine. "I know you said you didn't want to be my wife..."

Her chin pulls back, and her eyebrows clench. "I never said that!"

Chuckling, I kiss her fingers. "You kind of did."

"I said we couldn't get married just because we were pregnant," she argues. "We didn't even know each other then."

"What do you think?" I cock an eyebrow at her. "Do we know each other now?"

"We know each other a lot better..." She leans forward to put her hands on my face gently, then just as gently press her lips to my damaged ones.

Sitting higher, I cover her hands in mine then I pause, looking into her eyes, letting this feeling settle around us. "Good."

~

TWENTY-ONE DAYS.

The doctors couldn't rule out whether I'd suffered a concussion because I was out for so long, so our team trainers recommended we play it safe and follow standard concussion protocol, which means I'm on the bench for twenty-one days.

It's a freaking lifetime in hockey, especially at this time of the year. Mav's pissed. I'm pissed.

Placing my hands on the dining room table, I exhale heavily as I re-read the email on my phone for the tenth time. Yes, my recovery is important, but so is winning the championship.

I have a dentist appointment tomorrow to get my tooth capped, and the bruise on my head is still pretty ugly. But I'm so damn glad to be out of the hospital, back here with Haddy and Mav and Gigi and the dogs.

"Welp, I'm headed out." Knox emerges from the kitchen, where he was chatting with Mav and Gigi. "I've got to get back to New Orleans."

"Thanks for taking care of that for me." I hold out my hand to fist bump.

Knox secured the ring and held onto it for me while I was in the hospital, bringing it to me as soon as I got home.

"No problem, cuz." He bumps my fist then points at my face when I smile. "Next Halloween, *Dumb and Dumber*."

"No." My voice is flat, and I hear Haddy's snortle coming from behind me.

"That would be hilarious." She joins us in the living room holding Peepee under her neck.

She's adorable in a short, black cotton dress that hugs her figure and shows off her baby bump.

"Girl, look at you." Knox goes to give her a hug. "Gettin big."

Haddy rubs her hand over her stomach. "Mon petit chou."

"What does that mean?" he asks.

"My little cabbage." Haddy's nose wrinkles, and she's so damn cute, all my frustration melts away.

I walk over to pull her into my arms. "How do you say 'my little princess' in French?"

"Ma petite princesse."

"Hell, I didn't even know you spoke French." Knox grins. "That's cool."

"I wish I spoke Japanese," she muses. "*Arigatou.*"

"What's that?"

"Thank you."

"Ready?" Mav breezes into the living room.

Hugs are exchanged, and they take off for the airport. Gigi snaps a leash on Spanky to go for a walk. Haddy's still in my arms, and she leans her head back against my shoulder.

Bending down, I kiss the side of her neck. Her face turns, and our lips meet and part... and she quickly pulls her head away.

"Ouch." Putting her fingers over her lips, her eyes dance. "How soon do you get that fixed?"

"Tomorrow morning." I give her a disappointed smile.

It makes her laugh more, and she shakes her head. "You do not look like *Dumb and Dumber.*"

My eyes narrow. "I'm concerned you felt the need to tell me that."

Walking to the mirror, I smile at myself, and hell. I do look like that guy. Haddy walks up behind me, holding my waist and resting her cheek against my bicep.

"You have better hair." She's doing her best not to laugh, and if she weren't pregnant, I'd throw her over my shoulder.

Instead, I turn and pull her into my arms, arching an eyebrow. "I've got more than that."

"Yes, you do." She lifts her chin to kiss the side of my jaw. "And I can't wait to make out with you after your appointment."

Peepee hops around our feet, and she steps back, calling to the little dog. "I'll take her out. Let's eat!"

Dinner finished, movie watched, Peepee is in her crate, and we're getting ready to curl up in Haddy's bed. I hate to confess the trainers might be right, but I'm pretty exhausted right now.

Haddy complains about being tired all the time as well, so I guess it works out. She's in my arms, Lucy is in my hands, and that puck's not stopping me.

I'm already working on Plan B.

35

———

Haddy

"Can you believe Dr. Barry specifically said no more shower sex?" I'm standing in the bedroom reading the text I received from my OB/GYN. "She said with your injury and my center of balance off, it's too dangerous right now."

Time is flying, and I can't get over how big my stomach is getting. It's pretty terrifying to think I'm having a baby with Gavin the giant, even if it is a girl.

Aunt Liv gave me a pep talk over FaceTime a few days ago. She reminded me that Gina is Uncle Garrett's daughter, and he's six-foot-four. She told me she went through the same freak-out when she was pregnant.

Then I talked to Mom yesterday after I learned most women poop during delivery. That put the kibosh on water birthing for me. No floaters in my pool.

Now we've switched to all of my aunts' favorite method, hypnobirthing. It's basically learning to breathe and chant mantras when you really want to scream your head off and have a panic attack.

I'm not convinced it will work, but at this point, I'm doing my best to take a scientific approach. Women have babies every day with all varieties of men, and only a small percentage have problems. Breathwork and intense focus have been proven to help ease the pain of childbirth.

I can do this.

I wrote it on a Post-it note and stuck it inside my iPad cover. *I can do this.*

"Damn, that's my favorite kind of sex." Gav walks into the bedroom, smiling with his perfectly repaired front tooth.

I melt a little bit at how handsome he is, and despite my baby fears, I wouldn't change a thing.

"It's all your favorite kind of sex."

"Yeah, it is." He bends down to kiss me. "Get on the bed and let me taste that pussy."

Heat flushes through my body, and a horny giggle slips from my throat. "Maybe we could switch to bathtub sex."

His face scrunches. "I don't think either of us would fit in that tub, much less together."

Reaching up, I curl my fingers in his shaggy flow. "Sounds like we need a bigger tub."

His expression stills, almost like he's about to say something, but stopped himself.

"What? You didn't get my *Jaws* reference?"

"I want to show you something." His hand slides down my forearm to thread our fingers. "Get Peepee and come with me."

I reach down to scoop up our little dog, and he leads me down the stairs and out the front door. My feet are bare as I skip across our front yard to the sidewalk, hesitating to look both ways, then crossing the street.

"Where are you taking me?" I'm breathing quicker as I laugh.

He doesn't answer as he walks straight up the porch steps and into the house across the street. It's an adorable bungalow I've always admired.

"What are we doing?" I don't know why I'm whispering. "Why is the door unlocked?"

Inside, we're greeted by soft yellow-pine floors and white beadboard walls. The ceiling is also painted white with exposed, matching pine beams across the length.

I put Patsy down as we walk through, looking up and all around the completely empty house. The walls are painted in neutral colors, and it has arched doorways throughout. A wall of windows lines the living room, facing a flowering bush and tree-filled backyard.

"It's so pretty," I sigh, walking around and looking at everything. "I've always loved that giant sycamore out front."

"Check this out." Gavin leads me through a large master bedroom, to the master bath.

It's a luxurious suite with smooth tile floors. A beige stone, walk-in shower is in one corner and a door leading to a private toilet is situated across from it.

Gavin stops me right in front of a large jetted garden tub beneath a frosted, stained-glass window, and my heart picks up with excitement.

"What do you think about that tub?" He asks, studying my face. "Big enough?"

"It should be..." I put my hand over my thumping heart, not sure what all this means. "What are we doing here?"

"How would you feel about making this our home?"

I turn to walk slowly back into the master bedroom with its pine floors and exposed brick walls. "*Our* home?"

"I wanted to do this at the game, but it got all fucked up."

He reaches into his pocket, taking out a little blue pouch with *Tiffany's* stamped on the side.

From it, he removes a shining silver ring, and my breath disappears. It has a massive, pear-shaped stone in the center with two smaller baguettes on either side, and I realize when he slides it onto my third finger, it's in the shape of a crown. Tears immediately flood my eyes. He's giving me back my crown.

"I've known from the minute I met you, Princess, you were the only woman for me, and every day we've spent together, I've only known it more. And to top it all, you're having my baby? Damn, Haddy, nothing would make me happier than to have you as my wife. I don't want to live another day without you in it. I want to spend the rest of my life with you. Will you marry me?"

I have to tell myself to breathe. "Gavin..." My lips part with my inhale. "It's so beautiful... It's all so beautiful... I—"

"Is that a yes?" His eye squints, and I'm nodding hard, tears falling onto my cheeks as I laugh.

"It's a massive yes, a million thousand times yes!" I step forward to throw my arms around his neck.

Warm lips cover mine, and even Lucy gives my stomach a hard push, which makes my chin drop with a laugh. "We're all saying yes."

"Welcome home." His eyes meet mine. "I'll let the realtor know tomorrow. I can finally get my shit out of storage."

"And it's right across the street from Gigi and Mav!"

"I figured that might sweeten the deal." He's grinning, and I hug my body close to his side.

"You didn't need to sweeten anything. I'd have said yes even if we were staying in my bedroom."

"It's still your bedroom, only slightly larger and more private."

We walk down the hall, and I see what will make a perfect baby's room. "How did this happen?"

"I've been looking for places since I got here. You know that, but when things got more serious between us, I changed the location of my search." He shrugs. "It just so happened these guys wanted to move to the beach. They're headed to Malibu, and we're headed here."

Shaking my head, I scoop up Patsy, and pause at the front door, taking one more look at the warm, cozy space. "I can't wait to start nesting!"

"It's that time." He lifts my hand and kisses the back. "Fit it out with all the twigs and leaves and moss you want. Break the bank."

Rising onto my tiptoes, I kiss his scruffy square jaw. "You've always been so good to me, Gavin Knight. I love you."

His large hand cups the side of my face, and he kisses me gently. "I know."

Wrinkling my nose, I give the place one more look. "There will be no twigs or moss in our nest. It's going to be beautiful."

Gigi is waiting for us when we get to the house, iPad in hand. Spanky is hopping all around her like he always does when we FaceTime with the family.

"Did she say yes?" My cousin's green eyes are bright, and she's smiling so big.

I nod quickly, and I hear a rally of cheers coming from the device in her hand. She holds it up, and it's a group call with all the cousins, my parents, Gav's parents, everyone arranged in tiles on the screen.

"How could I not?" I cry. "He bought me a whole house, and look at this ring!"

I hold up my hand so she can capture it on the screen.

"It looks like a crown!" Elaine cries.

"It's perfect for you!" Kim adds.

"I helped pick it out," My mom calls, which makes me so happy.

"I love it—thank you, Mom!"

No one was with me when I carefully packaged the sash, crown, and scepter and sent them all back to the organization.

I still have all of my old pictures, and the things I achieved as a young woman. I treasure my memories of the good times, and what I have now, our little family, more than makes up for the few things I lost. I don't want them now anyway.

"I can't wait for you all to see the house," I continue. "It's so pretty. Gavin really outdid himself."

My big guy leans down to wrap his arms around me from behind, smiling at the screen filled with happy faces.

They continue talking and laughing, and he kisses the side of my cheek. "Are you ready for this family?"

His deep voice warms my insides, and I turn my face to kiss him right back. "I love your family. Are you ready for mine?"

Our eyes meet, and he nods, adding. "Now we're starting a new branch."

36

Gavin

"I haven't been up here since I helped you move in all that equipment." I follow Haddy across campus to the science lab.

Since I'm still on the bench, I've got plenty of time (and energy) to help her pack up her things, and we've been moving into our new house.

The semester is over, and yesterday she defended her thesis to the committee. I would've liked to sit in on that and listen to her being gorgeous and smart. It always makes me smile.

She said now all that's left is for them to decide if she passed. How could they not?

"Some master's degrees require an experiment, and then you just write up the results." she explains as we enter the building. "Since mine is mostly theoretical, backed by the data Daniel and I collected and the information provided by the institute, I basically argued in support of the strong correlation between wind currents and the seasonal outbreaks of the disease."

"Have I told you how hot it is when you talk science?"

Her cheeks turn pink and she shakes her head. "You're so crazy."

"It's true."

"I'm going to miss Daniel, even if we did have to use translation apps to communicate." She's back to being Science Haddy. "He invited me to visit the institute again, but when he saw how pregnant I am, he politely nodded and wished me good luck."

"He sounds like a good guy."

Her hand is on the door to the lab, and she sighs. "If only we could go for a few days..."

It hit me hard, and I pulled her to me. "We're going to go. Once Lucy gets here, we'll start making plans, figuring out what we need to do. Dr. Barry can help us with the timing."

"I never thanked you for paying back the IPW." Her chin dips, and I know it's an adjustment for my independent girl to let me take care of her.

Ever since my injury, she's come a long way with letting me spoil her. I think her dad had something to do with it.

Still, she has her moments. "You didn't have to do that."

I catch her chin in my fingertips, causing her to meet my eyes. "You had to give up your scholarship to have my baby."

Her pretty blue eyes twinkle. "*Our* baby."

"It was the right thing to do, Hads. I had the power to help you, and I wanted to."

She reaches up to slide her thumb down my lips. "Because we're a family now, and I'd do the same for you if the tables were turned."

"Wrapping up, Haddy?" Timothy's voice interrupts our moment.

He opens the door to the lab, and I do my best not to show my annoyance with his presence. Haddy gives me a little "be good" pinch.

"Yep," she answers brightly. "Defended my thesis yesterday. Now I'm just waiting for the final word."

"Wow." Timothy's brows rise. "You're really pregnant."

I want to pop him in the mouth for that crack, but Haddy takes it in stride.

"I sure am!" She puts a hand on her belly and rubs it up and down. "She's an active little lady."

"Hey there, Tim." I step up beside her, putting a large hand on her shoulder. "What's your deal here, anyway?"

"My *deal*?" His tone is so condescending, I want to pull that sweater over his head backwards. "Do you mean my *field of research*?"

"Sure." I stand straighter, emphasizing our height difference. "Let's go with that."

"Tickling."

The room falls silent, and I'm not sure if he's making a joke. I glance at Haddy, who's biting her lip and lining up the things she brought here. She could've warned me.

"I'm sorry... Did you say tickling?"

"I did." His tone is defiant.

"No offense, but what are you researching when it comes to tickling?"

"None taken, hockey boy." This guy. He has the balls to slap my shoulder, and I gotta hand it to him, I'm impressed by his bravery. "Have you ever wondered why you can't tickle yourself?"

"Not really."

"And how there are some people who aren't ticklish at all? While others can barely stand to be touched in certain places?"

My eyes narrow. "Is that something you can study?"

"Yes, it is." All of a sudden Timothy is as excited as Haddy gets about wind. "The results are directly correlated to increasing tactile responses in babies with autism spectrum disorder. Basically, we're making autistic children laugh."

That stops me. I lower my arms, finding a new respect for this nerd.

"Well, hell, Tim, that's pretty fucking amazing." I shake my head. "You never said you were helping babies, too."

"You never gave me the chance." He sniffs like he's offended, like he wasn't the one always leaving the minute I showed up. "I wanted to share the lab with Hayden because of the crossover nature of our work."

"Does that really cross over?" *Nice try, Mr. Rewriting History.*

He wanted to share the lab because he's got the hots for my future wife, and we all know it.

He shrugs. "We're both working to help children."

I look over at Haddy, who's continuing to pack without joining the conversation. She's very focused... and possibly trying not to laugh.

"That's very cool, Timothy. Keep up the good work."

"You've never used my full name before." He blinks a few times.

"I was wrong about you." I hold out a hand to shake. "I'm sorry I underestimated you. If you ever want to come to a hockey game, just let Haddy know. We'll get you in for free."

"Thanks..." I can't tell if he'll do it, but I pick up the box of Haddy's things.

"Good luck with your studies." Haddy steps forward to give him a polite hug.

I notice she's been very different around him this visit,

and I'm not sure if it's for my benefit or if something happened.

Then he stops her. "I thought it was shitty that they took your scholarship away... and your crown."

That seems to break the ice.

She steps forward, lifting her left hand. "I got something way better than a pageant crown."

"Oh..." He seems surprised when he inspects the ring. "I guess this means I was wrong about him."

"One of the most important things we can do is admit when we're wrong. And apologize."

He seems to be turning this over in his mind. His jaw works, and he puts his hands on his hips. Finally, he seems to make a decision.

"I'm sorry, Hayden." Then he looks at me. "I was wrong about your intentions. I hope you're both very happy."

Neither of us speaks until we're on the other side of the door. Then as soon as it closes, we fall back against it quietly laughing.

"Damn, Princess, you put that boy in his place."

She shakes her dark head. "I've had enough of his condescending attitude. He needed to apologize to you."

"I wasn't sweating it." I shift the box onto my hip as we walk down the hall. "But who knew a guy like that could be doing such good work? You should've warned me."

"I don't know." She holds the door for me. "I guess it's some form of redemption."

I glance back, muttering under my breath. "Never judge a dude by his fanny pack."

～

THE TIME HAS COME, and I'm finally off the damn bench.

I got back to lifting weights and skating and jogging and doing all my usual training as soon as I could after the accident so I wouldn't lose any ground. Still, I can tell I've been injured and away when I'm on the ice. My reflexes are a little slow, and I'm not as quick to steal the puck.

It's frustrating, but Donovan is there with the pep talk. "A few more games, and you'll be back on top."

The bruise above my eyebrow went from blackish purple to bluish purple to greenish purple to yellow before finally fading away. Now all that's left is a scar, which Haddy says is hot.

Sometimes when she's straddling my lap, riding my cock, she traces her lips over it while I'm sucking her breasts, and I like having a bit of an edge.

Mav sends the puck my way, and I quickly get my head back in the game. I pass it to Saxon when the sharp tweet of a whistle interrupts our practice.

"Get over here and meet your newest teammate," Coach yells at us in his deep, growly voice.

The three of us exchange a look before skating over to where a tallish guy with light brown hair stands waiting to meet the team. He's six-two, and he's got a friendly, yet cautious expression.

It's a good sign. The Champions are a close-knit team, so the last thing we want is an ego to show up on the roster.

"This is Owen Stone. He was called up from the South Carolina Stingers. He's one of the best forwards in the minor leagues, and I expect you all to get him up to speed."

"Good to meet you, Owen," Don is the first one to skate forward and shake his hand. "Welcome to the big time."

Owen exhales a laugh, and Mav glances at me. I'm pretty sure we're thinking the same thing. North Carolina, South Carolina, Alabama. We've probably got a lot in common, and not just moving from one side of the country to the other.

"Owen?" Mav skates up to him. "I'm Maverick Murphy, right winger. This is Gavin Knight, defense. How's it going?"

He shakes Mav's hand. "Nice to meet you. I've heard of Gav and Mav... Or Mav and Gav..."

I can feel his consternation, and I reach out to slap the top of his shoulder. "Either way is fine."

"It's Mav and Gav." Mav's tone is flat, and I can't help a chuckle.

He's such an only child.

"Where are you staying?" Mav asks.

Owen shakes his head, looking side to side. "A hotel room down the street for now. I haven't been able to find a place that seems right for my situation."

"What situation is that?" Now that I've met Maverick's mom, I understand a lot about where he got his inquiring mind.

He has a very friendly way of getting all the information from people.

"My little girl is living with my sister Heather back home. I'm trying to find a way to move them both out here, but I don't know the area too well."

"You don't say?" Mav glances at me with a nod. "Let's talk after practice. I might be able to help you with that."

Shaking my head, I exhale a chuckle. It's like we've come full circle with a new player joining the fold.

THE LAST OF our things are moved, and we're officially in our new home.

All week Haddy's been decorating the baby's room. The

walls are painted a warm peach color, and the pine crib is decorated in a mixture of cream and peach princess and hockey-themed motifs. Even the mobile hanging over it is hockey players and princesses.

"I had that custom made," Haddy explains.

Waiting for Lucy in the center of the mattress is a green axolotl Haddy's aunt Mimi crocheted by hand. Haddy showed me a picture of Axel, the one she had as a baby.

"She's going to love it." Leaning down, I kiss the side of her neck.

"I hadn't accounted for pregnancy when I got a tattoo on my hip." Her nose wrinkles. "Axel is very large right now."

"I can really see the details at this size." I catch her fist before it makes contact with my chest, laughing as I lead her down the hall to our bedroom. "I'm just saying, my mom's a tattoo artist. It's good work—much like you did with the house."

"Nice save."

Our bedroom shows off our two worlds as well. Framed pictures of our last months together are on the dresser and nightstands. My favorite is the one of me catching her that first day when she fell off the float.

She put it together with a mat that has the headline about me being a hockey player and a white knight in a large frame.

"Lucy's going to love that one when she's older," Haddy laughs, resting her head on my arm.

"She'll be our little princess." I place my fingers under Haddy's chin. "You're my queen."

Her eyes darken, and I lean down to pull her lips with mine. Our mouths open, and I slide my tongue in to curl with hers. She exhales a soft noise, and it registers straight to my cock.

Threading my fingers in her hair, I tilt her head to the side so I can kiss her deeper. She scratches, pulling at my shirt and I take a break to pull it over my head. Like always her eyes light, and she traces her finger down the lines of my chest.

"My knight," she whispers, placing her lips against my skin.

The tip of her tongue circles my hardened nipple, sending energy to my dick, and she kisses lower, moving to her knees and sliding her hands up my thighs.

"You shouldn't be on your knees," my voice is hoarse, and my body aches for her.

"I want to be." She blinks wide blue eyes as she takes my shaft in her fist, guiding my tip to her full lips.

One gentle suck, one circle of her tongue, and I bend forward, resting my palms on the side of the bed.

"Fuck, Haddy, that feels too good." It's a deep groan as she pulls me further into her warm mouth.

Her head bobs, and she moves her hand to meet her lips. Then she tilts her head, sucking the place right behind the tip and making me see stars. Another deep groan, and she opens her mouth, sliding the top of her tongue back and forth beneath my tip.

"Jesus, Haddy..." My fists tighten on the mattress. "Come up here before I come all over your face."

Her eyebrows rise, and she exhales a throaty laugh. "What's wrong with that?"

Shaking my head, I help her climb onto our king bed. "I don't think it's because I love you when I say you give the best head."

"I told you I studied."

"God, I love your scientific mind. Now lie back and spread 'em."

Her thighs fall open, and I kiss my way up the soft, inner skin, getting closer to her bare pussy as she squirms and moans on the bed. Then just before I get to the center, I stop and go to the other side.

"Gavin!" she pouts, making me chuckle as I do the same again.

Pausing on her inner thigh, I suck, flicking my tongue back and forth over the skin between my lips as she moans.

"If you make me go into labor, Dr. Barry is going to see that," she gasps.

"I'm sure she's seen worse." I lift my head inspecting the hickey on her inner thigh, then I kiss the bottom of her pregnant belly. "Buckle up, baby."

Covering her pussy with my mouth, I circle my tongue over her clit as her moans grow louder. I slide one finger into her core, then two... then three as I suck her clit.

"Oh, fuck, Gavin!" she shouts, and my rigid cock drips with precum.

"Yes, scream my name..." I give her center a slow lick. "We can make all the noise we want."

Focusing my attention on her center, I keep going, pumping my fingers in and out as she twists and moans. Her hands slap the sheets and pull as her heels dig into the mattress beside me. Another loud moan, another low swear, and I feel her inner muscles start to spasm and grab my sliding fingers.

Just before she breaks, I give her a kiss and stand, lining my cock up with her entrance and driving straight home.

We both moan loudly. My mind bends at the feel of her tight cunt gripping my cock. I'm too far gone to be gentle. Thrusting hard and fast, I rest a knee on the side of the bed.

Haddy moans and wraps her legs around me, arching her back and crying out. My vision tunnels, waves of pleasure snake up my legs, centering in the place where we're joined. I bend down to seal my lips to hers, and when our tongues collide, I feel her break.

Her body pulls me, shuddering, and I let go with a deep groan, pulsing and filling her, losing myself in the intense pleasure of our union. The mind-altering experience of flying through this place together, of fumbling down from ecstasy.

Gathering her body, I slide us higher to the center of the bed. Turning her in my arms, I hold her for a minute, spooning her against my chest as I kiss her shoulder, place my hands over her pregnant belly. Her full body has only become more attractive to me as time has passed.

"The nest is beautiful," I say, kissing the side of her cheek. "Just like you."

"I'm a whale," she laughs softly, covering my hands with hers and threading her fingers in mine.

"You're full of life." I kiss the top of her ear.

"I'm definitely full." Another snort. "Who knew the night you hung all those Halloween decorations we'd end up here?"

"I knew." I press my nose to the side of her head and inhale fresh jasmine. "You were made for me."

"You sound like your mom Kenny." She traces her finger around the ring on my thumb. "I want one of these. Would she do it for me?"

"We don't have to wait for her." I lift her slim hand.

"But I want to. It'll be more special that way, keeping it in the family."

"Anything you want." I kiss her again. "As long as we're together."

"That's the legend."

Only it's more than a legend. It's the sunlight filtering

through the leaves on the trees. It's the roots stretching deep into the soil, anchoring us to the earth and creating a foundation.

Haddy's mine, and I am Haddy's. It's our branch, the start of something new. The start of our forever.

EPILOGUE

Haddy

GIGI

I'm lonely.

HADDY

I'm right across the street!

GIGI

It's not the same.

HADDY

We have dinner together almost every night.

GIGI

Almost is a long time. It's so echoey upstairs all alone. Come see me

HADDY

I'm lying on my couch with a bowl of tater tots on my stomach and Patsy on my head.

GIGI

Why is she on your head???

HADDY

She's on the back of the couch, which puts her on top of my head.

GIGI

Walking is good for you, isn't it? It's how mom went into labor with me.

HADDY

You came out for a dog… which explains a lot!!!

GIGI

HADDY

Fine.

Heaving myself off the couch, I scoop Patsy under my arm and carry my bowl with me out into the twilight.

I'm in the last weeks of pregnancy, and I literally waddle like a duck when I walk now. I'm not overdue like Aunt Liv was, but I wouldn't complain if Lucy decided to come out now.

"You are too cute barefoot and pregnant." Gigi meets me at the door, taking Patsy from my hands.

"You could've walked over to see me." I grumble, eating another tot as I plop onto the couch and put my feet on the coffee table.

"I don't know." Gigi scoots in beside me. "It's sort of your little love nest. I don't think Gav would want me there when he gets home tonight."

"He'll be glad to be home. Mav's the one who's going to be sulky."

The two of us watched the championship game together last night on television, and sadly, the Champions lost.

The game was held in Edmonton, Canada, and I'm too far along in my pregnancy to fly. Otherwise, we'd have been in the arena in our Gav and Mav sweaters cheering for them.

It's been hard to watch Gav play since his injury. The last time he went in for a steal and got checked against the boards I had to cover my eyes. Then a fight broke out, and I had to leave the room.

I'm turning into Aunt Dylan, hiding behind columns while trying to watch our family football games.

At least he replaced his helmet with one that has a full plastic face guard and not just a strip around his eyes like before. That shot was one in a million, but I'm glad he's not taking any more chances.

"Where are they?" Gigi leans to look at my phone screen while she steals a tot.

"Almost home." I show her my tracking app, and the little car icon is bouncing along getting closer to our street.

"I gave Gavin a hard time for stalking you after Christmas." She pushes my arm. "You two are too cute."

Noises outside the house signals their arrival, but I'm too big to get up. It doesn't matter. Mav bustles through the door before Gigi even has a chance to get up.

The minute he sees me, he yells over his shoulder. "Haddy's at our place!"

Then he crosses the space to drop his bag in the laundry room, leaving the door open behind him. I can tell by his expression, he's still unhappy about the loss.

Chewing my lip, I decide against trying to make him feel better. I know my cousin, and he'll have to get through his emotions on his own.

Gavin, by contrast, smiles as soon as he sees me. "Hey, were you lonely?"

He walks over to the back of the couch, leaning down to kiss the top of my head. "I was pretty freaked the whole trip thinking you might go into labor."

Reaching up, I hold his face, dropping my head back for a real kiss. "Lulu knows better than to try and come out without her daddy here. Now, however, all bets are off."

Gigi hops onto her knees to face him. "Sorry y'all lost the championship. That Edmonton team was killer."

"We played well." Gav shrugs. "Just wasn't our year."

"Is it because you don't have a lucky charm?" I scoot to the side so I can see him.

"I think you're my lucky charm."

Warmth squeezes my chest just looking at him there, so tall and handsome in his suit, smiling that straight white smile, that bit of scruff on his square jaw. It was only a few days, but I miss him when he's gone.

"A person can't be your lucky charm." Mav stalks back into the room. "It has to be a thing, or a ritual. Hads is right. You need to get one."

Gavin's blue eyes slide to mine, and he just shakes his head, mouthing *it's you*. I duck forward, covering my laugh with my hand.

Just then, the doorbell rings, and Mav skips back into the living room, eyes wide. "Uh, Gigi, I have someone for you to meet."

My cousin's back straightens quickly. "What have you done?"

"You've been complaining about it being too quiet upstairs, so I found us a temporary roommate!"

"Maverick Murphy!" Gigi is on her knees on the couch facing the door as she argues. "We've talked about this..."

"Look how well it worked out last time," he argues, slapping Gav's shoulder. "You're going to like this guy."

"It's a guy?" My cousin is about to argue when Mav opens the door.

Standing on the steps is a handsome man the same height as Mav. He's got longish brown hair, and he's wearing a light blue suit that makes his blue eyes seem to glow. His shoulders are broad, and he has nice hands, one of which is holding a large bag and the other is holding the leash of a bloodhound dog.

I don't think it's pregnancy hormones when I say, he's pretty damn hot.

"Gigi, Haddy, I'd like you to meet Owen Stone." Mav holds a hand to him. "And Ladybird."

My eyes go to Gigi, and her green eyes are wide. Her lips part, and she sits down on her feet.

I decide I'd better jump in and save her. "Hi, Owen, it's so nice to meet you." I nod at the big dog. "I love Ladybird. She's a beauty."

"Nice to meet you." He ducks as he steps into the living room.

"That's an unusual name for a bloodhound. Is there a story?"

"Oh..." He exhales a light chuckle, and dimples appear in both of his cheeks.

My eyes widen as I look over at my cousin, who still hasn't said anything.

"She likes to sing along with Shania Twain," he continues. "It's actually howling. Loud, long howling."

"I can't wait to hear it." I laugh, putting my hand on the couch beside me to stand.

Only I can't seem to get up. I rock back and forth until Gavin reaches down to give me a push. Gigi snaps out of her trance, hopping in front of me to hold my hands and pull.

"You're turning into a team effort, Hads!" Mav laughs watching the three of us.

"Don't make me hurt you, Maverick." I cut my eyes at him when I'm finally able to stand.

He runs over to take my hands from Gigi. "Here, I'll walk you home. Where's Peepee?"

"I've got her." Gigi hands the little dog to me. "You're not going anywhere. You have a guest to situate."

"Gav can walk me home. I'm tired." Leaning forward, I kiss Gigi, hug Mav, then I wave to Owen. "I'll see all of you tomorrow."

"I'll whip up something spicy. See if we can't coax Lucy out of there."

"Maybe she likes cats?" Gigi skips over to me, holding my hand.

I lean to her ear. "Maybe you like bloodhounds."

She gives my arm a pinch, and I glance up to see Owen rubbing the back of his neck. "When my little girl was born, my late wife went into labor getting a foot massage."

Gigi and I freeze, clutching each other. A little girl? A handsome widower? We give each other the curious side-eye.

"You'll have to tell me all about your little girl tomorrow." I hold out my hand to shake his.

"Night, Owen." Gav puts his hand on my shoulder, and we head for the door.

Once outside, he chuckles, pulling me close. "You two are as obvious as... something really obvious."

"Well, he's got his work cut out for him." I hold Gav's arm, leaning on him as we walk across the street. "Gigi swore off men after her last love-bomber."

"What's a love-bomber?"

"A guy who acts like he's sooo in love with you, takes you

on all these elaborate dates, treats you like a queen, then ghosts the minute you sleep with him."

"Oh, you just mean a dick."

"That..." I point up at him, grinning. "That right there is why I should've known Karen lied to me. You're true blue Gavin Knight."

"I really love you, Princess."

"I love you."

Gavin

Warm water swirls around us, and the scent of lavender floats in the air. Haddy is in my arms, her back against my chest, and we're in our big, jetted garden tub.

"I don't know how much you paid for this house," she sighs, "But this tub makes whatever it was worth it."

Chuckling, I kiss her temple. "Anything for my queen."

"You know, if you said that in front of anyone, they would gag over how corny it sounds..." She tilts her head to the side, kissing my jaw. "But I love it."

"I know."

She snorts a laugh at my Han-Solo-ism. Her long hair is bunched on top of her head, and I reach down to put my hands on her hips, circling my thumbs over her lower back. "How are you feeling?"

"Like I don't care how awful it is, I'm ready to get her out of me."

"You're doing so good, babe." I kiss her again, thinking about the push present I've got waiting for whenever our baby girl finally makes her appearance.

"I'm sorry you lost the championship." Her voice is quiet, and she tilts her head to check my expression.

I kiss the tip of her nose. "Thanks, but I tell ya, I think that injury played a role." Shaking my head, I slide my hands up and down her arms. "It was so late in the season, I never had the chance to get back to my fighting speed. And I was worried about you here, thinking of you going into labor with me in fucking Canada... my head just wasn't in the game."

"To be fair, Canada is a nice place." She's teasing, and I exhale a low chuckle. "And that Edmonton team... I mean, it's Gretzky-town."

She knows my idol... hell, every hockey player's idol. I put baby powder on my stick for the first five years I played.

"Try telling your cousin that."

"Mav's just hates losing... Oh..." She shifts abruptly in my arms. "I think I'd better get out of the tub."

"Okay." I reach down, lifting the drain and holding her arms to help her stand. "Hang on... I've got you."

Reaching for a towel, I'm holding her hand when I hear her gasp. My eyes snap back to her wide blue ones, and my stomach drops. Her chin dips, and we both look down to where a gush of water rushes from between her legs.

"I think my water just broke!"

"Thank fuck I'm here!" I don't even try to hide my relief. "Hold my hand. We're ready for this."

Overnight bag is in my new Rover, the car seat is properly installed, I texted Dr. Barry, and we're heading up the 5 on our way to Pasadena.

"Oh, shit!" Haddy is in the passenger's seat, doing her best to breathe. "It hurts so bad!"

My chest tightens, and I reach over to hold her hand. "What's your mantra, babe?"

"I don't remember." She turns wide eyes at me. "All that practice... it was *relax*... oh, Gavin! It hurts so much!"

"Take it easy, hang on." I tap on the screen on my dash, searching for the number of her Aunt Liv who is the hypno-birthing pro. "I'll call your Aunt Liv to talk you through it."

At that exact moment, we meet up with Highway 134 and come to a complete stop. "What the fuck?"

My forehead is tight. It's after ten, and it's brake lights everywhere. Changing course, I tap in her mother's number.

"What's happening?" Raven's voice is tense. "Is Haddy okay?"

"As a matter of fact, we're in labor." My tone is equally tense. "What's happening on 134? We're trying to get to the birthing center."

"Where the hell is it?" I hear fingers tapping keys.

"Pasadena."

"Gavin! What the hell? Why is your birthing center in Pasadena?"

"Mom!" Haddy groans from the passenger's seat. "I found this place when we were hiding from the paparazzi. Then we met Dr. Barry."

"Well, you can't get there tonight. A semi carrying cheese turned over and both lanes are closed."

My throat closes, and I jerk the wheel to the right, garnering a ton of honks as I manage to catch the next exit off the freeway.

"What do we do?" My tone is even, and I'm doing my best not to freak the fuck out. "What's the closest hospital?"

"Gavin, no!" Haddy cries before she leans forward, her eyes squinted in pain.

"Let me see..." Raven's tone turns to calm, and I see in this moment how my girl is just like her mother. "Yes, there's Glendale Memorial!"

I quickly type the name into my GPS, and sure enough, we're minutes away. "That's where we're going."

"I'll be there as soon as I can get to you!"

We disconnect, and in under five minutes, I'm pulling into the circle drive. The emergency guys hustle out to tell me I can't park here, but as soon as I open the door and they see Haddy, everything changes. A wheelchair is brought out, and two large male nurses help Haddy into it.

"I'll be right back," I yell as they shut the doors.

It feels like an eternity, but it's actually less than ten minutes. I'm in the hallway, and they're showing me to the room. I can hear Haddy groaning in the hall, and my heart beats faster. She doesn't remember her mantra.

"This way, Mr. Knight." The nurse holds out a hand, but I'm taking out my phone and hitting Liv's contact information.

"Hello? Gavin?"

"Liv, we're at a different hospital." I rush into the room where Haddy is on the bed, face red. "Haddy needs you. She forgot her mantra."

"If I had a dollar for every time I heard that."

I don't waste time. "Haddy?" I put my hand on her shoulder. "I've got your aunt Liv here. She's ready to talk you through it."

Haddy's blue eyes meet mine, and it's a punch to the gut. I've never seen my girl afraid before. Swallowing my own fear, I force a reassuring face. "Talk to her, babe."

Digging in my coat pocket, I grab a pair of Air Pods to slip in her ears. Holding her hands, I look into her eyes as the doctor pulls up her information on the computer.

"I see her doctor is Mandy Barry?" I nod, and she continues typing. "I have her birth plan here..."

Sitting on the stool beside her, I hold her hands, doing

my best to help her through. I'd been there for the water birth classes, but I missed the hypnobirthing. Haddy changed it on us. Something about pooping in the water freaked her out.

"Soften..." Haddy's voice trembles, and I see her doing her best to focus. "Settle..." Her face tenses, and she leans into the contraction. The last word is somewhere between a whisper and a scream. "Relax..."

"You've got this, Princess." I hold her shoulders. "I'm here."

"Release..." She trembles, and the doctor smiles, looking up at us.

"We're ready to push. Are you ready?"

"It's time to push..." This part I remember. "Let's hum together."

She turns watery blue eyes at me, and my chest is a mixture of heartbreak and admiration. I can't imagine what she's going through right now, and all I can do is hum. Still, I remember from the birthing classes I did attend, being here is a lot.

Our hands clasp, and our eyes meet. She inhales, relaxing her shoulders and her jaw. Her face is red, but she's doing it. I rub her shoulders, doing my best to keep her encouraged. She groans a low hum, and she's doing it.

"She's crowning," the new doctor cries, smiling. "One more push. We're almost there."

Haddy's blue eyes hold mine, and I press my lips to the back of her hands clasped in mine. Another deep groan, another low hum, and she pushes hard.

All at once, the sweetest, strongest cry fills the room. New doctor lifts our daughter quickly from between Haddy's legs, placing her on her chest, and we're all fucking crying.

After all this time, all this dreaming, she's here, and she's as feisty as her mother. She's dark and purple and wrinkly and covered in white goo, and she's the most beautiful thing I've ever seen... Next to Haddy, of course.

The next several seconds are spent weighing, cleaning, and wrapping baby girl in a blanket. She's quickly returned to Haddy, where she takes a moment to check us both out. Her dark eyes are round and curious, and I'm officially in love. Big time.

Haddy drops the hospital gown off her shoulder, pulling our baby to her breast, and it takes a minute. The nurse steps over, reaching in to squeeze Haddy's nipple in a flat shape. It takes a bit of teamwork, but Lucy finally latches. After that, she's eating like a champ and keeping her eye on these giants surrounding her, smiling like love-struck fools.

"She's perfect." My voice is quiet, and I trace my finger lightly over her black hair.

I'm leaning close, and Haddy kisses the top of my head. "She looks just like her daddy."

Sitting straighter, I kiss Haddy full on the lips. "With your dark hair." My arms are around her, and while this wasn't how we planned it, it couldn't get much better.

Two days later, we're at our home. Haddy is in bed with Lucy happily having her dinner. I climb onto the bed beside them, holding out the long, light-blue Tiffany's box for Haddy.

"What's this?" Her brow furrows, and I kiss the top of our baby girl's head.

"Just a little something for all your hard work."

"Gavin Knight, did you get me a push present?"

"It can also be a 'Congratulations on earning your Master's degree' present." I arch an eyebrow, and she shakes her head.

Lucy finishes, and I take her from her mom, placing her topless little body against my bare chest as I lean back against the pillows and gently pat her tiny back. "Time for some skin to skin with Daddy."

Haddy's shoulders drop, and for a second, she only looks at us. "You know how swoony you are right now, right?"

Shaking my head, I kiss my baby girl's head. "I'm just bonding with my baby."

Haddy finally opens her present, cooing as she lifts out a silver chain with a floating axolotl on it. "I love it." She leans toward me, planting a kiss on my lips.

"I love you."

She holds the necklace in her fingers, turning it side to side. "Gavin Knight. I don't know what I'd do without you. You said you'd never let me fall, but I've been falling since the day you showed up."

"Except that one time in the bush." I can't resist teasing her. "You were pushed."

She pokes my ribs. "Spanky has always been on your side."

"He did give me a nice view of your naked body."

"That dog." She snuggles down at my side, and I lift my arm to wrap it around her. I've got my little princess snoozing on my chest, my queen at my side. How could life be any better than this?

"It's okay, love. That red string was thrown around my neck the moment you looked at me."

It'll stretch and tangle, twist and turn. Regardless of time or place, it will never break.

～

Thank you for reading *Pinch*!

Please use the QR code below to download your **Free Bonus Scene**.

Up next is *Cage*, Owen & Gina's single-dad, roommates-to-lovers, hockey romance.

Gina "Gigi" Bradford is a champion dog breeder, groomer, and trainer, and if there's one thing she knows for sure, dogs are better than men. Owen Stone is a star hockey player, single dad, bloodhound owner, and he's learned being on the ice is safer than being in a relationship. Until his psychic sister says the girl of his dreams is holding a dog, and his new teammate Maverick Murphy invites him to move in with him and his dog-groomer, breeder, show-judge cousin Gina while he looks for his own place.

Available in print, Kindle Unlimited, and on duet audio.

NEW TO THE FAMILY?
The Way We Touch is Logan & Dylan's small-town, brother's best friend, football romance. It kicks off the Bradford Boys series with quirky characters, found family, hilarious hot-pepper accidents, angst, and *all the spice* you crave.
Keep turning for a short sneak peek, or order your copy today!

Available in print, Kindle Unlimited, and on audio.

Learn about all of my books on TiaLouise.com/Books, including a **downloadable Reading Guide**.

Free Pinch Bonus Scene.

THE WAY WE TOUCH

BY TIA LOUISE

*My **brother's best friend** might be a **cocky wide receiver** with an ego the size of Texas, but I did not mean to almost kill him with a ghost pepper. He did that all by himself.*

Logan Murphy should come with a warning.
He's as hot as a Carolina Reaper on black asphalt in the middle of July.
With perfectly messy dark hair and smoldering blue eyes—and don't even get me started on the way that black tee stretches across his toned chest...

He's my brother's best friend.
He's also *a football star* on track to win the first wide-receiver MVP in league history.
Good thing I only date golfers... or I did.
Good thing he's only visiting for a month, because the more I see he's not a player, the harder it is to block him from running away with my heart.

I've always loved football, but after eight years pro, everything about it leaves me cold.

So when I agree to head south with *my best friend*, the last thing I expect is to have my face melted off by *his pepper-loving little sister*.

Dylan Bradford was supposed to be a kid, not a feisty pinup who looks at me like she's never seen a man before.

She's all curves and cutoffs, bare feet dancing in the warm summer night,

But I'm only in town a month, and she doesn't date football players.

Then late-night talks turn to sharing past hurts and future dreams, and shy looks turn to confident kisses.

The heat between us can't be denied.

It's spicy and sweet, and it melts us together.

Until *the way we touch* becomes more than friendly—*it's forever*.

(THE WAY WE TOUCH is a small-town, brother's best friend, sports romance with close proximity, hilarious "accidents," and a dirty-talking hero. No cheating. No cliffhanger. No third-act breakup.)

1

———

Logan

"So you want to fuck another man." I lift the tumbler of whiskey, jaw tight, despite the casual smile on my lips.

"Of course, that's the first place you'd go." The cool blonde sitting across from me crosses her mile-long legs, leaning them to the side beneath the table like a giraffe.

I admit, they were the first things I noticed about her. I'm a legs guy.

"Must you always be so cocky?" she continues. "Maybe if you acted like you cared once in a while, I wouldn't have to expand our repertoire."

"I prefer only one dick at the party."

"That dick being you?" She tilts her head to the side.

"Always." Stated with my usual bravado, my calculated cool.

A light laugh slips from her glossy-red lips, but it's insincere.

Natalia van Norse is a six-foot, size zero supermodel with

fake tits. Later, I learned she's also an author and a Midtown influencer, which pretty much makes her a U.S. influencer.

Tonight she's wearing a black dress covered in star-shaped sequins to match the décor of the restaurant, and her platinum hair is swept into an elegant twist off her neck complete with tiny gold stars scattered across the crown.

She's picture-perfect, ready to document the grand opening of Galileo's, the hottest new restaurant on West 53rd Street, which I was invited to attend. I'm invited to attend pretty much every opening, charity gala, red carpet affair.

I'd tossed the invitation aside, but she insisted we make an appearance.

The menu sounded like a prank, and I wasn't in the mood for camera flashes blinding me all the way inside as soon as our car pulled up at the door. But I acquiesced, and here we are.

The host whisked us away to a private alcove off the main dining room, and now we're nestled at a gilded table where midnight-blue velvet curtains separate us from the other, less-sought-after guests.

"You're so provincial, Logan, I swear, it's hard to believe you've lived in New York for eight years."

"I didn't know not wanting to share my bed was considered provincial."

I almost said my *girlfriend,* but that term hasn't felt right in a long time.

"And what about what I want?"

I roll a star-topped toothpick between my fingers thinking about the first time I saw this woman. I was out with Garrett Bradford, offensive lineman and my best friend, on our last free night before the start of the regular season.

I approached her purely out of ego. With her height and

style and reputation, I decided she was the type of woman "Lightning" Logan Murphy should have on his arm.

Logan Murphy, star wide receiver for the New Jersey Pirates, most completed passes in last year's season, and on track to win the very first MVP trophy ever awarded to a wide receiver in history—if the sports commentators are to be believed.

Our relationship was rocky from the start.

She was promoting her book of essays, and I liked to read. However, when I discovered her book was actually a collection of essays about how the modeling industry only cared about her body, I made the mistake of questioning the premise.

Isn't being a model and complaining people only care about your looks the same as me being a football star and complaining people only care about my athleticism?

Sure, I graduated with honors from the University of Texas at Austin with a degree in communications, motivated by the fact that my father owns all the sports radio stations on the AM dial from El Paso to Jefferson City, but nobody gives a shit about any of that when the ball is second and goal in the fourth quarter with ten seconds left in the game.

I'm simply a player who'd better catch that fucking pigskin and get it across the line.

Then online sports betting exploded, and I was dehumanized even more.

The last time a dickhead cursed me out in the comments section, threatening my life because I fucked up a measly twenty-dollar parlay by simply doing my job, i.e., *winning*, I turned over all my social media accounts to a handler.

I'm not complaining. Much. We signed up for this life. It is what it is.

Natalia only glared at me, called me an un-evolved caveman, and we've been on the slow train to *done* ever since.

Not that I have time for a private life during the regular season anyway.

Studying the menu, I'm even less enthused about being here. Tang? Freeze-dried beef *au jus*... "It's a quirky concept, but space food?"

"My hook will be, 'It's out of this world.'" Natasha waves down our designated waiter. He's dressed in a white uniform like he's part of NASA, and he hurries over as if his life depends on keeping us happy. "I'll have another stardust martini, and may I see the kids' menu?"

"Of course." He nods, hastening away, and our eyes meet.

"I thought you promised to eat more."

"I'm not eating this." She flicks the menu with her fingernail. "I hope the children's menu will have a cheesy pasta or some version of pizza."

I hold up my hands. "It's a smart idea."

Natasha isn't dumb. She only acts that way on social media.

The man returns with a small card, placing it on the bone china plate in front of her, and she lifts it, curling her nose as she reads. "Freeze-dried carrots, potatoes, and beef cubes—just add broth. Is it supposed to be a game?"

"That does it." I take the napkin out of my lap and put it on my plate. "I'm out of here."

"Logan! We can't leave. I promised to take pictures of all the dishes and post them on my accounts."

I hesitate in my chair, irritated by this entire night—by my entire state of affairs. Maybe I'm having a quarter-life crisis, but I keep asking myself why am I still with this woman? What am I thinking I'll get? A do-over?

Reaching across the table, I place my hand on hers. Her brow furrows, and she seems confused by my sudden display of tenderness.

I'm not confused. I feel nothing, and it's the moment of clarity I needed.

I make a decision. "What do you want, Natalia?"

"Sorry?" She shakes her head, and I return to her earlier question.

"Tell me about the new dick you want to bring into our bedroom."

"Oh," Her blue eyes light, and she wiggles in her chair as if she's been planning this for a while. "Aristotle Drakos."

"Wait..." I glance to the side. "I know that name."

"You met him with Brittany on his super yacht in March, remember?"

Perhaps I am provincial, because I need to clarify. "Brittany, as in your best friend?"

"Of course! I mean, if I were to have a best friend."

"I thought she was dating that guy."

Air puffs through her lips, and she takes a long sip of her martini. "They have an open relationship. Everyone's doing it now, very *en vogue*."

I trace my finger along the base of my tumbler and consider Galileo. "Call him."

"What?"

"Give him a call. Tell him to join us."

"Okay..." The side of her lips curl into a smile, and her thumbs fly across her phone screen.

Exhaling slowly, I glance at the galaxies painted on the ceiling overhead. Galileo was an astronomer. He looked into the night sky and proved the universe does not revolve around us.

We are not the center of the universe...

They threw him in prison for it.

I think about how weary I am of the nonstop appearances, the social climbers, and the fakery. Eight years ago, my dream came true. I was a first-round draft pick, which meant I was a big fucking deal. It meant my father was wrong, and I wasn't throwing my life away on a barbaric sport.

Two weeks ago, Natalia left for a modeling gig in Europe, and I realized how much I liked *not* having her in my space. I'd already decided to end things tonight, then she suggested a threesome.

"He's on his way." She lowers her phone, stretching like a cat waking from a long afternoon nap. "You're going to like Aristotle. He's very confident in a way that immediately sets you at ease."

"It sounds like you two have a history."

Her shoulder rises, and when our eyes meet, I realize she's fucked him already. I also realize she's on some sort of amphetamine. And I realize I don't give a shit.

She flicks her wrist. "He mentioned something about your father being a billionaire, and how he *must* meet you. *Must* was his word."

My brow lowers. "What does he want?"

She shrugs, shaking her head with a laugh. "I'm sure it's some sort of partnership or business proposal. Everyone knows you're considering retirement, and he's wanting to get more into media."

Pulling my chin back, I study her face. I'm not sure what to make of her sometimes. "I've told you I'm not interested in working for my dad. Did you lead him to believe I was?"

"No! I don't know. He'll discuss it with you."

I motion to our waiter, and he hurries over again. "Yes, sir?"

"We have another guest joining us. Let me know when he arrives."

"Of course." He nods. "I'll alert the host."

"And put this all on my bill."

He nods before scurrying away, and Natalia leans forward, wrinkling her perfectly-crafted nose. "You surprise me, Logan. I thought you'd require a little more convincing."

"How long until he gets here?"

She glances at her phone. "Any minute, I'm sure."

On cue, a familiar man with dark hair and olive skin wearing a bespoke suit strides confidently across the dining room in our direction. Our waiter shows him the way, and as he gets closer, the way his eyes roam my date confirms my suspicions.

Anger heats my throat, but it's not jealous rage. He can fucking have Natalia, but he disrespected me by sleeping with her while we were a couple.

"Mr. Lightning. Your reputation precedes you."

Standing, I catch his hand in a shake, gripping it hard and pulling him closer so he can feel my strength. He's a few inches shorter than I am, and his eyes widen with surprise.

"You crossed a line." My voice is low and level. "Good thing for you, I'm finished here. You can have her, but I know."

He exhales a laugh, holding up both hands. "My apologies. I was given wrong information about your relationship."

"Yes, you were." I pass him roughly, headed for the door.

A swirl of air around me, and Natalia rushes up to my side. "Where are you going?"

"Away." I do my best to keep my voice low, trying not to be overheard, but the entire room is craning their necks to look at us. "Have a nice life, Natalia."

"But what about our arrangement?" She looks around at our growing audience.

"We never had an arrangement, and your new dick is waiting for you."

The noise of cameras clicks all around us, and I have to get out of this spotlight.

The host meets me, and I follow him to the door, hurrying out to a waiting black Escalade. As soon as I'm inside, my phone is in my hand, and my thumbs fly over the screen.

LOGAN

Where are you? I'm hungry and I want to drink.

GARRETT

Lightning! Get your ass to Blondie's and get some wings. We've got a pool game going.

Garrett and I have been tight since he transferred to the team two years ago. He's a giant of a man, six-foot-four and two hundred and sixty pounds of pure strength, and he's the one person I can be completely myself around.

His family owns a pool bar and restaurant in his coastal hometown in Alabama, and that small-town, southern background is probably why we bonded right away.

He's also the best offensive lineman on the team. Without Garrett, I wouldn't be as close to the MVP trophy as I am.

LOGAN

Stop hustling the college kids.

GARRETT

Don't blow my cover, narc.

Exhaling a chuckle, I wrap it up with

LOGAN

On my way.

I tell the driver where to go, thinking how only Garrett could make me laugh after this evening.

It only took a few weeks of therapy to trace it all back to my dad, Kellan Murphy, billionaire CEO of MurKo Communications.

I don't come from a family of jocks, but I knew the first time I caught a football, the first time I led a team to victory, this was the life for me.

I'd found a group of guys who cared about me, who noticed when I wasn't okay and checked up on me. I had a real family.

My mother died before I was old enough to remember her, so growing up, it was just me and Kellan—and a string of housekeepers to cover the basics, a driver to take me to school until I was old enough to drive myself.

The only time I spent with my dad was at the formal dinners we shared every night in his sterile mansion in north Houston sitting at opposite ends of a long, polished oak table.

I would push the medium-rare steak around my plate wishing I could escape, and he'd try to think of questions to ask me.

How was your day?

Fine.

Did anything interesting happen?

No.

Silence.

Eventually, he'd give up, take his scotch, and leave, and I'd dash from the table, running down to the park where guys were always playing football. They didn't care who I was or how much money I had. It was all about the game.

I'd strip off my jacket and get in the middle, calling plays and throwing passes. I wanted to be a quarterback, but when Kellan got involved, he changed my direction.

When I first told my dad I wanted to play football professionally, he'd frowned like I told him I wanted to be a professional wrestler.

Then I started making headlines when I was in college, and he started doing the math. He realized he could use my football career to benefit his broadcasting business—provided I continued to be the best.

That's when his tune changed, and the pressure began. He said I should be a wide receiver because I almost never missed a catch and I was fast. If I could run, I scored.

No wide receiver has ever won the MVP, the Most Valuable Player award, in the league, and he said I could be the first.

Don't mistake that for him being supportive and encouraging. He was simply stating his wishes before he disappeared into his ivory tower again. I was still young and naive enough to think he cared. He had a point, and maybe it meant he would take an interest in me.

So I changed directions and became a wide receiver, not considering outside of the quarterback, the wide receivers take the most hits.

Garrett has taken a lot of hits to keep me safe on the field, and I've managed to avoid serious injury and run the ball all the way to the top of the game.

The black SUV stops at the Upper West Side bar, and I thank the guy before hopping out. Outside of openings and other big events, I'm mostly left alone by the media—unless

I'm dating someone interesting, like a fashion-model, author-influencer.

The bar is packed with a different game on every television, from baseball to soccer. It's a sausage party with gym bros shoulder to shoulder holding bottles of beer and talking about the upcoming season.

Garrett is impossible to miss in the back corner holding a pool cue. He spots me when I walk in and motions for me to join them. I stop off and order a whiskey neat at the bar and a classic Angus burger before heading to where he's clearing the table.

He makes a big show of not taking the guy's money before slapping my back and walking with me to a standing table in the middle of the loud space.

"LL!" He clinks the neck of his beer against my glass. "You look like you just got an extra week of vacation. What happened?"

"I ended it with Natalia." Now that I say it out loud, I actually do feel lighter.

"Thank fuck," he shouts. "Of all the boney-assed bitches you've dated, she was the worst. Always posting shit on her damn phone and always criticizing everything you did."

A petite waitress with red hair and curves hustles up with my burger and fries. She's working hard, focused, and she looks good—or maybe she's just bringing me food, and I'm starving.

"Yeah, I'm done with supermodels."

"Don't get it twisted. Some of those gals are a lot of fun. But not that one." He grabs a handful of my fries while I take a big bite of burger. "If she made one more crack about you being a country mouse, I swear to the almighty football gods... She's from freakin Hoboken!"

I laugh around my bite. Garrett is so damn loud, and I

love it. I don't even want to know how he knows where Natalia is from and I don't.

I exhale a groan as savory meat and cheese fill my mouth. "We started at that Galileo restaurant tonight."

"What did you think?"

"I can't tell if it's a prank or what. You're supposed to pour hot water over everything to rehydrate it before eating."

His brows tighten. "So it's like DIY?"

Shaking my head, I take another bite. "Hell, I don't know. I didn't stick around to find out."

My burger is gone in five bites, and he waves for another beer. "What now?"

Good question. Now that I have food in me, I can think, and I don't like my prospects.

We've got a month before training camp begins, the last thing I want is to hang around the city alone. It's as unappealing as going to Houston to work with my dad, as he keeps asking.

"Know anybody with a timeshare on the moon?"

Garrett grips my shoulder. "Come home to Newhope with me." My hand is already up, and I'm ready to argue when he cuts me off. "My parents' old house is huge, and it's right on the bay. There's plenty of room, and it'll be perfect for clearing your head."

"Last thing your family needs is another football player taking up all the space and eating all the food." I know what we're like.

"Dude, it's my brother Zane and my little sister Dylan, and she loves when we're home." He waves to the waitress, and she walks over.

"Another round?" She blinks up at him, and I'm pretty sure she's flirting.

"Just the check, Wendy." Of course he knows her name. "Logan Lightning, meet Wendy the waitress. She's a single mom, working to put herself through nursing school, and she will not make you wait for more beer."

"Nice to meet you." My voice is quieter. "Good luck with... everything."

She shakes her red head. "Don't tell my life story."

"It's a good story! You should be proud."

Garrett is a giant, cocky, friendly bear with curly brown hair and a thick beard. He's casual in a T-shirt and jeans, and his dimpled grin and merry blue eyes put everyone at ease.

By contrast, I'm lean muscle, dressed in a suit jacket with my dark hair styled and a light scruff on my cheeks. I study the world with my brow lowered, and there's not many people I trust. Life has taught me to maintain a buffer.

All that to say, we're pretty much night and day.

"Grab what you need and be at my place in an hour. I want to be on the road by ten." He's not giving me time to come up with an excuse, and I don't really want to.

Escaping to a small town on the coast sounds pretty good right now.

"You know my dad has a private jet service. We don't have to drive."

"Nah, I gotta have my truck."

Garrett and his truck. "I don't know anyone who drives a pickup in the city."

"They should. Most useful vehicle on the road."

"Well, if it isn't Low-gas Murphy." The annoying voice comes from behind me, and I turn to see Ricky Berke, wide receiver for the Challengers swaggering to where we're standing.

"Bro, that is the stupidest dunk. It's not even close to his nickname." Garrett leans on an elbow and still towers over Ricky.

My nemesis is undeterred. "I noticed you weren't at the White Party this year, Murph. Losing your cool, old man?"

In the race for MVP, it's down to me and this guy, three years in and completely full of himself. Just like I was, I guess, only I'd like to think I wasn't a total asshole.

"Actually, I was in Houston with my dad for the Fourth." And it was hot as the face of the sun and humid as a fucking rainforest.

"I heard you weren't invited." Ricky lifts his chin. "No surprise. Mr. Rubin only invites the best to his parties. Not sad ole has-beens like you."

"Whatever helps you sleep at night, Dick."

I don't bother defending myself. My father and I have been on the guest list for that annual summer party in the Hamptons since before I was in high school.

"I'm surprised you made the cut this year, *Dicky*," Garrett steps up beside me, crossing his arms. "I heard *Mike* likes ass-kissing copycats even less."

Ricky and I are the same height and build, but he has bright red hair, brown eyes, and pale skin covered in freckles. I'm a little faster than he is, and my secret weapon is Garrett covering my ass and helping me make the plays that keep the commentators talking.

"Like you know anything, Grizz." He looks past Garrett. "Where's Natalia?"

This guy is always swimming in my wake.

"I left her at Galileo's. She might still be there if you're interested."

"I heard she spent last month on a yacht in the Mediterranean with some Greek mogul." Ricky smirks. "And now

ESPN has you trailing me in the MVP race. It really is a drag getting old."

"It's better than the alternative." I slap his shoulder, not interested in engaging any further.

"And by *alternative* he means *you*." Garrett points at him, a laugh in his voice, and he's vibrating, hoping Ricky is dumb enough to take a swing at one of us.

He's always up for a good bar brawl—because he always wins.

I put my hand on my friend's shoulder. "Meet at your place at ten, right?" Turning to Ricky, I tip my head. "Natalia's all yours."

I don't bother adding *if it's not too late*, since she does have Aristotle on standby. Hell, he's probably fine. She's looking for a second dick anyway, and this guy is made to order.

Garrett can't let it go that easy. The little waitress walks up, and he wraps an arm across her back.

"Wendy, I'm sorry we have to leave you with this guy. He's a real piece of work, and a bad tipper." He grips Ricky's shoulder. "Try to resist the urge to spit in his drink."

"Hey!" Ricky's brown eyes widen in horror, but Wendy only laughs, waving him away.

"He's full of shit. Just look at that grin." She points up at my friend.

Garrett puts a hand over his chest like he's shot through the heart, but it's all an act.

I slip an extra twenty under our check just in case Wendy actually does get stiffed on her tips tonight. Then I drag him out of the bar ready to pack and see what the place he's always raving about looks like up close and personal.

~

AN HOUR LATER, I'm in the plush leather front seat of his maxed-out, gunmetal F-150 racing south on Interstate 95 with the radio quietly playing country music.

We're facing a day-long drive, and I'm booking a room for us to crash in North Carolina. It's the first time I've made a road trip like this since I moved to the city, if ever.

"I saw you slip Wendy that extra tip." He glances at me, returning his eyes to the road.

I stretch in my chair, doing my best to get comfortable. We're going to be here a while. "You made me worry about her."

That makes him chuckle. "You're a good man, LL. I knew it the day I met you, even if you do approach the world with your guard up."

"Likewise."

"This is just what you need." Garrett glances at the lights of New York City in the rearview mirror. "Newhope will clear your head, get you back to square one, the basics."

"Does the chamber of commerce have you on the payroll?" I tease because I love.

Garrett is the poster boy for his hometown. It's all he talks about, but the truth is, at this point, I'm up for anything to kick me out of this funk.

I think about what he's told me in the few times we've spent together, shooting the shit. He lost his mom young, like I did. He's one of four brothers—all football stars—and a little sister. Although besides Garrett, only his brother Hendrix is still in the game.

I don't know Hendrix well, but we've met. He plays for a team in Los Angeles, and he's a bit of a rockstar tight end.

His second oldest brother Zane was a career kicker forced to retire last year after getting nailed pretty bad during a fake field goal. It was a dramatic injury, his foot dangling at the end of his leg like a freak show while he roared in pain.

It's the kind of injury you like to pretend could never happen when you're headed onto the field each week, and they played it on reruns every five minutes. Fuck, I still get chills remembering it.

"Jack said he'll be picking his fall lineup while we're in town." Garrett's large hand is propped on the top of his steering wheel, and he has a toothpick in the corner of his mouth. "I told him we could help him out, maybe give the boys a pep talk."

His oldest brother is a retired star quarterback from Texas. I remember watching Jack Bradford on the field and wondering how anyone with that much talent could ever retire. He did, though, at the top of his game. A legend.

Now he coaches high school ball. Friday night lights.

"Sure. Whatever he needs." I glance out the dark window wondering what my nineteen-year-old self would think of meeting Jack Bradford in the flesh.

Then I travel back a bit more, wondering what I would say to my fifteen-year-old self today. What would he even be able to hear? Certainly not that life at the top isn't as great as it looks from the bottom. Or that no matter where you go, there you are.

Hell, maybe I'm just depressed. I haven't slept with a woman in a long time, and the last time I did, it was with someone who was more interested in her social media following. I'm not being a hater. There was a time it was all I cared about, too.

"Dylan said Zane is laying low, but he's healing fine." My friend's jaw tightens, and he shakes his head. "It's going to be the first time I'll have seen him since that accident, and it was a fucking nightmare."

"Tell me about it." My lips tighten, and my stomach cramps.

It's a big switch to go from the nonstop schedule of a big game every week, seven months out of the year, traveling all over the country, being a celebrity to a certain segment of the population, to nothing.

Full stop.

From the roar of a stadium, to dead silence. Forgotten.

I've heard guys talk about the shock of retirement, and I'm not going to lie, I'm not looking forward to it. Even if I have been floating the possibility of this being my last year. It all depends on that trophy, even if that trophy means more to my dad than it does to me.

"That just leaves Dylan, but she'll be working at the restaurant most days." Nodding, I picture a kid living on the coast in south Alabama.

My mind travels a thousand miles down the dark road ahead of us, far from the lights of Manhattan. I think about the life I left behind when I graduated from UT.

Taking out my phone, I pull up my contacts and select my father's name. In the glow of the dashboard light, I text him what I've been thinking for weeks.

I'm not going back there.

~

Get THE WAY WE TOUCH and fall in love with this small-town, brother's best friend, football romance today!

Available in print, Kindle Unlimited and on Audio.

AUTHOR'S NOTE

A word of thanks to one of my favorite podcasts, "Radiolab," which inspired Haddy's graduate research. I was on a flight in February 2025, listening to Episode 628, "Revenge of the Miasma," when I stumbled upon their discussion of aerobiology and viral transmission via wind.

They specifically discussed emerging research on Kawasaki disease, and it was so fascinating to me, not to mention, with Raven's obsession with meteorology and studying the weather to save lives, it made perfect sense it would fascinate her daughter Haddy as well.

If you'd like to learn more about this topic, check out Carl Zimmer's book *Air-Borne* or listen to the podcast at radiolab.org.

Thanks for reading!

BOOKS BY TIA LOUISE

ROMANCE IN KINDLE UNLIMITED

THE NEW BRADFORDS
PINCH, 2025*
CAGE, 2026*
FLOW, 2026*
ZONE, 2026*
CLAIM, 2026*
(*Available on Audiobook.)

THE BRADFORD BOYS
The Way We Touch, 2024*
The Way We Play, 2024*
The Way We Score, 2025*
The Way We Collide, 2025*
The Way We Win, 2025*
(*Available on Audiobook.)

THE BE STILL SERIES
*A Little Taste, 2023**
*A Little Twist, 2023**
*A Little Luck, 2023**
*A Little Naughty, 2024**
(*Available on Audiobook.)

THE HAMILTOWN HEAT SERIES
*Fearless, 2022**
*Filthy, 2022**
For Your Eyes Only, 2022
*Forbidden, 2023**
(*Available on Audiobook.)

THE TAKING CHANCES SERIES
*This Much is True**
*Twist of Fate**
*Trouble**
(*Available on Audiobook.)

FIGHT FOR LOVE SERIES
*Wait for Me**
*Boss of Me**
*Here with Me**
*Reckless Kiss**
(*Available on Audiobook.)

BELIEVE IN LOVE SERIES
Make You Mine
*Make Me Yours**
*Stay**
(*Available on Audiobook.)

SOUTHERN HEAT SERIES
When We Touch
When We Kiss

THE ONE TO HOLD SERIES
*One to Hold (#1 - Derek & Melissa)**
*One to Keep (#2 - Patrick & Elaine)**
*One to Protect (#3 - Derek & Melissa)**
One to Love (#4 - Kenny & Slayde)
One to Leave (#5 - Stuart & Mariska)
*One to Save (#6 - Derek & Melissa)**
*One to Chase (#7 - Marcus & Amy)**
One to Take (#8 - Stuart & Mariska)
(*Available on Audiobook.)

THE DIRTY PLAYERS SERIES
*PRINCE (#1)**
*PLAYER (#2)**
DEALER (#3)
THIEF (#4)
(*Available on Audiobook.)

THE BRIGHT LIGHTS SERIES
Under the Lights (#1)
Under the Stars (#2)
Hit Girl (#3)

COLLABORATIONS
*The Last Guy**
The Right Stud
Tangled Up
Save Me
(*Available on Audiobook.)

PARANORMAL ROMANCES
One Immortal (vampires)
One Insatiable (shifters)

Books by Tia Louise

ABOUT THE AUTHOR

Tia Louise is the *USA Today* and #4 Amazon bestselling author of small-town, single-parent, second-chance, sports, and military romances set at or near the beach.

From Readers' Choice awards, to *USA Today* "Happily Ever After" nods, to winning Favorite Erotica Author and the "Lady Boner Award" (*lol!*), nothing makes her happier than communicating with fellow Mermaids (*fans*) and creating romances that are smart, sassy, and *very sexy*.

Connect with Tia:
TiaLouise.com (signed copies)
Instagram, @AuthorTLouise
TikTok, @TheTiaLouise

GET THREE FREE STORIES!
Scan the QR code below to sign up for my newsletter and never miss a sale or new release by me!

www.ingramcontent.com/pod-product-compliance
Lightning Source LLC
Chambersburg PA
CBHW021412310726
48971CB00005B/1307